Praise for *Someone Else's Bucket List*

"This life-affirming tale reminds us that happiness is possible if we find the courage to reach for it."
—Jamie Beck, *Wall Street Journal* bestselling author

"*Someone Else's Bucket List* takes a poignant look at how the bonds of sisterhood can shape our lives."
—Namrata Patel, author of
The Candid Life of Meena Dave

"I loved *Someone Else's Bucket List*. It begins by breaking your heart then takes you by surprise by becoming uplifting and utterly galvanizing. Best of all, though, it's a stirring celebration of the power of sisterhood!"
—Matt Cain, author of
The Secret Life of Albert Entwistle

"Fans of Josie Silver and Cecelia Ahern will be taken by this story of joy after grief."
—*Publishers Weekly*

"[Matthews] has given her novel genuine depth, with characters who grow and love together even when facing loss."
—*Library Journal*

Also by Amy T. Matthews

Someone Else's Bucket List

BEST, FIRST, and LAST

AMY T. MATTHEWS

KENSINGTON
PUBLISHING CORP.

www.kensingtonbooks.com

KENSINGTON BOOKS are published by
Kensington Publishing Corp.
900 Third Avenue
New York, NY 10022

All Kensington titles, imprints, and distributed lines are available at special quantity discounts for bulk purchases for sales promotion, premiums, fund-raising, educational, or institutional use.

This book is a work of fiction. Names, characters, businesses, organizations, places, events, and incidents either are the product of the author's imagination or are used fictitiously. Any resemblance to actual persons, living or dead, events, or locales is entirely coincidental.

To the extent that the image or images on the cover of this book depict a person or persons, such person or persons are merely models, and are not intended to portray any character or characters featured in the book.

Special book excerpts or customized printings can also be created to fit specific needs. For details, write or phone the office of the Kensington Sales Manager: Kensington Publishing Corp., 900 Third Avenue, New York, NY 10022. Attn. Sales Department. Phone: 1-800-221-2647.

Kensington and the K logo Reg. U.S. Pat. & TM Off.

ISBN: 978-1-4967-4211-7 (ebook)

ISBN: 978-1-4967-4210-0

First Kensington Trade Paperback Printing: July 2024

10 9 8 7 6 5 4 3 2 1

Printed in the United States of America

For Su, my mother,
and for Beryl, my grandmother,
and for my kids, who will climb mountains because of them.

And for Jonny.
This one doesn't count, and I know it.

If you want a happy ending, that depends, of course, on where you stop your story.
—Orson Welles

I didn't fall in love. I rose in it.
—Toni Morrison

I may be a senior, but so what? I'm still hot.
—Betty White

Chapter 1
Bonnie

Tucson, Arizona

After the funeral, everyone went home. And Bonnie Jenkins was left alone in the big house on East Goldsmith Place, swimming about under the ten-foot ceilings like a minnow in an empty SeaWorld aquarium.

"I blame you for this," she told her late husband, who was sitting opposite her in the breakfast nook on this very early morning in March. Bonnie had given up pretending to sleep and had headed downstairs for coffee and toast in the watery predawn light. "If I'd still been in the old house in Phoenix, I wouldn't be lonely like this. I'd have my girls right there on my doorstep."

He didn't answer her. The cherry wood box just sat there. She'd chosen the cherry wood for his ashes because she'd been worried about breaking an urn. She'd promised Junior that if he upped and died on her, then she was going to carry him with her everywhere she went and talk his ear off. Even if his ear was no longer there. "If you die, you'll be coming to every choir practice, every lady's lunch, every shoe-shopping expedition," she'd threatened.

"You're not in a choir." He'd been unfazed.

"I'll join one." She'd been deadly serious. "I'll make sure your afterlife is anything but restful."

And she was keeping that promise, which is why he was in a box on the kitchen table, and not scattered to the four winds, like he wanted.

It had been a revelation to discover how many kinds of urns there were to choose from, she thought as she stared at the cherry wood box. Times had changed since she'd last lost a husband. The funeral home had sent her a link and when she'd clicked it open, she'd found a catalog of final resting containers: marble and brass, stone and steel, even crystal. Junior's daughter, Holly, had favored skipping the urn since they were going to be scattering him, but Bonnie wasn't giving into the scattering so easily. Holly was back in Vancouver with her polite Canadian husband and children, and Bonnie was the one here in the empty house with what was left of Junior, so she figured she had the final say. Bonnie had settled on the polished cherry wood box for him, which she'd had screwed shut, to make sure she didn't go spilling him everywhere. Particularly on nights when she'd had a couple of drinks at the golf club bar.

Ugh, the golf club.

She was only living out here in the deserty foothills of the Santa Catalina Mountains because of that stupid golf club. Junior had already bought the house (or at least the idea of the house, off a plan) when she'd met him, and he'd spent their courtship driving her out to the site to watch it go up, promising her a perfect sun-splashed life, with a pool sparkling in the courtyard and views of the mountains from every window. And a golf club just over the back fence.

"You can amble on over to the club and meet me for lunch after I finish my round of golf," he'd said gruffly, pulling her closer, in that beary way he had. He was a man of immense affection. It had its charm. Golf, less so.

He was the second husband who'd wooed her with a house. Funny how life had its echoes.

She missed a lot about Junior. His calmness. His twinkliness. The way he asked her opinion on things and then actually listened when she spoke. Even now, when he was reduced to a cherry wood box, he listened.

"Three dead husbands is beyond the pale," she complained around her mouthful of buttery sweet toast. What did it matter if she ate nothing but carbs, fat and sugar, and with her mouth open to boot. There was no one to see her. And nothing to stay healthy for. "One dead husband is a pity, two is a tragedy, but three? Three is a joke." She cast her eyes heavenward. "You tell Him while you're up there, Junior. A *joke*."

She'd made Junior put it in their wedding vows—the promise about not dying on her. But he'd up and done it anyway.

"And now I'm stuck out here next to a golf course, in a house that's too big, with my girls four hours away. I can't even pop by."

Bonnie missed her kids. She'd had Sandra when she was still just a kid herself, and it felt strange living so far from her. Like she was missing a limb. They'd basically grown up together, and when things were uncertain, there was always Sandra, giving her a reason to get out of bed in the morning. Jacqui had come later, when Bonnie was more sure of herself, and less bruised by . . . well, life. But now, here she was, bruised again, but this time with no daughters to drag herself out of bed for.

There was a splash outside. Bonnie perked up. It had come from the direction of the Ortegas' house next door.

"Bit early for a swim, isn't it?" Bonnie shot Junior's cherry wood box a look.

She'd always told him the neighbors were too close. These houses were so big they ate up the whole block. You could see into each other's windows, for Pete's sake. And who swam this early? And in *March*? Dawn was only just flushing the spring sky apricot. Bonnie stood and craned her neck. If she really stretched, she could just see over the fence, particularly now that Paula had trimmed the palms back. It was like the tropics over there. Bonnie would hate to see their water bill. And yet . . .

"I wouldn't mind some palms myself," she told Junior absently. "Instead of all that agave you put everywhere."

She rose on tiptoe and managed to catch sight of a well-muscled back and a pair of strong arms cutting through the water of the Ortegas' pool. Which was the exact same size and shape as her own pool.

"Who do you think that is, Junior?" It certainly wasn't her neighbor Steve, who was about twice as thick and half as toned.

She didn't wait for Junior to respond, but headed for the dining room, pulling her phone off the charger on the way. From the dining room window, she had a clear view into Paula and Steve's kitchen, and she was glad to see the lights were on and Paula was filling the coffee machine with water.

Bonnie turned on her own lights and pressed Paula's number on her phone. She watched as Paula reached for her cell, glancing over at Bonnie's place. Bonnie didn't miss the wry resignation as Paula gave her a wave.

"Can't sleep again?" Paula was sympathetic, or at least trying to be. She leaned against her counter and gave Bonnie her full attention through the window.

"There's a man in your pool." Bonnie didn't care about sleep. This wasn't her first rodeo. She knew how grief went. She'd sleep eventually, probably too much once the serious depression hit, so, until then, she'd just be glad she was awake and sad, but not in the black hole of despair. And unlike the last couple of black holes, which she'd suffered through alone, this time she'd had the good sense to keep Junior with her, for company.

"There is indeed a man in my pool," Paula agreed shortly as she went back to her coffee machine.

Bonnie didn't take pity on her. "It's not Steve."

"No." Paula was equally pitiless. It was why Bonnie liked her.

"Is this some kind of ménage à trois situation?"

"Yes, we're engaging in threesomes with young men on every second Wednesday of the month."

Bonnie managed not to laugh. "Well, good for you."

"It's only Owen."

"Your grandson?" Bonnie headed back to her kitchen. She slid open the courtyard door and stood on the step. She had a better view from here. There was the steady slapping of water as Paula's grandson did his laps. "I've not met him yet. Or seen any pictures of him on Facebook."

Silence.

"He's the journalist?"

"Photojournalist."

Bonnie could do silence too. Eventually there was a gusty sigh. "Would you like to come for breakfast?" Paula offered.

Bonnie tossed her toast in the trash. "Depends. What are you cooking?"

"Rice Krispies."

"Sounds divine. Give me a moment to freshen up and I'll pop over. I might have an avocado or two I can bring."

"For Rice Krispies?"

"And maybe some feta. You could throw a couple of poached eggs on top."

"Could I?"

"Don't go to any trouble for me, though." Bonnie heard a laugh as she hung up. "This is more interesting than toast," she told Junior, as she dragged him back upstairs so they could get ready.

Paula pursed her lips when she opened the door. She looked Bonnie up and down. "Well," she said, "you certainly did get fresher."

"What? Too much?" Bonnie looked down at her patterned skirt and pale-pink T-shirt. "I was aiming for breezy casual. With the urn providing a dash of grieving widow chic. You don't think I can pull it off?"

Paula rolled her eyes. She was still in her pajamas, which had sleepy iguanas all over them, and her steely gray hair was sticking up like a cock's comb.

"I can wipe the lipstick off, if you think it's too much?" Bonnie handed over the avocados and the tub of crumbled feta. "There's a lemon in there with the avocados too."

"Would you actually wipe the lipstick off if I said you should?" Paula asked curiously as she closed the door.

"Doubtful, but we'll never know unless you ask."

"Not my style." Paula padded back to the kitchen, Bonnie in her wake.

"Where's Steve?" Bonnie asked, continuing past the open kitchen and into the back room, where the sliding doors stood wide. From here she had a very clear view of the photojournalist grandson as he did a tumble turn and kept swimming.

"Asleep," Paula said.

"This is the grandson who has commitment issues?" Bonnie asked.

Paula grunted an irritable assent, clearly annoyed about it.

"The one who runs off every time he gets feelings for someone?"

"That's him." There was the sound of Paula yanking the refrigerator door open with some violence. "Although to be fair, he runs off even when he doesn't have feelings. He just runs. Like a dog at the damn track."

Bonnie glanced away from the grandson long enough to see Paula putting the avocados and feta in the fridge. The stubborn woman pulled out two bowls and a box of Rice Krispies.

"You don't have almond milk, do you?" Bonnie couldn't resist asking. What would she do without Paula to play with?

"I have half and half, or Steve's milk, which will lower your cholesterol."

"God forbid. I don't want to live any longer than I have to."

"Hence the almond milk?"

"How old is the commitment-phobic grandson?" Bonnie kept an eye on him as she joined Paula at the breakfast bar. She hadn't had Rice Krispies in years. She popped Junior down and accepted coffee and a bowl of cereal.

"Too young for you."

"Paula! As if I'm the kind of woman who'd hit on a young thing. And don't upset Junior. You know how he gets."

"Sorry, Junior." Paula blew on her black coffee. "But you know what she's like."

Bonnie was enjoying this much better than her lonely kitchen. She didn't feel like a minnow when she was with other people. "What am I like?"

"You're a flirt. Hell, you even flirt with Steve."

"Of course I flirt with Steve. The man needs it. It's good for his heart."

"Well, Owen's heart is just fine, so your services aren't necessary." Then Paula pulled a worried face.

"What was that?"

"What?"

"That." Bonnie mimicked the face.

"Nothing." But Paula shot a look at the swimming pool.

"Something *is* wrong with his heart," Bonnie deduced.

Something serious, by the looks of it, Junior agreed. She waved a hand at the urn. Now he talked? After torturing her with silence all night long?

"He's going through a breakup," Paula confided. "Again. Such a shame, we all thought she was The One."

No such thing.

Bonnie glared at the cherry wood box. Honestly.

I only mean there's more than one One, Junior amended hastily.

Well, there was that. After all, Junior wasn't her first love. Or even her second. She placed her free hand on the cherry wood box. Paula noticed, because she noticed everything.

"He's taking the breakup hard," Paula told Bonnie, turning back to her bowl.

"She left him, then?" Bonnie knew more than a thing about being left.

Paula shrugged. "I can't say I blame her. He's never home. Always off traveling."

"Well, he is a photojournalist."

"I doubt he was home one week of every month last year." Paula was disapproving.

"Why didn't she go with him?"

Paula shrugged again.

"I would."

"I'm sure you would. Just like you learned to play golf for Junior."

"That's different." Bonnie finished her Rice Krispies. She poured another bowl. "No one is worth golf."

Is that so?

"Besides, Junior didn't need me to play golf. He just needed me to rub the knots out of his lower back afterward." And more. *God, I miss that.*

Yes. Bonnie sighed. She did too.

"He says staying in one place makes him feel like one of those mammoths." Paula leaned her elbows on the counter and gave the grandson in the pool a dirty look.

"What mammoths?"

"The ones that fell in the tar pits in California. At La Brea."

"That's a very specific image." Bonnie appreciated that in a man; it was the sign of a good communicator. Which was a rare trait.

"He photographed them once. Says he's got no desire to be uncovered after the next ice age, preserved in his eternal misery."

"Maybe he should pick a tar pit that doesn't make him so miserable, then."

"He says he's not interested in tar pits anymore. Not after the last one."

"Are we still talking about women here? I've lost track."

Paula shrugged. "You've got granddaughters, don't you?" she said speculatively.

"None around here. They're all off being career women of the world. The closest is Heather and she's in Chicago. She's also got a guy. I've not met him yet, but Sandra tells me he's perfect." Not that her daughter Sandra had great taste in men. "I don't believe in perfect, myself."

"Shame."

"Not really. Imperfect is much more fun."

"I meant shame she's taken. I imagine any granddaughter of yours would make a tar pit interesting enough to get through an ice age or two."

"Does he like older women?"

"You're too old."

"Not me. I'm done with men—I told you. I'm just waiting to die now Junior is gone."

Paula snorted.

"I was thinking about my daughter Sandra."

Paula rolled her eyes. "Sandy's old enough to be his mother."

"So? It happens the other way around all the time. Look at Craig and Leanne from the golf club—she's young enough to be his *granddaughter*."

"Ew. But thanks for reminding me." Paula slid off her stool and pulled a calico bag off the door handle to the laundry. She fished around in the bag. "Here." Paula handed Bonnie a book. "Leanne picked the next book for the golf widows book club."

Bonnie looked down. *Eat Pray Love.*

"I told her it was a dumb pick because everyone read it years ago, but then I remembered that Leanne was probably in kindergarten when it came out."

"I haven't read it, but I might have seen the movie." Bonnie turned the book over to read the blurb. Book club was the bane of her existence.

"Maybe it'll inspire you to run off to Bali or to join an ashram." Paula topped up their coffee. "And you're down for bringing wine this time."

"What are you bringing?"

"She wanted me to make a green papaya salad. But I'm bringing wine."

"*Drink Pray Love.*"

"Something like that."

There was a sloshing sound as the photojournalist climbed out of the pool. Bonnie pivoted in time to see glistening lengths of young musculature.

"You sure he wouldn't be interested in a fling with a cougar?"

"You're too old." Paula was firm.

"Sandra," Bonnie reminded her. "God knows, she needs it." Sandra was stuck in her own personal tar pit, living through an ice age that seemed to never end.

"Owen," Paula called. "Would you be interested in a fling with a cougar?"

The photojournalist turned their way, the towel frozen halfway to his face. It was a very nice face, Bonnie noted approvingly. Strong, a bit broody, but not in the least self-indulgent looking.

"What?" Ohhh, more than broody. There was definitely an edge. Bonnie liked an edge.

You do?

Bonnie patted the box reassuringly. She'd *once* liked an edge, she amended. When she was young, before she knew better.

"A cougar?" Paula repeated to her grandson. "Would you be interested in a fling with a cougar?"

The grandson resumed toweling off. "Sure. I run a side hustle as a gigolo."

Bonnie laughed. She liked this one. He took after Paula.

"Owen, this is our neighbor Bonnie. Bonnie here has a daughter who needs cheering up." Paula poured her grandson a coffee.

"She's going through a divorce," Bonnie chipped in. "It's nasty." Although in Bonnie's opinion the marriage had been nastier than the divorce could ever be.

"How do you know that I'd cheer her up? I might make her more miserable." The grandson wrapped the towel around his hips and shrugged on an old blue T-shirt. His dark hair was damp and shaggy. He took the coffee mug Paula offered him.

"You'd make a poor gigolo if you were going around making women miserable," Paula said dryly.

"I didn't say I was any good at it." He leaned against the counter and cupped his hands around the mug. Lord, he was a looker. Cheekbones for miles. Big dark eyes. Sulky mouth but with a twitch at the corners, like you could easily coax a smile out of him. If you wanted to. This one didn't look like a helpless mammoth. The running made a lot more sense now that she was looking at him front on. This wouldn't be an easy man to hold down—this would be a man to run off with.

"Miserable would be a step up from where Sandra is," Bonnie observed. She was out of sorts now that she was thinking about Sandra. She pushed the mostly empty bowl of Rice Krispies away. Sandra had stopped answering her calls, which was never a good sign.

"Breakups suck," Paula's grandson said. He had the same frank dark stare as Paula. Only he was sultrier than she was. But who knows, maybe Paula had been sultry once. Before she lived next to a golf course with Steve.

"You should tell her to go traveling," Owen the photojournalist suggested. "It's the best way to get out of a slump."

"Isn't that what got you into your slump in the first place? Traveling?" Paula said, a touch sharply.

"Where should she travel?" Bonnie jumped in before Paula could ruin things. She was enjoying this and didn't want it to end. When it ended, she'd have to swim back to her empty aquarium and try and find ways to pass the day. Like watching the movie of *Eat Pray Love* so she could fake her way through book club again.

"Somewhere she's never been before in her life," Owen the Sultry said with conviction. "Somewhere totally new."

Bonnie liked the sound of that.

"Sometimes you don't need new," Paula interrupted, still being sharp. "Sometimes you can get out of a slump without running away."

"It's not running away," Owen told his grandmother calmly. "It's running *to*."

Running to. Bonnie felt the splash of the words like cool water on a hot day. Running to. Something you did when you were young, and the world was spread out at your feet like a summer beach. But what the hell could you run to when you were seventy? Golf?

Screw that.

"Is that what you're doing with this Machu Picchu nonsense?" Paula was genuinely irked with him. "Running to? And what are you running to, exactly? A life spent alone? Homeless and childless and destined for a lonely old age?"

"What Machu Picchu nonsense?" Bonnie butted in. She liked the sound of this *running to* business.

"He's off to Peru." Paula crossed her arms. "Climbing some hill to see ruins."

"It's one of the new Seven Wonders of the World." Owen the Sultry's lips were twitching up. He might actually smile, Bonnie thought, curious to see what that would do to his face.

"What's so wonderful about it?" Paula was really settling into a grump now.

"Why don't you come with me and find out?" Now Owen did grin and boy, oh boy. Bonnie liked the look of him even more. He had the kind of smile that had just enough wickedness to be interesting. Shame she *was* too old for him. He was just the sort of man she'd enjoyed when she was a kittenish young thing. Like her first love Jimmy . . . Ah, Jimmy. The best worst thing to ever happen to her.

Paula made a scoffing noise. "If I'm going anywhere, it's to Mexico to eat fish tacos and laze on the beach. There may or may not be margaritas."

"Send me a postcard." Owen winked at his grandmother, who was pretending not to be charmed. But how could she not be? "Are you coming on the hike with us this morning, Bonnie?" Owen asked her. He'd put his coffee down and was rummaging in the fridge.

"Hike?" Bonnie cocked her head.

"Does she look like she's dressed for a hike?" Paula rolled her eyes.

A hike. Not something she'd do on her own but . . . Bonnie and Junior had done some of the Santa Catalina trails before his heart attacks. She used to be a good hiker. So long as she had people to talk to while she schlepped.

Go on. You promised you wouldn't sit around moping after I went.

She hadn't promised any such thing. He'd demanded it of her, and she'd ignored him.

But of course she was going. It beat watching old movies and not reading old books. "I can get changed," Bonnie assured Paula's broody-charming grandson.

"You have hiking shoes?" Paula asked dubiously.

"Of course." Somewhere.

"You'd best get ready, then. We're leaving soon."

"There's time. The boy's still making breakfast," Bonnie said placidly.

"The *man* eats quick," Owen told her, spreading her avocado on his toast.

Bonnie didn't begrudge him the avocado. The Rice Krispies had been a treat.

"We'd best change plans about the route," Bonnie heard Paula sigh as she gathered up Junior. "We can do one of the longer easy ones, instead of doing Blackett's Ridge."

"Blackett's Ridge isn't hard." Owen gave Bonnie a speculative look.

"Hard enough for a grieving granny who hasn't hiked in forever," Paula told him firmly.

"Don't go easy on my account," Bonnie sang as she slid off the stool and headed home to change. "I'm tougher than I look. And I might be grieving, but I'm still hotter than any granny you've ever known."

"Don't forget your sunscreen! And water." Paula followed Bonnie to the door. "And here." She gave Bonnie the book club book, which she'd tried to leave behind.

Bonnie took it. "Maybe I'll read it aloud to you," she told Junior's cherry wood box as she took him home to get ready for their hike. "Serves you right for introducing me to the golf widows book club from hell. If I have to read it, so do you." She felt better than she had in weeks. "I'll do all the voices and everything."

But now that they were home, Junior had gone silent again. He had a nasty habit of doing that.

Chapter 2
Heather

Chicago, Illinois

"Your mother isn't answering her phone."

Heather wished she hadn't answered the FaceTime call. Her grandmother loomed at her, holding the phone too close as usual, so the screen was all big pink-lipsticked fish lips.

"Isn't she?" Heather strove for mildness, even though she felt the usual wave of stress at the mention of her mother. She stole a glance at the Post-it note stuck to the windowsill behind her computer. *All my emotions have a place at the table,* was scrawled in Sharpie on the lime-green square, *even the uncomfortable ones.* Heather took a deep breath and rose from her desk—calls with Bon-Bon were never quick. She felt her back crick as she stood; she'd been working, hunched over, for hours.

Heather kept her gaze fixed on the patchwork of Post-its that had built up on the windowsill and the wall since she'd downloaded her e-therapy app. *Don't look back, you're not going that way,* on brooding purple; *I am allowed to take a break,* on blue; *Good things are coming,* on Sunkist soda–colored orange.

Working at home hadn't been good for Heather. She spent all day on her ass, in sweatpants and a nice sweater (relaxed on the bottom, ready for Zooming on top), eating junk and sweating deadlines that only seemed to hide more deadlines. This wasn't how she'd imagined her life. She'd imagined herself in shafts of sunlight, the apartment clean and zen-like, an idyll out of *Architectural Digest*. But actually, working from home meant that she was stuck in her sloppy, ordinary life *all the time*. The hour when she used to commute just filled up with work. There was no more walking through the seasons—there was only watching clouds and rain and snow through her window. When she remembered to look up. She missed *Chicago*. Sitting here, staring at a screen, she could be anywhere at all. Or nowhere at all.

Be where you are, a yellow Post-it chided her.

"Are you listening to me?"

Heather tried to smile at Bon-Bon on FaceTime. "Yes, Bon."

"When was the last time you spoke to her?" Bon-Bon demanded.

"Who? Mom?" Heather carried her phone in front of her as she did a lap of her one-bedroom apartment, massaging her tight lower back with her knuckles. By the time she reached the bed she was walking a little easier.

"You *have* spoken to her?" Bon was getting sharp. Sharp*er*. Because when was Bon ever not sharp?

"Yeah, of course," Heather lied. She'd been dodging Mom's calls for a while. She didn't want to hear about Dad's affairs, or about the latest round of the divorce, which was a blood sport. He was her *father*. Sure, he was a lying, cheating, self-focused, immature dick, but he was still her dad.

It's okay to set boundaries. Many hours of late-night therapy with a series of calm online therapists had led to that pink Post-it. Boundaries certainly weren't a problem anymore with Dad, though, as he'd barely spoken to her since he and Mom broke up. It was as though when his marriage dissolved, Heather's relationship with him had dissolved too.

"When did you speak to your mother?" Bon-Bon demanded. Heather could see a flash of sky on the phone as Bon-Bon moved outside. God, look at that. It was clear blue skies in Tucson, with bright sunshine. So bright Bon-Bon slid sunglasses on.

Maybe all Heather needed was some blue skies and sunshine. She looked out her window at the gray day. As much as she loved Chicago, sometimes she missed Arizona, mostly during the slush end of winter, which dragged into spring.

"When?" Bon was relentless.

"I spoke to her a couple of days ago," Heather lied. She was lying a lot lately. Like when she'd told her now-ex-boyfriend Shawn there was someone else. It was the only way she could get him to accept the breakup. Although even now he insisted on calling it a "break" rather than a "breakup." The breakup itself was another result of *It's okay to set boundaries.*

"And how was she?" Bon-Bon asked. "Jacqui says she's bad?"

Oh, thank God Aunt Jacqui was talking to Mom. That made Heather feel a little less guilty about dodging her calls. Aunt Jacqui was the brisk type, she could manage Heather's mother, Sandy.

"She was the same the last time I spoke to her." That wasn't a lie.

"Bad," Bon-Bon said grimly.

"Bad," Heather agreed. Her palms were sweating. She hated the thought of Mom's sadness.

Bon swore and pressed her bright pink lips together. The image on the screen jostled as she lowered herself to the edge of her pool and sat down.

"It's warm enough there to get in the pool?" Heather focused on the sparkling blue water and unsuccessfully tried to stay in the moment. There was a terrace pool in Heather's apartment building, but she'd moved in at the beginning of winter and so she hadn't used it yet. She couldn't wait until summer to dive in. Even though she worried about avoiding Shawn at the pool, as well as in the corridors. . . .

Ugh, what had she been thinking, dating someone in her building?

And now here she was, falling into spirals of bad thoughts about Shawn again.

"I'm not getting in the pool, I'm just soaking my blisters. How I love you, Junior, for choosing a saltwater pool. So good for the blisters. Have you said hi to Heather yet, honey?" Bon-Bon turned the phone in the direction of a small wooden box. It contained her husband's ashes, which was equal parts romantic and gross.

"Hi, Junior." Heather felt a pang. She'd liked Junior. He'd been a big cuddle of a man, with a thick white head of hair and twinkling eyes.

Poor Bon-Bon.

Only poor Bon-Bon wasn't poor Bon-Bon, was she? There was nothing poor about her. She was there wearing pink lipstick, sitting by her pool in the sun. And she was a *widow.* Not for the first time Heather wished Sandy had inherited a dose of Bon's buoyant nature.

"Why *do* you have blisters?" Heather asked.

"Hiking," Bon-Bon said happily. "I've been hiking. Surely you've seen my pictures on Facebook?"

Heather couldn't imagine Bon-Bon hiking. She must have misheard. "I'm not on Facebook, remember?"

"What are you on?"

The last thing Heather wanted was her grandmother finding her on socials. "Nothing," she lied.

"Shame. You're missing out on some spectacular posts. I met a lovely young man," Bon-Bon said, "and he's into hiking."

"A man? Already?" Heather supposed she shouldn't be shocked. After her grandpa died Bon-Bon had brought home boyfriends. Lots of them. Until she met Junior.

"Not that kind of man. This one's just for being friends with. He's too young for me. Shame, because he's a hottie."

Heather laughed. "Is there such a thing as too young for you? How old is he?"

"He's more in your range than mine."

"Ah. That's definitely too young." Heather didn't want to think about Bon-Bon with a man Heather's age.

"I was thinking he might be good for your mother."

"Oh." That took a minute to hit. "Oh! *Ew.*"

"Definitely not *ew.* Quite the opposite. And did I mention he's Paula's grandson?"

"Who's Paula?" She shouldn't have asked, because now Bon-Bon was off and running. Conversations with Bon were hard to keep track of at the best of times, but now that she lived alone and was starved of company, forget about it. It was like being hit by an avalanche. Heather couldn't keep up with all the asides, except she somehow gathered that Paula was Bon-Bon's neighbor and that Heather might have met her at Junior's funeral. There was something about Paula having a daughter who lived in Boulder, and photography, and somehow Peru came into it . . . And hiking. Lots of hiking.

"I'm going to work up to the big hikes. Today we tackled Ram's Canyon. There's one called Romero Pass that takes all day—I'll be doing that by April, you wait."

Heather glanced at the time on her desktop. "I can't talk all day, Bon, I'm at work."

Bon-Bon wasn't pleased. "You work too much." She paused. "What do you actually do again?"

Heather couldn't be bothered explaining. "I'm in software," she sighed, as she always did. She'd given up trying to parse the details of software quality assurance with her family. "And I have a backlog, so I'll have to dash."

"Everyone deserves a break," Bon-Bon went blithely on, unknowingly paraphrasing the blue Post-it. "What's this about you meeting the perfect man? You haven't told me anything about it."

"I haven't met the perfect man." Heather went hot and cold. The thought of Shawn made her feel guilty and uncomfortable. *All my emotions have a place at the table.* Even the Shawn-shaped ones.

"I'm glad. Perfection is boring, if you ask me. Now, tell me about him. What's his name? What does he look like? What does he do?"

"We broke up," Heather blurted. And to her shock tears flooded in. Damn it, what was she crying for? *She'd* broken up with *him.* And she was happy about it. But she felt so wretchedly guilty, like she'd committed a crime.

Bon barely missed a beat, tears or no tears. "What did he do?"

"Nothing." Heather reached for a tissue. "He didn't do anything. I'm sorry, I don't know why I'm crying."

"No, you never were one for crying. You were always one for repressing."

Heather scowled. Well, if she was, it was because she'd been expected to.

"It's your mother's fault. She didn't leave you room to have any emotions; she took them all for herself. A girl has to get mad if she's to know her own mind."

That made no sense to Heather. She felt like she was always mad. Everyone was always telling her to lower her voice, to calm down, to get a grip.

"Your mother may be a grade A weeper, but she's never understood the value of a really good fit of rage."

The one benefit of Bon's chatter was that it gave Heather a chance to pull herself together. She pushed the tears away and wiped herself up.

"Which is quite an achievement, given she's the angriest person I know."

"She's not angry," Heather sighed, "she's passive-aggressive." And sad.

"Exactly. Passive aggression is just anger leaking through the cracks." Bon took her sunglasses off, her periwinkle-blue eyes kind. "Now, tell me. What happened with Mr. Not Perfect?"

Heather gave a shaky shrug.

"Did he leave you for another woman?"

"God, no." That was one fear Heather had never had. "Shawn would never."

"How do you spell his name? S-E-A-N or S-H-A-W-N?"

"The second one."

Bon pulled a face. "He wouldn't change it? *Shawn* sounds like someone who'd go and watch monster trucks."

Heather was startled into a laugh. "Not this one." She couldn't think of anything more ridiculous than Shawn, with his expensive bamboo T-shirts and perfectly trimmed fingernails, watching monster trucks.

"Well, that's something. So why wouldn't he cheat?" Bon-Bon sounded suspicious.

"He loves me."

Bon snorted. "Since when has that ever stopped them?"

"What?" Heather felt a sour spurt in her stomach. "Who cheated on you?" She hoped it wasn't her grandfather. A cheating father was bad enough without adding a cheating grandfather to the mix.

Bon-Bon waved a hand. "Stop trying to change the subject. Why did S-H-A-W-N leave you if he loves you?" She frowned. "Did *you* cheat?"

From the corner of her eye, Heather saw a reminder flick up on her computer screen. Thank goodness, she had only a couple of minutes before the next burst of meetings. "I have to go, Bon."

"You can't hang up yet, I haven't even got to your mother."

"Thanks for letting me know that Aunt Jacqui is checking in on her. It makes me feel less worried." Heather wasn't playing this game. "I really do need to go now." Before she lost control of her boundaries, which were still new and shaky.

But Bon-Bon bulldozed right over her. "We need a Zoom. The three of us. Tonight works for me. How about eight thirty your time? You'll need to email the link through—your mother won't answer if it comes from me, but she always wants to talk to you."

She always does, Heather agreed tiredly. She had strings of unanswered messages on her phone.

Bon was wearing an expression that made Heather's stomach squeeze with anxiety. You never knew what her grandmother might do next—she was the very definition of a loose cannon. "Don't worry," Bon assured her, "I'll handle your mother. I have a plan."

"A plan for what?"

But Bon-Bon was already saying goodbye. "Eight thirty! If you don't send the link, I'll call you back to remind you. And I want to hear more about S-H-A-W-N."

Then she was gone. Heather felt like all the air in the room had been sucked out through the phone. Bon-Bon had that effect.

Heather glanced at her computer. Her next meeting was about to start, but she was feeling all tangled up now, the way she did every time she interacted with her family.

She punched open her e-therapy app and stared at her options. Meditation. Chat. The sound of rain in the jungle at night. It didn't cut it.

She called her brother. Not FaceTime. She didn't want to control her face.

"Hey," Chris said. He sounded sleepy.

"Did I wake you?"

"Nah, I've been up for an hour or so." He was clearly lying. Chris was a nurse, and he pulled a lot of night shifts.

"Have you spoken to Mom?" she asked.

"Ever?"

"Very funny. Lately."

"About a week ago. Since then I've stuck to texts. Because . . . *Mom*." Chris was the one who'd recommended she try the therapy app. Because *Mom*.

"Has Bon-Bon called you?"

"Ever?"

"Stop being a smart-ass. Bon-Bon called *me*. Just now."

"Ah, how's she holding up? I feel bad I don't call her more, now she's all alone." But he didn't sound sorry enough to change.

"She's the same. But she called me to hassle me about calling Mom. Why isn't she calling *you* about that?"

"Because I'm a boy." He sounded smug. "It means I don't have to take responsibility for my mother, or bring pie to Thanksgiving, or talk about periods or how uncomfortable my bra is."

"Dickhead."

"But I do have to shovel snow, listen to Dad make remarks about hot women—"

"Gross!"

"And scratch my balls in public."

Heather rolled her eyes. "How *was* Mom last time you spoke to her?"

Chris sighed and Heather heard the same teeth-grinding tan-

gle of feelings in it that she felt, which was why she'd called him.
"The same," he admitted. "Depressed."

"Maybe she needs to see someone?"

"Maybe."

There was silence.

"Dickhead. You could suggest it. You're a nurse, it makes
sense."

"Yeah," he said dryly, "but you're the *girl*. She doesn't want
me to say it."

"I don't want to say it. I don't want to talk to her anymore. I
spent *months* talking to her after he left. I can't do it anymore.
Whenever she kicks Dad out, she wants me to fill the emotional
hole he leaves. And I just can't."

"Good, I'm proud of you."

Heather groaned. "I hate you." She hung up on him. Then
texted him, **Love you. Dickhead.**

He texted back, **I'm too busy scratching my balls to reply.**
Then, **Good luck with Mom.**

It took Heather hours to send the Zoom link. Before that she
ran the gamut of meetings, emptied her email inbox, stacked her
dishwasher and then went out to get coffee. Her homemade coffee wouldn't cut it—today she needed something with foam. She
checked the corridor before she dashed to the elevator, always
cautious about running into Shawn, even though he worked at
home only half the week and today wasn't a usual home day.
She sighed with relief when the elevator doors closed and she
was still alone.

As she stepped outside the wind hit her like a slapping wave,
straight in the face. The freshness of the afternoon was stunning. Marvelous. Heather took a deep breath. Already she felt
alive again, the skin on her face tingling. She left her mittens in
her pocket, enjoying the slap and chill of the afternoon on her
bare skin. She *had* to get out more. When she was home all the
time she got trapped in her head.

Heather avoided the closest coffee place. She hadn't gone
there since just after the breakup. It had been one of "their"

places, and the last time she'd gone Shawn had been sitting in their favorite booth, looking like he was still waiting for her.

Like a stalker.

Maybe that wasn't fair of her. He was just having coffee. Ugh. This was the problem with Shawn. With *men*. She had such a hard time telling a red flag from a green flag, because of the weird model of love she'd grown up with. Was it a sweet green flag that Shawn still had hope, that he went and sat at their coffee spot and pined? Or was it a screaming red flag that he wouldn't take no for an answer?

Heather headed for a coffee place a few blocks over that she'd been meaning to try for months. They roasted their own beans, and the smell billowed into the street as she opened the door. The place was as white as the inside of a cloud, minimalist, with rattan furniture and olive-green pottery cups stacked on shelves along the shiplap walls. The warmth was stifling, like sticking your face in a wool rug. Maybe she'd get her coffee to go and walk down to the park. . . .

"Heather!"

Shawn.

Couldn't she go *anywhere*?

Shawn and his roommate, Kyle, were standing at the counter. As always, they reminded her of the old Looney Tunes cartoons of the bulldog and the yappy puppy. That was mean, but she couldn't help it—she thought mean thoughts around Shawn now. Her app said that was okay, but she still felt horrible when she did it. A bulldog wasn't the right kind of dog to describe Kyle, though, she thought as she sized them up. Kyle was more like a massive cuddly Saint Bernard, all hair and beard and shoulders. Next to him Shawn was a lean cord of repressed energy. Kyle was chilled in the extreme; Shawn was so kinetic he vibrated. That intensity had been part of what she liked about him, at first.

Even away from their building, away from their corridor, away from their usual coffee place, she ran smack bang into him. Damn it. Damn it. Damn it.

And damn *him* for looking so good. The breakup really

suited him. He leaned into the romance of suffering. The scruff of his hair and the shadow of stubble along the planes of his face made him look decidedly sexier. She liked him better in the slouchy gray hoodie and sheepskin jacket too.

No.

She wasn't doing this. This was what happened. She saw him, and he did that face he was doing, and then he started talking, and she lost her resolve. . . .

Not this time. This time she was sticking to her guns.

"Heather." The thing was, when he saw her he looked so wretchedly *happy*. Just because she'd walked in. And it felt good to have someone be glad to see you, even when you felt horrible about the fact that you didn't necessarily want it to be *him*.

"Hi," she said grudgingly, giving Shawn and Kyle a limp wave. She could hardly turn and run, could she? She was already in the shop. Kyle gave her a pitying look.

How long did she have to be polite here before she placed her order and bolted?

"Getting coffee, huh?" she said lamely. She'd have to go farther afield in the future, she thought grimly. Or move.

Oh God. Shawn was staring at her with those huge hazel eyes, which were full of longing.

Red flag? Or green flag?

Why couldn't he just accept that they were no longer together?

Maybe because *she* couldn't seem to explain to him why they were no longer together. He'd begged for explanations, but she couldn't explain it. Hell, she couldn't even explain it to herself. He was *ideal*. The kind of man you dreamed you'd meet; the kind of man your parents loved; the kind of man who wasn't out of place beside you on a sun lounger at the poolside of your expensive apartment building. But . . . there were just so many flags. Red or green or tangerine, they were there. And she didn't want them. Or him.

Heather had been fighting the feeling for a long time. Because he was everything she was supposed to want. Mom was over the moon about him. She said he was everything Heather's father had never been. Given Dad was nothing but red flags, that was a good thing. Wasn't it?

Breaking up with Shawn made no sense to anyone but Heather. And because it made no sense, and she couldn't explain it properly, poor Shawn couldn't accept it.

Although to be fair, he probably also couldn't accept it because she kept slipping up and sleeping with him.

"Yeah, we're getting coffee," Kyle rumbled, stating the obvious when the staring got too awkward. "It's good here."

Heather dragged her gaze away from Shawn's naked adoration. She'd almost forgotten that she was in a conversation. That happened in these situations. Shawn's longing sent her tumbling into self-doubt.

Kyle scratched his beard and gave her a rueful look.

"You look amazing," Shawn blurted at Heather, as though Kyle hadn't spoken. His long-suffering hazel eyes said she looked more than good; those moody eyes said she was the best thing he'd ever seen.

Which was patently insane, because she was still wearing her sweatpants and her hair was a bird's nest from the wind. She was limp and colorless from lack of sun, and she was doughy from sitting at her desk all day. Nothing about her looked amazing.

"You might need to get your eyes checked," she joked. Then she felt like a complete witch when he winced. What was wrong with her? He was clearly still suffering from the break(up). She was a horrible, horrible person.

Shawn said she was afraid to let herself be loved. It worried her, because it felt true. But then most of what Shawn said about her felt true.

She didn't want to think about it—she was sick of thinking about it. Couldn't she get coffee without plumbing the depths of her defective emotional range?

"You look good too." She shouldn't have said it because he flared with hope. She didn't mean to give him false hope; she'd just been trying to atone for her stupid joke and her mean thoughts. Besides, it was true, he did look good.

Oh no. No. She couldn't do this anymore.

Heather stepped past him and made for the counter, knowing exactly what would happen next.

He followed her. "I have tickets for Kyle's show tonight, if you don't have one yet. . . ."

From the corner of her eye, Heather saw Kyle wince in sympathy. For both her and for Shawn.

"Oh, you have a show?" Heather asked Kyle, although she knew perfectly well that he did. She'd seen the posts on his socials. She prided herself on how composed she sounded. Which was an achievement when your ex was staring at you without blinking.

She ordered her coffee, extra-large, extra foam.

"Yeah, at that club you came to last time, the one in the basement under the pool hall," Shawn sounded desperately hopeful. He ran a hand through his hair, and it flopped in that way it did, in the way she used to like. Mentally she stressed the *used to.*

"Right." There was no way she was going back to that place. It was not her scene. It stank of stale beer and weed. And, also, Shawn would be there, and the last thing she wanted was to be in a dark club with Shawn and his naked longing for her, when he was looking this good, and she was feeling this shaky.

"You'd like it if you'd just loosen up." He read her mind, as always. He knew she didn't like the claustrophobic dimness, or the noise, or the crush of people, or the pills and the lines and all the rest of it. And sure, maybe she would enjoy it more if she loosened up. But also, maybe she also didn't *want* to loosen up.

"Order for Shawn!"

He didn't move, even though his coffee was up on the counter.

Sighing, Kyle collected it for him. "Come on, man."

"I'll text you the ticket," Shawn told Heather. He was in earnest.

Heather felt a surge of panic. "I can't tonight." She reached for the fiction she'd been pedaling. "I have a date."

God, it was like kicking a kitten. Look at his face.

"A date?"

"I told you I was seeing someone." Even though she wasn't.

But maybe she should, just to end this ridiculousness once and for all.

"Oh. You could . . . bring him along."

Sure. Good plan. She'd bring her imaginary boyfriend to Kyle's gig.

"He, uh, hates music." He hates music. Good one. Heather shot Kyle a desperate look.

"No sweat." Kyle was unruffled. "I have days when I hate it too." He held Shawn's reusable coffee mug out to him. "Come on, man. Let's leave the lady to her day."

"Heather!" The barista slid her cardboard cup up onto the counter. Damn it, she'd been hoping her coffee would take longer, to give Shawn time to leave.

"We'll walk you back," Shawn offered.

Heather hated the way her hands and feet started to sweat and the way she couldn't meet his eye. "I'm not going back," she said, trying to sound brisk. "I'm taking a break for a bit."

"Shawn, man, come on." Kyle looked uncomfortable.

"Right, bye." Heather snatched her coffee off the counter and left before Shawn could say more. She picked up the pace and headed for the park. The starkness of the winter gardens matched her mood and she stayed longer than she meant to, well after her coffee was gone, circling the park as her thoughts looped around themselves in discontent coils.

She felt all messed up when she saw Shawn. It didn't matter how many laps she did of the park, the messed-up feeling just wouldn't go away. It was only when she got a warning text from her grandmother that she finally headed home to send the Zoom link, dragging her messed-up feeling with her.

"You can't be serious." Sandy couldn't even summon the energy to sound outraged, although she clearly meant to.

"At least go comb your hair and slap some lipstick on," Bon-Bon ordered cheerfully.

Heather's mother, Sandy, looked terrible. She was in her oldest, baggiest workout gear, with her hair twisted up in a tight, ugly dark knot. She had deep circles under her eyes, and her shoulders were slumped. She was sitting at the built-in desk in the kitchen, on her laptop. The screen was angled so the camera caught her in an unflattering spear of light from the downlights. She looked old and sad and tired. In the background, Heather could see empty spaces on the walls, where pictures used to hang. Pictures that were now in Dad's condo.

Heather felt like crying. How could Dad have kept hurting Mom like that, for all those years? And why had she *taken* it? Heather was scrunched up with a toxic mix of anger and sadness as she looked at her mom. Sometimes, to her shame, she felt angrier with Mom than she did with Dad.

Maybe because Mom needed saving and Heather wasn't up to the task.

"Why wouldn't I be serious?" Bon was chattering. "You'd be much happier. Everyone's happier with a little lipstick on." Bon was the opposite of Mom. She'd changed her outfit since this morning, dressing for their catch-up in a turquoise shift dress and a pair of orange beaded earrings. She looked amazing. Heather noted that she'd also clearly discovered the "touch up my appearance" feature on the app.

"I look fine just the way I am," Mom said flatly. "No one's going to see me anyway."

Heather topped up her wine. She couldn't do these Zooms without wine. And a Zoom this stressful warranted an expensive bottle from her "cellar," which was a cupboard in a kitchen stacked with fancy wine she'd imagined drinking by candlelight, to soft music, with someone special. As usual, Actual Heather didn't live up to the dream. Actual Heather was using the fancy wine to numb herself.

"*We* see you," Bon-Bon complained. "What are we, chopped liver?"

Mom narrowed her eyes. "Fine." She turned her camera off. "Is that better?"

Heather didn't think there was enough wine in the world for this. "Well, this is fun," she said. "Great idea, Bon."

Bon pursed her coral-colored lips. "I might need a gin."

"Mom, why don't you get a drink too?" Heather suggested, a touch desperately. "We'll have cocktail hour together."

With her camera off, Mom had been replaced with a photo. The picture had been taken years ago, at Heather's twenty-first birthday; in it, a much happier Sandy was grinning broadly, looking fresh in a crisp white dress, her blue eyes sparkling. Cropped out of the photo was Dad, but his arm was still visible, draped around Mom's shoulders.

"Drinking makes me too sad. I've given it up." Mom's disembodied voice came from the screen.

"Well, I've given up giving things up." Bon's screen showed her empty living room. "Giving things up makes me too sad."

"Well, giving things up is not always a choice. Sometimes it's forced upon us."

Oh God. Mom was in fine form tonight.

Bon-Bon's head popped sideways into view. "You think widowhood is a choice?" she asked sharply. "Don't talk to me about sadness being foisted on you, Sandra Margaret. I've known more sadness than you ever could."

"Ohhhhh-kay," Heather interrupted, giving the time-out gesture. "If you two are going to fight, I'm leaving. You're ruining a good wine." That struck her as wise, and she reached for a Post-it and her Sharpie. *Don't waste good wine on bad company.* She stuck it to the windowsill and then ignored her own advice and took another gulp of wine.

Bon-Bon huffed rather good-naturedly and then disappeared. There was a splashing sound and, when she returned, she was holding a full glass.

"What did you want to talk about, Bon?" Heather asked.

"Good Lord, girl, don't you believe in small talk? We're supposed to chitchat for a bit first, not dive right in."

Mom's camera snapped back on. "Dive right into what?" She was suspicious.

So was Heather. They never did collective calls like this, so something was up.

"First, we'll ask Sandra about the state of her affairs, and then we'll ask Heather about her job and that boy she broke up with," Bon insisted. "*Then* we'll move onto the main thrust of things."

"I don't want to talk about the state of my affairs. I'm not the one having affairs." Mom snapped, and then she gasped as Bonnie's words sank in. "Hold on. What boy she broke up with?" All of Mom's limpness vanished. "Not Shawn! You didn't break up with Shawn?" She gave a despairing moan. "Honestly, Heather! What was wrong with *this* one?"

Why did Bon always have to stir her up? Heather watched, disgruntled, as Bon sat back to enjoy the show, while Sandy leaned forward, alive with displeasure, which was directed squarely at Heather.

"He was so nice!" her mother scolded.

"He still is, he's not dead," Heather said sourly.

"He treated you like a princess!"

Heather caught herself grinding her teeth. Why had she agreed to this? She could be watching Netflix right now.

"Maybe she doesn't want to be treated like a princess," Bon-Bon suggested.

"Who doesn't want to be treated like a princess?" Mom was a picture of sheer disbelief. "That's pathological."

"Maybe being treated like a princess isn't everything," Bon said sharply.

There was a chilly silence. When Mom and Dad were in the honeymoon stages of their cycle, Dad treated Mom like a princess. Heather remembered the flowers, the jewelry, the holidays, the cuddling and flirting. And then the cycle would turn, and he'd get restless, they'd get tense, his attention would wander elsewhere, there would be drama, *endless* drama, fights and tears, ruptures, explosions. Mom would kick him out. They'd suffer. Then he'd return and the sparks would rekindle, and they'd fall back into their ritual, honeymoons and flowers, and she'd be a princess again.

"Junior sure treated *you* like a princess," Mom reminded Bon-Bon tersely.

"No, honey, he treated me like a *queen*. There's a big difference."

"Alright," Heather jumped in before they could really kick off. Their bickering could be epic, more like siblings than mother and daughter. "That's probably enough small talk. Get to it, Bon. Why are we here, having this lovely moment of family bonding?"

Now Bon leaned forward, while Mom slumped back. Mom had her arms crossed and her lower lip was thrusting out. She looked like a petulant teen.

"Well, my little prickly pears, I don't know if you remember, but I just had an important birthday."

Heather winced. Junior had died two days before Bon-Bon's seventieth birthday. The extravagant party had been canceled, replaced with a wake at Junior's golf club. Not the ideal way to usher in your eighth decade.

"Of course we remember, Mom." Heather was glad to see her mother thaw into sympathy. Her face softened.

Bon waved away any nascent condolences. She hated sympathy with a passion—especially when it was directed toward her. "Yes, it was all very sad," she said promptly, "but I have an idea for how to make up for lost frivolity."

"You want a party?" Heather guessed. Bon always loved a party.

But Bon looked horrified. "Good God, no. I'm a *widow*."

Heather felt an inch tall. Bon was glib on the surface, but she felt things deeply, and of course she was still in the early months of bereavement—which was hardly the time for parties. "I'm sorry, I didn't think."

"*That* is exactly why no parties. 'I'm sorry' is all anyone will say, all night long. The wake was bad enough." She cast a sideways glance, and Heather knew she was looking at Junior's wooden box. "You don't get to be the center of attention at my party as well as yours, Junior."

"Oh, Mom." Heather's mother rolled her eyes. "Really."

"Really. I don't want to be the 'brave widow' at some awkward party where everyone is trying not to say the wrong thing to the poor suffering woman," Bon announced. "I want some damn fun. I want to embrace something different, to run toward something, rather than waiting out my final days watching the clock's secondhand tick toward death."

Heather took a sip of wine to hide her expression. Trust Bon to go all telenovela on them.

"Your final days," Mom scoffed. "*Your* father lived past ninety!" Mom was looking more like herself again. She pulled the scrunchie from her hair and ran her fingers through her dark waves.

Bon-Bon ignored her. "I want to have an adventure."

"Has this got anything to do with the young hottie you've been hiking with?" Heather asked dryly.

"Maybe." Bon was sly.

Heather laughed. "I knew it! I knew there was no such thing as too young for you!"

"What young hottie?" Mom froze, hands in her hair, all trace of her earlier thaw gone. "Please tell me you're not seeing someone already?" Mom covered her face with her hands. She was still wearing her engagement and wedding rings, Heather noted. It gave her a horrid shivery sick feeling to see. It would be so much easier if Mom would just move on. After all, she was the one who'd kicked Dad out. Why couldn't she make it a clean break?

"You always do this," Mom accused.

"Always do *what*?" Bon wasn't about to take criticism.

"You run from heartbreak straight into the arms of another man. You never take the time to grieve. You just ping from one man to the next like a pinball."

Heather winced. Seriously? That was low, even for Mom, who had a famously sharp tongue when she was in a mood. Bon was in mourning, for Pete's sake. Young hottie or no young hottie, the woman was carrying around her dead husband—and if that didn't tell you something about her state of mind, nothing did.

Bon's coral lips drew tight. Heather could practically see her wrestling with herself. Heather braced. She knew Bon would lose her battle to control her own tongue.

"Is that what you're doing? Grieving?" Bon said archly. "Because from where I sit it looks an awful lot like wallowing in victimhood."

And there we go.

"How apt, given I *am* a victim," Mom snapped. "And if you had an ounce of humanity, you'd understand what it must be like for me, to find out my entire life has been a goddamn lie." Mom leaned in until her angry face filled her camera. "You've never understood. You act like I can control it, like I'm somehow to blame. Like Nick's behavior was *my fault.*"

"I never said it was your fault, I said you made choices."

Mom made a noise like a spitting cat.

"Time-out!" Heather yelled, muting them both. Her stomach was all knotted up, and her chest was tight. She could see their mouths moving vigorously, but now she couldn't hear a word. Thank goodness, because she didn't want to hear any more. The mute button was one of the greatest inventions of the twenty-first century. Heather only wished she could mute people in real life.

"I'm getting off this call if you don't keep your tongues sheathed." Not for the first time, Heather felt like the only adult in her family.

Eventually they realized they were muted, and they turned their irritation on her, rather than on each other. They looked eerily similar as they scowled at her. "Here are the rules," Heather said firmly. "I'll unmute you, but if either of you so much as thinks about being mouthy to the other, then I'm ending the call. Understand? It's been a long day and I'm too tired for this garbage."

She unmuted Sandy first, her stomach twisting.

"We're not children, Heather." Mom was flushed with anger, but at least she wasn't limp and miserable anymore, or raging at Bon.

"Well, you can prove that by listening to Bon's plan for adventure without throwing any more fits, okay?"

Mom's eyes narrowed.

"I mean it, Mom. I will block your calls for a month if you don't behave. We've talked about this. Keep your calm." Heather's hands were clenching and unclenching, and she couldn't seem to find a Post-it that helped. Boundaries weren't enough; she needed a battlement or something.

Mom took her time to come to terms with the ultimatum. Heather could see her turning it over. But Mom knew it wasn't an empty threat.

"Fine," Mom sighed, "I'll listen."

And then she turned her camera off again. Heather wished she wouldn't, because it hurt to look at the old photo. Even though he'd been cut out, Heather was hyperaware of the space where her father used to be. She missed her father. Heather felt just as discarded by him as Mom did.

At least Mom's camera didn't stay off for long, so Heather didn't have to keep staring at Dad's disembodied arm. It snapped back on the moment Bon announced her grand plan.

"What do you mean, *we're* going to Peru?" Sandy didn't seem shocked so much as exasperated.

Heather, on the other hand, was blindsided. "Not Peru the *country*?" she said, confused. Maybe Bon was talking about a Tucson restaurant called Peru.

"Yes, Peru the country!" Bon was thrilled with herself. She was grinning from ear to ear. "You'll need to get fit before the trip, as we're going to be hiking. You only have a few weeks, so you'd best get to it. Walk. A lot. Maybe find a StairMaster to train on . . . And I'll email you a list of things to buy for the trip. And the itinerary. This is going to be great!"

"Whoa, slow down, Bon," Heather interrupted. "What do you mean, *Peru*?"

"What's not to understand? I want to climb Machu Picchu for my seventieth birthday, and I don't want to go alone. And neither of you have much going on right now."

"Are you insane? I'm not going to Peru, Mom," Mom snapped.

Neither was Heather! She couldn't have been more shocked if

Bon had suggested they go to the moon. *Machu Picchu?* Where the hell had that come from?

"Of course you're going. It's already booked. You're going to Peru and you're going to climb Machu Picchu with your grieving mother, to celebrate her seventieth birthday."

"I can't go climbing Machu Picchu either, Bon," Heather protested, unable to believe the scale of Bon's surprise. "I have work!"

"Take a vacation. Besides, you work remotely. If you work from home, then surely Peru can be home for a while. It's only a one-hour time difference. I looked it up."

"Right, so I'll take meetings while hiking," Heather said sarcastically. As if.

"I have work too," Mom reminded Bon sharply.

"No, you don't. Jacqui said you're on unpaid leave, and that all you're doing is watching Netflix and stalking Nick on Facebook. Trust me, you need this more than I do. Besides, the tickets are non-refundable, and they're in your names and non-transferrable too, so it's too late now!"

"Jesus Christ, Mom!" Despite her promise to behave, Mom exploded.

Bon was wrong about Mom never getting angry, Heather thought dryly, as she turned the color of an overripe tomato.

"This is completely nuts," Mom ranted. "You can't just drag people out of their lives like this. We have commitments. We can't just drop everything."

"Sure, you can." Bon sipped her gin, looking inordinately pleased with herself. "And I'm paying for it, so what's to complain about? I don't want to travel alone."

Heather's crazy grandmother was serious. She'd actually booked them non-refundable tickets to *Peru*. Without asking.

"I don't know anything about Peru!" Heather knew she sounded as panicked as she felt. She didn't want to spend an enforced vacation with her mother. She had boundaries now, maybe soon even battlements, damn it. How was she supposed to keep those in place if she was stuck with her mom twenty-four/seven?

"Take Jacqui if you don't want to go alone!" Mom snapped. At least she also didn't want to go.

"I don't want to take Jacqui; I want to take you."

Heather's mother was astonished. "You hate doing things with me."

Bon-Bon looked genuinely startled. "Since when do I hate doing things with you? We always used to take little trips together."

"When we went to Miami you accused me of ruining your whole vacation because I chose to read a book by the pool instead of going shopping, and in Palm Springs you said I was as much fun as a martini without the gin."

Bon flapped her hand. "You take things too personally."

"Well, I'm not doing it!" Mom was an immovable object.

Where even *was* Peru? South America somewhere, but Heather had no idea if it was in the east, west, south, north, or smack bang in the middle of the continent. And when Bon said hiking, how seriously did she mean it? Was she talking about a walk, or *mountain climbing*? Surely seventy was too old for serious climbing?

"It's not a discussion," Bon said blithely. "It's all organized. I'll be at your place on the second of May, Sandra. We'll fly out of Phoenix together. Heather, I booked your flight from Chicago. I hope you don't mind heading to Peru alone, but I want to catch up with Jacqui in Phoenix for a couple of days and spend some *quality* time with your mother before we get to Lima. Won't it be nice to have girl time?" Bon said sweetly to her daughter.

Heather felt like she was on a runaway train. "I might not be able to get time off work!" she insisted. Although part of her was stirred by the thought of traveling. She hadn't gone overseas in a very long time . . . And her work was task based, so she should be able to rearrange her schedule and knock off some tasks in advance. . . .

But God. Traveling with Bon and *Mom*?

"I mean it, Mother, I'm not going!" Mom insisted.

Pointedly, Bon pulled Junior's wooden box into view. She cradled it to her chest. "I lost my *husband*, Sandra. On my *birthday*."

"Not *on* your birthday." But Mom had winced, and Bon had noticed.

"What a present for my seventieth birthday . . ." Bon made sure the box stayed in the center of the frame. "And here I am, trying to make lemonade out of the two-ton truck of lemons dumped on my doorstep. . . ."

"You're so manipulative!" Mom complained.

"Is it manipulative to tell the truth?"

"I'm in the middle of a divorce, Mom! I can't fly off to Peru."

"What better time?"

"Why Peru?" Mom shook her head disbelievingly, the fight draining out of her.

"Why not? Have you ever been? I sure haven't. And I'm up for seeing a wonder of the world, aren't you? My life's in desperate need of a bit of wonder." She blew them a kiss, her coral lips puckered up like a grouper's. "Check your emails! We'll talk soon, my lovely girls. We'll need a quick planning chat before the trip!" And then she was gone, and Heather and her mother were left staring at each other in shock.

"See what I had to live with growing up?" Mom griped.

Chapter 3
Heather

Lima, Peru

By the time she landed in Lima, Heather had seventeen messages from Shawn. That was roughly one every half hour, although the time stamps showed that they had come in flurries.
She didn't open them. Because: red flags. As she exited the plane,
she rammed her phone down deep in her bag and tried to forget
the messages existed, to very little success.

It was her own fault. She'd slipped up again and ended up in
bed with him.

She put her fall off the wagon down to a dangerous cocktail
of guilt, loneliness, and anxiety about the trip. Last night, when
she'd been packing and repacking, feeling the pressure of the
coming vacation with her mother, Shawn had come knocking at
her door very late, bearing farewell gifts and his usual unadulter-
ated longing. He'd stood there, leaning against the doorframe,
his hair flopping over his forehead, looking at her with those
soft hazel eyes. He'd brought her a book for the plane (some author he'd been telling her to read for months—an author she had
zero interest in reading), and an Aesop "arrival kit," which was
full of luxury toiletries to make her arrival in Lima a botanical-
scented joy (green flag?). Although she suspected his motive was

less about her joy and more about getting her to think about him every time she used the products (red flag).

"I'm going to miss you," he said huskily. "Let me in."

He was like a sexy vampire, looming at the threshold, trying to gain entrance. And once he was over the threshold she was in trouble. She wondered if he practiced that longing stare in the mirror, or if he spent hours watching Edward in the *Twilight* movies, trying to master the exact wordless hunger that was supposed to make a woman helpless.

It didn't make her helpless exactly, but it did make her stupid enough to sleep with him. And, of course, he'd still been in her bed when she'd thrown her new Aesop toiletries into her suitcase and zipped it shut at the crack of dawn. She had a ridiculous amount of luggage—both a suitcase and a hefty hiking pack. Bon-Bon had paid for extra luggage on the flights and organized storage for their suitcases while they were off trekking, so they didn't have to limit themselves to just hiking pack and sensible clothes.

"I am not wearing hiking clothes the entire trip!" Bon had said scornfully. "Imagine wearing hiking boots to a nice restaurant in Lima. And I'm certainly not lugging heels up the mountains in a backpack."

So, a hiking pack *and* a suitcase it was. There would be luxury in Lima and roughing it from Cusco on.

"You'll thank me when we get back from Machu Picchu and you can change into some proper clothes again," Bon had said smugly.

But Heather wasn't sure she'd thank her during transit, when she had to lug two bags around. It was hard enough getting it all into the elevator, especially because she didn't want to accept Shawn's help. He'd followed her down to the lobby of their building as she booked an Uber. He'd been hastily redressed in last night's clothes, all rumpled from bed, and mournful because she was leaving. The streetscape outside only added to his drama; it looked like something out of an old movie, with unseasonable fog rolling in off the lake, billowing slowly through the buildings and along the street, making everything misty and romantic, like they'd stepped out into *Casablanca*.

Shawn's hand migrated to the nape of her neck as they waited in the suppressed morning light, his thumb caressing the bare skin under her collar. She shook him off. She hated when he did that. It made her feel like she was a dog being brought to heel.

"Shawn," she blurted, as they waited for her ride to arrive, "last night was a mistake."

He shook his head. "You always say that. Once is a mistake, Heather, twice might be a problem, but this many times? Face it, babe, this is destiny."

Or a pathology.

And she *hated* being called babe.

Why was she so *weak*? She didn't want him, but when he was there, handing out fancy geranium- and citrus-scented body wash (or flowers, like last time; or a bottle of pinot noir, like the time before), smoldering at her like a vampire in a teen movie, she couldn't seem to say no. Or rather she said no, but then he'd touch her, or kiss her, or tell her she was beautiful, and she was *useless*.

Peru was exactly what she needed. For a few weeks there'd be no Shawn knocking at her door. She'd go cold turkey on him and by the time she returned she'd be reformed.

"You should date other people," she told him firmly.

"There's no point. I know what I want."

Oh God. Where was her ride?

"Besides, dating other people hasn't worked for you," he observed. "It doesn't matter how many times you say you like this new guy, you still end up with me."

Yeah, well, that was only because the new guy didn't really exist. If he existed, it would be a whole different story.

Maybe what she needed *was* a real guy. A substitute, like the way people chewed nicotine gum to quit cigarettes. Maybe she could find the man version of nicotine gum in Lima? She could have a lusty fling with a gorgeous Peruvian. That might be all she needed to break Sean's spell/curse.

"I'm not *with* you," she corrected Shawn testily.

"Sure." He was unconvinced. And then, to prove his point, he'd given her a guerilla kiss goodbye. His hand plunged into her hair as he hauled her against him, his mouth hot and insistent. He seemed to expect her to melt into him, maybe because of the romance of the Hollywood fog, or maybe because he thought she'd be overcome with regret now that she was really leaving. Or maybe it was just the fact that she often *did* surrender to him. Something made her go limp around Shawn. A kind of emotional freezing response. Annoyed by his kiss, Heather planted her palm on his chest and pushed him away. Or she tried to, but he was in the throes of passion or something because he barely budged.

Shawn was suffocating the life out of her. So much so that she'd paid the fee to change the flights Bon had booked so she could leave early.

"I know you're afraid of commitment," Shawn said tenderly, when she eventually got herself unstuck from his kiss. "And I know it's probably because of your dad, and all that mess. Which is perfectly understandable. I'll wait. I know you're scared, but I'm brave enough for the both of us."

She couldn't get into the back seat fast enough when her car arrived. *Brave enough for the both of us?* Blerg. Shawn always devolved into talking like they were in a soap opera. Did he actually mean the garbage he spouted? If he did, something was wrong with him. But then, maybe something was wrong with her, not him. Wasn't she supposed to *want* a man who was this in love with her? Was she taking something that was good and whole and healthy and turning it into something else, because of her own emotional chaos? The idea terrified her.

Her mother always accused her of being unromantic, but Heather preferred to think she had a low tolerance for drama. Probably *because* of her mom's idea of romance . . . Shawn's passion often seemed a lot like drama, and with the drama she'd grown up with . . .

The thing was, she didn't trust herself at all.

Shawn told her to trust *him*—but she didn't want to do that either.

Oh, for the love of God, here she was in Lima, and she was still thinking about him! Damn him for texting her. Now her stomach was churning. He was ruining her vacation from more than three thousand miles away.

Well, she wasn't answering his messages. In fact, first thing tomorrow she was going to get a temporary Peruvian SIM card, and then he wouldn't have her number until she got back.

She was in Peru! This was supposed to be exciting. No more silent moaning. She was on an adventure. This wasn't Everyday Heather here in Lima, this was Adventurous Heather, and she didn't have to please anyone but herself.

"Hola!" A man hopped out of a small black hatchback as Heather reached the front of the cab rank. There was no taxi sign on the car's roof, or company name painted on the side, but that didn't seem abnormal here. The cab rank was a mix of official taxis and unsigned sedans and hatchbacks. There was even a dented lime-green van in the line.

"Hola," Heather said, wishing she'd paid more attention in her high school Spanish class. The cabdriver chattered at her as he took her suitcase and her new hiking pack and threw them into the trunk of his battered old car. He had more of a drawl than her old Spanish teacher and all the words ran together.

"*Hablo muy poquito español*," she apologized, pulling out her phone to find a translation app. She should have planned this better and learned some basic phrases, but the whole trip had been kind of hasty. "English? Do you speak English?"

"Miraflores?" he asked, holding the door open for her. "San Isidro?"

Right. This could work. She knew the name of where she wanted to go. "Barranco! Casa Suerte, Barranco," she said as she clipped her seat belt in. She fumbled with her cell phone and showed him the address. Then she checked her bad high school Spanish in the translator; she wanted to know how much the ride cost. "*¿Cuánto cuesta?*"

The cabdriver shrugged, which didn't seem promising. But he was driving off, with her and her bags onboard, so it was too late now. . . .

Heather tried to relax as the cab headed south. She'd never really traveled much on her own; she'd always gone with friends. This was quieter.

She'd best enjoy the quiet while she could, she thought with a snort, because there wouldn't be any quiet once Mom and Bon-Bon arrived. They were both talkers. Which would be fine if they simply chattered and let Heather listen, but they didn't. Talking to Mom and Bon was a contact sport. And Heather didn't always like playing.

But they weren't here now, and neither was Shawn. She was alone, and she didn't owe anyone anything for the next few days.

Heather felt her shoulders loosen as the cab reached the coast. The ocean beyond the cliffs reflected the city lights like smears of oil paint on a dark canvas. The cabdriver was a cheerful, fatherly guy, who gave a running commentary in Spanish. He threw the name of each suburb over his shoulder, and Heather snapped to attention when they reached Miraflores. This was where she needed to be when she met Mom and Bon. It was a shiny, modern district right by the ocean cliffs, and Heather could spot the glow of familiar hotel brands lighting up the night.

"*Turistas,*" the cabdriver said, with a smile in his voice. "*Bacán.*"

"Cool." She nodded and smiled stiffly, feeling keenly her lack of Spanish.

"*Sí! Bacán.* Cool." He turned to grin at her. "*Barranco cool también.*"

Barranco was the bohemian artists' district, and it had leapt out at her when she was trawling the web for places to stay in Lima. It was just as touristy as Miraflores, but in a different way. One hundred years ago Barranco had been a fancy little resort town, but these days the old mansions had been converted to *casonas* for the tourists. Heather loved the eclectic look of the neighborhood in the photos and the way the old-fashioned charm had neon-bright modern edges. Barranco was a vision of cobbled promenades lit by branches of globed streetlights; there were terraced gardens, and, best of all, the ocean lapped at its feet. Street art splashed the buildings, and there were pop-up galleries and bars and live music. It was young and colorful and *alive*, and Heather couldn't wait to dive in.

She'd booked a room in a gracious old casa that was like a luxe version of a hostel; it had a warren of both single and shared bunk rooms, a rooftop terrace with a casual bar, and there was a common breakfast room and lounge. She could imagine herself in those rooms, a newer and improved version of herself. Barranco Heather. In her mind's eye she was wearing flowing peasant skirts and chiming stacks of silver bangles, and she was thinner and prettier, bohemian, and radiant. This was the kind of casa where she could finally be the person she was meant to be. Or a version of her. Her Chicago fantasy was of being a sleekly successful career woman; her Barranco fantasy was of being a loose-limbed, glowing traveler, at ease with the world, wanting nothing but the present moment.

Neither of them was Heather as she usually was, which was short, plump, and overthinking everything . . .

After half an hour of wending along the coast, the cabdriver turned into Barranco, and Heather felt her mood soar. It was everything she'd hoped for. Bright graffiti murals were splashed across the sides of buildings, carnival lights glimmered in the alleyways, and an ocean breeze stirred the leaves of the spreading trees in the parks. She couldn't wait to get out into it.

"Casa Suerte," the cabdriver announced kindly as he pulled up in front of a slightly shabby yellow building, which was three stories high and overgrown with climbing bougainvillea. The flowers were dark purple in the orange streetlight, and between their thickets the windows were thrown open to the night. Casa Suerte was romantic in the extreme. It had a fading glamor that made Heather tingle. Up on the rooftop she could see a net of multicolored party lights strung between outdoor umbrellas, and she could hear the unmistakable pulse of reggaeton.

It was *perfect*.

"*Ciento diez*," the cabdriver called as he threw open his door. "Soles, not dollar."

Right. Heather dragged herself away from goggling at the

casa and found her currency converter. She was relieved to see it was a cheap ride. She dug out the soles she'd stashed away and counted the cash, including a tip, because she wasn't sure if you tipped in Peru or not. The driver had been nice, and he certainly deserved a tip for putting up with her insufficient Spanish.

Heather's cell phone vibrated in her hand as she waited for the driver to pull her luggage out of the trunk. Of course it was Shawn calling. Annoyed, Heather punched decline. Honestly. She hadn't even been gone a full day.

Did you get in safe? The message popped up on her screen.

Seriously?

She'd get that SIM first thing in the morning, she swore, as the cabdriver left her to the sunshine-yellow casa. She carried her bags into the foyer, which was eye-poppingly colorful. She was here, she reminded herself, and Shawn wasn't. Ignore him and *be* here. Like the purple Post-it said, *Don't look back, you're not going that way.*

The floor was a mosaic of orange and green tiles, and the ceiling was painted bright green, with a huge smoked orange glass pendant light suspended beneath it.

Heather loved the place, chipped paint on the walls and all.

Above, she heard the pattering of feet on the stairs and a woman appeared on the landing. She was wire thin, with a thick purple knitted headband wrapped around an impressive tower of dreadlocks. She brought the musky smell of incense with her as she descended. "Well, hi," she said, her accent thick but her English fluent. "You must be Heather—you're the last one due in today."

"That's me," Heather agreed.

"I'm Cristina." She swung around the newel post of the banister and reached for Heather's hiking pack. "No need to sign in or anything—we've got all your details online. Come on, I'll show you to your room."

Oh. Okay. Heather hefted her suitcase and followed. She struggled to keep up. Cristina was *fit*—she was halfway up to the second floor before Heather had reached the first landing.

Cristina grinned down at Heather. She was carrying the

pack like it weighed nothing at all. "You're a hiker?" she asked. "Come to Peru for Machu Picchu?"

"Is it that obvious?"

Cristina laughed. "Nine out of ten people come for Machu Picchu. I'm guessing by the pack that you're trekking and not taking the train?"

"I didn't know the train was an option," Heather said dryly. Bon sure didn't mention any train.

"It wouldn't be for me," Cristina called back over her shoulder. She was heading up to the third floor. "What's the point in coming all this way, if you're just going to sit on a train? When do you leave for Cusco? Hit me up for some recommendations before you go. I love Cusco."

"I don't know how long I'll be there before we head out on the trek . . ." Heather puffed. There were a lot of stairs in this place.

"You're second to the end here," Cristina told Heather, gesturing to a door the exact same shade of Sunkist orange as Heather's Post-its. *Good things are coming.* The doors alternated between green and orange all the way down the corridor.

"There aren't any numbers on the doors, so you'll have to remember which one is yours."

The key was hanging out of the lock. No swipe cards around here. Cristina took the key out of the lock and handed it to Heather. It was on a long tassel of yellow and red pom-poms. "So you don't lose it." Cristina laughed and lowered Heather's pack to the floorboards. "I'll leave you here to unpack and freshen up. If you shower, make sure you lock the door, so you don't get any nasty surprises."

Heather frowned. Wait, what did that mean?

Warily, she opened the door to her room, half expecting to be disappointed. Hotel rooms were always disappointing; the photos online were usually taken from weird angles, which made the rooms appear bigger than they actually were. She was expecting a place so small that she could touch every wall from the bed. But she was pleasantly surprised. Her little garret looked just like it had in the pictures online: stripped floorboards, pale-peach walls, a starburst art deco mirror above a narrow bed, which was covered with a hand-woven Peruvian bedspread. And that window. The window took up most of the wall next to the bed, a wide arch with mullioned panes. Through the glass, Heather could see the bougainvillea lapping at the window frame, the leaves nodding in the breezes eddying in from the ocean, the flowers like fat clusters of grapes. The lamplight gave the room an apricot glow, and everything was warm and welcoming. Someone, Cristina probably, had left a thick bunch of Peruvian lilies in a clay vase on the bedside table.

Heather realized that she was holding her breath.

This was exactly what she needed. She could feel a tremble of magic as she stepped over the threshold. This was a place where she could be happy. Heather peered out the window—she was facing the backstreets, which were a tumble of ramshackle buildings, a terra-cotta-roofed wonderland. She was itching to get out and explore. But she was going to wash the travel grime off first.

When she stepped into the bathroom, Heather discovered what Cristina's cryptic comment about locking the door meant. The bathroom was a shared Jack-and-Jill arrangement, a narrow shower room wedged between her room and the room next door. She didn't have her own bathroom—she was sharing with a total stranger. And there were only little hooks to lock the doors, not substantial locks.

Her bathroom-mate had left their door unlatched and slightly open. The room beyond was dark. Heather swiftly closed and latched it. Good Lord. The poor woman certainly didn't want to walk in on Heather showering. And Heather didn't want to walk in on her either.

Heather dropped her toiletry bag on the counter. She stared at the small Aesop box Shawn had given her. As much as she would love to use the luxury products, she couldn't bear to think of Shawn every time she lathered up. The whole point was to get away from him.

Heather grabbed a pen from her bag, tore a scrap from the magazine she'd been reading on the plane and scrawled a note to put on the box. *Howdy, neighbor. Please use. I'm allergic, so it's all yours.*

She felt guilty and hated herself for it. But it was hers to give away, wasn't it?

You're not allergic to me, you're allergic to commitment. Shawn's voice was clear and kind in her head. Kind-ish. Kind sounding. But actually goddamn annoying. Total red flag of a voice.

You get stressed just thinking about commitment, Shawn-in-her-head said.

She didn't. She got stressed thinking about *him*—they were two different things. Now that she was away from him, his vampiric charm had lifted completely, and she felt surer of her decision.

I'm not your father, Heather. I won't leave.

Oh, get out of my head, she thought, irritated. Heather left the box of toiletries on her neighbor's side of the sink and turned her back on Shawn's invisible voice.

Despite her vision of her new self, Heather didn't own any peasant skirts or silver bangles, so after her shower she had to settle for jeans and a light sweater. At least it was a nice sweater, a light pastel-pink knit. She blasted her long bob with the hair dryer to try and give it some volume and slicked on some lip gloss. She didn't look anything like a glowing, relaxed boho chick, but she didn't look too bad. Her hair was shiny and swung naturally perfectly straight to her shoulders, and her cheeks had a natural flush. While she looked a lot like her mom, she was glad she'd inherited her dad's southern Italian coloring. She liked her thick dark eyebrows and eyelashes, and the drama of her blunt-cut dark hair. She laced up her kicks, blew herself a kiss in the mirror, and headed up to collect the welcome pisco sour she'd been told about when she booked.

The rooftop was really a terrace. It ran along the street side of the building, backing onto an upper-story suite of bunk rooms. Yellow and pink tasseled beach umbrellas were unfurled over the tables, even though it was night, and overhead cobwebs of party lights glowed in bright colors. Potted plants proliferated, making the place feel like a jungle.

Every table was full, and laughter cut across the cheerful pulse of the reggaeton thumping from the speakers. Heather's shyness ramped up. She reminded herself that she'd never see these people again, and it didn't matter what they thought of her. But she was still intimidated. She headed for the makeshift bar at the far end of the rooftop. A pisco sour might calm her nerves. The bar was a plank propped between two ladders and was staffed by a bearded guy in a yellow T-shirt.

"Hey, *mamacita*," the bartender greeted her, grinning as she wandered up. "You must be our new American." His accent was heavy, but he spoke fluent English. "What shall it be? Pisco or beer?"

"Pisco, please." When in Rome, after all.

"Excellent choice. You always want the pisco when I'm making it, not when Cristina is." He winked at her. "Cristina is many things, but a mixologist is not one of them," he told her jauntily as he mixed her cocktail.

His cheerfulness was infectious.

"I thought I might grab some dinner after this," Heather said as she watched him splash pisco brandy into an old jelly jar, which she assumed was her glass. "Do things stay open late, or should I hurry?"

"Depends. What kind of food do you like? Some of the fancy places close earlier."

"I like whatever's local," she told him, accepting the pale-yellow foamy drink that he slid in front of her.

"Ah well, you can't go wrong with ceviche," he suggested. "You don't get more local than that. You can find lots of casual Cevicherias. There's a great little place just over the Puente de los Suspiros." He scrawled directions on a napkin for her. "The Bridge of Sighs. You'll want to see that anyway. You know if you make a wish and hold your breath as you walk across the bridge—don't let it out before the end, *comprender?*—then your wish will come true." He handed the napkin over.

"Seriously?"

"Cross my heart." He actually crossed his heart. "Know what you're going to wish for?"

Heather had no idea. It must have shown on her face because he laughed.

"Maybe to find love?" he suggested. "That's always a popular one."

Love. She had flashbacks of Shawn telling her how much he loved her. God, no.

"Or even just to have a bit of casual fun while you're in town," the bartender teased. "After all, nothing is forever."

"I might just wish for a nice dinner." She tucked the napkin into her pocket and toasted him with her drink.

It felt good to go for a walk after a long day in transit. She wound through the hilly maze of streets, past buildings painted rainbow colors (watermelon pink and spearmint green; burnt orange and sky blue; sherbet yellow and pale lilac), peering in shop fronts and pausing to listen to the live music spilling from the bars. The directions on the napkin led her downhill to a plaza, beneath towering palms, and the spreading branches of ancient Ficus trees. There were strings of golden lights and the sound of salsa and balladeers on their guitars. People flowed around her, ambling happily, soaking up the atmosphere. A series of wide steps led down through a terraced garden; everything was lush and smelled of grass and earth, and there was the occasional waft of woodsmoke and good things cooking. With every step Heather felt she was sinking further into enchantment. The claustrophobia of her apartment seemed like another life. Her skin tingled and she felt alive to the night.

When Heather finally reached the Bridge of Sighs, she was surprised to see how modest it was—just a narrow wooden bridge on a trestle. The name had led her to expect a whimsical stone folly, but this was a simple straight traditional bridge over a narrow ravine. The ravine itself had been cobbled into a promenade and was loud with restaurants and bars. Heather looked it up on her phone. The promenade below was Bajada de los Baños, the old fisherman's walk down to the sea. Gardens and bright buildings hugged the hillsides all around her, and the view from the head of the bridge was incredible—the city sprawled in all directions, a charming undulation of historic buildings in various styles (gothic, colonial, art deco, modern). In the distance Heather could see the fat hook of the moon shining on the ocean, and a lighthouse flashing rhythmically from a rocky outcrop; the Costa Verde coast curled away, a darkness against the sea.

She paused at the first plank on the bridge. The bartender had said that if you held your breath as you crossed the bridge and made a wish, your wish would come true.

But what should she wish for? Heather didn't have a clue what she wanted. She had the job she'd always wanted, the apartment she'd always wanted . . . Sure, her love life was a mess, and her parents had ripped her family apart . . . but she didn't want to think about them tonight.

She didn't know what to ask for. Something new. Something to look forward to.

Surprise me, Bridge, she thought abruptly. *Send me something completely unexpected and totally wonderful.* Then she took a breath, held it, and walked quickly to the other side.

Chapter 4
Heather

Barranco, Lima

The ceviche was good. That was Heather's first happy surprise. It was a cool, tangy, zesty, spicy plate of joy. The second happy surprise was that the beer was also good. Made in Barranco, it complemented the herby ceviche perfectly. The third and most surprising happy surprise was that she met someone.

Like, *she* met someone.

Like, actually walked up to a guy and introduced herself. Hit on him, to be precise; something she'd never done in her entire life, and never even imagined she'd be brave enough to do. She even used a terrible pickup line on him.

And it was all because of Shawn.

Well, Shawn-in-her-head. The annoyingly talkative residue of him. His invisible voice kept at her as she sat in the cute little restaurant eating her ceviche and drinking her beer, alone at a table.

You miss me, don't you?

She didn't. She was enjoying her night alone.

No, you're not. You're wishing you had someone to experience this with.

Fine. She was wishing—just a little bit—that she had someone to experience this with, as she watched the couples around her sharing food, gazing at each other over the candles, their feet tangling under the tiny tables. It looked nice.

Don't you wish I was there with you? We're meant to be, Heather, his stupid voice-in-her-head told her.

There's no such thing as meant to be, she argued with him.

She was driving herself crazy sitting alone, arguing with Shawn-in-her-head. Maybe she should have struck up a conversation with some of those tanned, pretty people back on the rooftop at Casa Suerte, and gone out to dinner with them? Because what kind of night was this, here all alone, arguing with her phantom boyfriend? Phantom *ex*-boyfriend, she corrected. Phantom *permanently* ex-boyfriend.

If I'm your ex, why do you carry me with you in your head? Doesn't that tell you everything you need to know? You can't forget me, because you need me.

I don't need you. I don't even *like* you.

The truth of it was shocking. Like a clean deep cut. For some reason (probably guilt) she hadn't been able to grasp it before. At least not with such clarity. *She didn't like him.* She didn't like the way he called her "babe" or, worse, "kiddo"; she didn't like the way he rearranged things in her apartment; she didn't like the way he breathed on her neck when they slept; she *hated* the way he made constant judgmental observations about her behavior. Hell, she didn't even like the way he smelled. He wore a scent that reminded her of her mother's linen cupboard. She guessed it was supposed to be lemony fresh, but it just stank of towels.

And he wasn't even her *type*.

My type is something like *that*, she told Shawn-in-her-head, staring at the very beautiful man sitting alone at the bar. And it was true. He was her type. She hadn't been able to stop stealing glances at him since he walked in. He was tall and lean, with broad shoulders, and long legs with strong thighs. She had a thing for muscular thighs, especially when they were hugged by well-laundered denim, the way this guy's were. She liked his face too. He had a square jaw, high cheekbones, and a wild mop of dark curly hair. His mouth was full-lipped and sulky. He was seriously gorgeous. And all alone. Eating ceviche and drinking beer, just like she was. Alone.

Him? Shawn-in-her-head was laughing.

Yeah, him. She even liked the way he drank from his beer bottle. He sucked on his lower lip after each mouthful. It made her stomach do floaty, twisty things.

Shawn-in-her-head was lethally matter of fact in his dismissal. *That guy is way out of your league.*

Heather clenched her jaw to keep from grinding her teeth. Is that so? That was the thing about Shawn. He blended absolute adoration with brutal negging. He'd be lovely as hell and then say something so hurtful it made her lose her breath. It was crazy making.

You couldn't get a guy like that in a million years. That guy dates hot girls. Not girls like you. Shawn-in-her-head had that tone Shawn got when he was punishing her.

That was what made her do it. That and the proper pisco sour she'd had when she sat down (actually drinkable, unlike the one at Casa Suerte), and the two beers she'd had with dinner. She felt reckless and rebellious, and she was sick of Shawn telling her that she wasn't good enough, and that she couldn't get anyone better than him. She was goddamn Barranco Heather tonight, and she could do anything and get anyone.

She made a beeline for the beautiful man at the bar. Her heart was raging in her ears, beating double time, but she refused to overthink this. She was riding a wave of anger and wildly unfounded confidence. As she reached the gorgeous man at the bar, she gathered scraps of her high school Spanish and managed to pull together a line as she leaned, maybe a little drunkenly, against the bar.

"*¿Oye hermoso, vienes aqui a menudo?*" Heather tried for a mix of seductive and cheeky. Her accent was genuinely deplorable, and the gorgeous man at the bar looked at her as though she'd just sneezed in his face.

Heather held her nerve. He was a complete stranger, and

she'd never see him again after tonight, so what did she have to lose? And maybe he'd find her cute. People did sometimes.

He swiveled on his stool and leaned on one elbow to look her up and down. Lord, she felt short standing here. She had to crick her neck to look him in the eye, even though he was seated. Not for the first time she wished for another few inches of height.

She felt the mad urge to run. What was she *doing*?

You're making a fool of yourself, that's what you're doing.

Oh, fuck off, Shawn.

The Peruvian dude wasn't running, so why should she?

He had the longest, curliest black eyelashes, Heather noticed, feeling a bit swoony as he examined her. He sure was taking his time looking her over. Her heart fluttered when his gaze lingered on her hips and chest. There were some benefits to being short and plump, she guessed. Curves. Men liked them, didn't they? When he lifted his gaze and met hers, Heather was stunned. Oh. Oh, *wow*. Look at those eyes. They were depthless, warm liquid darkness. *Confused* depthless, warm liquid darkness, to be sure, but they were admiring enough to make her run hot all over. One of his strong dark eyebrows rose in question.

Maybe it was her accent? Maybe he couldn't understand her.

Heather tried again, putting extra charm into it. But she was so disconcerted by his gaze that she'd slipped back into English without realizing it. "Hey, beautiful, do you come here often?"

His mouth twitched. "Yeah, I heard you the first time," he said in perfect English.

"Oh, you're American." Heather was disappointed.

"And beautiful, apparently." A trace of a smile curved that perfect mouth.

"Objectively so," Heather heard herself say. She flushed.

"Do you use that line often?" the gorgeous man at the bar asked. "And does it work?"

"It's the first time I've tried it," Heather admitted. She was painfully aware that she was still leaning against the bar like a sleazy pickup artist, but she didn't know how to get out of it. "I'll let you know how it goes. But to be honest, I thought you were Peruvian, in which case the language barrier would have worked in my favor. I think I'd benefit from the added mystery."

The trace of a smile became a proper one, revealing very nice white teeth. "Ah."

"I was just sitting over there—alone," she said, "and I saw you sitting here—alone—and I wondered if we could be less alone. Together." She couldn't do this lean against the bar anymore, especially since he was American. A sleazy lean had more charm if they were communicating across a linguistic and cultural divide. Clumsily Heather surrendered her pose and reached for an empty stool. "You mind if I sit here?" She climbed up. "And can I buy you a beer?"

He pressed his lips together and gave her an amused look. "Sure. It's not every day I get called beautiful in both bad Spanish and good English."

"Not to your face anyway." Heather wiped her sweating palms on her jeans and ordered them a couple more beers.

"What's your name?" he asked. He was polite, she had to give him that.

"Juliet." She wasn't about to give him her real name, not after behaving like a lunatic.

"Juliet . . . ?" He was dubious. Because she was obviously lying. She'd been trying for coy and flirty, but she suspected she sounded as sweaty and nervous as she felt.

"And you are?" She brazened her way through the nerves.

"Me? Romeo. Clearly." He gave her a sly grin that was sexy as hell.

"Clearly." Oh my God, the sexy man was flirting with her.

"Meeting must have been in our stars," he said as their beers were delivered. He lifted his bottle in a salute.

"I don't think Romeo and Juliet had the best stars," she reminded him as she clinked the neck of her beer bottle against the neck of his.

"As long as we don't tell our parents, I'll think we'll be fine," he said dryly.

"And no getting married, because that didn't work out well."

"Heaven forbid." But he leaned closer. He smelled spicy and salty and very, very nice.

Heather's insides were shivering. But she also felt powerful, because his dark eyes were appreciative. Of *her*.

Maybe he's drunk? Shawn-in-her-head said snidely.

Heather ignored him.

"Why *are* you alone here, Juliet?" Romeo took a sip of beer and did that mesmerizing lower lip suck again. With this guy Heather realized she didn't need to think about flags of any color. He was an adventure, not a life choice.

"I just got into town today."

"Traveling all by yourself?"

"Yeah."

"No boyfriend? Or husband?" His gaze flicked to her ring finger.

She helped him out by holding it up and wriggling it. "No husband. I broke up with a guy a couple of months ago, so no boyfriend either."

Took a break, not broke up.

Nope. Definitely broke up.

"What about you? No girlfriend? Or wife?"

He wriggled his finger back at her. "I also had a breakup a couple of months ago."

This was going too well. There must be a catch. "So, you're in Lima alone?"

"I am." He still had his stool swiveled, facing her. His soft flannel shirt stretched tight over his chest; the top few buttons were undone, revealing strong collarbones and a tantalizing curl of dark chest hair. She liked a bit of chest hair on a man. The thought of it made her buzzy. "But only for a few days," he said. "Then I'm off."

"What a coincidence. Me too." Heather tried to do her own lower lip suck and was rewarded by his gaze dropping to her mouth, where it lingered. "You have any recommendations for things I can do while I'm here?" Well, that came out more suggestive than she meant it to. Although she meant it too.

Those depthless inky dark eyes met hers again and her stomach just about dropped out of her. How could someone look so intense, and so amused, all at once?

"What are you doing now?" he asked.

"I don't know, Romeo, what am I doing now?"

Who the hell even are you right now? I have never once seen you be this aggressive.

A better version of herself, that's who the hell she was, even if she did feel vaguely ridiculous. So, take that, Shawn.

"You like dancing?" Romeo asked.

You hate dancing. Shawn was scornful.

"Sure, who doesn't like dancing?" Heather's heart was jumping around as she watched Romeo slide off his stool. She was lying through her teeth, but, hell, he was worth it.

"I was going to head to this little place down by the beach, if you'd like to come."

Heather nodded, even though she hated clubs. But she reminded herself that she was brave and adventurous Barranco Heather tonight and jumped down off her stool. She noted his eyebrows lift as he registered their height difference. She topped out just under five feet three, while he was easily over six foot tall. "Is this going to be a problem for dancing?" she asked, waving at their different heights.

"I can always hold you up so you can see the dancers," he teased, as he gestured for the door.

"Wait, what? *We're* not dancing?"

He laughed. "If you want to, we can, but I thought we'd go watch one of the local shows. I was reading about this place where you can see performances of La Marinera, and the scissor dance, and other traditional things. There are clubs nearby if that's more your scene, but to be honest, it's not really mine."

"Oh, thank God, because I hate dancing." Heather was so relieved. "I was just saying yes because I was being brave."

He gave her a sideways look.

"I actually really hate clubs," she confessed as they paid their bills and left the restaurant. "They're so loud. You can't talk to anyone. And they never have good wine. Everyone just pounds shots and grinds up against each other in the dark. It makes zero sense to me." Her mouth was running away with her. She forced herself to stop the nervous chatter.

"Grinding doesn't make sense to you?" he drawled, as they left the restaurant. He put his hands in his pockets and slowed his stride so she could keep up.

"I'm all for it in the right context," she amended hastily. "With the right person."

He laughed. "Good to know."

"So, it's not your scene . . . ?" she prodded.

He shrugged. "You've seen one club, you've seen them all. And I don't really get heading for a dark room when there's all this to see out here." He nodded at the neighborhood around them. "I mean, why come to Lima if you're not going to experience *Lima*?" He grinned. "Come on, Juliet. Let's go down Bajada de los Baños." He held his hand out like a grand gentleman inviting her to waltz; Heather put her hand in his and felt his touch through every last inch of her.

The night had taken on a sparkly, impossibly magic quality. She couldn't quite believe her terrible pickup line had netted her this beautiful man for the night.

He could be a serial killer. Shawn-in-her-head was still hanging around being a killjoy. She wished she could silence him.

"You're not a serial killer, are you?" Heather asked abruptly as they descended the stone steps into the ravine under the Bridge of Sighs.

Romeo almost missed a step. "No." He gave a startled laugh. "But I probably wouldn't tell you if I was, would I?"

"Fair point."

"*You* picked me up," he reminded her, "and you're pretty weird. If anyone should be worried about serial killers, it should be me."

"Weird!" Heather stopped dead on the bottom step.

I told you. He's out of your league.

"You think I'm weird?"

"Unusual," Romeo amended. He was still holding her hand, even though he was a couple of steps down from her.

"Unusual!" Heather didn't like the sound of that. But she did like the way his thumb was stroking the back of her hand.

Romeo considered her carefully. "It's not an insult."

"It's not a compliment either. I mean, I called you beautiful, and you're saying I'm *unusual?*"

He took a step up toward her and she had to tilt her head again to look him in the eye. "You said I was *objectively* beautiful," he reminded her teasingly.

"So, am I objectively weird?"

"Unusual," he corrected, and that stroking thumb made it hard to think straight.

"Objectively unusual?"

"I would have said subjectively a minute ago, but as this conversation progresses, you're only cementing the opinion."

Out. Of. Your. League. This is a pity date.

Heather flushed. She didn't want to be pitied. "I don't want to be unusual," she told Romeo. "I thought you were into me because . . ." She trailed off. Because what? She couldn't think why he *would* be into her. Because she bought him a beer? Because she was an easy lay? God, men sucked.

"I am into you because," he said, leaning in closer, "you're unusual." She could feel his breath on her face. He smelled sweetly of beer. "And because I'm alone, and you're alone, and you suggested being alone together would be more fun than being alone, alone."

"Are you having fun?" she asked huskily.

"It hasn't been boring so far," he said with a smile. "Now, are we going to watch this dance or not?"

"I guess if you're assuring me that you're not a serial killer, we are."

"I'll need your assurance too, weirdo."

"I can't promise anything. Not if you keep calling me weird."

He laughed. "I think I must have jet lag, because this is the strangest night I've had in a long time." He tugged her hand and pulled her on.

"I'll try and be less weird."

"Don't. I like it."

"Really?" Heather trotted to keep up as they plunged into the river of people in the Bajada de los Baños.

"Objectively," he assured her.

Heather surrendered to the night. In Romeo's words, it was strange. Unusual. Weird. But wonderful. They went to a bar-cum-theater by the sea, where they managed to squeeze in to see a series of Peruvian dances.

"Most of these dances are Andean," Romeo told her, lowering his head to speak quietly in her ear. The swirl of his warm breath against her skin was intoxicating.

As the final dance closed, she looked up and found Romeo smiling down at her.

"Enjoy it?"

She nodded, not sure she could put the pleasure into words. "Thank you for bringing me here."

"My pleasure, weirdo."

"I liked it when you called me Juliet better."

"A weirdo by any other name."

He was seriously gorgeous. The corners of his lips were pointy, always looking like he might smile. It was a tease.

"Fancy a beach walk?" he asked.

Of course she did. She never wanted the night to end.

R&B thumped from a beachside club as they ambled down to the shore. There was a line of people queuing to get into the club.

"So, what do you do for a living, Juliet?"

Oh no. No reality. She didn't want reality tonight. "My parents want me to marry this guy Tybalt, but I think he's a dick. I'm scheming to get out of it. That's basically how I occupy myself."

"Right. Noted."

"And how about you?"

"I guess I spend my days being all emo over some chick. I forget her name."

"Nice."

"It fills the time."

Bajada de los Baños led them across a garden strip planted with decorative flowers and stocked with statues, and down to a horseshoe beach with a pier. The cliffs towered over the ravine, sprinkled with city lights. The ocean was calm, swooshing against the sand like a series of sighs.

"You ever been to Lima before?" he asked, as they paused to pull their shoes off.

"First time," she confessed. "You?"

"Second. But last time I was working."

Heather was afraid that if they started talking about their real lives the magic would break. Software quality assurance wasn't particularly seductive. The sand was cool on her feet as she led the way down to the foamy frill of seawater. She rolled her jeans up and took a step into the water. They lapsed into quiet as they paddled along the beach. It was hard to talk when you didn't want to talk about work and real life, especially as work *was* her whole life.

Heather darted glances at him and shivered when she caught him darting glances back. Eventually she gave up stealing glances and just stared at him. Because she wouldn't be able to look at him after tonight and, God, he was fine.

"Are you spending your whole trip in Lima? Or are you seeing more of Peru?" he asked when he caught her staring. He didn't seem put off—he just stared back.

"More," she said. "But with family, not alone." She pulled a face.

"Looking forward to it, huh?"

"They're a lot," she admitted. "Like *a lot.*"

"Aren't all families?"

Heather shrugged. "I don't know what yours is like."

"Messy," he told her. The breeze was playing with his curls; they brushed against his eyebrows. He pushed them away and shot her a smile. "Which is why I don't travel with them."

"There's no need to be smug." Heather couldn't resist his smile. "It wasn't my idea."

"But you said yes and came anyway."

Heather couldn't argue with that.

He laughed. "I'm sure you'll have a blast. Peru will work its magic."

"So, this breakup of yours," Romeo asked quietly after a moment. "Was it your choice, or his?"

Heather didn't want to talk about Shawn. She'd only just shut his voice up. "Mine," she said simply. Curiosity got the best of her, and she couldn't resist asking, "And did you do the dumping, or did she?"

"She did."

Right. Heather heard the flatness of his tone and saw the way his jaw clenched, and decided this conversation was only going to ruin the night. "Is it a red flag when a guy starts talking about exes?" she asked lightly.

He looked startled and returned his full attention to her. "Probably." But his gaze softened, and that warm, languid feeling settled in again.

"Hey," he said eventually, "do you want to go get a drink, or do you need to get back to Casa Capulet?"

"Will you be at this drink?" she joked, not quite able to believe this magical creature wanted to keep hanging out. "Like, is this a together-alone thing, or an alone-alone thing?"

"Let's start with together-alone and see how it goes."

"Like whether one of us serial kills the other or not?"

"Exactly. I know a good wine bar—are you a wine person? Don't be brave, be honest. I don't want this to be another dancing situation. I want you to actually enjoy yourself."

"Wine is definitely my scene," she said honestly.

"Because we can easily opt for cocktails or beer if you'd rather?"

"Wine," she insisted. "I'm a wine person."

"Except when you're drinking beer and pisco sours."

"You saw me drink that pisco sour? You were watching me?"

"There was a mirror over the bar—I was watching the whole room."

"But I was in the room, so you were definitely watching me."

"You were in the room and drinking a pisco sour."

"Pisco is a thing you do in Peru, right? I was being polite."

"And the beer?"

"I never said I didn't like beer. I just prefer wine. And that place had a *terrible* wine list."

"It really did," he agreed.

"So, this place you know is better?" she asked as they climbed the stairs from the beach. Heather should have been exhausted from her long day, but she felt wired. Zingy.

"Much better." He took the stairs easily as they climbed, but she was puffing to keep up.

"How do I know I can trust you?" she huffed.

"Be brave. Isn't that your thing?"

Yes. It was. At least for today.

Romeo led her to an intimate wine bar and to a cozy booth with slightly shabby dark wine velvet upholstery. Soft music played, guitars and plaintive voices. Romeo ordered them a bottle of Argentinian malbec and sat back to gaze at her.

"A whole bottle? That's a big commitment," she observed.

"I don't do things halfway." That ghost of a smile was back again.

After the waiter poured the slightly chilled wine, Romeo swirled the ruby liquid in the glass. "What do you think?" he asked.

Heather swirled and sniffed. "Smells good."

He laughed. He clearly didn't think she knew anything about wine. "And how does it taste?"

She took an experimental sip and held it in her mouth for a moment before swallowing. "Oranges? Rind?"

The laughter faded. He took a sip too. "Definitely orange rind. And something woody. Sandalwood maybe?"

"Cherry and plum. And red tea tannins."

He reached for the bottle and read the tasting notes on the label.

"So you *like* wine," he said. He sounded pleased.

"A lot." That sounded bad. "But not in an alcoholic way. Just in an 'I like wine' way." That didn't sound much better. "You?"

"I travel a lot for work. I've been lucky enough to learn a bit about wine while on the job."

Heather itched to know what he did—but if he shared, then she'd have to share, and she really didn't want to be her regular self tonight. "I go to wine tastings at a fancy chain store," she confessed. "They do a wine and cheese event where they talk you through tasting notes. It was a fun thing to do when I got to Chicago and I didn't know anyone."

She saw him register where she lived, and she took a swallow of wine. No more real life. Instead, she kept the conversation focused on wine, hyperaware of his knuckles brushing hers across the narrow table every time he lifted his glass. His eyes were so dark that there was barely any delineation between iris and pupil. She kept getting lost in them. Now and then she came to, only to realize they weren't even speaking. He seemed okay with it. The music was a low tide pulling the night into ebb. The lyrics played at the edge of Heather's mind, slipping in and out of focus, the same way the real world kept slipping in and out of focus as she stared into Romeo's inky eyes.

Somehow they were still sitting there, staring, having fragmented drifting conversations, when the music faded and the malbec ran out, and the staff were flicking the lights to kick them out into the street.

"Time to go, lovers," the bartender called in heavily accented English.

Heather flushed. Lovers. She met Romeo's eye. He didn't look away.

Unsteady from more than the wine, Heather slid from the booth and prepared to be brave. She'd need courage to make a move. She'd also need it to face her disappointment if he didn't accept her advances.

"Well, tonight was an unexpected pleasure," Romeo said softly as they stood in the street, staring at each other. The orange streetlight was a fallen veil around them.

"Unusually so," she agreed, trying to work up her courage.

"Beautifully so," he corrected. Then he reached out and brushed her hair away from her cheek. His fingertips lingered on the curve of her face, sending swirls of pleasure through her.

Oh, wow. Was *he* making a move? Maybe she didn't need

courage at all. She'd stumbled into an evening that belonged to someone else, she thought dumbly. It was the kind of evening that happened to those long-legged boho girls at Casa Suerte, not to people like her. She wasn't even wearing a peasant skirt. . . .

"I'd love to know what you're thinking," he said, his fingertips still resting on her cheek.

She was thinking that she wanted to kiss him, very badly. And because she was Barranco Heather today, and she wanted to enjoy it before the magic ran out, she did. Very badly. She lunged on tiptoe and managed to catch the side of his sulky-lipped mouth with her lips. At least what she lacked in finesse she made up for with enthusiasm, she thought optimistically, as she plastered herself against his beautiful body, her legs hard against his strong thighs. She felt him smile against her. Then he angled his head, so that their mouths met properly, and kissed her back. He tasted like malbec, and salt. His mouth was hot as it opened under hers, and his fingers were just as hot as they slid along her face and into her hair, sending shivers down her spine.

Kissing Romeo was a revelation. He kissed her so slowly and thoroughly that her knees almost buckled. It was like sinking into honey. His tongue was a caress, inviting her to deepen the kiss at will, and the languidness of it was lethal. Heather wrapped her arms around his neck, as his hands trailed down her back to her waist. She held on for dear life, not sure if she could keep her feet. Was this how it felt to swoon?

Kissing him was a powerful narcotic. When he pulled away, she struggled to remember how to breathe. She gazed up at him, utterly dazed. "So, the line worked, then?" she heard herself say.

"Seems to have." His voice was a husky rasp that made her shiver.

"Any tweaks you'd suggest for next time?" Why was she talking? Her mouth had a mind of its own—and it was focused on the wrong things. It should be kissing, not talking.

"Send me the feedback form and I'll let you know." His hands were still on her waist, and they gave her a slow and intimate squeeze.

"It's more of a multiple-choice quiz than a form, per se." She was still on tiptoe, her arms looped around his neck.

"Multiple choice, huh?"

"Yeah. And the right answer is C, just so you know."

"Is it?

"C: Unusual is better than beautiful."

"I think I'll be ticking D."

Heather frowned. "Seriously? You're going to insult me *now*?"

"Calling you unusual *and* beautiful is an insult?" He closed the thin gap between them, and his lips were feather-soft against hers. When he spoke, she felt their soft movement. "Can I walk you back to your hotel? Or your Airbnb?" he whispered.

"Yes," Heather whispered back, her heart exploding into a mad gallop. "It's back over the bridge."

He reached up and grasped her wrist, untangling her from his neck. He turned her hand over and pressed a kiss to her palm and, oh my, who knew there were nerve endings in her palm that ran to *everywhere* else. "Come on, Juliet, before the lark starts singing."

Heather felt the raw energy pulsing between them as they walked up the hill, away from the ocean and back toward the Bridge of Sighs. "Do you know about the wishing thing?" she asked thickly as they reached the narrow bridge.

"The one about holding your breath across the bridge?" He was still holding her hand. She'd never met a man who held hands so much. What was even odder was how much she liked it.

It was so odd to feel this connected to a complete stranger. She didn't even know his name. "Have you made a wish since you've been here?" she asked.

He shook his head. "Not yet. You?"

She nodded, still feeling breathless. "I did it on the way to dinner."

"And did your wish come true yet?"

She nodded again, slowly, feeling the shimmer of moonlight like an evanescent web around them. Oh yes, she'd definitely been wonderfully surprised.

"Want to do it again?" he invited, eyeing the bridge in front of them. Earlier tonight it had been bustling with people, but now it was late, and the bridge was deserted. "It doesn't look hard." He considered her. "What are you going to wish for this time, Juliet?"

More. More of this. But she wasn't telling him that. "I can't tell you or it won't come true."

"It's like birthday wishes, you think?"

"All wishes are the same," she said firmly. "You can't go airing them, or they evaporate."

He nodded, looking amused. "Good to know. Got your wish ready?"

"Yes. You got yours?"

He nodded and she found she was desperately curious to know what it was. But she didn't want to risk it not coming true by asking—just in case it had something to do with her and the hours ahead.

"Deep breath," he ordered. His thumb was doing that stroking thing again on the back of her hand. She never wanted him to stop.

She took a deep breath, and so did he. Then he winked at her, and they started the mad dash to the end of the bridge. The sound of their feet on the bridge echoed through the ravine below. Heather's head was pounding. This was harder after a bottle of wine than it had seemed earlier. But she made it, a couple of steps behind him, their arms stretched between them like a guide rope. Heather exhaled in a burst. And then he kissed her. There was nothing languid about him this time. His mouth was firm, his tongue sliding into her. Heather gave herself over, melting into him. Every inch of her was tingling and aching to be touched.

"Take me home," she whispered against his lips, suddenly aware that she'd wrapped her legs around him and he was holding her up.

"Show me the way," he managed between kisses, as he lowered her to the ground.

They quickened their pace on the way back up the hill, but she noticed him slow imperceptibly when they turned onto her street. She glanced over, worried the magic was waning.

"Which one is yours?" he asked, sounding oddly suspicious.

"The yellow," she said, gesturing at Casa Suerte, which was much quieter than when she left it. There was no music pulsing from the rooftop, and the carnival lights were dark, as were most of the windows in the bougainvillea-covered frontage. She pulled the keys from her bag, the fat pom-poms swinging exuberantly from the key ring. She saw his surprise.

"I know, they're ridiculous. It's so I won't lose them—it must happen a lot. This place seems to attract a party crowd."

"Right." He followed her slowly to the front door.

She fumbled with the keys. The room key had an orange dot of paint on it, and the key to the front door had a green dot. But the fatal flaw was that it was hard to tell the difference under the amber glass of the front door light. Especially when you were cloudy-headed from wine and lust. It took Heather quite a few tries to get the door unlocked.

The casa was quiet and dim as the door opened. Everyone was either out clubbing or asleep. Expecting late-night revelers, Cristina and her bartender had left a lamp burning on the first-floor landing; they were clearly used to people stumbling home late. Heather held her finger to her lips and beckoned Romeo to follow her. She made sure the front door latched and then led him upstairs, aware that he'd gone very still and watchful.

Serial killer.

Oh hell, why was Shawn back *now*?

"You're all the way at the top?" Romeo whispered as she rounded the second landing and kept going. And then he stopped dead when she led him into the corridor. "You can't be serious?"

Something in his voice gave her pause. Heather turned to find him staring at her, with the oddest look on his face. "What? I know it's not fancy . . ."

"Is *that* your room, by any chance?" With remarkable instincts, he pointed directly at her orange door.

Heather looked back and forth between him and the door. "How did you know that? Wait. *Have* you been following me? *Are* you a serial killer?"

He shook his head, then stepped past her. "This is so weird."

"You really like that word."

"You'll never believe this." He tugged something from his pocket. Keys. And swinging from the keys were three fat green and purple pom-poms. Heather watched, stunned, as he took the key and opened the green door next to her orange one.

Wait, *what*?

He disappeared inside. There was a click as the door closed behind him.

No. No way.

Heather opened her orange door and stepped into her own room. She headed straight for the bathroom. As she slid the door open, she saw the door on her neighbor's side sliding open too. And standing on the other side of that door was . . . Romeo.

Romeo was her neighbor?

"What *is* this?"

They were both more than a little spooked.

"This is either a quirk of fate . . . ," he said. "Or you're going to kill me and keep my head in a freezer."

Heather was startled into a laugh. "It couldn't be both? You don't think serial killers deserve a bit of fate?"

"I don't believe in fate," he told her, but she didn't think he sounded too certain.

"It's just a coincidence," she said. "An out-there one, sure. But they happen. And I'm definitely not after your head. Look, I don't even *have* a freezer in here." She swept an arm at the room behind her.

"There are more than eleven million people in Lima. What are the chances that we'd be in rooms next to each other?" He ran a hand through his already tousled dark hair.

"Well, given we're tourists staying in a tourist district, it's not *that* impossible a quirk of fate." Was he having second thoughts? Because that didn't seem fair. It wasn't her fault they both liked to holiday in romantic old *casonas*.

"But right next door to one another?" he said, frowning.

"With a shared bathroom," she agreed. "It's definitely on the weirder, more fated end of the spectrum."

"I don't believe in fate," he reminded her.

"Let's say fate-*ish*, then." She cleared her throat. "Look, does this actually change anything? We were headed to my room, and here's my room . . ."

"And *my* room, as it turns out."

"It does kind of complicate the whole one-night-stand thing, I admit." She chewed on her lip. "But not much. I mean, I'm only here for three more days. How complicated can things get in three days?"

"With a shared bathroom?"

Heather's gaze drifted to the shower. Her mind was immediately full of tantalizing images, involving Romeo and hot, steamy showers. She gave him a sideways glance. "Look, if it's no good, there doesn't have to be an encore. You lock your door, I lock mine."

His gaze snapped to hers. He still wanted her. She could see it in the dark currents of his eyes. "If it's no good? Is that a challenge?"

"*¿Oye hermoso, vienes aqui a menudo?*" she drawled in her atrocious Spanish, adopting the same sleazy lean that had worked for her back at the bar.

"Does that line work?" he drawled back, copying her lean against the doorway.

"So far it's served me well."

"So far." His lips were twitching again. "But you might need to expand your repertoire."

"I'm more than happy to show you my repertoire, Romeo. Your room or mine? Or neutral ground." She was itching to put that shower to use.

"How about your room, then mine? *Then* neutral ground?"

Heather backed away from the bathroom, toward her bed. "How about *yes*."

"Who *are* you?" he whispered as he reached her. With both hands he smoothed her hair and cupped her face.

"Me? I'm just a weirdo," she whispered back, staring up at him. The moonlight fell through the arched window and silvered his beautiful face. "Please stop talking now and kiss me."

"A bossy weirdo."

Sure. Why not. Barranco Heather grabbed his shirt in her fist and yanked him to her. "Shut up and kiss me."

And in one last surprise, he did everything she told him to. And who even cared about flags at that point.

Chapter 5
Heather

Miraflores, Lima

"What's wrong? Why are you smiling like that?"

Heather rolled her eyes. Honestly. Why couldn't her mother just say *hello*?

Heather had arrived at the shiny luxury hotel in Miraflores an hour or so earlier and had been sitting in the sun-streamed lobby, listening to the splashing fountain, waiting for her mother and Bon. Who were late.

The hotel was expensive beyond belief—it was glossy and lush and as different from the shabby charm of Casa Suerte as it was possible to get. Here the lobby floor was polished hardwood, with enormous soaring plate glass windows looking out onto the lush gardens of the park; the gardens led straight to the cliffs, and to a view of the glittering South Pacific beyond. Above Heather's head, wrought iron chandeliers hung from cavernous ceilings, and beneath her feet was a Peruvian rug so huge she could have parked a bus on it. There was no pulsing reggaeton here; the place was as hushed and peaceful as a day spa.

Heather had been quite comfortable, sitting alone in the lobby on a buttery leather lounge in a pool of sunlight, listening to the fountain play, inhaling the perfume of the vast bunch of oriental lilies on the coffee table in front of her. She was feeling warm and loose and perfectly at peace with the world.

Until Mom arrived.

"I'm smiling because I'm glad to see you," Heather said brightly, trying not to lose the happy feeling she'd carried with her into the hotel.

Heather had been smiling because she'd been thinking about the morning that she'd spent saying goodbye to Romeo. In the shower. She opened her mouth, unable to resist telling Mom about him, but her mother cut her off before she could speak.

"What *is* that you're wearing?" Mom looked her up and down.

"A peasant skirt." Heather did a twirl and the skirt ballooned out, light as air. "It's new. I bought it at a market. It's made from alpaca silk."

"It's very bright." Mom was squinting.

"Mom, I—"

"You haven't spoken to your father, have you? I sent him an email before I left, and I haven't heard anything back."

Heather deflated. Mom had been here only two minutes and she was talking about Dad already. And no, she hadn't spoken to Dad, who hadn't answered his phone when Heather had called to tell him about Peru.

"Heather! You look *gorgeous*." Bon-Bon swept over from the check-in desk, clutching a fistful of hotel room swipe cards in little cardboard envelopes in one hand and Junior's wooden box in the other. "You look like a toucan."

"A toucan?" Mom rolled her eyes. "Honestly, Mom, is that supposed to make her feel good?"

Bon kissed Heather on the cheek. "Did I say toucan? I meant macaw."

"It's too bright?" Heather could feel some of the magic flake off her new skirt.

"There is no such thing," Bon assured her. "Besides, vacations are for brightness. For shaking it up a little. Say hi to Junior," she instructed Heather.

"Hi, Junior." Heather considered the box, genuinely surprised that he'd come along. "They let you into the country with him?"

"Of course. He's not a terrorist. But I did have to keep him in the carry-on luggage during the flight—which I'm sure he didn't appreciate."

"I hope you didn't spend too much on that skirt," Mom interrupted, frowning. "Tourist markets are so overpriced."

They were both in fine form today. Heather smoothed her hands over her skirt. She *liked* this skirt. But now she felt like a little kid playing dress-up. Especially standing next to Mom, who was in practical travel gear. She looked ready to hike right out the door and up to Machu Picchu.

Mom and Bon had arrived on the blue airport shuttle—the only people getting off at this stop. They'd been unmissable, squabbling like children. Bon had a mountain of luggage, but Mom came with just her hiking pack, even though Bon had explicitly paid for extra luggage. Heather had watched as the two of them fussed at the porter as he loaded their gear onto a baggage trolley, and as they bickered in front of the concierge's desk. She'd taken a minute to steady herself before they spotted her, but it didn't help much. They always managed to unbalance her, this time by mentioning Dad and picking at her about the skirt.

"You could do with something overpriced yourself," Bon told her daughter after she finished comparing Heather to a flamboyant bird. "Look at the state of you."

"The point of hiking is to strip things back to the basics," Mom said stubbornly. She stood out like a sore thumb in her outdoor wear, in the middle of the lobby of this exceedingly fancy hotel.

"Indeed. But we're not hiking right now, are we? I can't see why you need your boots to take an elevator up to a five-star suite."

"I'm wearing them in." Mom was looking mulish. "Besides, no one is looking at a middle-aged woman like me."

"Not dressed like that, they're not. Maybe Heather can take you to the market and find you something to wear to dinner." Bon was arch. "Cargo pants are hardly appropriate for the resort restaurant, and we have a booking tonight. And even if they were appropriate, they haven't been in fashion for decades."

"The market isn't likely to be open *now*," Mom said stiffly, "and I'm tired and want a shower."

"You'll have to wear something of mine, then." Bon was implacable.

"I can order room service if you don't like what I'm wearing."

"Alright," Heather sighed, feeling a familiar tension stiffening her shoulders. "Why don't we leave this argument until after we've unpacked and freshened up."

"Argument?" Bon looked startled. "Who's arguing?"

"Not me," Mom said grimly. "But Heather's right, let's stop talking until we've settled in." She headed for the bank of elevators at the far end of the lobby.

"Has she been this much fun the whole time?" Heather asked, watching her mother's military stride. Mom looked like she was heading off to battle.

It was supposed to be a *vacation*.

"Well, she's at the end of a long flight," Bon said, putting her arm around Heather and giving her a squeeze. "So she's tired out. She was *much* worse back in Phoenix, when she was fresh."

Heather laughed. "You deserve a medal for flying with her."

"I'm sure she thinks she deserves a medal for flying with *me*." Bon nudged Heather. "Five bucks for whoever gets Sandra to smile first tonight."

"Cut off at midnight?"

"Anything goes. Even cat videos on YouTube. I don't care what it takes."

"Deal." But Heather doubted cat videos would cut it.

"Wait till you see the room, chicken," Bon sang gaily as they joined Mom. "I spared no expense!"

"It's a waste of money," Mom sighed. "One bed is as good as another."

"Hardly. These have those expensive mattress toppers and

high-thread-count sheets. We have the most incredible view," Bon told Heather excitedly, "and just *look* at these elevators."

The elevators *were* pretty amazing. They were glass and chrome bubbles that ran up the outside of the building.

"Like in that old movie, *The Towering Inferno*," Bon said. "You ever see that one?"

Heather shook her head as the doors slid open and they stepped in. "Can't say I ever have."

Mom was holding on to the chrome rail with white-knuckled hands.

As well she might, because the ride up was vertiginous. And fast. The green park below whooshed away from them, and they were up in the sky, looking at the vastness of the ocean spreading out below. Heather's stomach was falling.

"Now that's a million-dollar view," Bon sighed happily.

The sun was lowering, casting a fiery orange blaze across the ocean. From here the seagulls were tiny dashes against the bronze sky.

"Oh, thank God," Mom breathed when they reached their floor, and she could escape the glass bubble of the elevator.

"If she hates heights, how is she going to manage the hike?" Heather whispered to Bon. "I saw online that some of the paths are right on the mountain edge."

"Oh, she'll be fine." Bon waved her hand dismissively, leading the way to their room.

Wow. Their suite was ridiculously fancy. The walls were painted a deep midnight blue, and everything was carpeted and plush; the deepness of the color served to draw the eye to the windows and . . . just *wow* . . . that view of ocean and sky. Heather felt a shiver of pleasure at the sight. She could look at that forever, she thought, creeping closer to the glass. At the edge of the terrace, a thick glass balustrade stood between them and nothing at all. Heather couldn't resist opening the doors to the rush of salt air and the sound of the waves on the shore. The wash of copper-gold evening light was warm on her face. It was like floating in air.

"Oh, Bon," she breathed, "it's amazing!"

Bon clapped her hands. "Isn't it! Don't you feel like a princess in a tower?"

"No," Heather laughed. "I feel like a *queen*."

"Close the door, Heather," Mom groaned. "It's giving me vertigo."

Oh dear. Mom was looking green.

"You'd best take the bed farthest from the window," Bon said practically, passing Mom her key card. "It'll save you girls arguing over who gets which bed." She winked at Heather, tossing her a key card of her own. "Junior and I are taking the king room." Bon opened the door to her room, revealing another plush midnight-blue oasis, filled with an expansive bed. "Oh, look, our bags are already here!"

They sure were. There was a mountain of them next to Bon's king-size bed.

"Wow, look at your en suite, Bon!" The door to the bathroom was open, revealing marble floors and walls, and a small crystal chandelier in the shape of an egg. "You've even got a Jacuzzi!"

"You've got one too." Bon sounded smug. "Go look."

Bon-Bon loved luxury, and her joy was catching. It made Heather feel like it was Christmas morning.

Heather took her suitcase with her as she went to check out her own bathroom. Mom was already there, standing on the threshold.

"Can you believe this?" Mom said. She was sounding a little grinchy.

Heather stuck her head in. The bathroom was a mirror image of Bon's, including the giant corner Jacuzzi. There was a large orchid in the corner, fat with flowers the size of small plates.

"Is this place bigger than your apartment?" Mom asked.

"Much," Heather assured her, "I could fit my kitchen and bedroom into just our room."

Their bedroom was big enough to comfortably fit two queen beds. There was another orchid on the table, the white flowers trembling on their stems in the air flowing quietly from the vents. There was a sliding door to the terrace in here too.

Heather opened it. She couldn't get enough of the salt air and the sound of the breathing sea.

The setting sun had turned the ocean molten bronze, and the palm trees along the cliff were streaming in the warm breeze. That loose, lovely feeling was back as Heather took it all in. It was gorgeous. Without stopping to second-guess herself, Heather snapped a quick photo on her phone and sent a message to Romeo. **Slumming it**, she captioned.

"Can you grab my pack when you get yours?" Mom asked from the dimness of the room behind. "I need a break from her for a minute or so." She sat heavily on her bed.

"Sure," Heather said absently. She'd noticed the flashing dots on her phone.

A message.

A photo of colorful fishing boats appeared on the screen in her hand. The boats were bobbing on a still bay, and the arid hills rimming the bay were glowing amber in the evening light. The bright colors of the boats—orange, teal, yellow, blue—reflected in the calm waters, doubling their charm. The sky overhead the bay was hazy, a pure blue streaked with orange and gold.

Romeo was off somewhere in Peru, watching the sunset. Living his best life.

Another message arrived.

Paracas.

He was living his best life, watching the sunset in Paracas. Without her.

Thought we weren't messaging . . . he wrote.

Stupidly, it stung.

We aren't.

Or they weren't supposed to be. They'd said their goodbyes this morning. They only had each other's numbers because they'd gone to get their Peruvian SIM cards together. Whatever it was they were to each other, it wasn't a thing that was lasting past their three days in Casa Suerte. Which they'd decided during their first night. This was a fateful fling.

Fated to be brief.

"I'm not one for permanence," he told her as they lay in

the darkness, watching through the mullioned window as the moonlight chased the terra-cotta roofs with filigrees of silver light. "I come and go too much. It wears people down."

He'd made himself clear, and yet here she was, messaging him only hours after they'd parted.

Missing me, huh?

And here he was, messaging back.

"Who are you messaging? Shawn?" The note of hope in Mom's voice was unmistakable. And jarring.

Heather hadn't thought of Shawn in days. "No," she said, more sharply than she meant to. "It's just a friend I made in Barranco." She bit her lip, wondering whether or not to tell her mom more.

"I bet the place you stayed in Barranco was cheaper than here," Mom said dryly, looking around at the antique furniture in their suite.

"Much cheaper," Heather agreed, tucking her phone in her pocket, trying to forget Romeo. She couldn't bear it if she told Mom and Mom ruined it. Romeo was her secret enchantment, and she didn't want it spoiled. She fetched their hiking packs from Bon's room.

"What have you got in here?" she huffed as she lugged her mother's gear.

"Not much," Mom sighed. "It's just a slightly heavier pack—but it got good reviews online."

"You ever done a hike like this before?" Heather asked her mom.

"I went to Europe with your dad after we got married, does that count?"

"Did you have to go up any hills?"

"We walked up to Sacré-Cœur in Paris." Mom gave Heather a rueful look. Then she sighed. "I never thought I'd be doing a trek like this for the first time at my age."

"You're only fifty."

"Almost fifty-one." Mom opened her pack. "If I have a heart attack, just leave me up there for the vultures."

"Jesus, Mom," Heather groaned.

"What?"

"Do you have to be so grim all the time?"

"It's *funny*. I'm being funny."

"Well, no one's laughing. Come on, Bon's spent a lot of money to enjoy this with us. Can't you at least *pretend* to have a good time?" Heather was sharper than she meant to be, but she had years of pent-up anger simmering—which was one reason she hadn't been answering her mother's calls. Her mom didn't need it right now. Heather had planned to deal with it herself and *then* talk to her mom. But now here they were, roomies, and within five minutes Heather had made her mom cry.

"You're right, I'm being useless." Mom's voice was tight and tender.

Heather's insides were all knotted up and she had a sour metallic taste in her mouth. Why did her mom do this to her? *She* was the kid here. What if *she* needed comforting? But old habits die hard, and Heather found herself stepping into the role of caretaker, as usual. "You must be tired," she said, switching gears and trying to sound brisk and cheerful. "I was wrecked after the flight in. Why don't you have a shower and get ready for dinner?"

Her mother nodded but kept her back determinedly turned. Even so, Heather didn't miss the way her hand darted up to dash away a rolling tear.

She felt terrible. She should be more sympathetic. Her mother had lost a husband too. And it was somehow worse for everyone that he was still alive and kicking.

"Here, I've got something for you." Heather unzipped her suitcase. She pulled the Aesop box out. Heather had hidden the products after her first night with Romeo, freaked out by the thought of him smelling like Shawn's gift. It was fine giving the box to an anonymous shower-sharer; it was not okay to give it to Romeo.

She held the expensive toiletries out to Mom.

"What's this?" Mom looked startled.

"A gift. Something to help you enjoy your arrival." Heather

felt a stab of guilt as she saw the pleasure on her mother's face. She wasn't sure if she felt guilty because of Shawn or because of Mom. Maybe both.

"Oh, honey, that's so thoughtful." Mom was welling up again as she opened the box. "Geranium! You remembered how much I love the smell of geranium?"

Well, she hadn't. But she accepted Mom's pleased thanks, glad she wasn't crying anymore.

"Baby." Mom rose from the bed and wrapped Heather in a hug, the Aesop box crushed between their bodies. "Thank you." Warm tears landed on Heather's neck.

Heather felt an inch tall. She resolved to be nicer to her mother as Mom gave a shaky sigh. Heather rubbed her back gingerly.

"What did you do, slip something in her water?" Bon whispered an hour later, as she watched her daughter lean into the mirror in the main room, applying a neat coat of red lipstick. "She looks happy."

Mom had changed into a pair of tight black jeans and a loose black knit top with batwing arms. She wore thin leather sandals, and she looked good.

"No, I just slipped her some fancy body wash," Heather whispered back.

"I thought you said you only brought travel gear," Bon needled Mom, unable to resist stirring her up. "And here you are looking fabulous."

"This *is* travel gear," Mom said, rubbing her crimson lips together to blot them. "You said to bring something nice to go out in. This rolled up small enough and didn't crease. And I can wear the jeans anywhere." She turned to them and raised an eyebrow. "Now please tell me the restaurant isn't on the rooftop, because I refuse to go any higher in those elevators."

"It's in the gardens downstairs."

"Oh, thank God." Mom tucked the tube of lipstick in one pocket and tucked her room card in the other.

"It's not even on the cliff edge," Bon said with mock innocence. She leaned in next to Mom and checked her own makeup, running a finger along the smudge of her eyeliner. Bon was smart in wide-leg forest-green trousers and a striped black and white top.

"Do you think I look okay, or should I change?" Heather was having second thoughts about her peasant skirt. She'd changed into a fresh T-shirt, cropped and tight, and thrown her denim jacket on. Earlier today, as she'd danced away from Romeo's farewell kiss, she'd felt bohemian and fine. But now the whole thing felt out of character, mismatched and kind of silly.

"You look stunning," Bon told her. "Like Stevie Nicks."

Heather wasn't reassured.

"Besides, you're young. You'd look great in a potato sack."

Now she really wasn't reassured.

As Heather followed Mom and Bon down to dinner, she felt the familiar prickly sweat of self-doubt. For a moment she imagined Shawn's reaction to her new clothes, which was a complete mistake, because now she'd invited him back into her head.

That skirt is really designed with taller women in mind. Shawn-in-her-head sounded thoughtful. That was what was so horrible about him. He framed every insult as though he was being helpful. And it was awful.

Heather was aware of her hem trailing slightly on the floor as she swished into the elevator. She *was* very short for it. She crammed her hands into the pockets of her denim jacket and kept her gaze away from her reflection in the elevator glass.

"Those are very flattering jeans, Sandra," Bon was telling Mom sincerely. "They do wonders for you."

"If you say one word about my weight gain, I'll sock you one, Mom. I mean it."

"Well, you'd never even know in those."

"Mom."

"Besides, big bottoms are fashionable these days. Not like in my day."

Heather's mom gave an eyeroll worthy of a teenager.

"At least she didn't compare you to Stevie Nicks," Heather told her.

"Heather Russo!" Bon-Bon was outraged. "I won't hear a

word said against Stevie Nicks. I first slept with your grandfather after a Fleetwood Mac concert. Although that was before
Stevie Nicks joined the lineup."

"Stop!" Mom put her hands over her ears. "I don't want to
hear it."

"Oh, gross." Heather was the first one out of the elevator.

But Bon wouldn't take the hint. "It wasn't gross. It was beautiful. And I was wearing a skirt much like that one. Only it was
Indian cotton."

"*Stop* talking." Mom still had her hands over her ears as she
crossed the lobby.

"Bon, you need to buy me at least a couple of glasses of wine
before you drop information like that," Heather told her.

"I'll keep that in mind." Bon was having a great time. She
had Junior's box in the crook of her arm, and she was grinning.
"This is so much more fun than sitting around back in Tucson,
next to that golf course. Thank you for coming along on your
grandmother's crazy vacation."

"Thanks for inviting me," Heather said honestly. "I'm loving
it so far."

"And we've barely even begun!" Bon gestured expansively
at the lush gardens, the palms spotlit against the plum-colored
night sky. "Ready?"

Heather was. Because she wanted to claw back the Barranco
magic. As they stepped out into the garden, she glanced down
the coast, to where Barranco was a glitter of lights on the cliffs.
But Romeo wasn't there anymore.

"And don't forget," Bon reminded her, "five bucks for the
first person to get your mom to laugh."

"I've got the cat videos queued up," Heather promised.

A couple were leaving the roped-off restaurant as they approached. The man looked Heather up and down and smiled.
Oh God. Was he laughing at the skirt? Heather curled in on
herself.

"Stop slumping your shoulders, Heather. You look divine.
Own it." Bon poked her between the shoulder blades.

Automatically, Heather straightened her shoulders.

"No one with a rack as good as yours should ever slump."

"Bon!" Heather flushed.

"What's she done now?" Mom asked. She was waiting at the velvet rope that cordoned off the hotel's outdoor restaurant, which sprawled onto a paved area in the gardens, beneath awnings that rippled in the breeze.

"She's talking about my rack," Heather told her quietly, still blushing.

"Mother!"

"I was giving her a *compliment*."

"Well, save the compliments till we're a few drinks in and can cope."

"You two need a few drinks. You're so uptight it hurts. Aren't they, Junior?"

"Don't you dare bring Junior into this. I don't want him anywhere near my daughter's rack."

"Mom!"

"What? I don't."

"Everyone shut up now," Heather warned. "The maître d' is coming."

Mom and Bon swiveled, polite smiles fixed in place, as the maître d' swooped in to take them to their table.

You'd never know what filthy old broads they could be, Heather thought, as they complimented the host on the table.

It was a great table, with a view down the lawns to the water.

"Three pisco sours," Bon ordered before the waiter even gave them the wine list. "And as soon as they're done, bring us three more. We're celebrating tonight." She gave the waiter a conspiratorial gesture, beckoning her closer. "You may be surprised, but this is my *seventieth* birthday present to myself."

"Happy birthday. And is that your birthday present from *them*?" the waiter asked in her heavy accent, nodding equally conspiratorially to the cherry wood box on the table in front of Bon.

There was a spiky silence as Heather and her mother regarded Junior's box.

"Oh no," Bon said. "That's my husband."

The waiter recoiled, horrified as Bon's words sank in. "*Lo siento,*" she stammered.

"Mom, why?" Heather's mother protested, as they watched the waiter beat a hasty retreat. "That poor girl."

"What? It's the truth." Bon seemed genuinely baffled by their responses.

"It's a bit unusual to have your dead husband on the dinner table," Heather told her grandmother.

"I'm sure it happens all the time." Bon-Bon was blithe.

"I'm so sorry," Heather's mom apologized to the waiter when she returned carrying a tray of cocktails for them.

The waiter waved the apologies away and, blushing, told them the cocktails were on the house. "Happy birthday," she said weakly, shooting alarmed glances at Junior's box.

"Put him away, Mom," Heather's mother pleaded. "It's probably a health hazard to keep him there."

"Don't be silly. He's sealed inside a lead casing in there. It's all perfectly fine." Bon patted the top of the box. "Besides, it's my birthday party and I want him here."

"Happy birthday, Bon." Heather raised her pisco sour, trying to pinch off another argument. She nudged her mother's glass closer to her hand and gave her a sharp look.

"Fine." Heather's mom picked up her pisco sour. "Happy birthday, Mom."

Bon toasted herself merrily and took a deep mouthful of the cocktail.

"Oh, wow, that's the best one I've had," Heather said admiringly after she'd taken a sip. Her phone buzzed in the pocket of her jacket. Surreptitiously, she slid it from her pocket and glanced at it under the table as Mom and Bon looked through the menu.

It was another photo from Romeo. This one showed a square-shouldered frosted-glass bottle of pisco and a shot glass.

Surreptitiously Heather took a shot of her cocktail and sent it back to him. *Snap.*

It was another one of those coincidences. Watching the same sunset over the water; drinking pisco at the same moment. Sure, they were tourists in Peru, and these were common things tourists did—but even so, it felt fateful.

There was a slow unwinding coil of anticipation in Heather's stomach. It was like she could feel him through the phone. But this was an anticipation that would be unfulfilled, she thought thickly as she hid her phone under her skirt. It buzzed again.

How's it going with the family?

Heather typed one-handed, lifting her cocktail with the other, to make it look like she was paying attention to her family and not messaging some hot guy she'd only just met. **Surprisingly well. They're ordering ceviche and scallops and there's no bloodshed yet.** She waited a beat. **I thought we weren't messaging.**

There was another beat. Then he messaged back: **We're not.**

And then her phone went silent.

"What are you smiling about?" Mom asked, sounding suspicious again.

"She must have been watching cat videos," Bon said, nudging Heather. "Go on, share."

"Not at the table," Mom scolded.

"I'll show you *under* the table, then." Bon took her own phone out and typed something in. Then she held her phone over Mom's lap and punched play on a video.

Heather couldn't see what was playing, but Mom's eyes bugged out of her head. Then she snatched the phone off of Bon and pressed it into her lap, to hide the screen.

"Mother!"

Bon took a sip of her cocktail and batted her eyelashes innocently. "What? It's a cat video."

Mom shook her head, trying to be outraged, but Heather could see that she had to press her lips together to keep from laughing.

"What?" Heather demanded. "What is it?"

"Nothing!" But Mom was struggling not to giggle.

Heather reached for the phone, but Mom held it away from her. Now she was starting to laugh.

"No!" she squealed. "It's not decent."

"For Pete's sake, Sandra, she's old enough. Hell, she's been busy sexting someone all night." Bon snatched the phone off of Sandy and dropped it in Heather's hands.

Heather was shocked. "I have not!" But then she saw the phone screen and was really shocked. "Bon!"

Mom was laughing in earnest now. She covered her face with her napkin. "I can't believe you, Mom."

"That's filthy." Heather was starting to giggle too, tossing the phone back to Bon like it was a hot potato.

"What? You've never seen someone stroking a little pussy before?"

"Mom!"

"Bon!"

Heather made the mistake of meeting her mother's gaze and lost control. Mom was turning bright red and starting to snort. Heather felt the tension of the last couple of hours drain away.

"That's five dollars to me," Bon told Junior smugly.

Chapter 6

Heather

Paracas, Peru

What were the chances she'd end up in Paracas, just a couple of days behind Romeo? It was another one of those uncanny echoes.

They'd reached Paracas midafternoon, on the Peru Hop red bus, which had a cheerful alpaca on its side. Bon had bought them passes on the hop on/hop off bus from Lima to Cusco, even though flying to Cusco was quicker.

"The whole point is to see things we wouldn't usually see," she told them as they climbed onto the bus. "I only bought us tickets with three stops. We don't have time for Lake Titicaca and the rest of it before we get to Cusco."

As they'd climbed onto the bus, Heather could see the poor Hop staff trying to deal with all Bon's luggage. Everyone else on the bus was traveling like Mom, with just a pack.

"Do they have to call us *hopsters*?" Mom complained. "It's infantilizing."

"It's supposed to be fun." Bon was enjoying herself. "We should play a game to pass the time," she said, as she settled into her seat. "How about twenty questions?"

"How about not."

"Heather?"

"Yes?" Heather was sitting behind them and had to peer through the seats to join the conversation.

"You only have three words to describe yourself. What are they?"

Heather couldn't think of a single one.

Bon wasn't pleased. "Fine. I'll give you another one. Three words to describe *me*?"

"Impossible," Mom muttered.

The Peru Hop took them out of Lima through the chaos of the slums, which were walled off from the richer neighborhoods nearby. The bus stopped at a couple of tourist sights on the way out of Lima: the Cristo del Pacifico, a statue of Jesus looking down over the ramshackle suburbs, which tumbled down the hillsides and onto the desert plains of Lima; and the San Jose hotel, a colonial-era building where enslaved Africans had been smuggled in through underground tunnels.

Heather felt oily guilt at the Cristo del Pacifico, as she stared down at the ad hoc stacks of makeshift buildings, and then again when they considered the violent past at the San Jose hacienda. How could things that were so dark, and so messed up, be tourist spots?

"Don't you think it's weird to come look at this stuff?" she asked Mom as they stood by the statue of Christ, watching the sea mist rise from the ocean far beyond the tumbling shacks. Nets of illegal power lines sagged and tangled over the flat-roofed houses, cutting through the sky.

"It is weird," Mom agreed. "But important, I suppose. Otherwise, you just swim in pools and order pisco sours and pretend that it doesn't exist." Mom put her arm around Heather. "It exists at home too."

"You're not going to tell us some awful story from work now, are you?" Bon sighed. The slums had depressed her, and she was hiding behind her big sunglasses.

Heather's mother was a social worker and spent her days (and nights, and weekends) as a case worker for kids in the foster system. She was prone to sharing her rage at family dinners. Which

Heather understood, but she didn't know what to do with all the anger her mother handed over, and neither did anyone else.

But that was the thing with Mom, Heather realized, wondering why it had taken her so long to see it. Mom handed her feelings over. If she was angry, she wanted Heather to be angry; if she was sad, she wanted Heather to be sad; if she hated Dad, she wanted Heather to hate Dad . . . and then when Mom was in love with Dad again, she wanted Heather to swallow down all that anger and sadness and hate too, and act as though love was the reality of their lives.

Mom and Bon argued about dark tourism and privilege for the rest of the bus ride to Paracas. Heather sat in the row behind them and pretended that she wasn't with them. She pulled up the map to see where they were headed next. And that's when she saw that the next stop was Paracas.

Where Romeo had been.

This kept happening. These little coincidences that didn't feel little or coincidental. They felt seismic, like they *meant* something. Like the universe was rolling them together, like marbles, trying to get them to collide.

As the bus drove into the small bayside town of El Chaco, Heather was glued to the window. The photo Romeo had sent her of the bay hadn't shown the vastness of the landscape around it. The town was a long, dusty curve on the flanks of the peninsula, and the peninsula itself consisted of wildly arid amber-gold cliffs and hills. Heather felt like she was reaching the edge of a desert world, although she could see pockets of green here and there along the coast, oases of palms and white buildings, the glass of the hotels shining in the sun. They were expensive luxury resorts, dotted down the coast, at a polite distance from the tiny dusty town.

When the bus pulled to a stop, and Heather stepped out into El Chaco, the weather was uncannily temperate, and not at all what she expected from the desert bay; it was a pleasant seventy-five degrees, and the breeze stirring across the water was delicious on her skin. Heather drifted away from the bus and her quibbling relatives. She inhaled the coastal air and listened to the lap of waves. The sun was blaringly bright off the water. Heather could feel Romeo's ghost standing next to her. Feeling like she was in a dream, she took a photo of the same cluster of colorful fishing boats that Romeo had photographed a couple of days before, and sent it to him.

There was no reply. No flashing dots. Nothing.

Maybe he thought she was stalking him.

But then the dots flashed, and her heart squeezed.

Are you on the Peru Hop?

Heather felt the most intense flare of something—happiness?—at the sight of his words. It scared her. She'd known him for three days, but didn't really know him at all, so why did he make her so damned happy?

Her thumbs weren't entirely steady as she typed back. **How did you know?**

The Hop always stops in Paracas at El Chaco. That's how I got there.

Heather turned to look at the red bus behind her. He'd caught the Hop too?

We've got to stop not-meeting like this, she typed.

Easy. Stop stalking me, killer.

"See? She's definitely sexting. Look at that smile." Bon's voice startled Heather.

"Leave her be. It's nice if she and Shawn are making up." Mom gave Heather an irritatingly pleased pat on the shoulder.

Heather ignored her.

"Well, save your sexts for later, chicken," Bon instructed. "We need a tie-breaking vote."

Heather sighed. "Can I vote that you're both crazy and be done with it?"

"This is serious," Mom told her. "I want to stay in a local B and B, and your grandmother wants to stay in another soulless resort."

They were both oblivious to the raw beauty of the desert bay in front of them, each fixed on winning their argument.

"Honestly, Sandra, can't you ever relax and enjoy the finer

things in life." Bon fished in her bag for her phone and punched up photos of the hotel she wanted them to stay in.

While Bon waved her phone at her daughter, Heather took the opportunity to look down at the message from Romeo. Oh *God*. It was a shot of a shower, with his long arm stretching into the frame to turn the water on.

You're not going to jump at me through the shower curtain, are you? he asked.

She wished. Instead, she was getting dragged into an argument she didn't want to be in.

"Stop!" Heather begged as they grew more heated. "Please stop. Honestly. You sound like a couple of overexcited parrots."

They both turned to her, outraged.

"The bus driver needs to know where to take us." Bon was terse. "He's waiting."

"Where did you book for tonight?" Heather sighed, holding out her hand to look at the pictures on Bon's phone. She was so sick of being the mediator in this family.

"An evil resort." Bon was being a snot now.

"Mom—have you looked at anywhere, or booked anywhere?"

"No," Mom confessed, still angry.

"We're going to the resort, then. And we can do a B and B next time." Heather cast another glance at the bay. "And before you get back on the bus, why don't you take a minute and actually look around this place. It's why you're here, isn't it? And it's pretty amazing." She strode back to the bus, aware of her phone buzzing.

The first message was a selfie of Romeo in a steamed-up mirror. He had a towel wrapped around his waist and droplets of water clung to his collarbones. The line of hair down his abs had curled into wet little whorls.

Guess you're not lurching through any shower curtains today, he wrote. **But I'll keep vigilant. Just in case.**

Heather had the urge to jump into the driver's seat of the bus and tear ahead a few stops. He was somewhere down the road, thinking of her . . .

*   *   *

Heather was contemplating telling Bon about Romeo, as they sat on the garden terrace of their room in the late-afternoon sun. Bon's resort was a travel-blogger's delight, a series of luxury villas dotted around an artificial oasis. Bon had allowed Mom to take the king bed in a separate villa, to salve Mom's fury after she didn't get her B and B, while Bon and Heather shared the twin. Mom had locked herself in her villa on arrival, and they hadn't seen her since.

The resort didn't have a view of the fishing boats, or the wild arid landscape of the peninsula. The place was a curated green oasis of white paths, palms, flowering oleander and Indian hawthorn, a garden out of time and place. Heather and Bon's villa had a private bamboo-roofed terrace, with cushioned benches built into the low walls and wicker furniture pillowed with deep sand-colored cushions. From where they sat on their terrace, they could see the sparkle of the ocean in the late-afternoon sun. It was lovely, but . . . well . . . *inoffensive* was the word that leapt to mind. It was like they'd pressed pause on the real world and had retreated to a set-dressed alternate reality. Resort World, rather than real world.

None of it was what Heather had imagined when Bon said they were going to hike Machu Picchu. All the websites, the guidebook she'd bought, the YouTube videos she watched— none of it showed the Resort World experience. She'd been expecting to hike through wild landscapes and to pass through villages, where she might eat with local people, and watch the mountains loom closer. She wasn't expecting high-end hotels, high-thread-count sheets, and high views of distant oceans. Heather thought she'd rather be paddling in the sparkling water than staring at it from an architecturally designed terrace. In truth, Heather would rather be back in Paracas, checking out El Chaco and watching the fishing boats putter in and out of the bay. With Romeo.

She bet Romeo wasn't doing the Resort World version of Peru. He seemed like a guy who liked the real world.

Oh, these feelings.

What *was* this? Was Romeo just a rebound from Shawn? A vengeance fling? A healing hookup? Or was he a form of self-sabotage? Was she just trying to screw up what should be a good thing with Shawn?

Or . . . was Romeo the real deal . . . ? Which was somehow even more terrifying.

She desperately needed advice.

"Bon . . . ?" Heather cleared her throat.

Bon looked up in relief from her book. She was still only a few pages in, even though she'd been reading for ages. "Yes?"

Heather braced herself. "How do you know when you're in love?"

Bon's periwinkle eyes grew wide. She snapped her book closed and Heather saw the cover. *Eat Pray Love*. How like Bon to read about traveling *while* traveling. Although she was really *not* reading while traveling, as she seemed to have been reading the one page this whole time.

Bon lit up at Heather's question. A secret little smile tugged at her lips. "Well, now you're talking. This is much better than reading about a bad marriage." She tossed the book aside with vigor. "If you want to know about love, you've come to the right girl. Did I ever tell you about Jimmy and the pool?"

Heather sat up straighter. She didn't know much about Bon's first husband, Jimmy. The family didn't tend to talk about him; Heather assumed out of deference to her grandfather, who'd been Bon's second husband. Heather didn't think she even knew Jimmy's last name.

Bon was grinning now. "I grew up in a place with one of those silly names that desert-dwellers love. Everything back then was 'Something Gardens' or 'Something Paradise' or 'Something Greens.'"

"I thought you grew up in Phoenix?" Heather frowned, wondering what this had to do with Jimmy.

Bon flapped a hand at her to be quiet. "It *was* in Phoenix. Anyway, we lived in a place with 'Gardens' in the name, even though there was no garden. But we all called it Shitsville."

"How did I not know that you grew up in a place called

Shitsville?" Bon talked *all the time*. It was weird to find out there was something she *hadn't* talked about. "You never told me about Shitsville."

"Hush up, I'm telling you now."

Heather hushed. She had no idea what her grandmother might say next. But that was true of just about every conversation she had with Bon.

Bon's expression grew dreamy. "Lord, the summer I met Jimmy, I felt like I'd won the lottery. I don't think we got out of the pool that whole summer."

Heather was already getting lost. "And the pool was in Shitsville?"

"No, not in Shitsville." Bon swatted Heather on the knee. "You're not paying attention. The pool was at Jimmy's place."

"You haven't told me about Jimmy's place! I don't even know how you met him at this point." Heather was trying to keep up, she really was.

Bon glanced at Junior's box. "Hold on, I can't tell this story with Junior here." She carried her most recent husband into the villa. When she came back out, she was carrying the room service menu. "Are you hungry? I could eat."

"I thought you were telling me about Jimmy?" Heather cursed herself for ever asking Bon a question in the first place.

"I am. But we can order food while I talk. Thinking about Shitsville makes me hungry."

"I thought we weren't talking about Shitsville? I thought we were talking about Jimmy's place? Isn't that where the pool was?"

"They're linked."

"Right." Heather shook her head. She could never keep up with the way Bon's conversations jumped around.

"Who is it who keeps sexting you?" Bon asked abruptly as she perused the menu. "Is he the one you're in love with?"

Heather's heart jumped at the word *love*. "No one is sexting me. And I'm not in love. I'm just asking how you'd know . . . if you were," she said lamely.

"I assume it's not that S-H-A-W-N sexting you?"

"No, it's not that S-H-A-W-N. That S-H-A-W-N and I have broken up, remember?"

"Aha, so someone *is* sexting you."

"Neither S-H-A-W-N nor not-S-H-A-W-N is sexting me. It's just a friend."

"Uh-huh." Bon rolled her eyes and then ordered up a bottle of chilled white wine and a bowl of fries. "Sure. Because friends make you all flushed when they message you and friends make you ask your wise grandmother how you know if you're in love."

"I'm not all flushed." That was clearly a lie.

"If I tell you about Jimmy, will you tell me about this not-S-H-A-W-N?"

"Only if the Jimmy story is good."

"Challenge accepted."

Chapter 7
Bonnie

Shitsville, Arizona, 1969

Meeting Jimmy Keays was like getting struck by lightning. It was the summer after high school, and Bonnie Brown was green as a new shoot in spring. She was working her first job, handling reception and bookkeeping for Arthur Slaughter's dental practice, right off Central in town. Doc Slaughter had given her the job because he was her pa's cousin once removed and he felt sorry for Pa, left alone in Shitsville with Bonnie still to feed. Bonnie's mom had lit out for greener pastures and Bonnie couldn't really blame her. Mom had been the main earner in the family, slogging through long shifts at the Spotless Sudz laundromat and also waitressing at the diner out by the interstate, until she was as wrung out as an old sheet. Bonnie's older brothers had both lit out too, the minute they were old enough, leaving Bonnie alone with the old man. Terry and Wayne were in Vietnam now, and neither of them were much for writing, let alone sending any of their pay home. Pa watched the nightly news from his old brown chair, keeping an eye out for Terry and Wayne in the endless streams of footage, but so far he hadn't caught sight of them. Although the snowy reception on their old television was so bad that Bonnie didn't think there was ever much chance of seeing them, even if they'd been on the screen.

"At least they ain't dead," Pa would sigh in his usual dusty way, when he failed to see his sons on the snowy screen. "Someone would have told me if they were dead." Then he'd light up another Lucky Strike and complain about how the boys were hanging him out to dry by not sending a nickel or two, given they were earning a regular paycheck on Uncle Sam.

Pa was what people in Shitsville called *down on his luck.* Everyone in Shitsville was *down on their luck.* The place was built for the luckless, and Bonnie hated it and was itching to get the hell out. Shitsville was the kind of trailer park that gave trailer parks a bad name. It wasn't a mobile home park, or a trailer estate, or luxury mobile living, like you saw in the shiny magazine ads, but a regular dirt-road trailer park, full of trailer trash like the Browns. Not all trailer parks were like Shitsville. Some of them had people who were *born under a lucky star.* Not far away, on the northwestern edge of Phoenix, there was a prime example of what Shitsville *wasn't. That* place was luxury mobile living. Both Shitsville and the other place had "Gardens" in their names, but one was laid out like an actual park, with actual gardens and even a pool, and the other . . . *wasn't.* Bonnie could never understand why she'd been born under a star that left her in the desolation of Shitsville with all the people *down on their luck*; surely she deserved the actual park, with actual gardens and even a pool?

The *other* Gardens was full of snowbirds flocking to the Arizona sun, their pastel double-wides taking up plots in the well-watered gardens, decked with awnings and ringed with picket fences. They had barbecues out on their little lawns, and the residents splashed about in their fancy chlorinated pool, enjoying retirement in the Valley of the Sun.

Shitsville, on the other hand, was none of that. While it also bandied about the name "Gardens," there wasn't a patch of green to be seen. Not a bush, not a flower, not a tree. It was a baking stretch of dirt, with aged, boxy brown and tan trailers slowly falling to bits on the desert flat. Bonnie was glad to get a job so she could get away from the claustrophobia of living practically on top of your neighbors. Oh, the noise of them all. The competing radios and televisions going at all hours; the ballgames called, the Elvis records Sally Nash played over and over and over again; and Mrs. Chisum's soaps, which tinnily screeched through the afternoon somnolence. Every. Single. Day. Well, bar weekends, when Mrs. Chisum watched *Songs of Praise* and took to singing hymns in her off-key wavering voice, which was surprisingly loud for such an old broad.

Bonnie was even more glad not to be home when Mrs. Chisum started yelling at the damn TV, cursing out one or more of the soap characters for their cheating, lying ways. Mrs. Chisum was *down on her luck*, having been permanently incapacitated by a hard-drinking husband twenty years before. He'd come home from the war with a temper problem and was prone to beating on Mrs. Chisum with whatever implement was close to hand. He had also been *down on his luck*. As was Nancy Miller, across the dirt road, who took gentleman callers to pay the bills. And Cora Buck, who was just about always pregnant, because her husband didn't believe in the pill. He said it was against God. And Mr. Buck's God seemed pretty determined to keep Cora knocked up, that was for sure. Knocked up and *down on her luck*.

Bonnie had decided long ago that she didn't believe in luck. She was going to live her life without it, and the first step was making good at this job with Doc Slaughter and saving some coin to escape Shitsville for good. Maybe even to somewhere like the other Gardens, because she liked the idea of a pool, especially during the blazing Arizona summer.

Bonnie met Jimmy Keays on the day that she cashed her first check, on the Friday of her second week of work. Jimmy Keays, the best worst thing to ever happen to her. Just imagine if things had played out differently, if she'd worked somewhere else, somewhere that expected her to be at her desk on a Friday after lunch . . . She never would have met Jimmy Keays, and she'd be a completely different Bonnie, living a completely different life. And even though Jimmy put her through hell, she wouldn't have wished it otherwise. Because: *lightning*. Jimmy struck Bonnie like a bolt from the blue, and he wasn't good luck or bad luck, he was just elemental. A force. And she was well and truly struck.

Although he would have said *she* was the lightning, and he was struck. And maybe it was true.

They only met because Doc Slaughter, it turned out, didn't take patients on a Friday afternoon, and he let Bonnie take an extra-long lunch break, so long as she was back by two to an-swer the phone. The doc told Bonnie she was to say he was busy to his wife or anyone else who called after two p.m., because, and Bonnie was sworn to secrecy on this, Doc Slaughter spent his Friday afternoons at the Playboy Club, which was over in the Mayer Central building. Once he'd told her that if she was just a bit taller, and just a little more dramatically proportioned, she might make a good bunny. They earned good tips, he told her. But Bonnie liked her current job just fine. The doc's clinic had real, honest-to-goodness frosty air-conditioning, just like a de-partment store, and he had a coffeemaker and never complained if she helped herself to a cup as she worked. It was good coffee too. And she was getting paid $57.50 *every week* just to sit there and answer the phone, and open mail, and greet the patients, and take the payments, and keep the books up to date. This was a plush way to live, and she wasn't about to give it up, especially to strip her clothes off for a bunch of men.

Besides, how good could tips be, to beat $57.50 *every week*?

The first thing Bonnie was going to do with her paycheck, she decided on that first payday, was to use her long lunch to get some new clothes. She had only two outfits, and she was sick to death of washing them. She knew exactly what she was going to buy with her money too. There was a yellow shift dress at JCPenney's that she'd first seen in an ad in *Seventeen* magazine. It was sleeveless, with a high neck and big white daisies on it, and it cost a whole fourteen dollars. Which she could now af-ford. As soon as she'd waved the doc off, she skipped to cash her check at the bank. And then she met her friend Dee at Bob's Big Boy for lunch before they went shopping, and for once she could afford to splurge a dollar forty-five on the fried chicken *and* thirty-five cents on a strawberry shake, instead of nursing a Coke and watching everyone else eat.

"One day we'll be out *there*, in a car," she told Dee, nodding at the cars lined up at the hop outside the window. She was sharing her fries with her friend and had shoved a second straw in her shake for her too. Dee wasn't from Shitsville, but close enough. She lived in a leaky old place with her sister Yvonne and Yvonne's husband and kid. They lived on beans on toast, and Dee watched her screaming snot monster of a nephew while her sister went to work at the same diner on the interstate that Bonnie's mom had run away from. Dee was *down on her luck*, but Bonnie was out to convince her that she didn't need to be.

"You wait," she said, cutting a big, juicy chunk of chicken off and handing the fork to Dee. "I'm going to be driving up in a whale of a Cadillac, the radio blasting, and I'm going to pull us up right there"—she pointed to an empty spot—"and we're going to get the full Big Boy combination burger *and* the hot fudge sundae. *Each*. And old Myra over there is going to hop it over to us and hang those trays on and we're going to have a time of it."

Dee rolled her eyes, but she ate the chicken. "Sure, and Peter Tork is going to pull up next to us and fall in love with me, at first sight, and whisk me away from the snot monster."

"You never know. The Monkees are coming to town for the state fair."

Dee had a burning crush for Peter Tork, The Monkees bass player. It had been burning since they were fifteen—she was nothing if not loyal. Bonnie herself had cycled through the band, crushing first on Davy Jones but lingering longest on Michael Nesmith. But in the end The Monkees couldn't compete with real-life boys, who could take her to the movies and buy her a milkshake.

"What color will your Caddy be?" Dee set to work on Bonnie's fries.

"You'll be expecting me to say pink, or cherry red, but I'd go for something classier. Like that yellow right there." Bonnie pointed to a buttercream-yellow Caddy pulling up in the empty spot in front of their window. This Caddy was bright shiny new, the size of a train car, and for a moment Bonnie had the eerie feeling she'd conjured it up.

"That's definitely the kind of car I'd expect The Monkees to drive," Dee said cheerfully.

"They're not going to be driving it, dumbo, I am."

"No, you're not. *He* is." Dee waved her French fry at the driver of the Caddy.

Bonnie had a clear view of the driver through his windshield, given he'd parked just in front of them, and he was something else. There weren't guys like him in Shitsville, or at Doc Slaughter's, or anywhere else Bonnie hung her hat. He didn't look like the guys from Luke Air Force Base either, or the boys she'd known from school (not the jocks or the nerds), and he certainly didn't look like Bonnie's brothers and their friends. He had a floppy head of shiny hair that went all the way down to his shoulders. He was wearing a striped brown and green T-shirt without a collar, and he had a leather cord tied around his neck like a necklace. She couldn't see much of his face because he was wearing a big old pair of aviator sunglasses. He was like those long-haired dropouts her pa ranted about when he watched the news. The kind from California who caused trouble. Maybe this guy was from California, she thought with a frisson of excitement. That might explain the fancy car—because he sure didn't look like the type to own a car like that.

He also didn't look much older than she was, so how did he get hold of a car like that? Was he someone famous?

"Who *is* that?" she asked.

"If it's not a Monkee, I can't say that I care," Dee sighed.

"It's second best to a Monkee." Bonnie watched as Myra, who'd been in their class at school and was now car hopping for a living, leaned flirtatiously over the not-a-Monkee-but-just-as-good and took his order. "Look at her drooling all over him."

And who could blame her. The guy slid his sunglasses down as he was talking to Myra and Bonnie whistled. He was some kind of fineness. Too good for the likes of Myra, who was the kind of girl to throw the medicine ball too hard in gym class. In short, a bitch.

"You think he's in the music business or something?" Bonnie mused aloud. "But he's so young . . . he doesn't look much older than us."

Bonnie drank her strawberry milkshake before Dee could hoover it up like she was hoovering up the fries, but she kept a close eye on Myra and the guy in the Caddy, only half listening as Dee talked about the trials and tribulations of babysitting the snot monster. "Just be glad Yvonne doesn't work Fridays," Bonnie told her. "Oh, my goodness, Dee, look. He got the Big Boy combination and a sundae!" Bonnie sat up straighter as Myra delivered the not-a-Monkee's order.

"He's clearly your destiny," Dee said dryly. She tugged the milkshake away from Bonnie and Bonnie didn't resist.

"You're joking, but he could be." Bonnie wiped the milk off her lips and watched the guy in the Caddy devour the whole burger and sundae. He sure ate like a regular guy, Caddy and pricey Big Boy combination or not. "That could be me sitting next to him next week, and then my vision will have come true."

Dee snorted.

But Bonnie genuinely believed it. And she didn't believe in luck, so she didn't see why it couldn't happen. Particularly if she *made* it happen.

"Where are you going?" Dee asked, as Bonnie slid off her stool. "You haven't finished your chicken."

"I'll be back." Bonnie straightened her skirt. "Maybe."

If only this was tomorrow, then she would have been wearing her new yellow dress from Penney's. She still looked like a schoolgirl in this stupid old homemade pleated skirt, and even more so in the short-sleeved shirt with the Peter Pan collar. She didn't look at all like the professional young woman she was. At least she'd chopped off her ponytail last week and had managed to snip her hair into something approximately resembling Goldie Hawn's on *Laugh-In*, a short pixie cut that was a gas. It had been worth the grief from her father, because she definitely looked older and more sophisticated like this. Her father had never watched *Laugh-In*, so he didn't understand how chic her hair was now, but Bonnie was sure the guy in the Caddy would appreciate it.

Bonnie glided out of the restaurant and into the blaring July sun. She tried to slink like Zsa Zsa Gabor, but she suspected her height made slinking incongruous. Being short made you seem cute, rather than slinky. Which was a crying shame. But cute worked for Goldie Hawn, didn't it? So maybe she should just embrace it.

"Aren't you worried about getting ketchup all over your upholstery?" Bonnie purred, as she slunk (cutely) up to the driver's side window of the Caddy. The dinner tray kept her from leaning in the window, which, ideally, she would have liked to do. "Seems dangerous to eat a burger in a car this fine."

The young guy turned to look at her. She could see herself reflected in his mirrored sunglasses. He must not have minded what he saw, because he examined her from head to foot, lingering on the bits boys usually lingered on. Now that she was up close, she saw that he was even better looking than she'd thought. What kind of guy had skin that dewy smooth? He also had a dimple in his chin, and she was a sucker for a chin dimple.

"No, honey, I'm not worried." He had a husky voice and an odd accent. She liked the way he said honey. It wasn't quite decent. "The ketchup wipes right off." And to prove his point, he scraped off a slap of ketchup from his burger and flung it on the bench seat next to him. "But thanks for your concern."

Lord, he was a sassy one.

"Yes, well, I'm a very concerning person," she told him. She wished she had a pair of mirrored sunglasses too, because she was squinting, and she was sure it didn't do much for her looks.

He grinned, and it was such a quick foxy expression that it quite knocked her off her feet. "I just bet you are."

Goodness, they *definitely* didn't make them like this around here. "Where's that accent from?" she asked. Her pa would be horrified by her forwardness, but she figured she'd never get to ride in a Cadillac the color of buttercream without a little forwardness. She reached over and snagged his aviator sunglasses and slid them on. There, that was better.

"I'm from Minnesota," he said. He'd leaned back and was giving her an amused look. He had striking silvery eyes that made her feel like he could see straight through her.

"Nice to meet you, Minnesota." She put extra pep into her voice. "Now, I don't suppose you could make a girl's dream come true and take her for a spin in this shiny new Cadillac?"

He was the one squinting now. He pursed his lips. "How old are you? Because I'm not into jailbait."

"I'm eighteen. Nineteen next March."

"All grown up, huh?"

"That's right." Bonnie tried to slink around the car to the passenger side. She could see Dee watching through the window, her eyes just about bugging out of her head.

Bonnie opened the car door, admiring the shine of the sunlight on that glossy buttercream yellow. And then she caught sight of the interior. The leather, the walnut on the dash, the state-of-the-art radio . . . and there was even air-conditioning. Not that it was on at the moment, but she could remedy that.

"I didn't say yes," Minnesota protested as she slid into the Caddy.

"You also didn't say no." Bonnie closed the door. Old Dee was just about to fall off her stool. And Myra was looking thundery. Bonnie grinned. She bet the both of them would tell everyone about this.

"Go on, eat up, so you can take me for a drive before you drop me back at work," she coaxed Minnesota the not-a-Monkee-but-just-as-good. She reached across him to whip a napkin off his tray and wiped up the splat of ketchup. She didn't want to get it on her skirt.

"You want me to take you for a spin?" His silvery eyes narrowed. And then a sly, foxy grin flickered over that mobile mouth.

Bonnie's stomach did a tumble, but she kept her cool. "I sure do."

"I reckon I've eaten enough, then." Minnesota pounded the horn to get thundery Myra to come clear away his tray. "And after we take a . . . spin . . . you want me to drop you at work? Where's work?"

"Near here. But we're getting ahead of ourselves. I don't know your name." Bonnie's heart was skittery with the thrill of adventure as he cranked up his window and started the engine. The radio wailed to life, playing something she didn't know and didn't like, and the blessed air conditioner puffed to life.

"Jimmy Keays," he told her, raising his voice to be heard over the music. "K-E-A-Y-S." He spelled it out, reaching over and stealing his sunglasses back so he didn't have to squint and drive. "What's yours?"

"Bonnie." Bonnie fiddled with the radio dial. "Because I am. Bonny, I mean." She searched for better music.

"Hey! Leave it be. I liked that."

"Well, I didn't." She stopped the search on The Archies singing "Sugar, Sugar."

Jimmy K-E-A-Y-S from Minnesota groaned. "You are too cute to have such terrible taste."

He thought she was cute, huh? Well, it wasn't slinky, but it would do. "The Archies aren't terrible!" Honestly. Who didn't like this song?

"I swear, this town missed out on the sixties, didn't it?" He was annoyed as he looked around Central as they drove. "Everyone's stuck with buzz cuts, and bad threads, and old music."

"This song only just came out," she scoffed. "It's not old. Maybe they're behind the scene in Minnesota, and you just haven't heard the new tunes."

"It may have just come out, but it belongs to the age of the dinosaur."

"It's better than that noise you were listening to." Bonnie propped her elbow on the back of the bench seat and turned to watch him as he pulled the car out of the Big Boy. He sure was nice to look at.

"That *noise* was Creedence, and it was bitchin'," he protested. "What kind of cultural slag heap am I in here?" He ran a hand through his floppy shiny hair, and it slid back into place like silk. Bonnie had the urge to run her fingers through it too.

"I've only been here a few weeks," he moaned, "and I'm going round the bend. It's so *square*."

Bonnie propped her chin on her hand. "Is this what you're choosing to do during our brief time together? Complain at me? Besides, you're from *Minnesota*, so you can't go complaining that *we're* square." She considered his long legs in their tight denim. His feet were bare and dirty. Interesting. "If you hate Phoenix so much, why are you here anyway?"

"Because I have to be." He couldn't take The Archies anymore, plainly, because he reached for the dial and changed the music. He skidded through Frank Sinatra and the Beatles before he was back to his wailing guitar noise. "Please tell me you like the Rolling Stones," he begged. "Because this song is balling."

Bonnie had heard the Rolling Stones before, but she didn't have a record player at home and her pa didn't let her listen to stuff like this, so she'd not heard a lot. She guessed that did make her pretty square. She wondered what this Jimmy Keays from Minnesota would make of her father and his Hank Williams obsession. It she was square, then her pa was *cubed*.

"Where do you want to go?" Jimmy asked, drumming his fingers along on the steering wheel to the music.

"Let's go out near the air base and watch the planes," Bonnie said on impulse. She glanced at the dash clock. She still had an hour. And who would notice if she was late back to the clinic? It wasn't like Doc Slaughter was there.

"Tell me the way," Jimmy Keays from Minnesota said.

Bonnie gave him directions and laughed as he put his foot down and the car shot forward. "This thing flies!"

"It sure does."

"Is it yours?" Bonnie asked, knowing it probably wasn't. He was too young. "Or your dad's?"

"It's not my dad's." He laughed like that was the funniest

joke he'd ever heard. Then he turned the music up. "God, it's hot out here. Even with the air-conditioning."

"It doesn't get hot in Minnesota? Or you're all just too cool to notice?"

He gave her a look. "Honey, I can be cool and hot all at once." She bet he could.

He had the most striking face. Hollow cheeks under strong cheekbones, a mobile wide mouth, and an expression so changeable it was like water moving.

"Is there *anything* you like about Phoenix?" she asked.

"I don't mind you." That foxy grin was back. It did loose and wonderful things to her insides. Things she was considering pursuing.

Bonnie wasn't a virgin. She'd taken care of that on prom night with Roy Madsen, and she and Roy had kept at it a few times, trying to get it right. So she wasn't unaware of the way Jimmy Keays was looking at her, or of the swelling in his jeans. She also knew what the floaty loose feeling she had was, and she was keen to follow its lead.

She was definitely going to jump him, she decided. In this car, out by the base. But she'd only go all the way if he had a rubber. If he didn't have a rubber, he'd have to settle for heavy petting. And so would she. Because the last thing she wanted was to end up like Cora Buck, all knocked up.

Lazily, Bonnie slid her hand along the back of the bench seat until her fingers brushed the back of Jimmy's neck. He twitched in surprise and gave her a sideways look from behind those aviators. She traced the line of the leather necklace he wore and then wound her fingers into all that silky hair. It felt as soft and shiny as it looked. It was a bronzy brown, with light streaks where the sun had kissed it.

"You're awful aggressive for a girl who dresses like she's going to church," he said.

"I'm dressed for work, Mr. Keays," she scolded him, sliding closer along the bench. She felt him stiffen as her thigh came to rest against his. She kept toying with his silky hair.

"Oh yeah? Where do you work? In a church office?"

"No." A giggle escaped her. "A dentist's office." She inched even closer, until her boob was squishing against his arm. She could feel the air in the car grow thick with feeling. The air wasn't the only thing growing thick with feeling either. She had a clear view of how much he was enjoying her company.

"You sure come on strong," he said, and his voice was tight. "You must be used to those *cool* Minnesota girls."

"We only just met and you're near about climbing in my lap."

"Are you complaining?"

"What's your game?" he asked suspiciously. "You going to mug me and take the car?"

Bonnie laughed. "I'm more likely to take you than the car. *Honey.*" She took note of where they were. "You know what? Pull over up here. There's a little dirt road, take it down to the stand of cypresses. If you park over there, no one's likely to see us."

Bonnie heard him swallow hard, but he did as she asked.

And then they were parked in the shade of the trees, all alone, the engine of the Caddy still purring away for the sake of the air-conditioning.

"I don't get it," he said, disentangling his hair from her fingers and pulling away as far as he was able, given that she'd backed him up to the door. "You come over to my car, even though we're complete strangers, and you climb in and order me to drive you about, and now you're . . . what exactly are you doing now? What is this? Some kind of tease?"

"I just liked the look of you," Bonnie said honestly. "And I was in a good mood. And I liked the car. It seemed like a fun way to pass a lunch break." She cocked her head.

"I ain't that kind of guy," he said stiffly.

"What kind of guy?"

"The kind to take advantage of a girl."

Bonnie laughed long and hard at that. "You aren't taking advantage of me, dumbo. *I'm* taking advantage of *you*."

"Well, I'm not that kind of guy either."

Bonnie cocked her head. "So, what kind of guy are you?"

"Not the casual kind." He lowered his sunglasses and his silvery eyes fixed on her. "I'm not a game you can play."

Her pulse was leaping madly. There was an energy coming off him that made her blood sing. He sure wasn't like the boys she'd known in school.

"I'm not a guy you can bait," he warned her. "And I'm not a guy you can catch."

"No?" Bonnie dared him.

"No." He took her chin in his hand. The feel of his fingers firm against her jaw made her shiver. His silvery eyes were locked on hers. They were somehow grave and gleeful all at once. He was a complicated one, that was for sure.

And then he kissed her.

And . . . *lightning*.

Bonnie felt the bolt snap through her. It was a violence.

This wasn't anything she'd experienced before. Jimmy Keays kissed like he was out to win a competition. There wasn't an inch of him that wasn't kissing her. His hands slid down her arms, his chest was hard against hers, his lips were commanding, his tongue intoxicatingly, wonderfully teasing. There was a sense that he was leashed, but not firmly. Like he might lose control or something. And Bonnie realized she was very green when it came to men like this.

When he pulled away, she was dazed.

"I don't do casual," he warned again. "If you keep chasing me, you'll get more than you bargained for."

"Is that a promise?" she breathed. Her heart was thundering in her ears, and she felt reckless and wild. It was a good feeling.

Bonnie never got to find out if it was a promise or not, because they were quite rudely interrupted. By the cops.

"You *stole* a car!" Bonnie's pa was a few cans of Pabst down and shouting up a storm, right in the front office of the police station.

"Calm down," she huffed, annoyed at him. "If you'd just listen, you'd understand that I didn't steal anything. I *rode* in a stolen car. It's completely different."

"We won't be charging her." The cop sounded tired. He was at the end of his shift and happy to let her go. "Or her little boyfriend neither. Mr. Bleasdale doesn't want to press charges."

It turned out Mr. Bleasdale, the guy who actually owned the Caddy, was Jimmy K-E-A-Y-S from Minnesota's grandfather. He'd come in red-faced and furious and was almost as shouty as Bonnie's pa was now. "I thought some punk had taken it, and now I find out it's you. I told you it wasn't for you! You want to go somewhere, you drive your gran's station wagon." Mr. Bleasdale was deeply tanned and was wearing a checked sport coat and a straw hat; he had the same funny accent that Jimmy Keays had. Bonnie bet he lived in one of the fancy retirement communities that kept springing up all over. Old people sure seemed to like Phoenix.

"No one *took* anything." Jimmy had been composed as all hell as he greeted his grandfather. "I borrowed it. I got bored. And no one ever cured boredom by driving a station wagon around."

Jimmy and his grandfather had left an hour ago, batting their argument back and forth as they went. Jimmy Keays had given Bonnie a lazy wave as he followed his grandfather out of the station. But he didn't say goodbye. He just left her there.

It put Bonnie in a bad mood. He hadn't even asked if he could see her again. And they had unfinished business. At least in Bonnie's book.

The cops wouldn't let her leave under her own steam, even though her pa wasn't easy to get hold of, which put her in an even worse mood. Pa had never hooked up a phone in their trailer, so Bonnie had to call Mrs. Chisum next door. The old woman wasn't happy about it, as it was prime time for her stories, but she was eventually coaxed into knocking on the Browns' trailer to see if Bonnie's dad was home. Bonnie could hear her yelling for Pa, but Pa wasn't there. So Bonnie set about calling all his buddies until she eventually tracked him down at the Ace High bar, after a tip from Howie Gough's wife, who complained long and loud about how Howie drank away their rent money instead of working like he was supposed to. Bonnie's father was a leopard of the same spots, so Bonnie wasn't at all surprised to find that he was holding up the bar next to Howie. The bartender was kind enough to force the phone on him.

Pa didn't own a car anymore and so had to come get her on foot, which gave him time to build up a head of steam. The beers had lubricated his tongue too.

"Oh, hush," she snapped, as they walked out of the police station. She couldn't take his stomach-aching. "Here," she handed over a dollar from her pay. "Go get yourself another beer at the Ace High. It's on me, for your troubles. That should settle you."

He forgot his speechifying immediately and peeled away to go get another drink. She doubted he'd be home before she went to bed tonight. Sighing, Bonnie headed for Doc Slaughter's clinic. There was still half an hour till close and she hadn't packed up her desk yet. She stepped in, put the coffee on and set herself up at reception for the last half hour of this sleepy Friday afternoon. She was out of sorts, the shine of her first paycheck tarnished by Jimmy Keays and his dumb stolen Cadillac. He'd gotten her arrested, and then all he did was *wave* when he left? And after all that "I don't do casual" nonsense? Leaving with just a wave seemed pretty damn casual to Bonnie.

She picked away at it like a scab as she waited out the last of the workday and kept picking at it as she packed up and locked up. There was only one phone call to the clinic that whole time, and it was someone who hung up on her. There was not one blessed thing to take her mind off her gripes and by the time she locked the front door behind her, she was a regular old thundercloud, knowing she still had a long, hot walk home. Today was the *worst*. But then she turned around.

And there was Jimmy K-E-A-Y-S, sitting on the hood of an old Buick station wagon, right in front of the clinic. Waiting for her.

Bonnie froze, caught somewhere between so mad at him she wanted to push him off the hood and so glad to see him she wanted to squeal with delight.

"I reckon it's got to be a hundred and five degrees today," he grouched, like they'd been right in the middle of a conversation.

"Even in the shade here." He was still barefoot, she noted, and still hiding behind his big, shiny, old aviator sunglasses.

Bonnie put her hands on her hips and fixed him with a withering stare. "Is that all you've got to say to me?"

"Hell. You only just came out. I have to start the conversation somewhere."

"Well, I'd suggest starting it with 'I'm sorry I got you arrested, Miss Brown. And I'm especially sorry I didn't so much as say goodbye when I ditched you at the police station. Where you were under arrest because I *stole* a car.'"

"Ah," he swatted her words away with a flick of his hand, "I didn't steal anything. I only borrowed it. And you weren't charged, so what are you whining about?" He slid off the hood and slunk to the passenger side, hopping a little on the hot asphalt. He opened the door and gestured to it. "Well, are you coming or not?"

"Coming where?" Bonnie put her nose in the air. "And how did you find me?"

"You said you worked for a dentist."

"There's more than one dentist in town."

"Yeah, turns out there's a lot of them. I called them all. And then I called here, and you answered."

"*You* hung up on me?" Bonnie was caught between astonishment and outrage, pleasure and annoyance. He seemed to have that effect on her. "Why didn't you *say* anything?" If he'd talked to her, she wouldn't be in this thundery state.

"So, you're not coming?" He jerked his head at the front seat of the Buick.

"Coming where?" She didn't see why she should make it easy for him, even though she knew she was most definitely getting in that car with him. But he didn't need to know that yet.

"To the pool," he said impatiently. "You got any better ideas on a day like this?"

"The pool?" She lost her battle with playing it cool right then. "You have a pool?" She cocked her head, suspicious that it was too good to be true. "Or are we stealing the pool too?"

"We're not stealing *or* borrowing—this is a straight-out honest pool. Come on, or I'm going without you."

"But I don't have a suit!"

"Can you just get in the damn car? It's a million degrees out here and my feet are cooking."

Bonnie debated with herself whether she could get him to stop by her trailer to get her suit, but she didn't want him to know where she lived. Not yet. There'd be time enough to show him the horrors of Shitsville—she didn't want to scare him off right out of the gate. Because his family, with their Cadillacs and pools, certainly didn't seem to be the *down on their luck* sort.

"Fine. But if I don't have a suit with me, I'll have to just paddle my feet." Bonnie did her best slink to the passenger side of the car.

"It's not that kind of pool, princess. It's an all-or-nothing kind of deal. There's no shallow end to paddle in." He slammed the door behind her after she slid into the Buick, and jogged around to the driver's side.

"Besides," he puffed as he joined her. "I took care of the whole suit problem already. I told you—I don't do casual. If I make a plan, it's made down to the detail." He reached into the back seat and grabbed a package. "Here you go. I had to guess your size, but I took a good look at you earlier, so I think I guessed right."

Too surprised to speak (which was rare for her), Bonnie opened the package. It was a *bikini*. She'd never owned a two-piece bathing suit before.

"The straps tighten, in case I was off on the sizing." He was watching her intently with those silvery eyes.

Bonnie held up the red and white gingham shorts and top. "I *love* it!" she squealed. She lunged across the car and gave him a smacking kiss on the cheek.

He grinned, and this time there was nothing foxy about it. He was like a kid. For the first time she noticed the freckles across his nose. "You do want a swim, then?"

"Oh, my goodness yes!" It beat walking home in the baking

heat to swelter all alone in her trailer. "Your folks don't mind?" she asked, as he drove the chugging old Buick out of town.

"My folks? They're back in Minneapolis. They don't mind a thing."

"Your grandparents, then."

"The pool's for everyone to use, isn't it? Why should they care if I bring a friend." He winked at her. "Although I may not have told Gran I was picking up a girl when I asked to borrow her car."

"You asked this time, huh?"

"After that scene in the police station? I'm a lot of things, honey, but dumb isn't one of them. Of course I asked this time."

Bonnie was stunned when she saw where he was taking her. It was the *other* Gardens! The luxurious mobile home park on the northwestern edge of town. "*This* is where your grandparents live?"

"I know. Square, isn't it?" He sounded embarrassed. "They're here most of the year now. And even though I don't rate Phoenix, it sure shits on Minneapolis." He darted a look at her.

Bonnie didn't think the place was square at all. The roads were paved, there were shade trees and green lawns, and all the trailers were just so pretty. The striped awnings rippled in the hot breeze, and . . . oh . . . *hold on* . . . Bonnie couldn't believe it. They had air-conditioning units! Wow. She thought of her own trailer, which was like the inside of a gas oven on days like today. Who knew you could air-condition a trailer?

When Jimmy took her into his grandparents' trailer, crossing a little porch under its peachy awning, Bonnie felt like she'd stepped into the pages of a magazine. The place was *split level*, with a wood veneer kitchen on the upper level, along with a little dining nook, and on the lower level there was a lounge like people had on the television sitcoms. It reminded her of Samantha the witch's house in *Bewitched*. There were pretty floral drapes at the windows, and a thick shag carpet on the floor. Bonnie had never been in a trailer like it. And it was cool as a fresh fall morning thanks to that humming air-conditioning unit. She craned her neck to check out the kitchen. Good Lord.

It had twin sinks, and robin's-egg-blue appliances. Even the refrigerator was blue!

Bonnie wouldn't complain about living in a trailer like this. The place even smelled good, like lemon-scented Pledge.

"Gran, I'm back." Jimmy tossed his keys onto the Formica bench in the kitchen. "My friend is just going to change for a swim in the bathroom, okay?" He turned to Bonnie and lowered his voice to a whisper. "Don't worry, she popped one of her pills just before I left. She'll be dozing until suppertime."

His gran certainly wasn't calling back, or coming to see what was going on. Bon bet it was fine to stretch out in bed in this fancy trailer on a hot evening, submerging yourself in the chilled air for a late siesta.

Jimmy led her down a skylit hallway to the bathroom. "Here you go, get changed and we'll go to the pool."

The bathroom was another joyful revelation. There was pretty wallpaper showing tiny bouquets of tight little rosebuds and daisies, and more robin's-egg-blue accents; this time the bathtub and the his-and-hers sinks were shiny bright blue, as was the shower curtain, which was fringed with white tassels. Bonnie wished fiercely that she lived somewhere this nice. One day, she promised herself. One day she'd find herself in a Gardens like this one—and not just for a visit.

She emerged from the bathroom shyly, her shirt with the Peter Pan collar loose over the new gingham bikini. Jimmy Keays had sized her up pretty well. It wasn't a perfect fit, but it was close enough.

Jimmy whistled when he saw her. "You're a stone fox, princess."

"You ain't so bad yourself." Bonnie looked him over approvingly. He was wearing a pair of tight navy swim shorts, with red and white stripes down the hips. And that's *all* he was wearing, except for the leather necklace. And he was all kinds of fine. There wasn't an ounce of fat on him; he was ropy with muscle, and tawny from the sun.

"Guess we make a pair, then," he said, his gaze sliding all over her in ways she liked.

"Guess we do."

He opened the door for her like a perfect gentleman and they eased out into the throbbing heat of the July evening. Avoiding the paved paths, which had banked the day's sun, they lazily crossed the shady lawns, heading for the pool, which was the mobile park's heart. Of course it was crowded on a day like today, mostly with old people, the women in bathing caps, and the men in singlets or T-shirts, but there were kids splashing about too.

"A lot of people here look after their grandkids for the summer," Jimmy sighed, "so the pool is always infested with kids."

Bonnie didn't care—a pool was a pool! And this one was a pretty aqua blue, so vivid it seemed to glow. It was set in the center of a concrete square, surrounded by picnic tables and cheery floral beach umbrellas.

And it was deliciously cold. The moment she got in, she felt her body tingle with the bright delight of it. "I may never leave," she sighed, as she surfaced, slicking down her wet hair with her hands.

"Don't," Jimmy said. "Stick around."

And he meant it. Jimmy Keays aimed to keep her and, as he'd promised, there was nothing casual about him. That first night, she stayed until almost midnight. They swam as the sun set, as people broke out their barbecues and the night air filled with the mouth-watering scent of beef sizzling on the grill. They accepted offers of burgers and pickles from the picnickers, who worried they were going hungry, and then they sat on the edge of the pool talking as people went to bed, the lights in the fancy trailers turning off, one by one. And Jimmy invited her back to swim the next day. And the next. And after work the next week he picked her up from the clinic every single day in his grandmother's Buick.

After that first day, there wasn't a day that they didn't see each other.

The old people got used to seeing them necking on their beach towels or making out in the front seat of the Buick. Sometimes, when Jimmy's grandfather was at his poker games and his grandmother had popped her little pill, they snuck into Jimmy's tiny room in the trailer and made love, silently. Bonnie's favorite times were lying sweaty and satisfied in Jimmy's arms, feeling the delicious wash of the air-conditioning over her naked body, soothed by the slow circles his hands rubbed on her back, as they whispered secrets back and forth.

At the end of the month, on the night Neil Armstrong walked on the moon, Bonnie and Jimmy had the pool to themselves. Everyone else was clustered around their televisions, reverently hushed as they watched to see if the moon landing would be a triumph or a tragedy, and Bonnie could hear the newsreaders' voices drifting from the open windows. That was the night Jimmy told her he loved her. And, as the whole world was watching a man step foot on the moon, which lit the sky above them with romantic silvery rays, Jimmy Keays proposed. They'd known each other only a few weeks, but neither of them had any doubts. They were young and struck by lightning. And as history happened, watched by all the people in the hushed trailers around them, Bonnie Brown said yes, and they made love in the pool.

The other Gardens was a magic place, out of time. The real world went away for that enchanted window of time with Jimmy Keays, in that artificially green garden in the desert. And for that magic time, in that unreal place, Bonnie was totally and completely happy. She was going to be Mrs. Jimmy Keays, and she was getting out of Shitsville. No one was ever going to say that Bonnie Keays was *down on her luck*. Instead, they'd look at her and think, *you lucky bitch*. And all because she slid into a yellow Cadillac that day and met Jimmy K-E-A-Y-S.

Chapter 8
Heather

"And you said yes? Even though you were only eighteen?" Heather wasn't convinced of the romance of it. Jimmy Keays was nothing *but* red flags.

"I was nineteen by the time we had the wedding." Bon was a million miles away, smiling at memories of times long past. "It was a cute little wedding. I wore a mini dress I bought from Penney's. It was ice blue and just the most darling thing. I had good legs back then."

Personally, Heather would have run a mile from a man like Jimmy Keays. *Boy* like Jimmy Keays, she amended.

"We were young," Bon said, her voice warm with memory, "and in a rush, as young people are."

Heather wasn't sure she'd ever been in that kind of rush. But then, she supposed, she hadn't grown up in Shitsville.

"We were so happy," Bon said, still all dreamy and far away. "You never saw two people who fit together as well as me and Jimmy Keays. I'm not sure I've ever felt such simple, strong love since. It just *was*, and it was good. Nothing's ever the same as your first real love, but when your first love is lightning . . . well, it's a hard act to follow."

Heather's first love hadn't been lightning. She wasn't even sure it had been love.

"Mom said Jimmy left . . ." Heather broke off as she saw the cloud cross Bon's face. Maybe it was best not to go there. Maybe it was best to stop the story here, in the brightest, happiest moment. Because Jimmy Keays hadn't been The One, had he? Lightning or no lightning. If he had been The One, he never would have left her. That was part of the deal.

"Yes, he left," Bon sighed. "I never even saw it coming."

Heather didn't see how that was possible. How could she not have suspected he might run? Judging by the story Bon just told, Jimmy Keays was practically the poster boy for men who leave . . . Impulsive, reckless, rootless . . . Or rather, he was the poster boy for *one* kind of man who leaves. Heather's father was another kind. Maybe a worse kind, because he'd left without ever really leaving.

"But that was Jimmy," Bon said, staring at the glitter of the ocean in the distance. "He was complicated. And I think it might have been different if he'd known about the baby."

"Wait. What? You were pregnant when he left?" This was news to Heather. She'd thought Mom was Bon's first kid.

"I most certainly was. Knocked up, all alone, and back living with Pa in Shitsville." Bon cracked a bitter smile. "I was so mad at Jimmy Keays about that. Madder than I've ever been before or since."

What happened to the baby? Had she lost it, or given it up? Heather searched Bon's face, looking for answers. "And did he ever turn up again?" Heather didn't know why she asked. She knew the answer, even without being told.

"Jimmy? No," Bon said softly. "When Jimmy left, he left for good."

"What a bastard." Heather felt a white-hot lick of rage on Bon's behalf. What was wrong with him? Who walked away from a woman who loved him, and who walked away from *lightning*? Lightning didn't happen every day.

Oh, listen to her. Until recently she wouldn't have believed in lightning . . .

Unbidden, the memory of Romeo kissing her after their run across the Bridge of Sighs surfaced, and Heather's heart tumbled over.

"Jimmy wasn't a bastard. He was just young and couldn't do better. He had a lot of demons." Bon took a sip of her wine. Her hand shook. Not much, but enough that Heather noticed it.

She knew she should drop it, but Heather had to know about the baby. "What happened, Bon? To Jimmy's baby? Did you have it . . . or not?"

Bon gave her an odd look. "Of course I had the baby. It was all I had left of Jimmy, and of us."

"But . . . where . . . I mean, who? What happened to it?"

"What do you mean what happened to it?" Bon seemed genuinely surprised by the question. "You know what happened to her. She's your mom."

"How could you not tell me?" Heather had gone straight to Mom's villa. She'd pounded on the door until Mom let her in. "Jimmy Keays is your father? Not Grandpa?"

"I didn't tell you because it doesn't *matter*." Mom was firm. She didn't want to talk about Jimmy Keays.

Heather refused to drop it. She followed Mom into her room, feeling hot and cold and just *weird*. "But this means Grandpa wasn't my grandpa!"

Mom rolled her eyes. "Honestly, Heather. Jimmy Keays wasn't my father. *Dad* was my father. For God's sake, I never even met Jimmy Keays. He ran off before I was born!" She headed for the bathroom and reached for her toothbrush.

"But—"

"No, no but. And no more. I refuse to waste time talking about a man who never showed any interest in me." Mom squirted a splat of toothpaste on her brush.

"Bon said he left before she knew she was pregnant, so how could he show any interest in you? He didn't even know you existed." Heather sat on the edge of the bathtub. She had no intention of letting the subject drop.

"Well, he sure didn't show any interest in your grandmother, then, did he? He brushed off his wedding vows, he brushed off the fact that Mom *might* have been pregnant, even though, surely, he knew how babies were made. And he just up and left. So, I don't see that he deserves any of my time or energy."

Mom was immovable on the subject. She thrust her toothbrush in her mouth and scrubbed fiercely. Heather had been upended. Grandpa wasn't her biological grandfather. He was Mom's *step*father. Aunt Jacqui was Mom's *half* sister. It was shocking.

Jimmy K-E-A-Y-S from Minneapolis, Minnesota, the man covered in red flags, was her grandfather. Not quiet, solid, sweet Dale Waller, the man she'd known and loved as her grandfather. Jimmy Keays, a person she'd never met, was in her blood. And Grandpa wasn't.

And they'd never *told* her.

Why not tell her? She examined her mother's face in the bathroom mirror, wondering if Mom resembled Jimmy at all, and in which ways. Mom was so much like Bon that it was hard to tell. Mom had Bon's periwinkle-blue eyes, not silvery ones like Jimmy Keays, and her hair wasn't brown and gold, but dark, like Bon's. She did have a slight dent in her chin, though. Heather was burning to see a photograph of Jimmy Keays. She wanted to see his face. Did *she* look like him at all? What would she have thought of him if she'd met him? Would she have been as charmed by him as Bon had been? And what would he think if he learned that he had a daughter and grandchildren that he'd never known about?

Didn't he deserve to know about them? He might have been a horrible husband, but he was still family.

Just like Dad.

The thought clung to her like a burr as they went down to dinner. It pricked her so much that she almost pulled out her phone and messaged her father. But what would she write? *I miss you?* And what if he didn't message back? That would hurt more than she could deal with right now.

She missed Dad so much. It was a familiar feeling, because Dad ran as hot and cold with her as he did with Mom, and he always had, even when Heather was a kid. But when he ran hot . . . there was nothing better in the world than being the center of his attention. It was like filling your veins with sunshine. But his sun always set, and it seemed to hurt Heather worse and worse each time it did. She put her phone back in her pocket, without messaging him.

That night, as Bon lay snoring in the twin bed next to her, Heather searched the web for a trace of Jimmy Keays. Was he still alive? What had he done with his life? Who had he become? Had he ever remarried? Did he have other children?

But Heather couldn't tell if any of the Jimmy Keays she searched was *the* Jimmy Keays. She thought about the way Jimmy had called all the dental clinics in Phoenix, looking for Bon, and wondered if she could do the same, calling all the Jimmy Keays she found online.

Unable to sleep, she messaged her brother. **You up? I have the gossip to end all gossip.**

But he didn't message back. He was probably on night shift.

Hey, Juliet, you awake? Heather jerked as Romeo's message landed on her screen, right in her hot little hand.

She hurriedly typed back, before he disappeared. **Wide awake.**

Can you see the moon?

Heather most certainly could not see the moon, as Bon had drawn the blackout blinds.

Go outside and look at the moon.

It's the middle of the night, she typed, but she was already out of bed and heading for the door. She'd do anything Romeo suggested at this point. She wished she knew his real name, so she could go hunting for him online, the way she'd hunted for Jimmy Keays.

She could just *ask* him his name . . . but for some reason it felt risky.

Part of the point, weirdo. The moon is often found at night.

Heather opened the door to a wash of russet-tinged light. It was bright-bright-bright outside. Time slowed the way it often did when Romeo was involved, and she stepped outside and off the terrace onto the lawn, gazing skyward. Above, the sky was so thick with stars that the darkness could barely peer through. And directly overhead was a swollen full moon; it looked like it was on fire, a reddish-orange ball so close that she felt she could see its scars and craters. Heather could hear waves pounding on the red beach at the edge of Resort World, a yearning, forceful percussion that made her blood race. The night was full of red magic. No wonder she couldn't sleep—this wasn't a night for sleeping.

It's the Flower Moon. A blood supermoon.

Heather had a hard time looking away from the moon to read the message.

The Inca believed a Jaguar was trying to eat the moon during an eclipse, he wrote.

Eclipse? I thought you said it was a supermoon? The red moon was reflected in the screen of the phone as she typed.

A blood moon is an eclipse.

Heather looked up at the sky. Then typed back, But there's no eclipse?

There is. We're between the moon and the sun right now. What you're seeing is the reflection of all the sunrises and sunsets happening on earth right at this moment. Somewhere right now, the sun rises as it sets. And the moon is watching.

Wow. Heather took in the collected light of sunrise and sunset the world over, lighting the dark face of the moon. The crash of the waves filled the night. How do you know all this?

I'm curious.

Objectively so, huh? Heather had a lump in her throat. Every nerve of her body yearned to be with him right now. She felt, somehow, that she was in the wrong place. That she'd missed her fate. It was a deeply unnerving feeling, overwhelmingly strong.

Are you curious? he asked.

Yes. She was. She was curious about *him*. Who was he? What made him the type of person who watched the moon? Why was he in Peru alone? Where was he going after this? What did his home look like? What did his *life* look like?

If she was brave, she'd ask him about himself right now.

Hell, what was wrong with her? She couldn't bring herself to message Dad, and she couldn't bring herself to ask Romeo an outright question about himself . . .

I'm as curious as the next person, she wrote. But was it true? She'd never asked Bon about her childhood, or about Jimmy before. And she'd never asked Dad any questions at all. She'd somehow known without asking why he used to sneak out to the garage to make phone calls at night, and why he was late home so often, and why Mom was crying when he went out of town on "conferences." But she'd never asked him about it, not even when he turned up to visit her in Chicago, with a woman in tow. Was that a lack of curiosity, or a well-developed sense of self-preservation?

Maybe both.

Heather remembered being fourteen and running into her father at the mall. He'd been with a woman, a young, peppy-looking brunette who was in tight jeans and an even tighter T-shirt. They'd been holding hands. Heather had frozen on the escalator, praying her friends wouldn't notice her father down there on the ground floor, walking along, holding hands with a woman who wasn't Heather's mom. Dad had seen Heather too. Had met her eye. He gave no indication that he recognized her; he didn't smile, or nod, or anything. But he let go of the peppy woman's hand.

And Heather had never said anything about it. She never saw the woman again and never knew if her father had either.

But she imagined he had. She'd lain wakeful at night, every muscle tensed, listening for raised voices, waiting for Mom to find out and erupt in pain. Heather imagined her dad and the woman at the mall, going to the same cinema he took Heather to, sharing popcorn, just like he did with Heather. And then she imagined worse things, until her stomach hurt so badly that she thought maybe she had stomach cancer or something.

In the mornings, she'd be exhausted from lack of sleep and possible stomach cancer, and she'd sit next to Dad at the breakfast bar, eating her cereal while he read the paper, never once asking him a single question about the woman at the mall.

And now she could barely even message her father to say hello.

Heather waited for Romeo's dots to appear, but her cell screen was still.

She had curiosity, damn it. She did. She *burned* with curiosity. About Dad and why he did what he did, about whether he still loved her even when he sapped the sunshine from her veins, and about *him*: Romeo. She wanted to know his name, and what he did for a living; she wanted to know where he lived, and why he'd broken up with the ex-girlfriend.

Only it seemed weirdly intimate to ask. Too much time had passed, and now it meant too much when she asked. It showed him what she was feeling, when she didn't quite know how *he* was feeling.

Where are you? she wrote instead.

A photo appeared on her screen. Moonlit sand; a bowl of dunes around a desert oasis; sparkling town lights clustered amid the dark palms. And the huge reddish moon of collected sunrises and sunsets hanging over it all like a burning heart.

I'm sitting on the crest of a sand hill in Huacachina, watching the moon. You still by the bay in Paracas?

Heather looked around Resort World. **Sort of.**

Missing me, weirdo? Want me to wait here for you to catch up?

Heather's stomach was somehow heavy and floating all at once. She glanced back at the villa, for a moment tempted to ditch Mom and Bon and to run and catch him up. **I wish,** she eventually typed, **but family, remember?**

I remember. But it was worth a try.

The phone went silent.

Romeo?

Nothing. Heather felt a wild beating panic.

Romeo?

Don't fret. I am wherefore art.

Funny. But was there an edge to it, or was she imagining it?

I wish I was on that sandhill with you, she wrote.

Me too. Last chance, Juliet. I have to meet someone in Nazca, so if I don't see you before then, we're out of luck.

Nazca. That was only two stops ahead . . . only one stop for him . . .

Heather felt the pull of him like the moon on the tides. But she stayed where she was, on the grass in Resort World, staring at the burning moon and feeling that disturbing frisson. The one that told her fate was slipping away.

A day later she was in Huacachina herself, filing off the Peru Hop with the other Hoppers. But too late, because he was gone. He'd sent her a photo from the road; he was back on another red Peru Hop bus, already bound for Nazca.

I had a great time with you, Juliet. Make sure those Capulets treat you right. And enjoy Peru x

And that was it. He was moving on. The magic was over.

How could he just sign off like that? Didn't what they had mean anything to him? Heather refused to believe that this was casual. It was too intense for casual. *She* didn't feel casual about it.

"You're very quiet," Bon told her, as they took in the tiny little resort town around the greenish waters of the Huacachina oasis.

"She's still ruminating over Jimmy Keays," Mom complained. "I don't know why you had to go stirring that pot, after all these years."

Mom had been in a foul temper all day. For all her protestations that she didn't care about Jimmy Keays, he'd clearly gotten under her skin. Because no one else was talking about him anymore. *She* was the one bringing him up.

"I didn't stir any pot. I shared my life with my granddaughter," Bon protested. "Stop ruining a beautiful moment. You know what you need, Sandra, is a little sexting. You should learn from Heather's example. If you had a guy messaging you the way Heather does, you wouldn't be so wound up all the time."

Mom scowled. "Mom. Don't."

"Don't what? Tell you the plain truth? You're *pent up*. You need to release some of that frustration in a way that doesn't involve screeching at the rest of us."

"I *knew* I shouldn't have come on this vacation. I knew exactly what it would be like. Why did I come?"

"I don't know," Heather said bluntly. "Because as far as I can see you're having no fun at all, and you're ruining it for the rest of us." She was in a bad mood too, and she was sick to death of Mom's bitching. She'd given up her last chance with Romeo for this, and all Mom could do was complain.

Heather was feeling heartsick as she took in the sandhills around the green oasis and the moonless blue sky. She felt like she'd screwed something up that should never have been screwed up. She could have been here in Huacachina yesterday, in time to sit beside Romeo on these dunes . . . she could have seen him at least one more time . . . But she hadn't. Because she was here for *them*. Because Bon had booked this trip, and had paid for it, and all Bon wanted was a little fun for her birthday, after a horrible, lonely few months. And it wasn't too much to ask, for your family to be there for you when you needed them, was it?

"I know things have been bad with Dad," Heather continued, unable to stop herself from unloading her feelings on her mother. "I know you're having a shocking time and it's an effort to even get out of bed in the morning. I know all that. And I'm sorry. But can you please at least *try*? Goddamn it, Mom, you're not the only one having a hard time."

Mom started to cry. And this time it was the full ugly cry. "Your dad met someone," she blurted.

"I know," Heather said tightly, feeling the usual wave of stress at her mother's tears, "that's what started this whole mess, remember?"

"No, I mean he's *met* someone. He wants to marry her." There she went. Ugly cry. "He wants to *marry* her."

Heather frowned. "What?" She glanced at Bon, who was oddly silent. "What's she talking about?"

Bon cleared her throat. "Why don't we go somewhere a little more private . . . ?"

"Oh, fuck private!" Mom exploded wetly. "What's private anymore, when it's all up on Facebook!"

Heather's head was spinning. "What's up on Facebook?"

"Honey . . ." Bon approached Mom gingerly and tried to embrace her, but Mom shook her off.

"No. I don't want your goddamn pity."

Bon didn't listen and hugged her anyway. Heather watched as Mom stiffened, rigid as a board, but something about Bon's unyielding affection must have gotten through, because Mom abruptly melted, collapsing against Bon's shoulder, sobbing fit to burst. Heather felt a hot stab of pure jealousy. *Mom* got comforted.

"What the hell is happening?" Heather demanded.

Bon flapped a hand at her. "There's time for that later. Let's just get her sorted first. Why don't you go look around Huacachina and I'll take her to the hotel."

Bon wanted her to go *sightseeing*? "What the hell is this about Dad?"

"Heather, honey. Give her a chance to calm herself and then we'll talk about it. Why don't you meet us back at the hotel in an hour?"

"Mom?" Heather felt stirrings of panic as she listened to the deep body wrack of her mother's sobs. What did she mean Heather's father was getting married? To *whom*?

It couldn't be true. He would have told Heather if he was getting married.

Only . . . maybe he wouldn't have . . .

Heather felt a scary black hole start to swirl in the middle of her, and that old familiar stomach cancer ache was back. How little did she mean to him? Little enough to turn cold on her and to not answer her calls, little enough that he didn't even tell her he was getting married?

He couldn't get married! He was still married. To *Mom*.

"Come on, Sandra, you're upsetting Heather," Bon said firmly. "Get yourself in hand."

Heather felt a messed-up welter of feeling as she watched Bon lead Mom away. They kept doing this to her. They threw their feelings at her and then they *left*. And now she was holding all these feelings that she couldn't even name. And they wanted her to go sightseeing?

Heather felt like kicking something.

So she called her brother.

"Did *you* know Dad was getting married?" she demanded as soon as he picked up.

"Is that the gossip you wanted to tell me? Because yeah, I knew. Thank God he finally told you. I've been pestering him for weeks."

"Wait. What? *Weeks?*" Heather felt a surge of emotion so strong she had to walk it off. She strode around the sandy edge of the tiny green oasis. It was so small she had to do laps; there were people out on the water in little boats watching her walk in circles.

"He didn't tell you that bit, huh?" Chris didn't sound pleased. "What did he do, pretend that it only just happened?"

"*He* didn't tell me anything. Mom spilled."

"Mom? So, he finally told her?"

"No." Heather picked up the pace, increasingly sure that what she was feeling was fury. "I think she found out on *Facebook*."

Chris swore. "I didn't know they'd put it on Facebook."

"Dad hasn't told me a thing. And apparently *you* didn't tell me anything either."

It wasn't the first time. Keeping Dad's secrets had kept them walled off from each other, and from Mom.

There was a deep, awkward silence. "No. Well. He asked me not to."

"Right. Well, if *Dad* asks you not to say anything, I guess you don't. Just like you always have."

"That's a low blow," Chris protested. "I mean, *you* knew he was cheating too, Heather. I'm not the only one who kept his secrets."

Heather felt like throwing up. The nervous energy bled out of her, and she sat in the sand like a dropped sack. "He's such a *dick*," she said weakly.

"Yeah," Chris sighed.

"So, who is it? The one he left Mom for?"

"He didn't leave Mom, Heather. She kicked him out."

"He was screwing around—it's the same difference."

"No, it's not. If it were up to him, he'd still be living at home, messing around. Ah, I really don't give a shit enough to argue the point. Frankly, I find our parents tiresome. So, ask me what you want to know and let's get this out of our system and move on."

That was so like Chris. He had an ability to draw a line under things and move on. Heather didn't think she had the same gene.

"I assume it's same one? The one Mom found out about?" She pulled her legs up, curling into a ball and resting her forehead on her knees. Please don't let it be the same one. Please don't let it be the woman with the lip fillers and the shiny long hair. Please not the one who he'd brought to Chicago. *Please.*

"Yeah, Heaths, you know very well it's the same one. Her name's Megan. Meg."

Call me Meg, the woman had said, looking around Heather's awful little studio apartment, the one that had a view of a brick wall. Dad had visited the month before Heather had decided to move. And he'd brought his "friend." It wasn't the first "friend" Heather had met, and she'd assumed it wouldn't be the last. "I should have told Mom," Heather said weakly. "Why didn't I tell Mom?"

Why hadn't she ever told Mom? If she'd told her, maybe Mom wouldn't have wasted so much of her life on him.

"Where do I even start?" Chris sighed. "Because she didn't want to know? Because telling her would have meant delivering the blow? Because this was their pattern, and it was just how it was? Who thought they'd actually break up?"

Memories were lodged deep in Heather's body.

Mom lying on the stairs, not crying so much as keening, her face all screwed up, terrifying in her distress: Heather being the one to comfort her, to pick up the pieces, even though her own heart felt like someone had smashed it to pieces. Dad's utter inability to stop cheating, or to leave. Feeling that home was made of paper and might blow away at any moment. The endless carousel of drama her parents generated, fighting and making up; him lying, her looking the other way. Her needing, him rejecting. And Heather and Chris standing sentinel, guarding secrets, and waiting for the axe to fall. It was exhausting.

Sometimes Heather thought the nights her parents weren't fighting were worse than the nights they were. The threat of the inevitable was terrible. The echoing memory of the hurt they inflicted on each other, the way she and Chris were always collateral damage, the bone-deep knowledge of impending loss, that was always more real than any fleeting peace. Knowing she'd have to keep it together and be the grown-up.

"Tell me what you know," Heather said flatly to her brother.

And Chris did. Because he was the only other person in the world who understood. "This time is different. Meg's been around for years. Usually he moves on, you know? He and Mom blow up and argue about it, he promises to turn over a new leaf, he's good for a while, and then there's another woman. But Meg's been around for too long to be just a side thing. Hell, Heaths, this was always inevitable. Didn't I always say it?"

"Yeah." He had. Ever since they were in high school, Chris had been sure this was in the cards, that eventually Dad would find a woman who filled the black hole at the center of him better than Mom did. Because Mom was sick and tired of it, bitter and spiky and no longer adoring. And if there was one thing Dad needed, it was adoration.

"Dad needs to be the center, you know that," Chris sighed.

Even his absence was the center of everything, Heather thought, her stomach aching. Heather was his daughter, not his lover, but she was still one of his girls. She remembered the trips to the movies, just the two of them, him happily seeing every teen film she chose, buying her popcorn and Milk Duds, putting an arm around her as they walked back to the car. And when they drove home, he'd sing along to the radio, serenading her. In those moments she never doubted his love for her—it was the best feeling in the world. Dad was the one to take her to her first concert (Taylor Swift, amazing) and to buy her a ticket to her most recent (Harry Styles, even more amazing), and he'd given her guitar lessons, adjusting her fingers on the strings patiently. Music wasn't her thing, but he'd never shown an inch of disappointment in her. Not once. When they were together, he showered her with love. And it was so addictive that the withdrawal she felt when she didn't get it was incapacitating.

Dad would always be her absent center, Heather thought helplessly.

"And you said he gave Meg Nonna's ring?" Heather felt a pang at the thought of her grandmother's sweet pavé diamond ring on Meg's finger. Meg had never even met Nonna. While Mom had sat with her through her last days, for God's sake. It wasn't fair.

"Yeah."

"I guess they posted that on Facebook too," Heather said grimly. "Jesus. Poor Mom. No wonder she's been a maniac."

Chris sighed. "So Peru's not helping?"

"Not so far."

"Look, Heaths, I love you, but you need to disengage. Mom's not your responsibility. I know when we were kids you got her through tough times, but she's a grown adult and can look after herself. You can choose not to do it anymore."

"Fine for you to say. You're home in the States, not hopping about a foreign country with her on a stupid red bus." Heather rubbed her forehead against her knees, her gaze fixed on the sand between her feet. "And I *had* disengaged before Bon sprung this trip on me."

Chris laughed. "Nooooooooo. Oh no, you hadn't. You *avoided*. You're great at avoidance. But you certainly hadn't disengaged."

"Well, how do I do that, smart-ass? Have you managed to do it?"

"Better than you." He paused. "But you're right, that's easy to say when I'm a thousand miles away."

"Three and a half thousand miles," Heather corrected.

"Well, there you go. You just need to put three and a half thousand miles between yourself and Mom."

Heather groaned. "We're going to have to go to Dad's wedding, aren't we?"

"You don't *have* to do anything, Heather. You're a grown-ass adult."

"Well, will you go?"

"Probably. But only so I can drink my share of the inheritance. He owes me."

"This is so screwed."

"Look on the bright side: he hasn't told you yet. Maybe he won't tell you until after he's married to her, and you can skip the wedding entirely."

Heather felt hot tears prickle at the very thought of it. Chris had always escaped the partisanship, because Mom didn't confide in him in the same way she did with Heather. As a result, Dad tended to think Heather was in Mom's camp. So, it was entirely possible Dad would invite Chris to his wedding, but not Heather . . .

"At least he didn't marry that Pilates instructor. Remember her?" Chris was trying to cheer her up, in his usual dry way.

"Oh God, the Pilates instructor." Heather rubbed her tears away. "The one who spoke like a fitspo meme. Hashtag live your best life with someone else's husband."

"Or Miss Bolt. Imagine if he'd married Miss Bolt!"

Heather laughed despite herself. Miss Bolt had been Chris's freshman homeroom teacher. Dad had attended a lot of parent-teacher meetings that year.

"Dad is an emotional black hole, Heather. His gravitational pull can suck you in. Mom has spent her whole life risking an event horizon—don't you do it too. Let him be a black hole for someone else." Chris sounded tired.

"It's just hard, you know."

"That's what he said."

"Ew, Chris! That's so gross." But as usual he'd made her laugh.

"So, is this the epic gossip you wanted to tell me? That Dad's taking vows to cheat on someone other than Mom?"

"Oh. Noooooo. There's something else."

"Is Mom getting married too? Because nothing would surprise me anymore."

"Wanna bet?" It was a bet he would have lost, because Chris was just as floored as she'd been to hear about Jimmy Keays.

"What is *wrong* with our family?" he groaned.

"Too much to start listing."

"Right. Well, how about I call Mom right now, to take the heat off you for a bit? I imagine she's in a state, dealing with Dad and you finding all this out."

"You'd do that for me? Call her?"

"I would. On one condition: you promise me you won't be like the other women in our family. No shit men. You promise?"

"I promise," Heather said fervently.

"That includes Shawn. I don't like him, and I haven't even met him."

"One hundred percent."

"And, Heaths?"

"Yeah?"

"I'm sorry Dad hasn't told you. That really sucks."

Heather scrubbed at her eyes. She didn't want to cry in public.

"And," he said softly, "I'm sorry I didn't tell you either."

"We're not staying," Bon told Heather when she reached the lobby of their hotel.

Heather had walked the tiny town for a good hour, hoping that between them, Bon and her brother could calm Mom's eruption. "What?"

Bon was surrounded by their bags. "I know you're probably keen to see Huacachina, but we're going." She checked the time on her phone screen. "Come on, help me get the luggage out before the Hop comes. I called them and told them we'll take the afternoon bus to Nazca."

Nazca. Heather's heart jumped. That's where Romeo was.

"Are we leaving Mom behind?" Heather asked, jangling with feelings.

"No, she's coming. She's just in the bathroom trying to find a way to look like she hasn't just cried her face off. Now, come on, grab some bags."

"Do you think we could have a day on this trip that isn't full of drama?" Heather begged, as she followed Bon, weighed down by packs and wheeling her suitcase. "And why exactly are we running off to Nazca already?"

"Because it's time for plan B!"

Heather dumped the packs under the awning outside the hotel. She had a sinking feeling. "And what, exactly, is plan B?"

"Plan B is where we knock some joy into your mother."

Heather shook her head. "And how exactly do you plan to do that?"

"By reminding her that she's still *alive*, damn it."

"Right. Well, if Peru hasn't done it, what on earth do you think will?"

Bon grinned.

"Oh no." Heather knew that look. "If this is about what I think it's about, you can forget it."

"In times of crisis you need *life*," Bon exclaimed. "Life, and love, and a good, sweet—"

"Okay, stop right there." Heather held a hand up.

"It's a fact. Trust me, I've been through it enough times."

"I don't think you and Mom are the same," Heather said tactfully. "Mom is a one-man woman."

"Well, she's a one-man woman who picked the wrong man and is now a no-man woman." Bon was blunt. "So, what's she got to lose?"

"Her dignity?" Heather suggested.

"Ha. What dignity? Her husband is posting all over Facebook about how he's never been in love before he met his latest fling. What do you think that does to a girl's dignity?"

"Maybe she doesn't need or want a man right now."

Bon considered that. Then she shrugged. "It's all I've got left."

Heather groaned. "Please don't."

"You'll change your mind when you see what plan B is."

Heather doubted it, but she couldn't be bothered arguing.

She was utterly spent. It was a familiar feeling from childhood; you reached this point where you'd fried your emotional nerve endings. Shorted out. Gone blank.

She decided that she'd climb on the bus and just leave Bon to it.

Romeo was in Nazca . . .

A horrible thought occurred to her. He'd said his farewells, he'd told her he was meeting someone in Nazca . . . All of a sudden Heather was certain it was a woman. It made her feel sick to think about. He was meeting a woman, and she was going to show up like a creepy stalker. Like *Shawn*. Oh my God, *she* was going to be Shawn.

"Here she comes," Bon hissed. "Act normal."

"The word *normal* doesn't belong in the context of our family," Heather hissed back as Mom emerged from the hotel, her face shiny and red behind her sunglasses. She was slump shouldered and exhausted.

"We might need to give her a makeover when we get there," Bon murmured. "I wonder if they have a day spa or a salon . . ."

Heather ignored her. "Hey, Mom." She gave her mom a hug as she joined them by the luggage. "How are you feeling?" She'd lapsed back into false cheer and caretaking, she thought, feeling like she was watching herself from a great distance. Like she wasn't suffering too.

"Chris called," Mom sighed. "He said he told you the details. He said you didn't know either."

Abruptly, Heather realized that she was going to cry. It felt like it came out of nowhere, but of course it hadn't. She'd been pressing the tears down for the last couple of hours. She swallowed hard. "Yes," she said, her choked voice giving her away.

"Oh, honey," Mom said, squeezing her tighter.

Heather scrunched her eyes closed. She wanted her mom's sympathy so much it was a physical pain. She leaned into the hug.

"I can't believe he'd treat his own daughter like this." Mom was vicious with disgust.

Oh no. No. Heather didn't want to be turned into a weapon. She pulled away.

"Darling. None of this is your fault," Mom said fiercely.

"I didn't think it was," she snapped. Honestly. Heather took a deep breath. "Bon has a plan to cheer you up," she said quietly.

Bon wasn't pleased. She swatted Heather warningly on the butt. And not gently.

"It's supposed to be a surprise," Heather continued, ignoring Bon's pique. "But I told her that you might want to have something to look forward to on the drive."

"Heather!" Bon warned. "I want it to *stay* a surprise."

"I don't like surprises," Mom reminded her. "You know that. I get enough of them with Nick."

"We want to treat you to a spa day when we get to Nazca." Heather kept her voice even, ignoring the latest barb about her father. "Bon thought you could use some pampering."

"A spa day?" Mom blinked. "Do you think there'll be one in Nazca? It's remote, isn't it?"

"Since there seems to be a five-star hotel in every corner of this country, yes," Heather said. "Besides, it's a small city, not the complete middle of nowhere."

"You'll be a new woman, Sandra," Bon declared, "after a massage and a facial."

"What did I do to deserve you both?" Mom was overcome.

"Very nicely done," Bon whispered once Mom had hugged and kissed the life out of her and had greeted the arriving Peru Hop bus with a renewed smile. "I thought you were going to rat me out."

"I heartily approve of the spa idea," Heather whispered back. "It's the rest of the plan I don't like."

"You will. Once you see it in action." Bon was smug as she followed Mom onto the red bus.

"I doubt it."

The bus wasn't full, so they each took a row to themselves. Heather watched as Bon unpacked Junior's box and buckled him into the seat next to her. Heather didn't think she'd ever get used to the way Bon carried her dead husband around.

Heather put her headphones on, threw a playlist on shuffle, and tried to find her equilibrium. This was why she'd moved to

Chicago, she reminded herself. To get away from her family. She loved them best from a distance; with a little space, she could keep herself on an even keel. She remembered what one of the e-therapists told her: you're on your raft, they're on their rafts; you're tethered together, but separate. When you hit whitewater and you feel like they'll smash you against the rocks, loosen that tether. You're responsible for keeping your raft afloat; that's your task; they're responsible for their own rafts and, in calm water, you can bring them close again, when there's no risk to your safety.

Heather visualized it. She was on her raft. And as the music curled around her, forming a private bubble, she felt herself slide out of the whitewater and along the tumbling stream. She was still afloat, she reminded herself, feeling calmer. Her task was to stay afloat. That was all she had to do.

Her mind drifted to Romeo. Heather rested her head against the window, feeling the bus's vibrations travel through her. She bet he was rafting on calm waters. With another woman tethered to him.

Chapter 9
Heather

Nazca, Peru

"So, there's something I need to tell you," Bon said as soon as they'd deposited Mom in the day spa.

It had been a near-impossible task to find somewhere for Mom to get her massage and facial. It turned out they were staying in an old converted farmhouse, the first place Bon had booked that *didn't* have a day spa attached. It was a traditional rustic hacienda, built around a courtyard with spreading shade trees and verandas with terra-cotta tiled roofs. It was utterly charming, but not the least bit luxurious. It didn't even have a restaurant or a bar. It had the same shabby enchantment Casa Suerte had, Heather thought, taking in the cracked terra-cotta tiles and the scruffy grass around the fountain. There were chickens bobbing around, and peacocks perched on a low wall, dozing. There was a pool, but it was half empty and mostly green with algal bloom.

"This doesn't seem like your kind of place," Heather said mildly, when they reached their shared room, which was utilitarian in the extreme. It had dark beamed ceilings, dusty tiled floors, and unadorned whitewashed walls. There was a small bathroom with chipped tiles and a shower without a shower curtain.

"A friend recommended it." Bon didn't look terribly impressed by the two stacks of bunk beds. "I suppose the veran-dahs are very pretty. And the courtyard would be lovely with some mowing and clipping . . ."

Bon had immediately gone online and booked Mom into a full afternoon of wraps and scrubs and facials and massages. Heather envied her mom's afternoon. Especially now that she was alone with Bon, and Bon had her scheming expression on. Heather should have booked herself for a massage too. . . .

"I don't know if I can take more today, Bon," she sighed as they left Mom and the luxury hotel spa behind. She just wanted to go and sit in the shady courtyard outside their room and watch the peacocks.

"You'll like this bit of today, I promise."

"Has it got anything to do with your plan B? Because if it does, I don't like it just on principle."

"It does, and you won't just like it, you'll *love it*. Principles be damned." Bon took Heather by the arm and propelled her back to the farmhouse. "So, your father . . . ," she began.

Heather sighed. She wanted to forget Dad existed. "Do we have to talk about him? Seriously, let's just move on."

"Exactly. We want to help your mother *move on*. And I know just the person to do it."

"Bon. I'm tired. I'm struggling here. Just talk straight. I don't have the energy to try to guess what you mean."

"I've got a man lined up."

"What?"

"A man. For your mom."

Heather groaned. She hadn't misheard. "Please tell me you haven't hired some kind of male escort."

Bon laughed. "No, no escort. But he is pretty enough to be one, if he wanted to be."

"Who is this guy you're foisting on Mom?" Heather asked as they passed through the charming arched gate of their farm-house and into the shady courtyard. "Who is he, and *where* is he?"

"He's my hiking friend from Tucson. And he's here!" Bon

smiled at Heather like she'd just handed her a winning lottery ticket.

"Oh my *God*." Heather stopped dead. "Your hiking friend? You don't mean your neighbor Paula's *grandson*?"

"That's the one! He's young enough to be fun, and old enough to be mature about it."

"About *it*?" Heather echoed.

"Exactly."

"I can't believe you, Bon." But she could. That was the problem. "You're seriously talking about hooking Mom up with your friend's grandson?"

"He's perfect. He's smart, he's kind, he has a sense of humor. But most of all, he's not likely to break her heart. He's the kind of guy who'll understand the situation, if you know what I mean."

Heather took in her grandmother's sparkling excitement. "Bon, not everyone gets over heartbreak the way you do."

Bon pursed her lips. "Well, your mother's way isn't working, is it?"

She had a point there.

Heather sighed. "And you convinced him to come to *Peru*?"

"No, he was already coming to Peru."

"So, what, we're crashing his vacation?"

"No, of course not. He invited me. Not on his whole vacation—originally just the hike to Machu Picchu. He had this whole thing about *running to* something that appealed to me, and I thought I might as well run to Machu Picchu with him as sit home on the couch in Tucson watching—I mean reading— *Eat Pray Love*. He asked his grandmother too, but she wasn't interested."

Good Lord. What kind of guy wanted to travel with someone else's grandmother? Voluntarily. "What do you mean, originally? So, we're crashing *this* bit of his vacation?"

"I *asked* first," Bon said defensively. "I didn't just turn up here. He didn't seem to mind. He said he was getting lonely and wouldn't mind the company."

Again, what kind of guy wanted to hang out with his grand-mother's friend?

"And he's just fine with you foisting your middle-aged daughter on him?" Heather asked, disbelievingly.

Bon looked cagey at that.

"You are genuinely the craziest person I've ever met," Heather told her, "if you think some hot guy my age is going to take a swing at Mom. Especially if he doesn't even know she's coming! I mean, it's one thing if he's interested in being set up with an older woman he's never met, but *this* . . ." Heather threw her hands in the air.

"Your mom is a good-looking woman."

"A good-looking *almost fifty-one-year-old* woman."

"Haven't you heard, men like cougars these days," Bon said blithely.

"Does *this* man?"

"I don't know, but we'll find out. The main thing is, your mom will be around a beautiful younger man for the next couple of weeks. She'll have a chance to be a woman. Not a wife, not your mom, not my daughter. A *woman.* Just trust me, will you? Even if nothing happens between them, he's lovely and kind and very charming. It won't be a chore for her to hang out with him. Or for you. But you keep your hands off, you hear? He's not for you. You've got your sexting, let her have this."

"Trust me, the last thing I want is your friend's grandson," Heather said dryly. "My life is complicated enough as it is. And I'm not sexting anyone." Her heart pinched at that. Somewhere here in Nazca was the man she wasn't sexting. . . .

"Good. About keeping your hands off, not about the sexting. You should be sexting at your age. Now, are you ready to play nice? He's waiting for us."

"What? He's here *now*?"

"Of course. Why else do you think we're in this godforsaken farmhouse?" Bon clucked as she looked around the rundown courtyard, with its dribbling fountain and tired peacocks.

"I like the farmhouse," Heather told her. She'd grown tired of shiny, hermetically sealed luxury. She liked feeling like she was actually in the country she was traveling through.

"I'd like it better if it had a Jacuzzi, but we can't always get what we want. Now, let's go rustle him up and have a drink while we wait for your mom to come back all relaxed and glowing. And amenable," she added. "We'll find somewhere with a dash of romance, so when she comes in, he'll be open to seeing her charms. And vice versa."

Heather sighed. This vacation was going to be the death of her, and they hadn't even started the trek yet. "And then what? We all merrily head to Cusco and hike up to Machu Picchu together?"

"Of course. I only decided to go to Machu Picchu in the first place because of him."

"You mean this whole thing is just a scheme to get Mom a boy toy?" That seemed ridiculously convoluted. Surely there were hot young men in Phoenix?

"Don't be daft," Bon huffed as she crossed the courtyard. "Machu Picchu is for *me*. This stuff with your mother is just a bonus."

Right. Some bonus it was, Heather thought, as she watched Bon cross the courtyard. Why couldn't her family just be normal? Wasn't it enough to be in Peru? Heather really didn't want to hang out and be polite to Bon's neighbor's grandson. Or watch Bon play matchmaker. With the grandson and *her mom*. Gross.

But she followed Bon anyway. Because that was what she was here for.

"Now, he said he was in room 10," Bon muttered, checking her phone to make sure she'd remembered right.

"That's literally right next to us," Heather said, pointing.

"Well, that's convenient, isn't it?" Bon hooked a sharp left and made for room 10.

Room 10's casement windows were thrown open, and the unbleached muslin curtains shivered in the stirring breeze. Heather could hear soft music playing. It was something that teased the edge of memory, a plaintive voice over a slow thudding bass guitar. Something eighties sounding.

She knew it but couldn't place it. *I've lost you . . .* Repeated. She *knew* this. How did she know this? Heather paused by the window, trying to find it in her memory, but it just kept slipping out of her grasp.

Bon marched right up to the thick wooden door just as the bass guitar kicked into a winding solo, and she gave the door a military knock. "Yoo-hoo!" she called.

After a beat, she pounded again.

The door swung open, and Heather froze. "Hey, you made it!" Stepping over the threshold of room 10, and hugging her grandmother, was *Romeo*. As in, *her* Romeo.

Heather couldn't move. She felt like she'd been struck by lightning, fused in place. Like sand that had been blasted into glass on a beach during a lightning storm. She was frozen and breakable all at once.

"Well, hello stranger," Bon said, hugging him back like he was her own grandchild.

Something tumbled in the lock in Heather's head, and she knew where she'd heard the song. It had been playing in the wine bar in Barranco, when they'd shared a bottle of Argentinian malbec, caught in the eerie web of magic that kept throwing them together. It was a cover of "Age of Consent," the old eighties song by New Order. It was more wistful than the original; the offbeat wistfulness suited Romeo, Heather thought dazedly.

Still hugging Bon, Romeo flicked his gaze in her direction, and he was *struck*.

He froze too, her glass equal.

This was what Bon had been talking about with Jimmy Keays. *Lightning.* Wordless, senseless, irresistible. Kind of frightening.

"Despite the dramas, we made it," Bon chattered gaily. "What is *with* this farmhouse? I told you I liked comfort. What kind of girl do you take me for?"

Romeo pulled away from Bon, his gaze fixed on Heather.

He was wearing the same jeans and the faded blue T-shirt she remembered from Lima. His hair was the same tussle of curls, and his inky eyes were fixed on Heather with that intensity that made her float.

Bon seemed to realize that she'd lost his attention and followed his gaze to Heather. "Oh, that's right, you haven't met my granddaughter. This is Heather. Heather, this is Owen."

"Heather?" he drawled. His pointy lips twitched in that amused way they had, and one dark eyebrow rose lazily. Her memory hadn't done him justice. "So, you're *Heather*." And then he smiled, a white, slow, slightly dazed smile.

Heather broke out of her glassy freeze. "And you're *Owen*." Owen. He didn't look like an Owen. Owen made her think of stoned surfer dudes, not . . . him.

"Owen Ortega León," he said, regarding her curiously.

Heather took a breath. "Heather Russo."

Bon shot her a dirty look and Heather blinked. Oh. She'd forgotten for a moment what was happening. This was Bon's Owen. Not her Romeo. Or rather it was Bon's Owen *and* her Romeo.

"Stop smiling at my granddaughter like that," Bon scolded him, slapping him on the arm. "You'll have her all in love with you and I won't allow it. Besides, she's taken."

Romeo—um, Owen—lost his smile at that.

"No, I'm not," Heather said hurriedly.

"She is. She's been sexting madly this whole trip."

Heather turned bright red. "I have not!"

Romeo—*Owen*—seemed caught somewhere between amusement and confusion.

"Besides, I've got someone else I want you to meet," Bon said brightly. "Come on, put some shoes on and turn off that racket. Let's go get a drink." She pushed him back into his room, and while he obediently, and somewhat dazedly, gathered his things, Bon leaned over and hissed in Heather's ear. "You have one job," she ordered, "and that's to keep your hands off him. He's not for you, he's for your mother."

"No," Heather blurted, horrified, "he most certainly isn't."

Bon's periwinkle eyes flared wide. "Don't you dare tell me you've fallen for him already? I mean, I know he's ridiculously good looking, but you only just met him!"

"Bon," Heather pleaded, trying to get a word in edgewise.

"No." Bon covered Heather's mouth with her hand. "I won't hear it." And when Romeo—oh God, *Owen*—emerged from his room, Bon took him by the arm and frog-marched him ahead, leaving Heather to follow.

Owen turned to see if she was coming with them and in his expression she saw wary, starry, black amazement.

Because this kept happening to them. They were endlessly colliding marbles.

Heather gave him a helpless shrug. God, if he hadn't thought she was a stalky serial killer before, he really might now.

"You know, Heather's very tired," Bon said abruptly, when she realized he was glancing back at her granddaughter. "She's had the worst day. Why don't you take the time to rest in your room, honey, while Owen and I catch up." It might have been worded as a question, but Bon's tone was imperative.

"I'm not tired," Heather protested. "Not anymore."

"She should definitely come," Owen said. He slowed his step so she could catch up and Bon scowled at her. *Go away*, Bon mouthed.

"Bon," Heather sighed. "There's something you need to know."

An hour later, Bon glowered at them both over the rim of a huge frosty margarita. It was her second. She hadn't taken the foiling of plan B very well. "I wasted all that money on massaging your mother too," she muttered.

Heather had confessed that she and Romeo/Owen had already, ah, *met*.

Owen took the weirdness of the situation in his stride, and Heather guessed he'd known her grandmother long enough not to be shocked by her.

They'd found a little bar a couple of blocks away from the farmhouse. It was a retro wonderland straight out of the seventies, with heavy wooden furniture and orange tiles on the floor. They sat at a table out the front between potted olive trees, in the buttery late sun.

"I can't believe you've been sexting Paula's grandson," Bon

accused Heather over her first margarita. "You knew I had plans for him."

"I haven't been sexting," Heather told her shortly, blushing again. "And I didn't *know* he was Paula's grandson."

Owen was annoyingly sanguine, sipping his beer and watching the drama play out. He rested his chin in the palm of his hand. "To be fair," he said lazily, "you never *asked* if I was Paula's grandson."

Heather rolled her eyes. "Forgive me if that's not my first question every time I hit on a man."

"Best add it to the multiple-choice quiz."

"Sure. Are you (A) Paula's grandson, (B) Not Paula's grandson, or (C) Prefer not to say?"

"I'd pick D. Paula's grandson *and* prefer not to say."

Bon glanced back and forth between the two of them, eyes narrowed. "You two haven't *just* met," she accused. "You're too familiar for that."

"It's been more than a week," Owen acknowledged. "But we only spent three days together."

"Clearly a lot can happen in three days," Bon said tartly, taking a gulp of her margarita.

Heather reached for the wine list. She'd stuck to sparkling water so far, wanting to keep her wits, but she'd run out of stamina for this situation now.

"What are you getting?" Owen asked.

"I feel like chardonnay."

"Get a damn bottle of the stuff," Bon complained. "If I have to sit here and watch you flirt with my plan B, I'll need some too." She polished off her margarita.

"I'll split a bottle with you." Owen leaned back in his chair.

Heather headed inside to order. She felt flushed and overwhelmed. *Romeo* was here. And he knew Bon. It was surreal. She ordered the wine and checked her appearance in the mirror on the wall next to the bar. She was as flushed as she felt, her cheeks glowing like she had a fever.

"You look good."

Oh God. He appeared behind her in the mirror.

"I thought I'd come help you carry the wineglasses. Bonnie said you'll need one for your mother too." He stepped close behind her, his hands finding her waist. He dropped his head until his lips were against her ear. "We have to stop meeting like this. *Heather*."

The way he said her name made her shiver. She met his gaze in the mirror. "Do we? *Owen*."

"But I'm not sure we could stop it," he admitted, pulling her backward an inch until she was hard against him. He rested his chin on the top of her head as they stared at each other in the mirror. His hands gave her waist a squeeze. "I could run to Antarctica and probably find you there among the penguins. You just keep turning up."

"Like a bad penny?"

"Like an *unusual* penny."

His body was warm against her. It felt good. Right.

"And now we're climbing Machu Picchu together?" she asked, transfixed by the idea.

"Looks like it. Us and your grandmother."

"And my mother," Heather groaned, closing her eyes and thudding the back of her head against his chest. "Oh God, this is a nightmare."

"Should I be offended?" He didn't sound offended.

"Not because of *you*. Because of *them*. They're . . ." She groaned again. "You're going to *see* them. And I don't like people to see them till they know me." And sometimes not even then.

"I know you," he said, pulling away as the bartender put the wine and glasses up on the counter.

"No, you don't. You know this forward, fun person named Juliet, who wears peasant skirts and drags you into the shower. But that's *Barranco Heather*. Those people"—Heather gestured jerkily outside, where her mother had joined Bon at the little table under the potted olive trees—"*those* people come with Regular Heather, and they're a fucking mess. *I'm* a mess around them."

"I'll make a note," he said, gathering up the glassware. "Good choice of wine, by the way. Chilean chardonnay is great. Chalky. Acidic. Really interesting."

"Stop it," she begged, snatching the bottle of chardonnay off the counter. She thanked the waiter and headed outside.

"Stop what?"

"Stop being so perfect. It's not fair. At least try and even the playing field. I can't keep up with perfect when they're around."

"I could see if my grandmother will do a FaceTime call? Would that help? You could add my crazy family to the mix and meet Regular Owen."

"I don't believe you have any crazy," Heather grumped. "You're just trying to make me feel better." She paused at the threshold; Mom had joined Bon at the table. "Okay, get ready for it." She gave him a sympathetic look. "And I'm sorry."

"What for?"

"Everything that's about to happen." Heather plastered a smile on her face and headed into the fray, Owen following, still annoyingly calm. He just didn't know better.

"Hi, Mom."

"Hello, darling." Sandy was all shiny and loose from her massage and facial. Her skin had a rosy glow, and her smile was hazy. Heather hadn't seen her this relaxed in years. "And who is this?" Her periwinkle-blue eyes drifted to Owen, who was putting the glasses down on the table.

Heather glanced at Bon. "You haven't told her?" she asked waspishly as she slipped into her chair.

"Told me what?" Mom was giving Owen a curious and appreciative once-over.

Heather could see Bon's sourness as she noticed Mom's appreciation. She knew exactly what her grandmother was thinking: *Plan B would have worked.*

Well, a day spa clearly worked too, judging by Mom's demeanor.

"This is Owen," Heather said nervously. How was she going to explain this . . . ?

"Well, hi, Owen." Mom fixed him with a coy smile and held out her hand for him to shake.

Bon kicked Heather under the table.

"Lovely to meet you . . . ?" Owen paused, waiting for her to fill in her name, but she just kept giving him that daft, coy smile.

"Her name's Sandra," Heather said shortly. This was so wrong, watching Mom fawn over her . . . her what? Her Romeo?

"Lovely to meet you, Sandra." Owen shook Sandy's hand with infinite politeness. He didn't give any sign that he knew Heather's mom was hitting on him as he took a seat at the table.

"Lovely to meet *you*." Mom registered that he'd joined them and shot Bon and Heather a quizzical look. But she was relaxed enough to take it in stride. "I'm sorry for the state of me, I've just come from the spa."

"Nothing to apologize for. You look very serene."

"I am." Mom gave a breathy laugh. "You know, I realized as I lay there that I haven't been touched in *months*."

Oh God. Just *no*.

"This is Paula's grandson," Heather told her mother. "The one Bon's been hiking with in Tucson. Remember?" She gave her a significant look.

Mom's forehead furrowed, and then a light switched on. "Oh. *Oh!*" She gave her own mother a disgusted look. "He's far too young for you."

Owen didn't so much as flinch. He simply splashed the chardonnay into their glasses.

Bon rolled her eyes. "I never touched the boy."

"I can vouch for that," Owen agreed, passing Mom a glass of wine.

"But Heather can't say the same." Bon was even sourer about it, now that she had evidence her plan might have worked.

"I can also vouch for that," Owen agreed. He grinned at Heather as he passed her wine too.

"You're not helping," she warned.

Mom was frowning as she tried to take in what was happening. "I don't understand."

"This is the guy Heather's been sexting, and right under my nose." Bon ignored the glass Owen was holding out to her and reached for the one left on the table, in a pointed snub.

"No, she hasn't," Mom protested. "She's been sexting Shawn."

Owen's eyes narrowed.

Heather shook her head at him. "I haven't been sexting anyone. They're just sex obsessed."

Mom doubled down. "Sure. And that's why you keep messaging under the table at dinner? It has nothing to do with messaging Shawn?"

"And under the covers in bed when you think I'm sleeping," Bon agreed.

"I was messaging *him*," Heather snapped, jerking her wineglass in Owen's direction.

"And the spiciest it got was when she photographed boats," he said mildly, taking a sip of the chardonnay. He nodded appreciatively. "Good choice, Juliet."

"Uh-oh, Sandra, they've got pet names already. You know what that means," Bon said ominously.

Heather gave Owen a disgruntled look. It had got spicier than boats. He'd photographed himself getting out of the shower. Her gaze dropped to his chest, hidden beneath the soft blue cotton, remembering the sight of the water droplets clinging to his collarbones and the wet whorls of dark chest hair.

"What?" Heather's mom's serenity was evaporating, fast. "What do you mean you were messaging *him*?"

Heather felt herself slouching like a teenager. "I don't see that it's your business."

"But how? Is he from Chicago? Is that how you know each other? And what about Shawn? And why is he here, in Peru?" Mom's gaze was flicking between Heather and Owen.

"Pet names mean love," Bon declared. "Don't they, Junior?"

"Aren't you going to drink your wine?" Owen asked Heather, his lips twitchy with amusement. The shadows from the olive trees shivered across his face, and he held his wine loosely in one hand, looking for all the world like he was on the most peaceful holiday of his life. The man could be a seasoned politician, Heather thought sourly, he had such grace under pressure.

"Oh my God, is this why you got that peasant skirt?" Mom gasped, as though she'd just found the answer to an ancient riddle. "I *knew* something was up!"

Heather took a deep breath. She was on her own raft, she reminded herself, as she took a sip of the wine. "Wow, it's chalky," she said.

"All minerality," Owen agreed. He slid his sunglasses on as the sun glinted between the shivering shadows. Heather wondered if it was also to help him hide his expression, as her family ramped up their craziness.

It was a good move. Heather fished her own sunglasses out.

"I can't believe you're cheating on Shawn," Mom accused. Her face was flushing sunburn red.

"You know some mothers are happy when their daughters meet an eligible guy," she told Owen, pretending her mother wasn't there.

"How do you know I'm eligible?"

"We are still here, you know," Bon told them archly. "It's obscene to flirt like this in front of us."

Heather felt her raft catching on the rocks.

"Especially when neither of us have anyone to flirt with."

"You have Junior," Heather reminded her sharply.

"Oh, he's no fun. He never flirts back anymore." But she gave his cherry wood box a reassuring pat, to show she was only teasing.

"When did you start this affair?" Mom demanded. "Is this why you and Shawn keep taking breaks? He says you've been acting weird."

Heather caught herself grinding her teeth. "We broke *up*, Mom. We didn't take a break." Damn Shawn. "And why have you been talking to him?"

"He's distraught. You know how much he loves you."

"I don't think I gave you enough of an advance apology," Heather told Owen. "I should have said I'm deeply, *truly* sorry."

"You don't need to apologize to him—his family holds a torch for his ex too. Paula's always telling me that she was The One," Bon assured her.

Heather glanced at Owen, but he was unreadable behind his sunglasses.

"And, honey, while I'm annoyed you upended my plan, I can't blame you." Bon saluted Heather with her wineglass.

"What's this plan you keep talking about?" Owen asked Bon.

Heather met her grandmother's eye. "Don't you dare tell him."

"Is this that cougar/gigolo thing from the first day I met you?" Owen asked, exasperated.

"Oh *God*. You already *told* him?" Heather covered her face with her hands and wished she could just disappear.

"Relationships take *work*, Heather." Mom hadn't even registered their conversation. She was still off down her rabbit hole with Shawn. "You can't just run off and have an affair every time things get hard, like your father does."

"Did," Bon corrected. "Past tense."

Heather clenched her jaw so she wouldn't grind her teeth. Trust Mom to twist Heather's life into a mirror image of her own, and one in which Heather was cast as Dad. "I am not having an affair," she said stiffly. "We've *broken up*."

"Shawn doesn't seem to think so."

It's okay to set boundaries. Violent, necessary boundaries.

Heather pushed her wine away. "If you keep talking about Shawn, I'm going back to the hotel."

"Farmhouse," Bon corrected.

"Honey, he loves you," Mom said.

Heather took a deep breath. "I'm leaving now."

"You don't know how *valuable* that is. Not all men are like your father. Shawn is loyal. He's a good man. Don't screw it up because of Nick."

"Me breaking up with Shawn has *nothing* to do with Dad."

"Of course it does."

Heather stood. Her heart was hammering with rage as she grabbed her bag.

"I'll walk you back," Owen volunteered.

"I'm sorry about this," she apologized again. She couldn't read him behind the sunglasses. It made her nervous. What must he be thinking?

God, she missed Barranco. Life had been simpler when she was all alone with him.

"There's no point in sorrying all the time," Bon told her. "We're spending the next couple of weeks all together. If you keep sorrying every time we embarrass you, you'll never say anything else."

"She's not wrong," Owen told her, draining his chardonnay and rising to his feet.

"Poor Shawn." Mom sounded despairing.

"No, not poor Shawn," Heather snapped. "Shawn is just fine."

"Owen," Mom said, leaning forward and fixing Owen with an intense stare. "Take note of how easily she throws him aside. It will be you next."

Mom's words cut her to the core. She had to work hard to blink back the tears. "I'm not doing this, Mom. You're being completely insane. If you love Shawn so much, why don't *you* date him." She was done. "I'll see you back at the hotel."

"Farmhouse," Bon corrected.

Heather ignored her. As she strode off, she heard Bon sigh.

"Go on then, Romeo, go chase her down," Bon said. "I'll deal with Miss Misery here while you two enjoy yourselves."

"You weren't wrong," Owen said, catching up to her halfway down the block. "They are a lot." He'd taken his sunglasses off and hung them from the collar of his T-shirt, and his dark eyes were sympathetic.

"They're insane." Heather was tense, her body full of chemical stress.

"Eccentric, definitely," Owen agreed.

"No." She stopped dead and turned to him. "Don't minimize it. You'll never survive if you minimize it. You need to recognize it for what it is."

"And what is it?" He seemed genuinely curious.

"Toxic bullshit," she exclaimed, exasperated. "It's generational *trauma* is what it is." Heather ran her hands through her hair and tried not to cry.

"Right." He reached out and gently removed her sunglasses too. He tucked them next to his, hanging from the collar of his T-shirt. "Well, you're away from it now. Take a breath."

"I'm not away from it! I'm in a bunk room with it, and then on a trek with it."

"And with me," he said in a low voice, stepping closer.

She had to tilt her head to look up at him. "And with you."

"It's weird, isn't it?" He saw her frown at the word and his lips twitched. "Unusual," he amended. "The same bar in Barranco, the same casa, the same corridor, the same bathroom, the same Hop, the same trek. Our grandmothers, side by side in Tucson. What do you think it means?"

"It means that you'll keep finding yourself thrown under my bus?"

He laughed and took her face in his hands. "I like your bus." He lowered his head and brushed the lightest of kisses on her lips.

Heather felt like she'd been stung by a thousand bees all over. She was shivery and hot and cold with the force of his presence. "How?" she asked. "How is it *you*? Here?"

He shook his head. "I don't know. But here we are."

"Here we are," she agreed, distracted by the way the pads of his thumbs were stroking her cheeks as he held her face in his hands. God, it felt good to be touched with such tenderness.

"Admit it, you'd rather trek up to Machu Picchu with me, than all alone with them." He kissed her again, feather light, the tip of his tongue the lightest of teases against her lower lip.

Heather was floating and heavy all at once.

"What if," he whispered between feathery kisses, "we just surrender to this thing? Let fate do what it does and see what happens?"

"You say it like we've been fighting it," Heather managed to sigh. She felt drugged.

"We have. We went our separate ways in Lima." He gave her a slow, deep kiss. "And didn't share anything about ourselves."

"That's not true," she protested weakly, as she slid her hands up his firm chest to loop her arms around his neck. "You know I live in Chicago." And she knew he was still ruminating about his ex.

"*Heather*," he said her name like it was a charm. "What if . . ." Oh, more kisses. Kisses so languid and perfect she couldn't think. "Aren't you curious to see where this takes us?"

"I think it's taking us up to Machu Picchu with my crazy relatives."

The talking faltered as they grew increasingly more invested in the kissing. Romeo—oh, *Owen*—wrapped his arms around her and lifted her, until her feet were dangling. Heather took his advice and surrendered.

"I think we should continue this 'what-if' in private," she managed to say between kisses.

"I'll surrender to that," he said thickly. He looked as drugged as she felt. "Come on, *Heather Russo*. Let's get back to the hotel."

"Farmhouse," she corrected.

He laughed and lowered her to the ground. "I'm never living that one down, am I?"

Nazca was a dream. Adding Owen to the dynamic changed everything for Heather. She and Bon and Owen had a great time flying over the Nazca lines, awestruck by the massive glyphs, the curling tailed monkey, and the stabbing beaked condor (although Heather got a little sick in the bumpy little plane), and then checking out the Paredones Ruins and the aqueducts, which were more than a thousand years old.

Owen, as usual, was a fountain of information about all of it.

"How do you know all this?" Bon demanded, after he'd described how the still-working aqueducts had been built, detailing the engineering of the spiraling channels. "You could be a tour guide. Or write for an encyclopedia."

Now that she knew his name, Heather had stalked Owen on

Instagram. He was a photojournalist and seemed to spend his time being professionally curious. He'd been everywhere. His feed was a mix of gorgeous travel shots and really disturbing images of war zones, floods, fires, earthquakes, and the catastrophes of climate change. It was a far cry from her life, where she spent her time at a desk in a one-bedroom apartment. The most dangerous thing she did was eat yogurt that was a day past its use-by date.

They were about as different as people could get.

It couldn't possibly work long term.

Could it?

Mom certainly didn't think so. She was still being a pain in the ass, a loyal batter for the defunct Team Shawn.

"I don't understand what's wrong with Shawn," she complained, ambushing her in the farmhouse courtyard.

"Nothing is wrong with him," Heather said stiffly. "He's just not for me."

"Did he cheat on you?"

"No." Heather was feeling that deep insidious guilt again.

"He didn't hit you?"

"Mom! No. I just don't want to be with him."

Mom looked profoundly wounded on Shawn's behalf. "You just don't *want* him." She looked like Heather was rejecting *her*.

"Let her be," Bon advised after the interaction had blown up into a proper fight, which had ended with Mom in tears. "She's got a lot to work through."

"And what about me?" Heather snapped.

Bon looked surprised. "You? Well, you're fine, aren't you?"

Heather didn't even know how to respond to that.

"You don't want S-H-A-W-N," Bon reminded her, eyes narrowing. "So, you're fine. . . ."

Yes. She was *fine*.

But even if she *was* fine, she wasn't *always* fine.

The thing was, she had liked Shawn at first. She liked them all at first. Then came a point where she freaked the hell out. And with Shawn it came at a club one night when she went outside to get some air and found Shawn in the alley talking to a blonde. And it was stupid, but her whole body had gone numb. Shawn hadn't been cheating—the blonde was dating Kyle, and he was there too, slouched against the brick wall on the phone to someone. But before she'd seen Kyle, Heather had felt that same cold flare of horror she'd felt seeing her dad holding hands with the woman at the mall when she was fourteen, and she'd felt an urge to run so strong she couldn't resist it. *Get out*, every nerve ending screamed. *While you still can.* She'd run and she and Shawn were (mostly) over after that.

If she really loved him, she would have fought the urge (wouldn't she?).

But the visceral power of that inner voice screaming *Get out* revealed a swamp of feeling she could only begin to guess at, and couldn't hope to get to the bottom of, let alone explain to anyone else.

It was just easier to say she was fine.

Nazca was the last stop they had time for on the Hop. After taking in a busy day of sights, they were back on the bus for an overnight drive to Cusco. Mom tried to sit with Heather, but Bon was having none of it.

"Stop getting in between the lovebirds," she scolded, dragging Mom off to the back of the bus instead. "You were young once. Have some sympathy."

"I was young and had you for a mother," Mom grumbled. "You never left *me* alone."

"You said the other day that I neglected you. Which is it, smother or neglect? Make up your mind."

"It was both. You were never consistent."

"They'll keep this up all night," Heather sighed as their voices faded to the back of the bus.

"Oh, you never know," Owen said, sliding in beside her. "They might kill each other before midnight."

"Don't get my hopes up." She watched as he neatly unpacked his bag. Phone, headphones, and book into the pocket in the back of the seat in front. Water bottle out. Light sweater out, just in case. "How come you're not carrying a camera?" she asked. "You're a photographer, but I've never seen you with a camera. Just your phone."

"I'm on vacation," he said, smiling. "You're not . . . doing what you do. What *do* you do?" His brow furrowed as he realized he'd not asked her.

"You haven't looked me up online?" Heather was surprised. It was odd for a man so curious. She felt a warning bell toll.

He shook his head. "No, I haven't. Come on, Juliet. Spill. What do you do?"

Juliet. The intimacy of it warmed her up. She had nothing to worry about, she soothed herself.

For now anyway. She was sure if they ever had to deal with each other in regular life that there would be plenty to worry about.

"I'm a software development quality assurance analyst."

His eyebrows went up. "Wow. That's a mouthful."

"Yeah. And not as glam as your job," she admitted, equal parts bashful and defensive.

"I wouldn't know. I'm not really sure what a software development quality assurance analyst is." He sat back and waited for her to explain, as the Hop pulled out of Nazca and hit the road to Cusco.

"It's boring," she said. "You don't want to hear. I test software, basically."

He kept watching her, waiting for her to continue.

She groaned. "No really. No one's interested. It's boring."

"I'll tell you if I get bored."

Heather dreaded seeing Owen get the same unfocused look of utter boredom Shawn used to have, as she explained the tests she designed and activated; the training programs she ran; the protocols she created.

"Hold on," he interrupted, "you mean you have to work out what kinds of things might possibly go wrong with new software?"

"Yeah."

"Wow." He cocked his head. "So, it's a bit like playing a really complex game of chess, without being able to see all the pieces."

"I guess so."

"Or maybe more like working out all the moves the chess pieces can make and all possible permutations of the game?"

"Were you on the chess team or something?" Heather asked, worried he was about to keep talking in chess metaphors. She wasn't into chess.

"Yeah," he said sheepishly. "Captain of the team."

She laughed uneasily. "I was picturing you as a football player or something."

"Baseball and basketball."

"Were you the captain of those too?"

"Only the baseball team."

Heather groaned. "We're so incompatible. I was never captain of anything. Although I did once go to a meeting for the Coding Club. But they weren't my type of people."

"What type of people were they?"

"Guys. Like all guys. And I walked in, and it was like I was the latest release game and they all wanted to play." Heather pulled a face. "I was just there for the coding, you know?"

"I get it. I left the photography club for a similar reason."

"Seriously?"

"Yeah, but it wasn't because of the guys. It was because of Cami Walker. That girl was a serious stalker. You got any idea what it's like to be stuck in a darkroom with someone, only to discover they're developing photos they've taken of you? Photos you didn't even know they'd taken."

"Well, you are very photogenic. Objectively speaking."

"Am I?" He leaned closer, his smile wolfish. "Tell me about that."

"You just want me to stop talking about software QA," she laughed.

"No, I'm curious to hear more about that too."

"Liar."

"Heather," he said, his dark eyes warm, "I never lie."

She snorted. "Sure."

"I don't."

"Everyone lies sometimes. It's human."

He nodded. "Right. Okay. So I might tell a white lie now and then. Like if someone asks me if their butt looks big."

"Oh my God, are you telling me my butt looks big?"

"Your butt is perfect."

"See, you're perfectly capable of lying."

He put his arm around her and hauled her closer. "Come on, tell me more about software QA. I want to hear it."

"Liar."

"We've got a long drive ahead. Prove me wrong."

Heather settled in, under the curve of his arm, feeling her breathing slow and her mind settle. He had a way about him, that was for sure. He was solid, but not in a stuffy, intractable way. He was solid in the way that a tree is. A quiet, living solidity, radiating calm. He seemed awfully grounded for a man who wandered the world. The opposite of her. She was stuck in place but roiling like a raft on whitewater.

She wondered if she'd turn into a tree like him if they made this thing they had a longer-term thing. Or if her raft would just go smashing into his tree.

"Cusco was the major city of the Incan Empire," Encyclopedia Owen told her as they pulled into the city the next morning. They were still tangled together on the bus seat, his arm around her. They hadn't slept much. They'd talked softly, and made out like teenagers, and dozed lightly, then made out more. Heather thought she could probably have kissed him forever.

"It's beautiful," Heather sighed, taking in the ancient city at the foothills of the Andes. The breaking sunlight made the stone buildings glow gold and the terra-cotta tiled roofs burn orange. "Why don't you read me the rest of the encyclopedia entry?"

"Smart-ass," he said, dropping a kiss on the top of her head. But then he did, reciting a potted history of Cusco for her. He seemed compelled, like he couldn't have stopped himself even if he wanted to.

"Does your brain ever turn off?" she asked.

"No. It's a curse." He paused. "And a blessing. But most things are both, aren't they?"

"I don't want to get off the bus," Heather pouted when the Hop pulled over and Bon called down the aisle that this was their stop. "I *like* it here. I don't want to share a room with them."

"So, ditch and come join me."

"You're staying here too, right?" It wouldn't be hard to ditch, like the way she'd stayed in his room back in the farmhouse.

Owen laughed. "Too rich for my blood." He disentangled himself and slid out of the seat, so she could exit. "But I'm not far. I looked it up on Google Maps. It's within walking distance."

"What's wrong with her?" Bon asked, as she and Mom reached them.

"She's missing me already," Owen said lightly, but he wasn't meeting her eye.

Heather had a bad feeling about this.

"I'll drop my stuff off and come back later to hang out," he told her.

"You're definitely coming back?" she asked suspiciously. She hated how needy she sounded.

"Don't worry, Juliet. The universe would only send me careening back if I tried to get away." He laughed and got back on the bus, waving at her through the window as it took off.

"Heather." Mom blocked her path as she headed for the front door. "Wait." She gave an awkward, nervous laugh. "I don't want to fight."

"Me neither." But she also wasn't going to stand here and listen to Mom talk about Shawn.

"I've got a surprise for you, honey." Mom gave Heather a suspiciously shiny smile. "I know we've been rubbing each other wrong lately, but you must know I just want you to be happy."

Heather hoped this surprise was a solo room. Maybe then she could convince Romeo to stay. . . .

"It's just inside," Mom said, gesturing to the arched doorway of the whitewashed *casona*.

Heather got about four steps inside before she registered who was standing there, waiting for her.

Shawn.

He was standing in the middle of the tiled entry hall, with a nervous, hopeful look on his stupid face. He was dressed in designer jeans and one of his bamboo T-shirts, and he was holding a giant bunch of Peruvian lilies.

Heather was too shocked to speak.

"Look who it is!" Mom said excitedly, grabbing Heather by the shoulders from behind and practically squealing with joy, all trace of her earlier dark mood gone. "It's Shawn!"

"Hi, Heather," he said, his usual naked longing radiating at her.

Heather wondered what the penalty was for murder in Peru.

Chapter 10
Heather

Cusco, Peru

"What are you doing here?" Heather said coldly, refusing to take the lilies from him. She had goose bumps, and all the hair was standing up on the back of her neck.

"I heard about your dad," he said quietly, stepping toward her.

She took a step back.

"And I thought you might need me."

Right. Heather wasn't sure how she was feeling right now, but it was a big, cold, black feeling. She turned on her mother. "How did he know where I was?"

Mom didn't look guilty. In fact, she seemed to think this was a wonderful surprise. "He was so worried when you didn't answer his calls." Mom seemed caught up in the romance of it all. A romance that Heather wasn't feeling. "I thought he'd feel better if he knew where you were."

"You thought *he'd* feel better," Heather said numbly.

"He just wants to make you happy," Mom told her earnestly.

"You are so far out of line that the line isn't even in sight anymore," Heather said fiercely.

Mom blinked at that. "He came three and a half thousand

miles. For *you*," she said. She seemed genuinely taken aback by the fact that Heather wasn't melting with joy.

Hadn't she heard a word Heather had said? And what about *Owen*?

Oh God, Owen. He was coming back soon.

"He came all this way for you, Heather," Mom pleaded.

"Like a stalker," Heather's voice was flat, but only because she couldn't take the reins off her rage for fear it would be too much for her to handle.

"A stalker!" Mom was offended on Shawn's behalf.

"It's okay, Mrs. Russo," Shawn said patiently, "she's going through a lot right now. I understand."

"Don't call her that," Heather snapped. "She's not Mrs. Russo anymore."

Mom flinched.

"What the hell have you done, Sandra?" Bon was drawn from the check-in desk by all the drama. "And stop shouting in public. We're not acting like trash in front of these fancy people. Go sit your asses down in the breakfast room and get some coffee. I'll be right there, and we'll sort this mess out."

"There's nothing to sort out," Heather said, "Shawn's leaving."

Shawn blanched. Heather refused to feel sorry for him. Who turned up on someone's vacation, uninvited?

Only he *had* been invited, hadn't he? By her damn mother.

"Maybe it's best if Heather and I talk alone?" Shawn suggested as Bon went back to the check-in desk, glaring at them over her shoulder.

"There's nothing to talk about," Heather insisted. What was he not getting? She didn't want him there. She didn't want him, period. She'd been right to listen to that little voice screaming *Get out*, she realized as she watched him standing there holding a fistful of unasked-for Peruvian lilies. That little voice had been right. Maybe the urge to run wasn't a flaw in her character . . . maybe the little voice belonged to her better self, and it was looking out for her. Because Shawn was quite clearly a creep.

"Ah, sorry to interrupt . . ." A nervous voice came from the door next to the check-in desk.

Heather couldn't believe it. *Kyle* was here too?

Shawn's roommate Kyle was looking exceedingly sheepish as he hulked in the doorway, resembling a Saint Barnard more than ever. "Sorry," he rumbled. "But they're going to clear off the breakfast buffet in a minute. Did you still want me to hold the table?"

"What's he doing here?" Heather demanded.

"I asked him to hold us a table," Shawn said quietly. "I thought you'd be hungry after your all-night bus trip."

"How thoughtful," Mom gushed.

Heather felt like pushing her. She took a few steps away, worried she wouldn't be able to restrain herself. "I meant in *Peru*."

"I came just in case." Kyle scratched his beard and didn't seem to know where to look.

"Just in case what?" Heather asked tightly.

"Just in case it went like *this*." He gave Heather a sympathetic look.

Abruptly, Heather wanted to cry. It was his sympathy that did it. It helped when someone else saw the crazy.

"Guess you haven't slept," Kyle rumbled. "Buses aren't great for sleeping."

No. But *Owen* was the reason she hadn't slept, not the bus. Oh God, Owen. She needed to get this sorted and get Shawn out of here before Owen turned up. Heather pulled her phone out and sent him a quick message.

Going to breakfast before we go up to the room. Give us a few hours?

She felt oily with guilt as she sent it. She felt like she was cheating on him to be standing here with Shawn, who was still holding out the purplish-red lilies.

Going that well with your mom, huh?

Heather swallowed. How the hell was she going to explain this?

"Look, the table's just through here," Kyle coaxed. "There's coffee and food. Everything will seem manageable with some food in your stomach." Heather wasn't sure if he was talking to her or to Shawn.

Heather didn't want to go sit down with Shawn. She wanted to storm off and pretend that he didn't exist. But she needed to get rid of him before Owen showed up.

"Fine," she said, but she still stormed a little, stalking past Shawn without taking his lilies.

"Oh, isn't this place romantic?" Mom said as they stepped into the central courtyard, where the breakfast tables were set out under wide umbrellas. The two-story casa cradled the courtyard, which glowed with golden morning light.

Heather sat at the table Kyle had reserved for them, ordered a strong black coffee and put her sunglasses on, to hide her anger.

"Would you like a vase for the flowers?" the waiter asked politely, in accented English. She gently took the lilies from Shawn as Mom ushered him into the seat opposite Heather. Mom kept giving Heather the most infuriating encouraging looks. They were awful in their wrongheaded empathy. Mom clearly thought Heather was, or should be, overcome with the romance of Shawn's gesture. But, in Heather's opinion, Mom had always had a misplaced sense of romance.

"Why don't we get food for the table?" Mom said to Kyle. She hadn't even been introduced to him yet and she was bossing him around.

Heather found herself alone with Shawn at the linen-covered table in the romantic Peruvian courtyard.

He was looking nervous. As well he should.

"I know you're mad at me," he said softly.

"Mad doesn't even begin to cover it," she told him, crossing her arms.

His hazel eyes were pained. "I didn't mean to show up out of the blue—but you didn't answer my messages."

"I got a Peruvian SIM, to save money," she told him shortly. "I haven't been *getting* your messages."

"I didn't know that." He was staring at her with enormous tenderness. Tenderness she didn't *want*.

"You didn't *have* to know that. We're not together."

Shawn flushed. "If we're not together, why do we keep ending up together?"

"We don't. *You* keep chasing me. It's different." Ending up together was her and Owen, in adjoining rooms, with adjoining grandmothers, thrown together even though they didn't know each other's names. Shawn was something else. "And sex isn't ending up together, Shawn. Sometimes it's just sex."

"Heather," he said patiently. "You arrived in my life, in my corridor, at my coffee shop, and life has never been the same since. It was like being struck by lightning."

Heather flinched. "Don't say that."

"Like what? I'm just telling the truth. Remember the weekend we met?"

Of course she did. It was only a few months ago. He kept talking like they were in some grand affair, but they'd only dated for three and a half months. With a few slips afterward.

They'd moved into the building on the same day, three doors down from one another, and the super kept mixing up their boxes. He'd delivered all Shawn's records to Heather's place, and all Heather's computer hardware to Shawn's place.

Heather had been dreaming about the move to the new apartment, desperate to step into a new life, and immediately the new life had come with a charming neighbor who wore designer clothes and collected vintage records, who seemed to think she belonged there, in the fancy building. With him. She softened. It wasn't Shawn's fault she didn't feel like she'd been struck by lightning.

Maybe it was possible for one person to be struck, and the other to be immune?

"You were upset," he continued, "because your mom had just found out your dad was cheating on her."

She'd been on the phone with Mom as she'd packed her boxes in the old place, and by the time she got to the new place she'd been enervated and edgy. Shawn had come in like a welcome distraction.

"We spent the whole weekend together, remember?"

He'd helped her unpack, putting together her flatpack desk, stacking her books on her new bookshelf, setting up her TV. And he'd ordered food, and rubbed the kinks out of her back, and played her some of his records, sticking to the low-key stuff: Elliott Smith, Jeff Beck, Mazzy Star. He liked 90s music, and he almost shook with excitement when she said her dad had been in a mildly successful 90s band called Torn. She'd been surprised to find he'd heard of them. And even more surprised that he was desperate for a copy of their first album, *Chosen*, which he'd been scouring eBay for.

"I can get you a copy," Heather had said. "Mom has a box of them in the garage."

Torn had been a pretty average band, in Heather's opinion. And they'd done only three albums before they broke up. It was something Dad had done in the pre-Heather world, and she found the old posters Mom hung in the TV room kind of embarrassing. There were a couple of Lollapalooza posters from the mid-1990s and some really cringy posters of the Torn album covers. The worst one showed her dad posing like some kind of sleazy grunge heartthrob.

Shawn had assumed she must love music and had started dragging her to gigs, in all these seedy clubs, with bands who were trying to be the new century's Nirvana. She wasn't really into it. And she was pretty clear, pretty quickly, that she wasn't into Shawn either.

As Shawn reminisced about their early days, listing good times at gigs (which she'd hated) and listening to records at home (which she tired of quickly) and being able to pop in for coffee during the workday (oh, he was suffocating), Heather's mind drifted to Owen. Who, unlike Shawn, was *not* good on paper. He was rootless, always traveling, often in dangerous situations, and *out of her league . . .*

But *lightning.*

"Did you really feel like you were struck by lightning when you met me?" Heather blurted. Did he actually mean it? Or was it one of those sweeping romantic proclamations he was prone to, like he was to sending flowers and delivering grand gestures. Grand gestures like flying three and a half thousand miles to surprise her in Peru.

Shawn didn't get a chance to answer her question, because Mom and Kyle returned with the food.

"The waitress is bringing toast," Kyle said, as he put down plates loaded with bacon and scrambled eggs.

"Look at this, they have rice pudding for breakfast!" Mom set the little glasses of pudding on the table.

"Arroz con leche," Heather sighed. The fight was draining out of her. She wished it wouldn't, but waves of adrenaline were always followed by low chemical ebb.

Casa Suerte had served arroz con leche for breakfast, she thought tiredly. And Romeo had also taken Heather to a little family place in the neighborhood that made the traditional rice pudding, sweet but with a cinnamon and lemon zest edge, and they'd shared it, along with an empanada and strong black coffee. She wanted to keep the magic of Barranco, but with Mom and Shawn at the table, it was getting harder.

"Well, this is becoming a regular party, isn't it," Bon drawled as she joined them. She stood at the head of the table, looking unimpressed. "And from memory, this is supposed to be *my* party."

Shawn's chair scraped on the flagstones as he stood. "I'm so sorry," he said, all charm. "I didn't mean to cause such a fuss. I thought Heather would be glad to see me."

Bon frowned. "Why?"

Shawn was nonplussed. "What do you mean, why?"

"I mean, why did you think she'd be glad to see you?"

Heather's phone vibrated. Owen was calling. "Excuse me." She all but ran from the table. "Hey," she said breathlessly, escaping the courtyard and heading out through the foyer to the street. "Where are you?"

"At my casa." He sounded guarded. "So, how's it going there?"

"*Horrible*," Heather wailed. "You'll never guess what happened!"

"Shawn turned up." His guardedness softened a bit. "Bonnie told me."

"Bon told you! *She* knew he was coming too?" Heather was outraged.

"No. She called a few minutes ago to warn me. She didn't want me walking in on it all."

"Oh, thank God. For a minute I thought she was in on it."

"In on what, exactly?" He was careful.

It didn't look great, she had to admit. She tried to imagine if his ex-girlfriend had come crashing in.

"My mom's scheming," Heather told him.

"Your mom's scheming, with your boyfriend Shawn . . . ," he said softly.

"With my *ex*-boyfriend Shawn," she corrected. "Who I dated for about five minutes, by the way."

"This is a long way to come after five minutes of dating . . ." He cleared his throat. "Expensive too."

Heather wished she could see him. She couldn't read his voice. "Where are you? Can I just come there now and explain?"

"Leaving your ex-boyfriend of five minutes with your mom and Bonnie?"

Heather groaned.

"Maybe it's best if you get your side of things sorted out first?"

Heather could feel the Barranco magic slipping further and further away. She didn't like it. "Romeo—"

"We haven't slept," he interrupted. "Everything's a bit heightened. Let's take the day to get things in order, huh? I'll grab food and sleep and you . . . do what you need to do. I'll call you later, okay?"

No. Not okay. Not okay at all. Heather was feeling exposed and stressed, and she couldn't read him, and today had just gone to hell and back.

"Juliet?" he prodded, his voice husky. "Okay?"

"Okay," she said miserably.

He took pity on her. "It will be okay, weirdo. It's just a lot."

"It's always a lot," she sighed, rubbing her face. "I warned you."

"Maybe when we catch up you can fill me in on this guy you dated for five minutes, and why everyone keeps saying you're sexting him," Owen said quietly.

"I'm not sexting him!" Heather felt like strangling her mother and Bon. "I was messaging *you*."

"It's a pretty big deal for a guy to turn up in Peru like this."

"I swear on my mother's grave that I have zero interest in Shawn. *I* broke up with *him* and he's being a total stalker right now. Like that Cami Walker girl in your photography club."

"Your mother's grave? She isn't dead."

"She's about to be."

She was trying to make him laugh, but Owen sighed, and it was a weary, exasperated sound that filled Heather with dread.

"Alright," Heather said quickly. "I'll handle it and call you later."

"Good luck." He was wry.

"Owen . . . ?"

"Yeah?"

"You can trust me," she said quietly.

"I know."

"You do? How do you know?" Her heart was squeezing.

"Because you answered my call. And you were going to tell me straight up." He paused. "And Bonnie told me I could trust you. She said you were furious. And that you wouldn't take his flowers."

"I am furious. And I didn't take his flowers." Not this time.

"And you wanted to come straight here, to me."

"I do."

"So, relax, Juliet. What will be will be."

"Relaxing isn't natural to me," she admitted.

"Makes sense." There was a smile in his voice. "You spend your life imagining possible problems."

"And their solutions," she reminded him. "I'll fix this. I promise."

But, of course, it wasn't that easy. Because people were less predictable than software.

* * *

When she got back to the table, only Kyle remained.

"Where is everyone?" she asked, surprised.

The courtyard was empty, the tables all cleared away, except for theirs. Kyle was picking at the fruit platter and finishing his coffee.

"Ah, it all blew up," he said in his usual sleepy way. You'd never know Kyle was like Animal the Muppet on a drumkit. Off the kit, Kyle was slow moving and sweet. His big brown eyes looked up at her over the coffee cup. "Your grandmother really let your mom have it. I'm surprised you didn't hear it."

"She deserves it," Heather said bluntly.

"Yeah, well, your mom ran off crying to her room. And your grandmother said she was going to have a long bath and forget that we all exist."

"And Shawn?"

Kyle sighed. "I don't know. He went upstairs to our room. Maybe he's writing you a love haiku or something."

Heather gave a startled laugh.

"Want some fruit?" Kyle asked, pushing the remains of the platter toward her. "You haven't eaten."

Heather took a slice of pineapple and collapsed in a chair. "What a day."

"And it's only nine a.m."

"What the hell are you guys doing here, Kyle?" Heather moaned. "I mean, *seriously*?"

"I know. It's nuts." He shook his shaggy head. "But I couldn't let him come alone."

"You shouldn't have let him come at all!"

"I'm not his keeper, Heather. I'm just his buddy." Kyle took a slice of pineapple too.

"What's his deal?" Heather asked. "Why won't he take no for an answer?"

Kyle cocked an eyebrow and fixed her with a disbelieving look.

Heather huffed. "Fine. It's my fault for sleeping with him. But I never promised him anything. In fact, I told him *not* to have any hope."

"And then you slept with him. Again."

"Yeah." Heather slumped. "It was dumb. But he kept chasing. Every time there's a knock at my door, it's him, bearing gifts."

Kyle held his hands up. "We're only human, right? I'm just telling you why. I'm not judging."

"*I'm* judging," she grumbled, snatching a bunch of grapes off the platter. Now that she'd eaten something, she realized how hungry she was. "I don't know why I keep doing it."

"You don't think he's right? That you actually like him? That you're just skittish because of your folks' issues and stuff?"

Heather shook her head. "No." She picked at the grapes. "I think it's more that I have issues of my own." Heather felt a wave of exhaustion rising. "I think he just turns up when I'm lonely and I'm scared and I'm having a really hard time, you know? And I . . ." Heather swallowed hard. "I'm using him."

Kyle sighed.

"Do you think that makes me a horrible person?" she whispered, scared to look him in the eye. But she did, and all she saw was kindness.

"Nah," Kyle said. "He's using you too, so it all balances out."

Heather frowned. "What do you mean?"

Kyle shrugged. "I love him, you know I do. He's one of my oldest friends. But he's also forever falling madly in love with women who don't want him. That's *his* issue. And he chases and chases, like a moth flinging himself at a flame. You're not the first."

For some reason that stung. "Oh," she said. Like Dad, she thought. Dad's adoration wasn't unique either—or at least not singular. Dad just loved women loving him; Mom had loved him the hardest and the longest, but it hadn't kept him. Heather loved him too, and her love was genuinely unique (unless he had another daughter out there somewhere, which honestly, at this point, she wouldn't put past him) and it still didn't keep him. Love poured into Dad and poured right back out again, like he was a bucket with a hole.

She wasn't special to Dad, and she wasn't special to Shawn.

"It will pass. If you stop giving him hope," Kyle said significantly.

"I'm done," Heather assured him, feeling stupidly heavy with rejection, even though she was the one doing the rejecting.

"Good. Because it would be nice for him to find someone who likes him back." Kyle cleared his throat. "He might need to work on the stalker behavior first, though."

"Definitely."

"Hey," Kyle said with studied casualness. "Can I ask you a question?"

"As long as it doesn't involve me and Shawn." Heather smiled wanly.

"No. I was just wondering . . . your mom . . . she's the Sandy from the song, right?"

Heather groaned. "Not you too. Shawn was always wanting to talk about Dad's band."

"I love that song."

"Yeah, so did Mom."

Kyle grinned. "I mean, it's no 'Sally Cinnamon,' but it's pretty cool."

"I don't know what that is."

"The Stone Roses?"

"Kyle, you've got the wrong girl. Talk to my mom if you want nineties music trivia."

"Man, your mom is *the* 'Sandy Swears.'"

"You want her? You can have her," Heather offered. She yawned. "I'm going to go catch a nap."

"Oh, here, your grandma left this for you." He tossed her a swipe card.

"Thanks."

"You think your mom would autograph my CD?"

"She didn't write the thing, Kyle. She's just the muse." Heather got to her feet. "I guess I'll have to talk to Shawn today, huh?"

"Yeah. You want a chaperone, so you don't go sleeping with him?"

"Fuck off, Kyle," Heather said kindly, blowing him a kiss.

"Thanks for the pineapple. And, you know, for being you." She squeezed his arm. "Still good neighbors after this?"

"Sure. I'd do anything for that autograph."

She laughed. "See you later. Tell Shawn to book flights home and I'll talk to you when I'm rested."

"I mean it about the autograph," he called after her as she left the courtyard.

Bon had put Heather in with mom again. She was either hoping they'd sort it out or she was sick to death of them. Heather sighed as she saw her mother stretched out on the bed closest to French doors, which were open to a sunny terrace.

It was a nice room. It had more character than the Resort World places Bon usually booked. It was a simple sunny whitewashed room, with a beamed roof, Spanish-style wooden furniture and Peruvian cloth cushions on the beds.

Mom heard her come in and turned. She'd been crying again.

Heather sighed. She heard Kyle's voice in her head. *We're only human, right?*

"Mom?" Heather sat heavily on her bed, her mind tumbling over the events of the morning. Her anger had calcified, and her knotty emotions were bunched up, low in the pit of her stomach. As she stared at her mom, who was still crying, she felt deeply afraid.

Was this her future? Didn't it get better? Couldn't you grow up and find solid ground?

If only she could know which choices were right, and which were wrong.

"Mom?" She took a deep breath. "Did you feel like you were struck by lightning when you met Dad?"

Mom was confused. "What?" She'd obviously not been expecting Heather to be talking to her at all, let alone to be asking her about Dad.

"Did you know he was The One?" It seemed desperately important all of a sudden to know. Did Mom get struck, the way Bon had been by Jimmy Keays, the way Heather felt struck by Owen?

Because it hadn't worked out well for Bon and Jimmy, and she knew it hadn't worked out well for Mom and Dad. . . .

"Or," Heather said quietly, "did you talk yourself into it . . . ?"

Was Dad Romeo? Or was he Shawn? Which fucked-up issues were at play in her parents? And what did she need to watch out for in herself?

Mom raised herself up on one elbow.

"Please," Heather asked. "I just need to know. Please tell me."

Chapter 11

Sandy

Austin, Texas, 1992

Love makes you crazy. Sandy Keays had scrawled the graffiti on the toilet door at The Club, when she was crushing on Nick Russo, the lead guitarist of Torn, a band that was touring the college circuit. He was older, cooler, and sexier than any guy she'd dated before. And he'd seduced her with ease in her freshman year of college. She thought about it every time she went into that club toilet and saw her graffiti. The sight of it always made her smile.

She'd been at UTex only a semester the first time she hooked up with him. She'd gone out with some girls from her dorm; there were always bands from out of town headlining the local clubs, and Sandy lived for music.

She still remembered what she'd been wearing: a red and black tartan skirt, Doc Martens, and a well-worn black T-shirt with a ragged hem. She wore her hair long, with sharp-cut bangs. Sandy made her friends come to The Club with her to see Torn, even though they were keener on Cherry Bar and the lineup of synth-goth bands there.

"You have to let me see Torn," Sandy begged. "They're from Arizona, and you know how homesick I am!"

"Homesick," her roommate, Melissa, scoffed. "You don't even want to go home for the break."

"If you had my parents, you wouldn't either." Sandy didn't want to think about her parents. Or rather, her mom and her *step*father. That was the year she wasn't talking to Dale, who she'd disowned because he was a jerk for cheating on her mom. She called him Dale to his face, which he hated, and she went by the surname Keays at college, which he hated even more.

"I adopted you," he complained. "Your name is *Waller*."

Not in Austin it wasn't. And she didn't ever want to use his name again.

Sandy had never seen Torn live, but she'd heard them on the radio, and they were good enough to line up for. Even if the lineup did have a bunch of normies in their orange and white Longhorns gear in it. "Oh my God, some of these people look like they'd go to a Bryan Adams concert," she said, taking in the frat boys and shiny trendy girls.

"Worse, Richard Marx," Melissa said, nose wrinkling.

"Take That," Lori giggled.

Sandy laughed. "They've probably even got the T-shirts to prove it."

"They probably *wear* the T-shirts."

"This is what you get for picking The Club over Cherry Bar," Melissa sighed.

Sandy popped a stick of gum and passed the pack around. She'd given up smoking a couple of weeks before and it was still a grind to get through a night out without a puff. "It could be worse, I could have asked you to go boot scootin'." Which was totally a thing around here.

The Club was pounding that night, with normies and with the cooler indie kids. Torn was one of those bands that played to wider audiences, like the Chili Peppers or REM. Once Sandy and her friends had slid in, gliding through the velvet rope thanks to their short skirts, they headed straight for the dance floor. None of them were old enough to legally drink and they didn't have fake IDs, so they had to wait until someone offered to buy them booze. Which usually didn't take long.

Sandy usually kept to just a vodka orange juice or two. Melissa, on the other hand, was prone to getting hammered.

"You're in charge of her tonight," Sandy yelled at Lori over the music. "I don't want to miss the show." She left her friends and pushed her way to the front row of the mezzanine, where she had a perfect view of the stage.

It was hot and steamy in the windowless club, so much so that it felt like sweat was dripping off the walls. Which might explain why, when the band came out, they were minus their shirts. The lead singer and the drummer were completely bare from the waist up, and the singer had a total Anthony Kiedis vibe. But it was the lead guitarist Sandy noticed. He'd caught her eye when he sauntered out from the wings. He was sex on legs, lanky and muscular, in an unbuttoned red flannel shirt, which hung loose to his hips. His jeans hung low, revealing razor-sharp hipbones and a dark shadow of hair beneath his navel. And, oh God, he had abs like Keanu Reeves. He glanced up and saw her at the rail. She saw him clock her and felt a thrill when his gaze slid all over her.

He was *hot*.

They weren't the best band she'd ever heard (that honor went to Nirvana, who she saw at the Sun Club in Tempe the year before), but they were pretty good. Really thick guitarscapes. Just weak on the rhythm section, which was a shame as it made them janglier and looser than suited the songs. They needed to be toughened up.

But still, it was better than your usual gig. And worth it for that lead guitarist.

That very hot, very aggressive lead guitarist, who came straight for her after the show, carrying a couple of plastic cups of beer. He didn't say a word, just passed her the beer, and gave her a look that could have melted the Arctic.

"Hi," Sandy said, a little breathlessly, taking the cup, even though she didn't like beer.

"Hi." He leaned against the rail.

Sandy couldn't believe he'd singled her out. She was only a freshman. He was so confident. Like he wasn't scared of anything. Sandy mimicked his pose and took a sip of the beer, try-

ing not to pull a face at its sweaty hoppiness. He still had his
shirt open, and she couldn't stop looking at his chest.

He slid along the rail until they were close enough that she
could smell him: sharp, tangy sweat, beer, and the powdery,
piney scent of cheap body spray. "I'm Nick." His voice was
deep and rough. He seemed so *grown up*, slightly dangerous,
not someone you could tease.

"Sandy." She introduced herself, trying to sound casual.
He had dark brown eyes, and they were looking at her like he
wanted to eat her.

"Sandy? Like in *Grease*?" He slid another inch closer.

No one had hit on her like this before. It was like something
out of a movie.

"Yeah, like in *Grease*. Virginal. Can't you tell?"

He cracked a smile at that. "I don't believe you're a virgin."

Sandy liked the way he was looking at her. It made her tingle
all over.

He'd slid so close his chest was brushing hers.

"You guys sounded good tonight," Sandy said. She flicked
her hair, feeling the faint friction of him against her breasts as
she moved.

"I know." Then, without preamble, he kissed her. There was
no asking for permission. He just kissed her.

And hell, he was good at it. This was a dude who'd had a lot
of experience kissing girls. He was straight in with the tongue,
but it wasn't forceful.

"You want to get out of here?" he asked.

Did Sandy want to get out of there? With him? Yes, Sandy
did.

She loved the way people watched them as he led her out of
the club. People had been watching them make out too. She felt
flushed and horny and desirable as all hell. That's what Nick did
to her. He made her feel like the hottest woman in the room,
like every guy was watching them, envying him. And she *knew*
every girl was envying her.

They hooked up in his van, and the guy actually went down

on her. Which she'd read about but not actually had anyone do to her before. It was *transcendental*. A little awkward at first, because it was beyond intimate (and a little anxiety inducing) to have a guy put his face right between your legs, but once he got going she couldn't think, let alone feel any awkwardness or anxiety. She felt like a goddess. It was amazing.

He didn't run off after either. He pulled her into his arms, and they lay in the back seat of the van, their clothes tangled around them. She could feel him breathing hard, and then his breath slowed, like an ebbing tide. He toyed with her hair, winding it around his finger.

"Thanks," he said. Like she'd just played a good game of tennis with him or something. And then he drove her home and walked her to her dorm.

"Nice to know you, Sandy-the-not-a-virgin," he said, kissing her goodbye.

"Hey," she called as he walked off. "Don't be shy next time you're in town?"

He gave her a salute. "We're back in spring."

Sandy made sure she was back in spring too, right there at the rail on the mezzanine of The Club. The exact same spot as last time. That time he got her number after they hooked up, and now and then he actually called. He'd fill her in on what he was up to, and then he'd get hot and heavy on the phone, and it was just as hot as when he was there in person. By then, Sandy was obsessed. No one compared to Nick Russo. Certainly not the guys in her classes, or at the clubs around campus.

She went back to The Club a lot, and stood at the rail, and had vivid daydreams that Nick would walk in and see her, and slide along that rail, and then take her all the way to heaven.

But of course he didn't. He was touring. Or at home in Arizona.

With his girlfriend.

Sandy found out about the girlfriend when she was home for summer break, housesitting for her parents in Phoenix while they were off on vacation. She'd refused to go on vacation with them. Mom had rolled her eyes about it, but Dale had been furious, asking how come she was happy to accept her education from him, but not a vacation.

"Leave her be," Mom said, trying to soothe him. "She'll get over it. She's just being a teenager."

"I'm in college," Sandy had called out. "I'm not some damn kid." She was so goddamn *mad* at her mom for going on that vacation. How could she forgive him? She'd always thought her mom was so tough. But she wasn't. She was pathetic.

So Sandy stayed home by herself while Mom and Dale took Jacqui to some resort in Florida. She spent most of the summer reading books and listening to CDs, keeping an eye out to see if Torn was playing anywhere nearby. Eventually, in late August, she found them listed in the gig guide, playing as a support act at the Mesa amphitheater.

Sandy dressed casual, like she wasn't out to impress, but there was nothing casual about it. She wore her new denim cut offs, with a tight white tank, no bra, and her Docs. She'd recently cut her hair into a Winona Ryder–style blunt bob and was looking forward to debuting it to Nick. She looked fresh, but with an edge. And she couldn't wait to surprise him.

The gig was enormous. A proper summer concert, the air perfumed with weed, and the beer flowing freely. Sandy couldn't get anywhere near the front. Fine. She'd hit up the security guard backstage after the concert to tell Nick she was here. She was sure Nick would see her. He always did.

Torn had grown in popularity in the last few months. They'd had a couple of singles that had scraped the bottom of the charts, "Scoring Points" and "Hot Line," and had been landing higher-profile support gigs, like this one. Sandy's heart was in her mouth as she saw the band come out. There he was, his hair longer and shaggier, his shirt still unbuttoned. She felt an absurd burst of pride as she watched the gig. She *knew* him. And he knew her. And all these people around her would die of envy if they knew.

But then the unthinkable happened. A girl ran from the wings with a bottle of beer for him. She was tall and leggy, in a skintight cami dress, and her thick crown of henna red curls bounced as she ran. Sandy watched, horrified, but not entirely surprised, as Nick—*her* Nick—kissed the leggy girl in front of everyone. There were tongues involved, and the crowd cheered them on. It was only as she heard the murmurs from the crowd around her that Sandy realized who the girl was—Rachel Kelly, the lead singer of the headlining band.

And even though Nick had never promised her anything, and they clearly weren't dating, Sandy felt like the world had just fallen out from under her feet. It was dumb. Because *of course* he had other girls.

When the headliners took the stage—that hennaed hot girl up front on a mic—Sandy left her to it and headed backstage.

"Can you tell Nick Russo from Torn that Sandy Keays is here to see him?" she asked, keeping her shoulders back so the security guard got a good view of her braless tank. Security were always nicer after they copped a look.

The guy passed her message along on his walkie-talkie and then just stood there staring at her boobs. Sandy moved to stand against the fencing, her heart pounding. She didn't know if she'd be able to pull Nick away from the gravitational pull of the red-head on stage or not. She could hear the redhead singing. She was good. Her band was definitely better than Torn.

Sandy shifted restlessly in the heat. It was an oppressively hot August night. She wished she'd worn flip-flops instead of her Docs. Only there was nothing tough about flip-flops, and she needed the edge to be confident enough to approach Nick like this.

"Well, hey."

Sandy went hot with pleasure when she saw Nick at the back-stage gate.

"How you doing, Sandy the not-a-virgin?"

The security guard smirked at that.

"I'm good. You?" She bit her lip, trying to contain her grin. He was glad to see her.

"I'm good. Now." He was doing that dropped head, peering up through his floppy fringe thing that he did. "What are you doing outta Texas?"

"I live around here," she said, feeling weirdly shy. "Or my folks do."

"Is that right?" He hooked his fingers into the chain link fencing behind her head.

"Yeah. You're from Arizona too, right?" She tilted her head to accept his ducking kiss.

"I am," he breathed, leaning into her. "Phoenix born and bred."

"Me too." This was everything she'd hoped for.

But then he broke away. "Ah," he sighed regretfully. "I can't. My girl's here tonight."

"Your girl?" Sandy could taste ashes.

"Yeah, I mean what happens on tour stays on tour, you know? But not when she's on tour with me . . ."

"Right. Rachel Kelly."

"Yeah." He still had his fingers linked into the chain link fence over her head and his body was all but brushing hers. "God, it's hard not to touch you, though."

Sandy shivered. His gaze was full of longing. For *her*.

He ducked his head and pressed a kiss to the column of her neck. "How long are you here for?"

"Only another few days, before I have to go back and get ready for school."

He touched his forehead to hers and stared deep into her eyes. She could hear him breathing heavily.

"I'm home alone . . . ," she told him. "My family's all on vacation."

"Is that so?" He rubbed the tip of his nose against the tip of hers. "I might have some time on Monday . . ."

Nick spent more than just Monday with her. He arrived on her doorstep, rumpled and tired from too many late nights, and he didn't seem to want to leave.

"There's something about you," he said as they sat on the edge of her parents' pool drinking iced tea and talking about not much of anything at all. The Nick Russo who'd turned up that Monday was different from the one she hooked up with after gigs. This Nick Russo was tender with exhaustion, boyish, and weirdly vulnerable.

"What's the something about me?" Sandy asked, desperate to know. Was it beauty? Style? Wit? Cool?

Nick shrugged. "I don't know. You like me or something. I mean, you're happy to hang, not just fuck."

Oh. Sandy wasn't sure she liked that answer.

"I'm just a dumb guy when I'm off stage. I'm not fit for much other than sex."

Sandy was shocked. How could Nick Russo be insecure? He was *Nick Russo*. "You're not dumb," she protested.

"Yeah, I am. My mother says I was back of the line the day brains were handed out." He drained his iced tea and put the glass down with a gentle *clink*.

"I have never once thought you were dumb," Sandy told him honestly.

"Well, I'm no college kid like you. The closest I get to college is playing in campus bars."

"You could go to college if you wanted." Sandy moved her bare feet through the bright blue pool water. It was oddly thrilling to see this side of Nick. She wondered if she was the only person that he'd shown this side to, or if Rachel Kelly had access to him too. . . .

"Nah. No money. And no hope of a scholarship. Besides, could you imagine me in a classroom?" He pulled a face.

His dark eyes were sad. It tugged at Sandy's heart.

"Want to go for a swim?" she asked.

They spent the rest of the day lazily drifting in the pool and talking about music. Nick stayed all night, and the next night, and the next. They spent days together, just the two of them, eating cornflakes and drinking coffee; swimming and watching TV. It was regular and really nice. There was nothing of the rock star about him as he watched *Melrose Place* with her and helped her finish the crosswords in Dale's newspapers.

After he kissed her goodbye and went back to his band and his girlfriend, Sandy went back to Austin and tried to focus on her studies between his visits. Which was hard. Because she thought about him *all the time*. And while she was happy for him that Torn was booked onto national tours as an opening support act, she missed him. Torn had outgrown The Club, so he was never in Austin anymore. After a while his calls grew infrequent too, and she began to suspect he'd be a memory from her college years that made her smile, and nothing more. *Love makes you crazy*. The graffiti was a record of their mad hook-ups, and it still made her smile every time she saw it on the toilet door at The Club. It was proof they'd happened.

In junior year she started dating Scott Torres. One of his frat brothers was seeing Melissa, so they were thrown together all the time, at parties and weekends away, concerts and gigs. And he was hot and friendly and fun. She couldn't see any reason not to date him. He was a good kisser and good in bed, he liked live music, he liked reading, and he was interested in her when she talked about her studies. Which she did a lot, because she was enjoying her social work degree. She *believed* in it and had big plans.

Besides, it was nice having someone around all the time. Instead of a lover who was always somewhere else in the country. *With* someone else. If Nick could do it, she could do it too.

Only Scott wasn't an after-gig fling. He was deadly serious about her and looking for exclusivity. He even bought her an amethyst necklace for Christmas—it was an unpolished amethyst on a black thong that was so cool she never took it off. Sandy really liked him, and she really liked that he liked her.

So she committed to it. She even took Scott home to meet the 'rents. And month by month the *love makes you crazy* graffiti became an artifact of her past.

Until spring of '92, when Nick called.

"Hey, Sandy!" Melissa beckoned her to the phone, giving her a significant look. "It's *Nick*." As she handed the phone over, she touched her forefinger to the amethyst dangling from the leather choker at Sandy's neck.

Sandy rolled her eyes. *As if I would*, she mouthed. But her heart was thumping away like a runaway horse. She turned her back on Melissa, who pointedly sat down and opened a magazine, her big ears listening in.

"Hi," Sandy said, managing to keep her voice calm.

"Hi yourself." It was the same deep and dangerous flirty voice.

"I haven't heard from you in a while," she said mildly. "How's the touring?"

"Oh, you know, constant. Just about to ramp up again for spring too. And then we've got shows booked all summer."

Right. Of course. Sandy felt a stupid stab of disappointment. She didn't know what she expected. That he'd called to say he'd realized how much he missed her and was giving it all up for her? Sure. And pigs were going to fly.

"I guess you're calling because you're coming to town?" she said, sounding calm and mature. Even though she felt the opposite.

"Something like that."

"You'll have to tell me when you're coming," she kept her tone light, "so my boyfriend and I can come see you." She put emphasis on the word *boyfriend*.

There was a beat of silence. "Cool," he said, but she could hear a new tension in his voice.

Good.

"Be great to meet him."

Not good.

"What's his name?"

"Scott." Sandy turned and faced Melissa again. Her friend had given up all pretense of reading the magazine and was staring, engrossed in Sandy's side of the conversation.

"Scott?" Nick Russo sounded completely unimpressed.

"He's studying mechanical engineering," Sandy said blithely.

"Is he, now?"

"I think you'd really like him."

"I'm sure I would." Another beat. "Are you and Scott living together, then?"

Sandy frowned. He wasn't sounding at all upset now. He was taking it in his damn stride. "No. He's Greek."

"He's *Greek*? Like as in *Animal House* or *Revenge of the Nerds* or something?" Nick Russo made it sound deeply uncool. "So, he lives in a frat with a bunch of other dudes, instead of with you?"

Sandy almost giggled. This was more like it. He was jealous.

"So, Scott the Greek isn't there with you right now, then? He's off at a kegger with a bunch of bro-dudes?"

"He's in class, if you must know. He has late classes."

"Right. Engineering things."

"When are you coming, so Scott and I can put it in the calendar?" she asked coolly.

He told her. "Best make sure it doesn't clash with a kegger," he drawled.

"We'll make sure," she said sweetly. "And give my love to Rachel Kelly. I saw she's gone solo."

"Yeah," he sounded disgusted, "she sure has. We broke up."

Sandy jumped like someone had given her an electric shock. What? *They broke up*, she mouthed at Melissa.

"Uh-oh," Melissa groaned. And then she jabbed her finger at the amethyst.

Sandy glared at her.

"Anyway, Sands, it's been nice to chat. Talk again soon?"

"Oh, wait," Sandy panicked. It was too quick. She didn't want this to end yet . . .

But he was already signing off, and then she was just holding the buzzing receiver, standing there like an idiot. She dropped it in its cradle with a clatter, feeling empty and angry and full of bad feeling.

But then there was a lazy rapping at the front door.

Sandy and Melissa looked at one another.

"He wouldn't . . . ," Melissa said. But they both knew he would.

Sandy dashed for the door.

And there was Nick Russo, leaning against the wall outside

the front door of her share house. She'd moved off campus in sophomore year, and given him her address, just in case. Now and then he sent postcards from wherever he was.

Nick was wearing a pair of John Lennon–style round sunglasses and a flannel shirt open over a gray T-shirt. He was a study in casual cool and was giving her a wolfish smile.

"Hey," he said.

Hey. Like they hadn't just talked on the phone.

"Hey," she said back, also playing it cool. "Didn't know you were coming to town."

"Well, it was a sudden thing," he drawled. "I was home in Phoenix, and I went past your folks' place and, wouldn't you know it, I just got to missing you."

The thing about Nick was, you kind of knew he was playing you. But you didn't care. *She* didn't care. Because he played so well. And maybe there was a part of him, that boyish and vulnerable hidden part, that wasn't playing at all.

"I guess you want to come in?" she said, opening the door to let him in. Her whole body was singing to be in his presence.

"I always do." He lowered his sunglasses, and his dark eyes gave her an appreciative stare. Oh, she'd missed that look. No one else looked at her that way, not even Scott. Nick Russo looked at her like she was *delectable*. Irresistible. Just what he'd been hungering for his entire life.

He slid past her, his body brushing hers.

Melissa was in the hallway glaring at them.

"You remember Melissa?" Sandy was nervous under Melissa's judgment, but unable to refuse Nick. She *wanted* him there. More than she wanted Melissa's approval.

Nick was like nicotine. She knew she shouldn't want it, but she did. No matter how many times she quit, no matter how many times she suffered through withdrawal, she wanted it. She thought she'd always want it, even if she never smoked another cigarette, even if she never let Nick in ever again, she'd still want them both on a cellular level.

Once an addict, always an addict.

"Sure," Nick said. He put his hands in his pockets and stared straight back at Melissa. And then he smiled, that deeply sexy smile.

And even Melissa flushed and melted. She was still unhappy about it on Scott's account, and maybe on Sandy's account too, but she kind of understood.

"You want anything?" Sandy asked, gesturing to their little kitchen. The place was a rundown old 1920s bungalow that they rented for peanuts. But it was a whole house, big enough for four of them to share, and it was close to campus.

"Show me your room?" he suggested.

Sandy didn't need to be asked twice. She was glad she'd cleaned up on the weekend, she thought as she swung the door open. Her room was at the back of the house, with a window facing directly into the yard, with its overgrown grass and spreading live oak. Her room was furnished with thrift store finds, and she'd covered the bare globe that hung from the ceiling with a fat white rice paper shade that she'd bought for four bucks. There were books on every surface.

As she led Nick in, she noticed she still had a CD playing on the stereo, the Smashing Pumpkins' *Gish*. It was on "Crush," which seemed appropriate.

She saw him clock the poster of himself opposite her bed, and a ghost of a smile chased across his face at the sight of it, and then he prowled her room, examining her books and opening her lecture pad to read her notes. She closed the door quietly, feeling shy now that he was in her space.

"Who's this? Scott?" He lifted a framed photo from the mantlepiece.

Clearly not. The photo was old.

"That's my dad." Sandy was glad that was the only photo she had out. Jimmy was cool. Not like Dale. He was so normie it hurt. But Jimmy Keays wasn't. In that photo, her only photo of him, he was young, wearing aviator sunglasses and a cocky expression. He had long hair and tight jeans, and he had *attitude*.

"Oh yeah?" Nick held the photo closer and examined it. "He doesn't look like you."

"No, I look like my mom." Sandy pulled a face.

"I wouldn't complain," he said, shooting her a flirty look. "You got some good genes."

"Not good enough to warrant a visit from you lately." She wondered if he ever thought about their stolen few days in Phoenix, the easy comfort of it, the lack of pretense. The cornflakes and all.

He put the photo of Jimmy Keays down and sat on her bed. He patted the mattress next to him. "Well, I'm here now."

"For how long?"

He considered her. "How long do you need?"

Without thinking, Sandy blurted out the truth. "How long can you give me?"

His eyebrows shot up. "Oh yeah? And what about Scott?"

Love makes you crazy, Sandy thought. And what did she have to lose? "I'm only with Scott because you're not around."

"Lonely, huh?" He flopped back on her bed. "Yeah, me too."

And there he was, the Nick from Phoenix, appearing from behind the mask.

He rubbed his face tiredly. "It's a bummer being on the road all the time. It's fun for a while, but, I don't know, after a while you want to get beyond first conversations with people, you know?"

Sandy's chest tightened. He looked exhausted. "What about Rachel?"

"What about Rachel?"

"You clearly got past first conversations with her." Was he lonely only because they'd broken up? Or was he here because he longed for the ease of his few Phoenix days with Sandy? Did he want more than just sex?

"I guess." He stared at the ceiling. "She never really got me, though. You know?"

Rachel hadn't had access to *this*, then, Sandy thought triumphantly. Because you couldn't understand Nick until you saw him without his mask. Nick was just a lonely boy.

"She was cool and all. And fun. But . . ." He turned his head, and his dark eyes were more vulnerable than she'd ever seen them. "We're just not on the same frequency." He reached out and took her hand, entwining his fingers with hers. "Not like with you."

Sandy wanted to believe him, even though she knew a line when she heard one.

She had a choice to make, she supposed. She could choose to believe him, and lay down next to him on the bed, and keep this wild magic thing going. Or she could choose not to believe him, and say goodbye to Nick Russo.

Or . . . maybe she could choose to *kind of* believe him, and kind of not?

Because maybe he *kind of* believed his own bullshit too, and kind of didn't? And maybe he needed someone who kind of believed, and kind of didn't? Because it was lonely *kind of* believing all by yourself.

He sighed, squeezing her hand like he'd read her mind. "I've got issues, I guess."

"Don't we all," she said dryly. Then she cocked her head. "What kind of issues?"

He laughed. "How much time have you got?"

"All the time, for you." She crawled over him and lay next to him, taking his hand again as soon as she was comfortable.

"Just the usual shit, I guess," he said, still staring at her ceiling. "Parents who broke up when I was a kid, dad who ran off, mom who needed me to be her everything but who had nothing to give me in return."

"My dad ran off too," Sandy blurted as he trailed off.

"That guy in the picture?" He turned to regard her curiously. She nodded.

"They're fuckers, aren't they, dads."

She nodded. "Every year on my birthday I used to check the letterbox to see if there was a card. Like one year he'd realize how much he was missing out on me, and he'd post something." She paused. "But there was never any card."

"I'll tell you what, Sands," he said, rolling over. "I promise you I'll send you a card every year on your birthday. Fuck dads, right?" He ran a finger down the line of her cheek and Sandy felt like crying with the tenderness of it.

"What about you?" she asked softly.

"Oh, I don't need cards," he breathed, wriggling closer.

She laughed. "I know what you need."

"No." He laughed too. "Well, yes. That too. Always."

"What, then?"

"Just love me," he said. "And don't leave me. Everyone always leaves."

"I swear," she said fervently, wanting to give that to him so bad it hurt. "I swear I will love you, and never leave you. If you don't leave me too."

"It's a lot to ask of you," he admitted, staring into her eyes. "You don't even know me."

"I know you," she protested. "Or at least I'm starting to." And she wanted to love someone so badly. Someone who would put her in the center and never leave her. It could be her and Nick, and no one else. "You're worth it," she told him, leaning forward to kiss him, but what she was actually thinking was that *she* was worth it. He made her feel worth it. He could have any girl he wanted, and yet he had showed up here at *her* door, begging for *her* love.

"I'm not," he warned her. "I'm a fuckup."

"No." She wouldn't hear it. "You're everything." And she'd be everything too. They'd be everything for each other. And she wouldn't be alone anymore.

"When you say it," he sighed, looking like a little kid, "I almost believe it." And then he relaxed back into her pillows as she kissed him. And that was that. She ditched the rest of junior year and went on tour with him.

And, true to his word, every year Nick sent her a card on her birthday. And he never left her for good. It mattered.

Chapter 12
Heather

Cusco, Peru

Her dad was just a total fuck boy, Heather thought in disgust. And her mom had gone into their relationship knowing it. Not just knowing it, but kind of loving it.

It was infuriating. Heather wished she could go back in time and shake some sense into her mother. And maybe slap her father upside the head and tell him to get a therapist.

The worst bit was when she'd asked her mother if she'd take it back. If she'd have stayed with Scott instead.

"Of course," Mom had said, but the thought made her cry. "I mean, I should have stayed with Scott. He would have been a good husband."

She didn't sound convincing, not even to herself, Heather thought.

"But I wouldn't change any of it," Mom blurted it. "It was the best thing that ever happened to me." She wiped her face. "I can't even describe it properly . . . the feeling. Of being young and alive and in love."

"In lust," Heather countered, her stomach sinking. Mom hadn't said anything about her and Chris. That falling in love had led to *them*. But that was the thing about Mom and Dad, they were so intensely focused on themselves and their feelings for each other, that the rest of the world fell away. Including their kids.

Mom had shrugged. "Whatever it was, it was magic." And then she started crying again.

It wasn't any kind of magic Heather wanted in her life. It sounded like textbook acting out childhood trauma to her. And her mother was a *social worker*. She *knew* about this stuff. But she was still sitting there, getting misty about it.

Where she'd been wrong about her parents, Heather thought as she left Mom to her memories and took herself off for an angry walk through Cusco, was in thinking of Mom as a victim. Mom had chosen the shitshow knowingly. She wasn't Dad's victim so much as his accomplice. Their version of love was nothing but codependency.

Heather tried to walk off her feelings, but they weren't walking off. She was immune to the charm of the old imperial city, barely registering when she reached the main square. She was still thinking of her parents. Of their car crash of a relationship and of her father's total narcissistic need.

But . . .

Ah hell. Heather felt like crying as a thought pushed toward the surface. *But* . . . she kind of understood why her mom had fallen for Nick Russo. Because Dad was charming, and openly affectionate, and when he pulled you into a hug you felt like you were the center of his whole world and that he adored you. Dad made you feel like you were his secret treasure. And Heather missed it.

He had fucking *issues*, he'd said. No joke. He was nothing *but* issues. There was a hole in Dad that could just never be filled, no matter how hard he tried to screw his way to wholeness.

But as Kyle had said, they were all human, weren't they?

Dammit, she was going to cry. Heather scrubbed her face with the sleeve of her sweater as she walked the streets of Cusco. Why did people have to be such hot messes? Why couldn't there be a single person out there who had their shit together? Someone she could trust and not have to defend herself against; someone who didn't adore you, then ignore you; or demand you put their needs over yours; or make you be the grown-up to their child. Someone who cared what *she* wanted, who . . .

Heather stumbled to a halt, shocked.

Because, walking toward her across the square was a familiar long-legged figure.

Romeo.

She felt like she'd summoned him. And then he lifted his hand in greeting, and her heart felt like it lifted a couple of inches in her chest.

"Hey," he said as he approached, and he was smiling. "I saw you from across the square."

Heather burst into tears.

"Whoa." He looked surprised. "Hey." He took her shoulders and bent down to peer into her face. She saw her reflection in his sunglasses. "Hey, what's going on?" He didn't look impatient, or put off, or annoyed, or any of the things people usually looked when she cried. He didn't tell her to calm down. He just made a low noise of sympathy and pulled her into a hug. "Bad day, huh?" He rested his cheek on the top of her head and squeezed her close, rocking a little from side to side.

"You're going to think I'm nothing but drama," she hiccupped.

"Maybe. It's too early to tell." He kept rocking. "But maybe I just think you're human."

"Kyle said something like that."

"And who's Kyle? Another ex-boyfriend I have to contend with?"

Heather cried harder. She burrowed into his chest and wished all the feelings would go away. "I miss my dad," she said helplessly.

"Right. That's new." He pulled away and bent down again so he could see her face. He lifted his sunglasses so she could see his eyes. "Want to fill me in?"

Heather nodded, rubbing the tears away with the heel of her hand. "I'm not usually like this," she apologized.

He smiled. "You know your lips go all swollen when you cry? It's sexy as hell."

"Stop it," she groaned. "No one is this perfect. I know you're going to be an axe murderer or a Moscato drinker or something."

"I have been known to enjoy a Moscato from time to time."

"I knew it."

"And while I'm drinking Moscato, I might also spend my life on the road, neglecting people," he said seriously. "Come on, let's go walk around the square and I'll tell you the history of things and you can tell me why you're missing your dad."

The weight of his arm around her shoulders was soothing. Heather leaned into his body.

"Take a breath, Juliet. Look around. The sun is out and you're in the ancient city of Cusco." He rubbed her shoulder.

She nodded, taking a shaking breath. "Okay. Bore me about this square thing we're in."

"Square thing?" He was appalled. "This is the Plaza de Armas. The Incans called it Huacaypata or Aucaypata."

Heather let the sound of his voice wash over her as he went through his encyclopedia entry on the square.

"And up here we have the cathedral, flanked by the churches of I-can't-quite-remember."

Heather laughed, delighted he'd forgotten. Then she tugged on his shirt. "How did you know I needed you?"

"I didn't," he said, still holding her close to his side. "I was just out for a walk." He rubbed her arm. "But tell me about this needing me thing. Has it got something to do with the dad thing?"

Heather told him, the words coming in a flood. They sat on the steps of the cathedral in the sun, watching the flow of tourists crossing the square and picking their way along the paths through the gardens. She told him about her charming, feckless, fuck boy of a father, and her adoring, permanently wounded mother. About her childhood of keeping secrets. About her dad's impending wedding, which he hadn't bothered to tell her about. About how it felt to be forced onto her mom's "side." About how it felt to be collateral damage. About how much she'd distrusted Shawn's adoration as a result. About how even

if she'd liked Shawn, which she didn't, she wasn't sure if she'd
have accepted being loved anyway.

And when the deluge of words trickled to a stop, Owen made
a thoughtful noise. And then all he said was, "Yeah, that's a
lot." But he was holding her hand in both of his, and he lifted
it to his mouth and kissed it. And then he changed the subject.
"Fancy some street food? Hungry?"

"That's *it*?" she said, astonished. "That's all you've got to
say? 'That's a lot.'" She paused. "And yes, I'd like some street
food."

"Cool. There's a guy down that street over there grilling
something that smells great. Some kind of beef on a stick." He
stood and pulled her to her feet. And then kissed her lightly.
"And yes, for now that's all I've got to say. It's a *lot*."

He was compassionate and kept hold of her hand, but he
said nothing more. He left her holding her own feelings. This
was what having boundaries looked like, she realized. This was
what it looked like *not* to be enmeshed.

"You'll work it out, Juliet," he told her kindly, pulling her to
her feet.

And then he took her to eat beef on a stick. And to see Cusco.
Because he was there, and she was there, and Cusco was there.
And for now, that was enough.

When Heather got back to the room, Bon was lying in wait.
She was sitting on Heather's bed, Junior's wooden box sitting
next to her. Mom wasn't there, but Heather could hear the
shower running.

"Hi," Heather said carefully, closing the door behind her.

"This whole thing is supposed to be about *me*," Bon told her
sternly.

"I thought it was about Mom being some kind of emergent
cougar."

"Don't be smart." Bon lifted Junior and put him on her lap
and patted the bed beside her for Heather to sit down.

Heather sighed. She just wanted a shower and some rest. But
she went and sat next to her grandmother on the bed.

"Nothing ever goes to plan," Bon complained.

"Seems not."

They stared at each other, and then Bon tapped Heather lightly on the cheek. "A wise man once told me that when times are hard, it's better to run *to* something."

Heather nodded, as though that should make sense. Maybe it would make sense after a shower and a nap.

"We came to see a wonder of the world," Bon said firmly. "And instead we're dealing with your harem of men." She sighed. "It's probably my fault your mother did this. Or her father's. It's always the parents' fault, isn't it? Well, if that's the case, we can probably go all the way back and blame my pa. Or possibly his pa . . ." Bon gave Heather the side-eye. "Feel free to disagree with me."

"I just feel like there are so many traps," Heather blurted, and she wasn't talking about Bon's grandfather. "I mean, inside me. I'm full of traps: mousetraps and bear traps and trap doors—all lying in wait for me to take a wrong step. What if I put a foot wrong? What if I fall into loving the wrong person, because of Mom and Dad and the mess they made of me?"

"Oh, for Pete's sake." Bon was exasperated. "First of all, your parents didn't make a mess of you. You, honey, are all you need to be, and I, for one, *like* who you are. And second, there are no wrong people. Or right people. There are just people. You're overthinking things. Trust me, there's no rulebook and no map of traps. You meet people, you love them or you don't— or you love them *and* you don't—you stay with them or you don't. Sometimes they leave you and sometimes they stay with you, and sometimes they leave and stay all at once. Stuff is just stuff."

"Romantic."

"It is romantic. When you see people for what they are, not for what they could be to you, then you love them. That's what love is. Trust me, because I didn't learn this lesson the easy way."

"You think Mom and Dad only loved each other for what they could be to each other, not for what they were?" Heather was crying again. Her parents' split hurt worse than she'd thought it would. She'd expected it her whole life, and in a weird way had wondered if it might not be a relief when it finally happened, but it wasn't. It was bad.

"Oh, honey." Bon stroked her hair.

Heather leaned into her. It felt good to be comforted.

"I have no earthly idea. Who knows what happens in the secret terrain of a marriage?" Bon pulled her closer. "But I like to think they loved each other. That they tried. Your dad isn't all bad, you know. He's just in a lot of pain and incapable of seeing past himself."

"And Mom?"

"Your mom doesn't even know how much pain she's in. She got hurt so young she grew up with it and thinks it's normal."

Heather closed her eyes and just enjoyed Bon's one-armed hug for a while. It felt so nice to surrender.

"You're okay," Bon said, dropping a kiss on the crown of Heather's head. "But we do need to fix this *Love Island* situation of yours."

"Yes, well, Shawn's going home." Heather opened her eyes and reluctantly sat up straight. She was glad Bon kept her arm around her; she wasn't ready to relinquish the comfort yet.

Bon cleared her throat. "Did you know they brought their hiking gear? Him and the big bear of a friend."

An ice-cold wave swept Heather from head to toe.

"And they're booked on the exact same trekking tour that we are."

Heather could have screamed. She glared at the closed bathroom door. Goddamn her mother.

"That's one besotted little stalker you've got there," Bon said dryly, pulling away from Heather.

Heather let the words sink in. "Thank God you can see it," she exhaled. "Mom seems to think it's romantic."

"Romantic is a man listening when you say no," Bon sniffed.

Heather groaned. "What do I *do*?"

Bon put her hand on Heather's knee and squeezed. "Stop sleeping with him."

Heather flushed.

"The big, shaggy one told me you keep leading him on. And so did your mother."

There was no way in hell Heather was ever sleeping with Shawn again, and she certainly wasn't trekking up to Machu Picchu with him. Especially not with Owen here—it was deeply unfair to *him*. "I'll talk to Shawn," she said grimly.

"No," Bon said shortly. "That's what he wants. You need to suffocate the energy out of this thing. You don't sleep with him, and you don't talk to him. You put an iron curtain between you and that boy. He needs to know you're done. Stop running around trying to manage him. You're not responsible for other people's feelings—especially when those other people are your exes."

"But I don't want him here," Heather said, appalled. "I *have* to talk to him."

"How are you going to stop him by talking at him? He hasn't listened to you so far."

Heather didn't know.

"Besides," Bon continued, "I've already sorted it."

Heather had a sinking feeling. "You what?"

"I've sorted it. So, it's lucky you didn't want him, because you're not getting him. I've sorted *all* the distractions. I came here to spend some time with you and your mom. And with Junior," she added, stroking the lid of his box. "I can be very resourceful," Bon said mildly, but the look in her eye wasn't mild at all.

"What are you going to do?"

Bon gave a sharp laugh. "Do? It's already *done*."

"You mean Shawn's going home?" Heather felt relief so strong it stole her breath. She went to hug her grandmother, but Bon put a hand on her shoulder and held her back.

"Hold it. I don't want you in a strangling position when I tell you the next bit."

Heather had no idea what Bon was about to say next, but she knew it was going to be bad, because Bon had her imperious expression on. The one that brooked no discussion.

"I called the tour company," Bon said, her hand still on Heather's shoulder, in preparation for an attack. "And upgraded us. It cost a fortune, so you're welcome."

"What do you mean, 'upgraded us'?" Heather asked suspiciously.

"We're getting the private trek experience. Just the three of us." Bon pursed her lips. "No Shawn and his furry friend."

"But that's great!" Heather didn't see what the catch was, or why Bon's hand was keeping her at bay so strongly.

"*Just* us," Bon repeated.

And it sank in.

Just the three of them. And no Owen.

"You're telling me I'm going to be trekking with your boyfriend?" Owen wasn't taking it well. "Without you."

"My *ex*-boyfriend," Heather corrected.

"While you three go off on your own . . ."

"Don't take it out on her," Mom said sharply. "This is my mother's doing."

"No, it's *your* doing," Heather growled. "And he's not taking anything out on me. He's justifiably angry."

Heather had planned to have a quiet drink with Owen so she could explain the situation as calmly as possible. But, of course, Mom and Bon ruined it by crashing. They'd followed Heather to the bar, refusing to be shaken off. And now the four of them were crammed around an intimate little table in a romantic little bar, and Owen quite literally had his back to the wall.

"I'll take the blame," Bon said stoically. "Even though Heather is right, Sandra is actually to blame."

Sandy ignored her. "Shawn was with Heather long before she met you, Owen. They were still together the night before she flew out."

"I think that's Heather's private business," Owen said firmly. "And I'm not angry at anyone. I'm . . . surprised." But there was a muscle twitching in his jaw. He played with his beer bottle and maintained his careful quiet. Heather wished she knew him better and could read him. She didn't know what he was thinking—she only knew what *she* would be thinking in this situation. And it wasn't good.

He glanced up and met her eye.

"It's a pretty weird situation," he said quietly.

"No," she disagreed. "It's not pretty weird. It's batshit crazy and totally out of line."

He nodded. "Yeah, that's more accurate." He pushed his beer away. "Look, you ladies have a lot going on."

Another radical understatement.

He ignored Mom and Bon and leaned forward, clasping his hands together and staring Heather straight in the eye. "I had a great time with you in Barranco," he told her.

The hair rose on the back of Heather's neck.

"But I really don't do drama," he told her firmly.

Heather's heart sank.

"I don't know this guy you're talking about, and I could probably not care less if he's trekking at the same time I am," he admitted. "So long as I'm not tangled up in his bullshit." He leaned back in his chair.

Heather felt tears prickling.

Owen took her hand, unhooking her fingers from the stem of her wineglass. He linked his fingers through hers. "You've got to listen to the universe's hints, I suppose," he told her wryly. "And they've been pretty clear today."

"You were in the square when I needed you," she reminded him. "Doesn't that count for something?"

"Oh, for heaven's sake." Mom sighed gustily. "You'd think we were in some kind of Shakespearean tragedy. We'll be back here in Cusco within a week."

Heather felt a blast of shame at her mother's rudeness. "Alright," she snapped. "That's enough. No one invited you to this drink, so off you go."

Bon pursed her lips. "Sorry," she apologized, mostly to Owen. "I just wanted to tell you that this is my doing, not Heather's. She's innocent in all this."

"Noted," Owen said coolly.

"Come on, Sandra." Bon grabbed Sandy by the arm and all but hauled her out of her chair.

"Your family's not great at boundaries, huh?" Owen said after they'd left.

Heather shook her head. "I'm not sure they even know what boundaries are."

"That's why you moved to Chicago?"

"Yeah. Only now I'm going to have to leave Chicago too."

"Because of this Shawn guy? The ex you were still sleeping with right up until you flew here?"

Heather sighed. "Yeah." She had no defense to that.

"You know you get to sleep with someone and not owe them anything, right?"

"I know," she said bluntly. "And I know it wasn't fair to him. That I just confused things."

"And your mom? You know even though she's your mom you don't owe her anything either?"

Heather felt that stomach cancer ache again. "She's . . ."

"A lot?"

"Messed up about this stuff." Heather gave a helpless shrug.

"We all are. But you get to have privacy, you know. You're allowed boundaries."

"I know. I'm just not good at it. I'm better at running away."

"Practice makes perfect." He took a sip of his beer and did that delicious lower lip suck again. "And I can't judge. I run too." He slid into his thoughts, looking troubled.

"So, I guess our Barranco magic ran out." Heather didn't understand the scale of her sadness. She hardly knew him and yet she felt like she was losing something precious.

He shot her a look. "You always give up this easy?" He drummed his fingers on the tabletop. "You know when I run, I don't run *away*, despite what everyone thinks. I run *to*." He met her gaze, his eyes midnight dark. "And I keep waiting for someone who'll run with me." He drained his beer and gave her one of his twitchy almost-smiles. "We're only at the trailhead, Juliet. There's still a whole mountain to climb, so don't go giving up yet."

"You said you don't do drama," she reminded him.

"I don't," he acknowledged with a shrug. "But you might not always come with drama."

Heather felt the world turning upside down. What did that mean? Was he saying they might have a future?

"Enjoy your trek," he said huskily. He stood and looked down at her with those sultry eyes. "Who knows, maybe the trail will help. And, like your mom said, I'll see you back here in a week or so."

"You will . . . ?" Heather's heart was swelling up.

"Adios. Heather." He bent down and gave her a brief, fierce kiss. And then he was gone.

Chapter 13
Heather

Cusco, Peru

"I'm not talking to you," Heather said to her mother, dropping into a seat at the dinner table.

Bon had booked them a table at a little place upstairs on the Plaza de Armas. They were seated on the balcony, overlooking San Blas, the old quarter of the city. It was a table for three, with no Owen, and no Shawn and Kyle. It was cold out, and the air was clear and sharp, blue with falling night; the lights were turning on in the winding tumble of streets, blurs of gold, an impressionist painting brought to life.

"I think that's an extreme reaction," her mother told her stiffly, keeping her attention on the wine list.

Heather rolled her eyes.

"After all, you came here to spend time with *us*," Mom continued. "I don't think hooking up with strangers was on the itinerary, so there's no need to be such a thundercloud."

"Sandra," Bon interrupted. "Stop annoying her and order a bottle of wine."

"Me? Annoying *her*?" Mom's head snapped up from the wine list. "*She's* the one who walked in all huffy."

"I'd take issue with that, but I'm not talking to you." Heather took the wine list out of her hands. "And I'll order the wine."

"Spend as much as you want," Bon told her. "I'm paying for it and it's my last hurrah so don't worry about the price."

"Oh, please, Mom, don't be so dramatic," Mom grumped. "You're only seventy. This is in no way your last hurrah. I'll bet you fifty dollars you're climbing Everest this time next year or riding a camel across a desert in Jordan or something."

"No, I'm done." Bon considered the menu. "What do you think alpaca tastes like?"

"Ew, Mom. Really."

"What do you mean *ew*?" Bon was nonplussed. "How is it any different to eating a cow?"

"Red wine, then, if you're thinking about red meat." Heather went back to the wine list.

"Is alpaca red meat? I've never tried it."

"I'm going to order something Peruvian. We haven't had much local wine." Heather was just glad not to be talking about the whole Owen mess. It only made her angry.

"Do they make wine in Peru?" Mom asked, trying to get Heather talking to her, like it was a game she wanted to win.

Heather didn't respond.

"Fine." Mom wasn't one to be ignored, though. She called the waiter over. "Excuse me," she said brightly. "*Hablas Inglés?*"

The waiter did.

"Oh, good. Does Peru make wine?"

"We have the oldest vineyards in South America," the waiter said politely. "Some of our grapes date back to the sixteenth century."

"Wonderful." Mom shot Heather a look. "My daughter was hoping you could recommend a nice red."

Heather folded the wine list. She smiled courteously at the waiter but resented being dragged into this three-way conversation with her mom. "A malbec maybe," Heather told the waiter. "I was thinking about having the trout." She kept her attention squarely on the waiter.

"One of the Vitor Valley malbecs would be a good choice," the waiter suggested, and she and Heather fell into a conversation about the terroir of the region and the unique qualities of Peruvian wines made in the European style. Heather took childish pleasure in locking her mother out of the conversation.

"Since when do you know so much about wine?" Bon asked, astonished, once the waiter had dug up a fancy bottle from the cellar and decanted it at the table.

"Since she moved to Chicago," Mom muttered, slouching like an angry teen.

"I joined a wine club," Heather told her grandmother.

Bon sipped the wine, impressed. "You're a dark horse, aren't you?" She took another sip and then sat back in her chair. "Alright, ladies, listen up. This trip hasn't started out on the right foot. Things need to change."

Heather didn't know about that. She'd liked her beginning in Barranco. It was the rest of it that wasn't working out.

Bon put her hand on Junior's box, which was on the table, as usual. "I'm not spending all this money so you can ignore your mother, Heather," she said sternly.

Heather blinked, shocked that she was the one in the firing line. "Wait. What? You're mad at *me*?"

"Hush. I'm mad at both of you. Honestly, you're grown women and you're acting like children."

Heather thought that was some nerve, given the way Bon and Sandy bickered.

"I can't believe we got to the point where you weren't answering your mom's messages, Heather."

"Can you blame me?" Heather couldn't believe Bon could say this, after the stunt Mom had just pulled. "She doesn't have any sense of appropriate boundaries!"

"She's your *mother*."

Heather's mom was gazing at Bon, gratified. "Thanks, Mom."

"And *you*," Bon snapped at her daughter. "You haven't been answering *my* messages, so you don't get to be all smug."

Mom flushed. "You *know* why I'm not answering your messages."

"Because you want to wallow."

Heather reached for her wine. "And you told me *I* was acting like a child," she muttered.

"You're both acting like children."

"No," Heather snapped. "I'm putting boundaries in place. Which I'm allowed to do. She just doesn't like it."

"And is that what you're doing with me, Sandra? Putting boundaries in place?"

"No," Mom exhaled angrily. "I just don't want to talk to you when I'm depressed. Because you tell me to pull myself up by my bootstraps and I just *can't*. You've never been able to just let me be."

"I was worried about you."

"So? So, you're worried. You'll cope. I'm just fine, wallowing under my bedclothes without showering for a while. My marriage just ended, goddamn it. I'm allowed a bit of wallowing."

"I don't like wallowing," Bon said, her hand tensing on Junior's box.

"So don't do it. No one is making you wallow."

"I don't like *you* wallowing."

"Well, tough." Mom took an angry sip of wine. "It's *my* life."

Bon made a *humph* sound and sat back in her chair.

"I don't know why *you're* not talking to *me*, though." Mom turned on Heather. "It's not like I tell you to pull yourself up by the bootstraps."

"No," Heather said tightly, "you just invite my stalker exboyfriend along on our vacation."

"He's hardly a stalker!"

"*This* is why I don't answer your calls. Because you don't listen to me. You bulldoze right over me, insisting that what you want is what I want. I know what I want, Mom, and it's not Shawn. And he *is* a stalker. I don't like him chasing after me; I've said no; and he still does it." Heather was surging with adrenaline. She had the urge to get up and run. She could barely sit still, the feelings were so strong. "And as for you: you dump your emotions on me, and I don't want to be an emotional dumping ground. I'm a *person*, with my own thoughts and feelings, and I'm sick of being your carrier bag for nasty feelings. If you're mad at Dad, you dump it on me and expect me to carry it; if you're distraught, you dump it on me; if you're bleak, you dump it on me. I don't get the nice stuff. *Dad* gets that. When Dad's giving you flowers and making up with you, you disappear in a haze of happiness, with him. I only get you when he doesn't want you. And what I get is the *dregs*." Heather didn't know where it all came from. The words poured out of her like pus from an infected wound.

Mom looked stunned. "That's not true."

"It is. It is true!" And then Heather burst into tears.

There was a moment's silence and Heather held her napkin up to her face, still angry, but also something else. Something deeper than anger. *Hurt*.

"Well, at least she's talking to you again," Bon told Mom.

At that, Mom burst into tears too.

"Is everything alright?" The waiter approached the table nervously, as though she were approaching a table of hungry lions.

"Better than it's been all week," Bon said cheerfully. "Don't mind them, they're grieving." She patted Junior's box. "This is my husband, and we're here to say goodbye to him."

"*Dios*, I'm sorry!" The waiter was stricken.

Heather bit her lower lip and tried to stop crying, but now that she'd started, she couldn't seem to stop. And neither could Mom.

"It's better to cry than to bottle it up, don't you think?" Bon said to the waiter, sanguine.

"Of course. I'll fetch some tissues," the poor woman said, dashing off.

When she came back, she brought not only two boxes of tissues, but also a bottle of pisco and three shot glasses. "This looks like it needs something stronger than wine," she said sympathetically. "It's on us."

"You're too kind." Bon readily accepted a shot. "Here's to family!" She shot a sharp look at Mom and Heather and downed the shot.

* * *

Two hours later they were still on the balcony, more than a little drunk on wine and pisco, and quietly depleted from all the emotion. The other customers had dwindled, and the blue night had become an icy darkness. The waiter had brought them alpaca blankets and turned the heat lamp up as far as it would go. She'd offered them a table inside, but the three of them were enjoying watching the lights of San Blas and didn't want to leave the balcony.

"Aren't you glad you didn't eat an alpaca?" Mom said tiredly as she stroked the blanket on her lap.

"Not really." Bon sounded dissatisfied. "I was curious. The lamb was lovely, but I know what lamb tastes like."

Now that Heather had spat out her feelings, she felt empty. She pulled the blanket around her shoulders and watched the moon rise over the slanting rooftops. None of them had spoken about their argument after the waiter had delivered the pisco shots and a febrile peace had formed, like a rime of thin ice forming over a winter puddle. Nothing was solved, but nothing seemed to be broken either.

"You can feel the cold of the mountains here," Bon said, lifting her face to it, like she was sunbathing.

"It's beautiful," Mom sighed. "Too beautiful to seem real."

"It's a UNESCO World Heritage Site," Heather told them. She'd learned that from Owen, as they'd sat in the plaza below.

"I can see why." Mom stood and moved to the balustrade of the balcony.

"You're blocking the view," Bon said dryly.

"No, I'm just part of it."

Bon laughed and then called the waiter over. "Hey, honey, could we have three of those hot chocolates I keep seeing you carrying around? They look magnificent."

"Really, Mom, I couldn't eat another thing," Sandy protested.

"It's just a little drink. Besides, you can't say no to Peruvian chocolate in Peru. It would be rude."

The waiter rushed off to fetch their drinks while a sleepy Heather huddled under the blanket and let their voices wash over her.

"Mom?" Sandy said thoughtfully. "You know, Heather asked me about when I met Nick. And I realized afterward that I've never asked you about Dad. How you met him."

"Which Dad?"

"*Dad* Dad." Mom sounded a touch annoyed. "The dad who raised me."

"Dale, you mean?"

"Is there another man who raised me?"

"You said a Fleetwood Mac concert or something," Heather said drowsily, trying to head off any more conflict. She didn't have another fight in her tonight.

"No, not a Fleetwood Mac concert or something." Bon was put out. "I said I first had sex with him at a Fleetwood Mac concert. But that's not where we met."

Heather groaned. "This isn't a story with more sex in it, is it? I've heard enough about your sex lives to put me in therapy for the rest of my life."

"Where *did* you meet?" Mom prodded. "I can't believe I don't know."

Bon was suspiciously quiet.

"Bon?" Heather poked her in the arm. "Come on, spill."

"Fine. But don't judge me."

Oh, this was going to be good.

Chapter 14

Bonnie

Phoenix, Arizona, 1974

Dale Waller got Bonnie fired from the Playboy Club.

Bonnie had worked there for only a few months, drawn by the sizable tips Dee was earning. Dee had turned out to be something of a surprise. Once she hit twenty-one, all that baby fat melted plain off (probably because she couldn't even afford a soda at Bob's Big Boy and Bonnie could no longer afford to spot her one, now that she had a kid to feed), and it turned out that Dee was statuesque as all hell. She'd been scouted one day when she was wrestling the snot monster into a trolley down at the Alpha Beta market, with the guy asking her flat out what her measurements were; Dee had told him to buzz off, but he'd still given her his card.

And before you could say Hugh Hefner, Dee was earning enough to move out of her sister's place and leave the snot monster behind.

"You should do it, Bonnie," Dee told her. "And wouldn't it be a blast to work together?"

Bonnie was dubious at first, but Dee swore the guys weren't allowed to date a bunny, let alone touch one.

"It's classy," Dee said. "The *mayor* was there last night." She looked Bon up and down. "And your measurements are alright. Hell, you wouldn't even know you'd had a kid."

Bonnie took a good, hard look at her situation. She was earning only $61.50 a week, up from the $57.50 of five whole years earlier, and still living in Pa's trailer in Shitsville, but now with a kid. A kid who went through bread and bananas and milk like nobody's business. Hell, if Bonnie didn't do something soon, Sandra was going to spend her entire childhood in the same crappy trailer that Bonnie had grown up in, wearing the same kind of homemade clothes and patched-up shoes, and thinking a glass of milk and a banana was a treat, not a staple. And Bonnie would get old, and her life would be over, and she'd still be listening to Mrs. Chisum's soaps blaring over from her trailer, because the old woman would probably live to be a hundred. And so would Pa. He was so pickled he barely seemed to age, preserved like a goddamn onion in a glass jar.

Bonnie desperately wanted to get a better job, but the economy was in the toilet, and she didn't have any education, or any prospects. Her brothers had come back from Vietnam and settled in California and Oregon, and pumped out kids of their own, so they were no help at all. So sure, Bonnie didn't want to dress up like a bunny and smile at men like Doc Slaughter, but what choice did she have? She didn't want to live in Shitsville either.

So Bonnie squeezed herself into one of those corseted satin bunny suits, her boobs shoved just about all the way up to her chin, and tottered about on her first pair of stiletto high heels, fetching drinks for Doc Slaughter, and the mayor, and a bunch of city councilmen, and even the cop who'd arrested her and Jimmy Keays in that Caddy a lifetime ago. And trying to smile the whole time like she was having the best day of her life.

The club itself was a fine enough place to spend a shift. It was on the eighth floor of Mayer Central, with huge plate glass windows looking out onto Camelback Mountain and a terrace with a view right down the valley. There was always a jazz act playing, top-shelf booze being served, and the air-conditioning was good enough to stop the clouds of cigarette and cigar smoke from choking her to death. The guys stared but didn't touch, just as promised. Now and then, someone got too many drinks in them and tried to get handsy, but the manager dealt with it so quickly Bonnie barely noticed it happening. This was a classy joint. You had to treat the ladies like ladies. Even if they were dressed up like sexy pets, with their breasts hanging out.

Some of the guys developed sweet little crushes. There was one man, Dale Waller, who worked in town planning, who came every Thursday lunch shift, and he was polite as anything, studiously avoiding looking at her rack, while blushing profusely. He hated everything about the club, except for Bonnie. The first time he'd come, he'd been reluctantly dragged there by his boss, and he'd been itching to leave from the moment his butt hit the seat. He'd turned the color of ketchup and stared at his hands and just looked like a kid caught doing something he shouldn't.

Bonnie thought he was cute. For a guy who came to the Playboy Club.

"I'm guessing we won't be seeing you back here," she teased him, as she handed him a souvenir matchbook on his way out, amused by the way he almost fell down the stairs backing away from her.

But she was wrong. He came inching in the following week, blushing that red that made her think of ketchup squirted on a hot dog, and sat down, awkward as hell. He mumbled a drink order and kept his gaze on the tabletop. Except now and then he'd dart glances at her and turn even redder.

"You got an admirer there, Bonnie," Dee laughed, when he came back the following week. And the week after that.

"Trust me to get an admirer who can't even talk to girls in a club like this, where they're paid to listen," Bonnie said ruefully. Besides, she wouldn't date a man who came to a place like this. Not in a million years.

Dale would order one martini and nurse it for exactly one hour, trying to snatch a minute or two with her as she passed his table.

"You know if you ordered more drinks I'd be back here more often," she teased him.

He went redder than normal when she teased, his ears going the color of Twizzlers. He was a big guy, built like a linebacker, stuffed into a white shirt and tie and a checked sports coat. His hair was buzzed like the guys from the naval base, and he wore a gold pinkie ring that caught the light when he played with the knot on his tie. Which he did a lot, like it was choking him.

Bonnie liked Dale. He was nice. And he tipped well. Not as well as some, but better than others. He was reliable. Like a family car: a Buick Estate or a Ford Fairlane or something; no Caddy, but he'd get you from A to B in comfort and never break down. Bonnie got comfortable enough with him that she'd strike up a conversation, ignoring his Twizzler-colored ears, and passing the time with a friendly chat. She didn't even mind his minimal replies. Dale wasn't much of a talker.

"You ever think it's weird how much a guy will pay to look at a girl?" she asked Dale one afternoon, when the club was quiet, and she had time to hang about his table. "Don't you think it's odd? There was a guy yesterday who slipped me twenty dollars and I didn't do anything but smile and ask him how his day was going. So, all he was paying for was the look of me."

"Men always want what they can't have, I guess." Dale stole a glance at her.

Bonnie knew about wanting what you couldn't have. She was always wanting what she couldn't have. New dresses, her hair styled by a fancy hairdresser, a decent trailer in a park as fancy as the other Gardens, a color TV. Jimmy Keays.

She still had dreams that Jimmy came back and told her that it had all been a terrible mistake. He'd roll into town, in those aviator sunglasses, his hair swinging at his neck, and he'd give her that grin that said life had no boundaries, and he'd say, *Hey, Bon. What you been up to?* She woke up from those dreams crying fit to die. Crying like she hadn't cried since he'd left her. Those dreams seemed so *real*, and she was so completely happy in them, a happiness so bright and hot and pure that it made her remember a time when she was loved, and life was looking on the up.

But she couldn't have Jimmy, and that was that. There was no point in wasting her life away wishing for it, was there? And hell, she was only twenty-three years old. Far too young to be on the shelf. So, she let herself enjoy flirting with Dale Waller, who made her feel better than she had in years, less like a tired, directionless single mom and more like a cheeky young thing with prospects.

The biggest problem Bonnie had with her new job was getting someone to sit for Sandra, especially when Jimmy's grandparents went back to Minnesota for long stretches. She wasn't about to leave Sandra home with Pa when he was drinking, and the club wouldn't let her skip out on shifts just because she couldn't get a sitter. Which was why she had to take Sandra to the club a couple of times, squirreling her away in the kitchens and telling her not to make a peep. Sandra was a good kid and would curl up in a chair, drawing on her secondhand (and slightly busted) Etch A Sketch, and then she'd fall asleep. *She's an angel*, the other girls would coo. And mostly she was, although she'd sure be ratty when Bonnie woke her up to take her home.

The problem was Sandra was a talker. She was four, and talked a mile a minute, like some kind of wind-up toy that never wound down. And she went and blabbed everything about the club to Jimmy's parents, the next time they came to town for one of their visits with their unexpected grandchild.

Jimmy's parents, Don and Louise Keays, hadn't come to the wedding, so they'd met Bonnie only after everything had gone to hell. They didn't like Bonnie, and they certainly didn't like Shitsville, but Sandra was their blood, so they towed the line in order to see their grandchild. They thought Bonnie was a big part of the reason that Jimmy had gone off the rails, but as far as Bonnie could see, Jimmy had never fit on any rails in the first place. The straight and narrow wasn't his scene. After the baby was born, his parents were prone to suggesting that Sandra would be better off with them in Minnesota. Which, Bonnie swore, would happen only when hell froze over, but the Keayses sure got frosty enough to freeze hell when they heard about the Playboy Club.

They accused her of gross indecency and threatened to lawyer up. Bonnie couldn't afford a lawyer to fight them off and she was complaining about it to Dale one day at work, standing with her tray on her hip, getting pretty Twizzler-red herself as she worked herself into a state.

"Strikes me," Dale rumbled, "is that what you need is to prove you can provide a stable home, just as good as the one they've got up there in Minneapolis."

"Oh, trust me, Dale, my home is plenty stable." The trailer was rusted to its damn blocks and certainly wasn't going anywhere.

"I mean, you might want to consider a husband."

"I *had* a husband, that's what got me into this fix in the first place."

"But you don't have a husband anymore . . . ," he said, risking another glance. His glance snagged on her pushed-up-to-her-chin boobs and he flinched, like he'd put his hand on the stove. He had very nice pale-blue eyes, she noticed, the same kind of blue as washed-out denim.

"No, I don't. Again, Dale, that's part of what got me into this fix in the first place, the whole having a husband, then *not* having a husband thing."

"I'd do it," he blurted.

Bonnie frowned at him, not following. "Do what?"

"Marry you."

Bonnie was amused. "Have you had more than one of those nasty cocktails today? What's got into you?"

"It's not the cocktail. It's you. I can't stop thinking about you." Oh, he was so earnest it hurt.

"You don't even know me," she scoffed. But she remembered meeting Jimmy, and the feeling of not caring whether she knew him or not. She'd wanted him. Bonnie felt the old thrill as she thought about it, and she examined big-shouldered, barrel-chested Dale Waller, as though for the first time. He sat here every Thursday, come rain or shine. Was he feeling that thrill over her?

"I want to know you," he said determinedly.

Everything about Dale was earnest and determined. Bonnie wondered if he was always like that, or if it was just the over-whelming effect of the Playboy Club. The sight of pushed-up boobs and a bunny tail did strange things to men.

"Well, I'd recommend you get to know someone before you go proposing marriage all over the place," Bonnie suggested, reaching out to give him a soothing pat on the back.

"Can I get to know you, then?" he blurted.

Bonnie gave him an exasperated look. "Honestly, Dale, what's got into you? You know bunnies aren't allowed to date the clients."

"But I mean, would you," he stammered, "if you weren't a bunny and I weren't a client?"

Bonnie considered it. "You know what, Dale, just maybe I would." She was in the stage of life where a Buick might be just what she needed. God knew, she wasn't getting any other kind of ride. "But unfortunately, I *am* a bunny, and you are a client." She scooped up his empty martini glass. "You sure you won't have another?" He didn't. Because he never did.

Bonnie guessed she'd seriously underestimated Dale Waller. It was his mild-manneredness that tricked her. She didn't quite realize the depths it hid. Or the determination. He was like Clark Kent, his cape bundled up out of sight.

The thing was, Dale had taken to driving her home some-times. The first time, he'd been waiting for her in his car as she came out the back door of Mayer Central, in her jeans and jacket, her bunny tail hung up for the day. She'd been shocked to see him there. Partly because he was in a purple Dodge Chal-lenger, which wasn't at all what she expected. The Challenger was surprise enough, but *purple*? He just didn't seem the type. But also, she was shocked because clients weren't supposed to approach bunnies, and Dale had struck her as a man who followed the rules. But, of course, that was before she knew about the purple Challenger.

"Hey ya, Dale," she'd said, keeping it light, as she zipped her jacket up to the chin to keep out the fall chill. She gave him a wave and started walking.

"I can give you a lift home," he called, as his car came cruising along beside her.

"You know I can't say yes." It would have been creepy if another customer followed her like this, but it somehow wasn't with Dale. There was just a trustworthy kind of vibe about him.

"It's a lift, not a date," he said patiently.

And wouldn't you know, it started to rain right then. And Bonnie was tired, and Shitsville was a long walk home, and she didn't see much point in getting wet and cold when there was a purring Dodge Challenger right here next to her, with a nice man offering to be her knight in shining armor.

"Fine," she said, getting in, "but don't tell anyone." She considered asking him to drop her on the corner around the street from the trailer park, but it was pelting down by then . . . Besides, what did she care what Dale Waller thought? He'd seen her dressed up like a pornographic rabbit, how much lower could it get?

"I should warn you," she said, "that I live in Shitsville."

He hadn't heard of it. But then, no one who didn't live there had. To his credit, he didn't flinch when they turned down the drive and all the dilapidated trailers rose into view.

"Thanks, Dale. That was sweet of you," she said, sliding out of his car once he'd stopped in front of her depressing little trailer.

Dale didn't protest. He just gave her a wave good night and waited there in the car until she got in safe. And then he showed up after her next shift, to do it again. And the shift after that. And because it was a cold and wet October, and he was sweet, she kept accepting his lifts. And then, because it seemed rude not to after a while, she started asking him in.

"You're big. Are you a giant?" Sandra asked the first time she met him. She was sitting at the chipped Formica table eating the SpaghettiOs that Cora Buck's oldest kid, Tina, had heated up for her. Tina was picking Sandra up from preschool and getting her fed before Bonnie got home, for ten bucks a week. Ten bucks that Bonnie could afford now she had guys tipping her twenty dollars just for copping a look at her boobs.

"Not a full giant," Dale rumbled in his usual sweet way. "Only part giant."

And then he'd pulled up a chair next to Sandra and hung out. He didn't talk much, but he didn't need to; Sandra talked enough for everyone. Bonnie paid Tina and sent her home, and then whipped up an omelet for her and Dale, and her heart melted a bit when Sandra asked to swap some leftover SpaghettiOs for some of his omelet and he did it.

He was just so *nice*. He never made a move, never so much as tried to kiss her. Just drove her home and sat with Sandra for a bit, listening to her talk about preschool and *Sesame Street* and random obsessions, like the fact snails could live up to twenty years.

"Is that true?" Dale asked Bonnie.

"How the hell would I know?" she asked, exasperated. "You see any garden around here, let alone any snails?"

Sometimes he'd eat the food Bonnie offered, but mostly he shook his head and said he'd eat at home. He didn't want to take food off their table.

"Where's home?" she asked once.

Home, it turned out, was Royal Palms Estates, in a whole three-bedroom house.

"You live there all by yourself?"

He grunted, never much for talking, but certainly not one for talking about himself.

"Wowee, a Dodge *and* a house. You're doing alright for yourself, Mr. Waller."

He turned ketchup red again and she laughed.

"You and Sandra wouldn't want to come to my place for dinner tomorrow, would you?" he asked them nervously one hot Friday afternoon. It seemed to have taken him a lot to build up the courage to ask them. "It's going to be even hotter tomorrow. We could barbecue."

Sandra's eyes lit up. "Barbecue!"

Dale cleared his throat, looking even more sheepish. "We could eat out by the pool . . ."

"You have a pool!" Sandra squealed, just about falling off her chair with excitement.

"You have a *pool?*" Bonnie echoed.

Dale nodded sheepishly, as though a pool was something to be embarrassed about.

Bonnie watched Sandra launch herself at Dale, who caught her, looking awkwardly delighted by her affection.

"I *love* pools," Sandra was telling him, squishing his face between her palms until he looked like a fish. "My grandparents have a pool!" And then she was off and running, telling him all about how she could swim better than any mermaid and maybe even as good as a dolphin, but not as good as a whale.

Dale's faded denim eyes met Bonnie's and as she looked at his face, squished between her daughter's hands, she felt a soft uncoiling. Not a thrill exactly. Not lightning. But something warm, like sliding into a hot bath.

The next evening, Bonnie and Sandra were waiting in their bathing suits, towels and potato salad packed. Impatient, Sandra ran off to stand out front of the trailer, just about hopping on the spot, she was so excited.

"Who is this guy?" Pa asked from his chair in front of the television. He was slurry from a hot afternoon of drinking.

"Just a friend. You've met him, remember? The big guy who drops me home after work?"

Pa grunted. "Men aren't ever just friends."

Bonnie didn't want to hear it. She fetched him another can of beer from the refrigerator and put her sunhat and shades on, heading out to join her daughter. "Try and put yourself to bed before you pass out," she told him, letting the door slam behind her on its hinges.

Bonnie was feeling oddly nervous. She fidgeted with the button on her jean shorts, which she had on over the new blue-and-white-striped one-piece swimsuit she'd bought that morning. She was too proud to wear the slightly threadbare red and white bikini Jimmy had bought her all those years ago. And it didn't seem right—like she was being disloyal to Jimmy. Even though he was nowhere nearby to be disloyal to.

Every time they heard a car, Sandra pogoed up and down, but there was no sign of the purple Challenger. Hot and growing bored with the waiting, Bonnie didn't really register the bronze Buick until it had pulled to a stop right in front of them. But she sure leapt to attention when she saw who was bashfully climbing out from behind the steering wheel.

"I knew it!" she blurted. This big, solid, reliable Buick was exactly what she'd imagined he'd drive.

He was blushing again as he approached them. Bonnie had never seen him out of his work clothes before. He was in a pair of tan shorts and a pale-yellow polo shirt with an orange and brown stripe across his broad chest.

He wasn't cool in the slightest, especially compared to Jimmy. But there was something about him, and Bonnie felt her heart kick up as he approached.

"What happened to the purple car?" Sandra asked, disappointed.

Dale cleared his throat. "Well, uh . . ." He rubbed the back of his neck. "I might have borrowed the Dodge from my buddy Joe." He met Bonnie's gaze, searching to see if she minded. "I thought you'd like it."

"Sure, it was cool," Bonnie said shyly, shrugging. "But I like this just fine."

"You do?" He seemed genuinely worried. "Because, uh, this is my actual car."

"Are you kidding? I've never owned a car in my life. This is luxury."

As he took the shopping bag containing the potato salad and a bottle of soda from her, he gave her the sweetest smile. And then he opened the door for her kid, like Sandra was a princess and this was a golden carriage. Bonnie felt a pang, remembering the days when she'd dreamed of buttercream-yellow Cadillacs. She'd been young and stupid. From where she stood right now, this Buick was just peachy.

"And now for the queen," Dale said, closing the door on Sandra, who was bouncing up and down on the leather back seat. He opened Bonnie's door for her and bowed. He was a doofus, she thought fondly. A really nice one.

"Can we put the radio on?" Sandra asked, leaning over the bench seat as Dale took the wheel.

"Well, sure, Princess. What do you want to listen to?"

"I like David Cassidy and The Partridge Family."

Dale shot Bonnie a lost look. She laughed and took over the radio dial. "We'll put it on the pop station, kiddo, and see what happens."

"Right, everyone buckled up?" Dale asked.

Sandra settled back and sang along to just about every song: The Jackson 5, Sonny and Cher, Elton John. Bonnie didn't know how she did it, but she remembered the lyrics to everything. The kid was only in preschool, for Pete's sake.

"She likes music, huh?" Dale said. He relaxed as he drove, and he was smiling as he listened to Sandra belt out the words to "Crocodile Rock." "Are you going to start her on an instrument?"

Bonnie looked at him like he'd grown a second head. "Sure. She can learn piano on the family baby grand." She gave a tight laugh.

He registered her sarcasm but didn't respond to it. "I learned piano," he told her mildly. "And then guitar. I was in the school band." He grinned. "For about five minutes."

"You were that bad?"

"Nah, it clashed with football practice."

"I knew it." Bonnie laughed. "I picked the Buick *and* the football." She swiveled on the bench seat and sized him up.

"You've been thinking about me, then," he teased nervously.

He was flirting with her. It was a nice surprise that he could flirt. "Yeah, I've been thinking about you. I see you just about every day."

"What else have you been thinking?" He had a pretty great smile, with lots of white even teeth.

Well, right now, she was thinking about his arms, as she watched the muscles flex as he turned the wheel. But she wasn't telling him that, at least not yet. "I've been thinking your house probably has a palm tree or two, given it's in Royal Palms Estates."

"Try a bunch of them," he said, pleased. "Big ones too."

"And I've been thinking it sounds like a big house for a man alone," she prodded. "Seems like the kind of house that would hold a wife and kids."

"No wife," he said firmly. "And no kids."

"I've been thinking it's strange there's no wife. And no kids." Bonnie straightened as she realized they were reaching Royal Palms Estates. There was a sign at the entrance to his suburb, and he sure wasn't lying about the palms. The place bristled with them. Their fronds streamed in the hot summer breeze, pretty as streamers against the steely blue sky. Wowee. If Jimmy's grandparents' place put Shitsville to shame, this place put their Gardens to shame. Look at these houses with their luscious green lawns.

"I guess I never met the right girl," Dale said gruffly, answering Bonnie's question as he pulled into the driveway of a low ranch house. It was custard yellow, with a big pink hibiscus bush by the front door; rising behind it were almost a dozen elegant palms, swaying in the breeze. The car rolled to a stop under an open carport, and the shade was thick and cool.

"You have a puppy!" Sandra tore away from the car and bolted to the sliding doors, through which they could see a big chocolate-colored dog, its tail wagging wildly as it watched them through the glass.

"That's Oh Henry," Dale told her, ambling over to the door. "You know, like the chocolate bar?" He slid open the door and the dog bounded out, firstly jumping up on Dale and then sniffing Sandra and making her giggle.

"Heya, Henry," Sandra said, running a tentative hand over his head. He licked her.

"Not Henry," Dale corrected pleasantly. "*Oh* Henry, like the chocolate bar."

Sandra and Oh Henry the chocolate bar of a dog were clearly taken with one another.

"Is he safe with kids?" Bonnie asked. He was a big dog, part Labrador by the looks of it, but also something else. He had big, floppy ears and a slightly shaggy tail, which was decidedly not like a Labrador's.

"I don't know," Dale admitted, "I don't think he's ever hung out with a kid before. We'd best keep them with us."

Bonnie hovered, keeping a close eye on the dog, but it just followed along, its tongue lolling and its eyes rolling with pleasure whenever Sandra scratched at its ears.

"You want to see the house?" Dale led them inside. He showed them a kitchen that looked like something you'd win on a game show, an open living room with sliding doors onto an actual garden, two empty bedrooms, which had large windows looking out onto the front lawns, and a third bedroom, his, which featured a big bed and inbuilt wardrobes. It looked like he'd just moved in, but he said he'd been there more than a year.

"Mom, he has a bath! Just like in Gran's trailer!" Sandra was taken with Dale's bathroom. She slid open the glass doors to the shower and stood in there, admiring the yellow tiles with their brown and orange floral patterns.

"It's a beautiful house, Dale," Bonnie told him admiringly. "You're lucky."

"But where's the pool?" Sandra left the shower, pushing Oh Henry out of the way, and stared up at Dale. "You said there was a pool."

"So I did." Dale offered her his hand. "Come this way, Princess."

Bonnie followed them slowly, Oh Henry plodding along after her. Gosh, this was a house and a half. One day, Bonnie promised herself, one day she'd have a house like this. Imagine waking up in a room like Dale's bedroom every morning, she thought, with its big picture window to the side of the house, looking out onto a grassy area with a palm tree spurting from the center, sunshine splashing in, turning the whole room golden.

She heard Sandra squeal with delight and sped up, not wanting to miss the pool. She stepped out of the sliding doors, onto a concrete patio, and her heart soared. Oh *my*.

It wasn't a big yard or a big pool, but it was perfect. The pool was a glittering bright aqua oval, lined with palms. The patio was under a striped awning and was just big enough to hold a picnic table and a barbecue. Over the back fence Bonnie could see other houses just like this one, with the mountains a pastel haze beyond.

"Mom! Look!" Sandra grabbed her by the hand and pulled her to the pool. "He doesn't have to share it with anyone! Not like Gran and Pops. He gets it all to himself."

"I can see that," Bonnie laughed. "He's a lucky man, isn't he?"

"Can we swim now?"

Bonnie glanced at Dale. "I don't know when we're eating . . ."

"God forbid I make her wait." Dale grinned. "You get in with her, and I'll get cooking. I'll give a yell when it's ready."

"Are you sure? I should help. . . ."

"Get in, Bonnie honey," he laughed. "You're my guest."

Bonnie honey. She liked the way he said it. And she liked being taken care of. No one had cooked for her like this before. As she and Sandra splashed in the pool with Oh Henry the dog, Dale fired up the barbecue. He brought out a transistor radio and tuned it to the station Sandra had enjoyed in the car, and popped the tabs on a couple of beers, passing one to Bonnie. He mixed up a jug of Kool-Aid for Sandra, smiling as he listened to her sing to the dog. Bonnie watched him surreptitiously as he set the table and brought out her potato salad and a green salad that he must have tossed himself. When the hot dogs were ready, they sat under the awning, watching the evening sky streak hot pink and burnt orange, eating to the sound of the Top Forty countdown on the radio. Sandra managed to correctly guess most of the Top Ten, much to Dale's amusement.

"You should be a disc jockey, kiddo," he said admiringly,

passing her a napkin to mop the ketchup and mustard off her face.

After dinner, they swam as the pink sky darkened, and the moon rose like an orange ball into the starry sky.

"This has been the best night of my whole entire life," Sandra declared with a weighty sigh, when Dale finally bundled them back into the Buick to take them back to Shitsville.

"I'll take that as a challenge," Dale told her lightly. "Let's see if we can top it next Saturday. If that's okay with your mom?"

That was just fine with Sandra's mom. Bonnie hadn't thought she could ever be happy again after Jimmy Keays, but here she was, nothing but smiles. Because of slow and steady old Dale Waller.

Sandra was asleep by the time they got back to Shitsville. Bonnie stayed in the front seat after Dale turned off the engine, wondering if he'd try and kiss her. She was planning to let him if he did. She'd sure liked the look of him in his bathing suit tonight. Lord, when he'd come out in just his shorts after dinner she'd gone hot all over. He'd once reminded her of Clark Kent, but stripped off like that he was nothing but Superman. The muscles on the man . . . Bonnie felt something awaken in her at the sight of him, something she'd thought dead and gone.

So she waited on the bench seat of his Buick, sure that he'd make a move.

"Thanks for coming tonight," he said huskily.

He wanted her. She knew he did. It was in the slow thickening of the atmosphere between them, and the way his gaze clouded as he met her eyes. She could see his breath catch unevenly.

"I had a wonderful time," she murmured, inching ever so slightly closer.

But to her surprise, he inched back. And glanced at Sandra. "Guess we should get her inside, huh?" He cleared his throat.

And that was it. No kiss. After he'd gone, Bonnie lay in her bed, in the room she shared with Sandra, and stared at the ceiling, unable to sleep. She hadn't quite realized how much she'd wanted his kiss until she hadn't got it.

He had a long, thin upper lip and a plump lower lip. She'd studied his mouth as he failed to kiss her goodbye. How had she never noticed how sexy it was before? Or how sexy the shadow of his stubble was, or the square cut of his jaw . . .

If he didn't kiss her next time, she might have to take matters into her own hands.

That was about the time the shit hit the fan. Bonnie's manager at the Playboy Club happened to look out an upstairs back window just in time to see Bonnie climb into Dale's reliable Buick the first evening she worked after their barbecue. How was she to know the men's room had a window to the back of the building? The little girl's room sure didn't.

If she'd had a phone, it would have been ringing by the time she got home. But she didn't, so she didn't know she was fired until she turned up for work the next day.

"He just drove me home," she told her manager, exasperated. "Since when is that a crime?"

But the club rules were firm. No dating. And no one believed her that Dale wasn't a date. He was just a friend. One with beautiful, faded denim eyes and lips she'd started dreaming about.

"Guess I should have hit you up for a date," she told Dale dryly, when he arrived to check on her at the trailer, worried because she hadn't been there when he came to pick her up after work. "Since I got hanged for it anyway."

He took the whole thing harder than she did. "I didn't mean to get you fired."

Bonnie rolled her eyes. "You also didn't *not* mean to get me fired," she said. "I mean, you did turn up and offer me a lift all those times, and you knew the rules too." She was angry-cleaning the piece-of-shit trailer, while he sat at the Formica table with a mug of instant coffee. She wasn't angry-cleaning *at* him exactly. Just *near* him. Because he got to go home to Royal Palms Estates, didn't he? While she was stuck here in Shitsville, without rent money. And he hadn't even *kissed* her. She'd been punished for something she hadn't even got to enjoy.

"I'll fix it," Dale rumbled. "I will."

"Did you go to college, Dale?" Bonnie asked abruptly, dropping into her dad's old brown chair, her arms full of Sandra's thrift shop Barbie dolls. She'd been thinking about the state of her life lately and the dead ends it had thrown up as she tried to navigate it.

He blinked and nodded, unsure about her change of tack. "Arizona State."

"You played football?"

He nodded.

"Go Sun Devils," she said dryly, flopping back in the chair and looking at the ceiling. "I can't even imagine what college must be like. I never knew anyone who went before."

He sat there nervously, uncertain where she was going with this.

It was kind of nice to have someone just sitting there, listening to her.

"What the hell am I going to do now? Work at the diner out on the interstate, or down at the Spotless Sudz?" Just like her mom. And then what? She'd get wrung-out like an old sheet, just like her mom, and skip out on Sandra?

Never, she thought fiercely. She would never leave her kid. She wasn't like her mom, not one bit. And she wasn't staying here in Shitsville, and neither was Sandra. She was getting out of here.

"I can fix this," Dale told her. "This is my fault. Let me fix it."

And the next day he turned up on her doorstep, smiling broadly, holding a bunch of red carnations, and telling her he'd gotten her a job in the clerical pool in the town planning department, where he worked.

"The clerical pool?" Bonnie was astonished.

"You said you worked for a dentist once? So you can type and file? You can do clerical . . ." His blue eyes pleaded with her. "It's my fault you're in this situation. Please let me do this for you."

Bonnie accepted because she was desperate, and because the job paid well. And because Dale said he'd drive her to and from work every day, and her heart turned over at the thought of working in the same building that he did. There was one thing she was certain of, and it was that she wanted to get to know Dale Waller better.

"You can't pick me up every day, I'm not even on your way," she said, but she didn't mean it. She wanted him to pick her up in that bronze Buick every day for the foreseeable future. God help her, she was catching feelings for him, and they hadn't even kissed.

"Bonnie, no matter where you are, you're always on my way," he said, and he was too earnest for it to be a line. He meant it.

"Jesus, Dale." Bonnie put her hands on his chest, grabbed his shirt and yanked him close. "When in hell are you going to do it?"

"Do what?" He seemed genuinely bemused.

Bonnie swore and then she kissed him, hard.

He made the most adorable little moaning sound, like he was melting. And then he kissed her back. And he kissed like he'd been saving it up for a good long time. He all but hauled her off her feet and bent her backward. Bonnie felt like she'd been hit by a Mack Truck, and it was only in that moment she knew why he'd held off kissing her for so long. Because once he started, he wasn't stopping.

Chapter 15
Heather

Cusco, Peru

"You know why it happened, don't you?" Mom said as she opened the package that had arrived from their Machu Picchu tour guides. She and Heather were having breakfast in their room, out on the terrace, quarantined from bumping into Shawn. Bon had taken it on herself to go and break the news to him and his "furry friend," as she kept calling Kyle, that they'd be going on their trek without Heather.

"You know why what happened?" Heather turned her face up to the sun and closed her eyes. It was cold outside, and she was wearing her thermals and her fleece jacket and had pulled the quilt off her bed and wrapped it around her. If it was this cold here, she could only imagine how cold the mountains were going to feel.

"Why Dad cheated," Mom whispered. "I never got it at the time, but I was just a dumb kid. It's so obvious now." She opened the brochure from the tour company and swore. "Oh my God. This is *proper* hiking. Look at this map!" She turned the brochure so Heather could see the map. It was a jagged line, like a heart monitor graph, peaking in three steep jags before sliding down to Machu Picchu.

"I'm not going to read that," Mom decided aloud. She

snapped the brochure closed and tossed it onto the table next to their uneaten toast. "I'll be suffering whether I know about it now or not, so I'd rather just dive in."

Heather squirmed an arm free of her quilt and reached for the brochure. "What do you mean, why he cheated? You mean Grandpa?" She had a sick feeling in her stomach. She couldn't believe he *had* cheated. What hope was there, when even sweet and devoted Grandpa was a cheater?

"It was because of Jimmy, don't you see? Mom never stopped loving Jimmy, and Dad always wondered if Mom had only married him for his house. For security."

"Maybe he was always a cheater," Heather said, feeling depressed as she opened the brochure. "I mean, the guy met her in a Playboy Club."

"You heard her, he got dragged there the first time. And afterward he only went for her." Mom spread a thick layer of jelly on a slice of toast. "I'm telling you that it ate away at him. He loved her more than she loved him—he always did."

"Did you see the height of these climbs?" Heather blurted, distracted and more than a little daunted by the map. "The first one is almost fourteen thousand feet!" What the hell was Bon thinking? She was seventy years old!

"My whole life Jimmy Keays cast a long shadow," Mom said darkly, waving her triangle of toast. "Imagine how Dad must have felt, in his shadow! Did you know that Junior even asked me about him?"

"What did Junior want to know?" Heather turned the page. "This says we need to carb-load today."

"So eat some toast. I guess Junior wanted to know if he should be worried. He wanted to know where Jimmy was now—he said Mom wouldn't tell him."

"Do *you* know?" Heather sat up straighter. "Because I went hunting online for him and I couldn't work out which Jimmy Keays I was looking at."

"Do *I* know?" Mom snorted. "I've never even met the guy! I have one photo of him from the late sixties. I'd be the last person to know. Mom would barely talk about him when I was a kid. She said Dale loved me and was the only father I'd ever need."

"So, you don't know why Jimmy left?"

"No." Mom sounded disgusted. "Dad didn't know either. I asked him once and he was as in the dark as I was. He didn't like it either, that she kept secrets about Jimmy. I mean, who would? All Mom ever said to either of us was that he was gone and that was that."

Heather stared sightlessly at the itinerary in the brochure. "If Junior was asking about Jimmy, then Bon didn't tell him either . . . Does *anyone* know what happened to Jimmy Keays?"

"Junior said Bon talked about Jimmy in her sleep and would wake up crying. I mean, don't you think that's weird? Crying about a guy who left you fifty years ago?" Mom gave Heather a significant look. "Something made her start thinking about him again."

Heather closed the brochure. "You think she knows where he is?"

"Maybe." Mom ate her toast. And then she sighed. "Although I might still be crying about your father fifty years from now, so who am I to judge."

"You'll be one hundred years old and still crying about Dad?" Heather felt a spurt of disgust. "Or you can get a life," she suggested. "Bon's right, Mom. You're still young. Why don't you get a little cougar action? Move on from Dad. He's not worth this." Especially because Dad sure as hell wasn't sitting around pining for her. He was well and truly moving on . . . from all of them.

"Cougar action." Mom laughed. "No one wants a fifty-year-old woman with twenty extra pounds and a truckload of baggage."

"Puh-lease." Heather had no time for her mother's self-pity. "Junior met Bon when she was in her *sixties*, and those two had a lot of fun together. And screw your weight, I think you look great. When you bother to shower and all."

Mom threw a crust of toast at her. But she was thinking about it. "Junior *was* fun for her. Until he upped and died anyway."

"Well, maybe yours would live to ninetysomething like your pa."

"Pa the Pickled Onion," Mom laughed.

"Yeah, you might like pickled onion."

"I'd rather something fresher," Mom giggled. "You know who I wouldn't mind getting to know? That Kyle. Shawn's friend."

Heather was stunned. *"Kyle?"*

"Yeah. He's hot, don't you think?"

"No!" Heather laughed. "But each to their own. He's a nice guy." She paused. "And actually, probably perfect for you, except he's too young."

"Too young!" Mom scoffed. "And how old is your dad's fiancé, huh? Twelve."

"She's forty. Kyle's only thirty."

"That seems perfectly acceptable. What's the calculation? Half your age plus seven?"

"What are you talking about?"

Mom was coming alive in this conversation. Her blue eyes were snapping, and she had a smile that caused dimples to leap in her cheeks. She looked brighter and younger and full of energy. The fact Heather was talking to her again had lifted her mood immeasurably. "There used to be a calculation for it. You can go younger so long as you stay within the bounds of half your age, plus seven."

Heather did the math in her head. "He's too young for you. By three years."

"I could lie about my age?"

Heather laughed. She hadn't seen her mom this relaxed and playful for an exceedingly long time. Usually she was only like this when she and Dad were in the "making-up" phase. It was nice to see that she could get to this place on her own, without Dad. Now she just needed to get here without *Heather.*

"So tell me why you think he's perfect for me?" Mom asked, pulling her knees up toward her. "What does he do, love bomb and fuck around?"

Heather laughed. "No, just that he's a musician. And he has

an unhealthy obsession with nineties grunge, and he's fanboy-ing over you being the Sandy in 'Sandy Swears.'"

"It is pretty cool," Mom said smugly. "It's one of their decent songs too. What does he play? Tell me he's not a lead guitarist."

"He's not a lead guitarist. He's a drummer. Graduated from the music program at Columbia and is good enough to make a living teaching and playing. He does session stuff a lot."

"Musicians seem to be my lot in life," Mom said lightly. "Is he single?"

"As far as I know." Heather tried to picture Mom dating Kyle. She kind of could. "He wants you to autograph his Torn CD," she said with a laugh.

Mom giggled again. "Your dad would love that. *Me* signing his CD."

"About as much as he'd love you hooking up with a guy young enough to be his son." Heather paused. "But go gently, hey? I like Kyle. Don't break his heart or anything just to hurt Dad."

"Heather, you're talking as though a woman my age could actually attract a thirty-year-old man." Mom rolled her eyes. "I was just playing. I'm not actually going to do anything. Can you imagine? I'd look ridiculous."

"You know what, Mom? I don't think you would."

Mom took that in and smiled.

"So, when did the Fleetwood Mac concert happen?" Heather asked Bon, as they ambled through the San Pedro markets. "I thought you said you got it on after the concert, but last night you said you were hooking up in your trailer."

"We didn't hook up in any such place," Bon said, once again appalled at Heather's listening skills. "We kissed in my trailer. That's not hooking up."

"You said once he started, he didn't stop."

"Okay, stop there," Mom ordered. "I don't want to hear about my parents hooking up."

"Why not, it was beautiful." Bon was offended. "He was a gentle lover."

"No!" Mom howled. "No-no-no-no-no-no." She put her hands over her ears.

"What? You'd rather hear he was rough?"

"Talking to your kid like this is child abuse."

"You're middle aged."

"Rude." Mom veered off to look at a stall.

The markets were just a short walk from the Plaza de Armas, through a gated entrance; they were a chaotic blaze of noise and color, with literally hundreds of stalls crammed together. Bon had led them to the gastronomy section first, to start their carb loading for the trek ahead.

"Your mother seems happier," Bon said suspiciously.

"Yeah, she's thinking about becoming a cougar." Heather paused in front of a food stall. Every dish seemed to come with soup.

"Look, they've got baked guinea pigs," Bon said, pointing.

"If Mom wouldn't let you eat alpaca, she's certainly not going to be happy about guinea pigs."

"She needs to be more open to other cultures."

"She's just an animal lover."

"So am I. I'm just a carnivorous one."

"There's a whole juice section!" Mom announced, returning with juice. "This one's the Combinado," she said happily, passing it to Heather.

It was bright reddish orange. Heather took a sip. It was intense. It wasn't watered down; it was a blast of tropical flavors and something earthy. "Are there beets in this?"

"Good guess! Beets, papaya, banana, and orange. What's it like?"

Heather handed it back and accepted the next one.

Bon was holding something green. "What the hell am I drinking?" she asked, nose wrinkling.

"Aloe and alfalfa. It's supposed to be medicinal."

Heather tried the milky pink one. "Oh, I like this one. I'm keeping it."

Mom laughed. "That's just strawberries and milk."

"I thought we were supposed to be carb loading."

"We are." Mom and Bon swapped their juices back and forth as they kept walking. "I saw empanadas over that way?"

"Let's get corn on the cob," Heather suggested, liking the look of the bristling red and yellow cobs, so different from the smooth corn she was used to at the supermarkets back home.

"I like the look of the pastries," Bon disagreed.

In the end they ate all of it. They shared plates of fried potatoes and plantains, hot oily noodles, salty corn, and fresh-baked pastries.

"I'll climb all the hills in the world if I can eat like this every day," Bon said happily, as they wound their way out of the gastronomic section, heading for the textiles to look for souvenirs. "Oh, look, Junior, they have boxes like yours!" Bon held Junior up to look at the carved wooden jewelry boxes, which were stacked up in a pyramid.

"Bon," Heather blurted. "Don't be offended, but how long are you planning to carry Junior around with you?"

"I'm not offended. I'll carry him around until it's time to let him go. I told him I would if he upped and died on me, and I'm a woman of her word."

"And how do you think Junior feels about this?" Mom asked, curious.

"He doesn't feel anything, honey. He's dead."

"You must miss him." Heather couldn't imagine what it must be like to be a widow.

"I miss them all," Bon sighed. "Three times a widow is too much."

Heather startled at her words. "Wait. What? What do you mean *three*?"

"Not now, honey." She patted Heather's arm and wandered off to look at a stall of beaded jewelry, holding Junior close.

"Mom?" Heather hissed, leaning into her mother. "What did she mean widowed *three times*?"

"I don't know . . ." Mom was equally blindsided.

"Is there a husband I don't know about?" Or . . .

242 Amy T. Matthews

"Mom," Mom called sharply, striding over to where Bon was toying with bracelets. "You can't drop something like that and just walk off."

"Sure, I can." Bon held three slender bracelets out to the vendor. "I'll take these." She paid for them, tucked the little paper bag in her pocket and gave Heather and her mom a reproving look. "Not here, and not now," she said firmly. "Today is for fun." And she left them, headed for a stall of traditional Andean bowler hats.

For some reason Heather's stomach was in knots. Three dead husbands could only mean Jimmy was . . .

Mom was deathly pale. "Maybe that's why Junior asked about him," Mom said shakily.

"You think Bon found out that Jimmy had died?"

"Maybe that's why she was dreaming about him. . . ."

"But how did she find out? If he died, how did she find out?" Heather hissed.

"Why didn't she tell Junior?" Mom had gone from pale to slightly gray. "And why didn't she tell *me*?"

"Your mom's moody again," Bon sighed. "I thought she was cheering up." She was bent over her luggage, making sure she had everything she needed in her pack, for their trek the next day. Their suitcases would be shipped on to Aguas Calientes, where they'd be waiting for them when they got down from Machu Picchu in a few days.

"She's not moody," Heather defended her mother. She sat on Bon's bed, knowing she should be sorting her own luggage. The mystery of Jimmy Keays was eating at her. Just as it was eating at Mom. "She's upset. About Jimmy."

Bon startled, looking up from her pack.

"You said you were widowed *three* times . . . ," Heather prodded.

Bon's expression drew in on itself, like a blind closing.

"And Mom said Junior asked her about Jimmy, not long ago. . . ." Heather didn't think it was her imagination that Bon's hands were shaking as she lifted them from her pack.

"Yes, he said he'd asked her about Jimmy." Bon stood. "Junior always told me everything." Her gaze moved to Junior's box.

The air seemed colder and the room a touch darker. Heather felt like she was standing on the edge of the precipice, and abruptly she wasn't sure if she wanted to know what was at the bottom of it.

But she couldn't help herself from asking, "And did you tell *him* everything?"

Bon didn't meet Heather's eye. And when she spoke, she spoke about Junior, not about Jimmy.

Chapter 16
Bonnie

Phoenix, Arizona
A while ago

John Jenkins, Jr. went by the name Junior, and if that didn't tell you everything you needed to know about the guy, nothing did. He was the kind of comfortable rich boy who'd aged into a cheeky and cheerful captain of the universe. Bonnie was fascinated by him and had been since she'd met him at a town planning and real estate development "luncheon." They called it a luncheon, but it was a stand-up networking event, and there wasn't enough food to qualify as lunch. When Bonnie met Junior, she realized she'd never known anyone so at ease in the world. It came from never having to fight for scraps, not money-wise or lovewise.

Junior was on the board of a multinational building company and glided through the room like a swan gliding through water. Bonnie could see that he was a man to know. She was also a man to know, but no one ever knew it, because she was a woman.

"I'm retired," he laughed when Bonnie finally met him and they got to talking, "but it's not sticking. The board's supposed to be a hobby."

Junior was big. Not beefy and linebackery like Dale, just tall and broad shouldered—the kind of guy who took up space. He had a thick head of silver hair and sparkling brown eyes in a deep net of smile lines. She eyed his clothes: expensive. And his watch: *very* expensive. And his ring finger: wedding ring.

He caught her looking. "My wife's been gone for fifteen years, but I still wear it," he said, holding his hand out and looking at it. He had a nice tenor voice, clear and lively.

"Does that line ever work?" she asked lightly, refraining from rolling her eyes.

He smiled, cocking his head and regarding her with open curiosity. That was the thing about Junior: he was wide open, all the time. That's what growing up rich and happy would do to you—Junior had no need for defenses, even though he'd known his share of loss. "It's the truth," he told her gently. "Breast cancer, stage four by the time she was diagnosed."

"I'm sorry." And Bonnie was. She held up her own hand. "My husband: aneurysm. A few years ago. I don't wear the ring anymore."

"I'm sorry."

"Thanks. It was a nice ring, and he was a nice guy." Bonnie could talk about Dale now without any wobbles. It had taken a while, but she was finally there.

"The first few years are the hardest," Junior said kindly.

"I know." She smiled. "But you're not here to talk bereavement, you're here to meet people." She stepped aside, so he could move on and keep networking.

"You're not people?" He refused to move.

"I am, but you might be the first to think so," she said in disgust. She was about done with these events. She was retiring too, and not sad to see the back of a bunch of people who didn't think she was worth talking to.

"You're here because . . . you work in real estate?" His gaze swept her cobalt-blue suit.

"Not quite."

"You're in town planning?"

"No, but I used to work in the clerical department once."
"Development?"
"Kind of."

He was immensely curious now.

"I'm in mobile homes." Bonnie put him out of his misery. "I develop trailer parks." She waited for the usual polite-but-distant expression to form, and for his gaze to drift away to someone else, but Junior's lively brown eyes stayed fixed on her.

"Well, well," he said. "That's very interesting. I was just reading an article in the *New York Times* about mobile homes being the solution to the growing housing crisis. I think it even mentioned Phoenix."

Well, well, Bonnie thought, this *was* very interesting. A man taking her seriously at one of these events. Usually she was the invisible old woman in the room. They tended to think she was someone's PA, or an organizer of the event. If she was lucky, someone might assume she'd inherited some real estate and patronize the hell out of her by giving her development advice. But Bonnie hadn't inherited a thing. Her husband had been a public servant. It was Bonnie who made them wealthy.

"I was quoted in that article," Bonnie said coolly.

And then Junior shocked the hell out of her by quoting her to herself. He really had read the article. And he really was interested in knowing more about trailer parks. And there was nothing Bonnie liked better than to talk business, especially with a good-looking man.

"A mobile home is a good starter for a lot of folks," Bonnie told him. "Particularly for the kinds of people who are usually priced out of the market: single parents, low-income earners, older people. They're not making more real estate, and building is expensive, but a mobile home is a bargain. I've got land for people to put their homes on, and the land rental is reasonable. It's better business to have long-term renters than to price people out, so I think of it as a happily symbiotic relationship."

"Can I see one of your parks?" he asked, and it wasn't a

pickup line. Bonnie knew pickup lines—she'd been dating a lot the last couple of years, including online, and she'd heard more than her share of bad pickup lines.

"Sure," she said, trying not to give away how excited she was that he'd asked. "Just name a day."

"Today?" He leaned in conspiratorially. "I'd be forever grateful if you could rescue me from this event."

Bonnie laughed. "You looked like you were enjoying yourself."

"I am now."

"Well, okay, then. If you want to see a trailer park, you're talking to the right girl."

She took him to Sandy Gardens first. It was the biggest one, modeled on Jimmy's grandparents' place, only fancier. It had an artificial lake smack bang in the center of it (a nod to Jimmy's pool), and paved roads, with streetlights and everything. There were three pools—two for the adults and a kids' paddling pool—and a gym. And the trailers were neat double-wides, on their own patches of lawn, with strips of garden for people to plant as they wanted. Palm trees lined the streets, and everything was kept clean and classy.

"Just because people aren't rich, doesn't mean they don't deserve somewhere nice to live," Bonnie said, as she drove Junior around.

"What was here before you developed it?" Junior asked. He was impressed by the suburban dreaminess of her park, she could tell.

"It was already a trailer park. I just made it nicer." She shot him a sideways glance. "It used to be known as Shitsville."

He laughed. "Well, good thing you changed the name. I can't say I'd want to live somewhere called Shitsville."

"The streets are named after the people who used to live there," Bonnie told him. "Some of them still do live here." She gestured to her left. "Down that way on Chisum Street is a woman by the name of Tina who used to babysit my girl Sandra when she was little. She lived right over the road from us."

She watched as he digested that, waiting for him to get that distant polite look. But he didn't.

"How did you do all this?" he marveled. "This is a big undertaking."

"Well, like I told you, I worked in clerical in town planning and learned a thing or two. And my husband Dale was a city planner, so I learned a thing or two more from him. And, when the kids were in school, I went and got myself an education, including an MBA from the University of Arizona, and this just seemed to me like an idea that had legs." She gave him another sideways glance. "You got no idea how despairing you feel living in a place like Shitsville. But somewhere like this assures you that you're a human like all the others, with all the same potential."

"How many of these places have you developed?" he asked.

"Three so far. Sandy Gardens, Mountain View, and Waller Palms Estates. Waller Palms Estates was the first one."

Bonnie parked her Caddy down Chisum Street, within view of the lake. "No more now, though. My daughter Jacqui is taking over the day-to-day running of things. I'm ready to slow down." She drummed her fingers on the wheel. "I've never had a lazy day in my life, and I wouldn't mind trying it out. It looks like fun, lazing about."

"I'm supposed to be slowing down too," Junior admitted, "but my buddy asked me to be on this board and I couldn't say no. He's my old college roommate, you know how it is."

"Not really. I didn't go to college until I was thirty."

"Hey, you don't play golf by any chance, do you?" he said abruptly.

Bonnie laughed. "God, no. You think they had golf in Shitsville?"

"If you're interested in trying it, I was going to ask you out on a date."

"To play *golf*? How long were you married? I think you've forgotten how dating works. You want the girl to *enjoy* herself."

"Quite the contrary—you don't want to set the bar too high, or you've got nowhere else to go," he joked.

"Honey, your bar is on the *floor.*"

"So, no golf?" He sounded thoughtful. "How about dinner?"

"Let me guess: at a golf club?"

"Potentially."

Bonnie laughed. She'd been feeling glum about handing the parks over to Jacqui. Even though she'd still be the primary shareholder, she'd be stepping back, and she didn't know what she had left in life, now Dale was gone, and the kids and grandkids had their own lives. She certainly didn't want to take up golf, but taking up a *golfer* was something else entirely.

If Jimmy Keays was lightning, and Dale Waller was a slow dawning, Junior was a new day, even though he came in her sunset years. Junior faced everything like it was a fresh morning, full of expectation. Not even grief had dulled that in him; in fact, he claimed it had sharpened it.

"Every day could be your last," he was given to saying, often after a bourbon. "You've got to love it while you've got it."

"Don't you talk about last days," she threatened. "You promised you wouldn't up and die on me."

"I promised I'd stick around as long as I could—that's not the same thing."

"You're just tempting fate now. Stop talking about it." She didn't like death talk. It brought restless dreams.

The thing you didn't know when you were young was that death didn't erase people. When you were green, you thought of death as a finality—but in Bonnie's experience, there was nothing final about it. When people died, it was like they were still around somewhere, but you hadn't seen them in a while. It was like they were just down the street, around the corner, just out of reach. But they weren't *gone.* And they visited in dreams, dreams so vivid that for a moment you were sure they were real.

Sometimes, she woke up from her dreams, sure Dale was in the bed with her. And it was a feeling of sharp and sap-green relief. Like something wrong with the universe had been put right. Junior understood, because he dreamed about his Sarah too. He said he dreamed he could smell her face cream, and the smell was the smell of perfect happiness.

It was okay to talk this way with Junior, because he was an open book. And there was no upset in him, no jealousy. He just opened his arms after she woke up crying and held her close. And she did the same with him.

The only time they ran into trouble was when she dreamed about Jimmy. Because Jimmy she refused to talk about. And Junior, who kept no secrets, couldn't understand.

She hit the roof when he told her he'd asked Sandra about Jimmy.

"You had no right," she raged. She may have thrown a cushion at him. And the cushion may have bounced off his chest and hit a vase, which may have shattered on the floor. It may have been his wife's vase, and Bonnie may have felt so guilty that she got even madder.

"You were talking in your sleep. I didn't know he was her father," Junior said regretfully. He didn't rage back or defend himself. He just knelt down and gathered up the shards of Sarah's porcelain vase. "I didn't mean to upset the apple cart."

"That's why you don't go talking behind my back, because *you don't know*." Bonnie had been flooded with feeling, unable to stop herself from shaking. It wasn't all rage. Some of it was the usual Jimmy feelings that never seemed to go away, not even after all these years.

"Sandra was very kind about it," Junior sighed. "She's a nice girl."

"She never knew Jimmy Keays," Bonnie said tightly. "She sees Dale as her father."

"She said." Junior took the vase shards into his study. Bonnie knew he wasn't going to throw them away. Not yet. He'd have to work up to it. She felt terrible about the vase.

When he came back, Bonnie had gone outside to the pool.

"I'm sorry," he said miserably. "I was wrong."

"Sandra doesn't know anything about Jimmy," Bonnie said, feeling sick about her daughter, and Jimmy, and Junior's dead wife's vase. She was worried she was having a heart attack. Her chest was tight, and her heart was racing.

"Honey." Junior did what came natural to him and hugged her. Hugging was his instinct when people were hurting. He was nothing but a big ball of love. "Honey, I don't understand."

No. No one did. It was a chasm through the middle of her, losing Jimmy. It always had been, and always would be.

Bonnie burrowed into Junior's chest, even though she was still angry with him. She loved the comfort of him. No one had ever comforted her the way Junior did. "I never told Dale about Jimmy either," she reassured him. "Jimmy is just my private thing. Can you understand that?"

"Sandra said you don't know where he is," Junior rumbled. "Is that true?"

Bonnie shook her head. No. It wasn't true.

Junior just stood there hugging her.

Eventually, Bonnie gave a shaky sigh. "I know where he is," she confessed. "But I can't tell you. Because I can't tell Sandra. And if she can't know, you can't know." She pulled away and looked up at him. "I really can't tell you, Junior."

"Just tell me one thing," Junior asked, his brown eyes serious. "Do I need to worry about this guy?"

Bonnie gave a bitter laugh. "No," she said honestly. "Jimmy is gone."

"Gone, but you know where he is?"

"Junior?" Bonnie took his face in her hands and kissed him. "Jimmy is gone."

Junior nodded. He didn't like that part of her was closed off from him, but he accepted that it was her right to open or close herself as she wanted to.

"Don't you ever leave me." Bonnie was fierce as she squeezed his face between her hands. "I swear to God, Junior, I won't stand for another man leaving me."

"I'm not planning on it," he managed to say, even though his face was all squished up.

She kissed his fish lips. "You're my new day, Junior. Don't

dwell on old times. And please don't ever ask me about Jimmy again."

He promised. And he kept that promise.

But he didn't keep the one about not leaving her—he died the following year.

Chapter 17
Heather

Cusco, Peru

There was a message from Owen.

Heather's phone lit up, and she saw its blue glow immediately because she'd been unable to sleep. She'd been awake most of the night, fitfully dreaming that she'd been lost in the markets, chasing someone who was always just out of sight, and out of grasp.

Mom had been tossing and turning too. They were both going to be tired on this trek.

Just before dawn, Owen's message arrived, spilling blue light into the murky early morning. Heather's breath caught when she saw his name pop up. Or rather, the name *Romeo* pop up. She punched it open.

Heading off to Ollantaytambo now on the bus. Not sure when you leave but wanted to wish you luck. Ready to set foot on a road that's more than five hundred years old?

Heather missed him on a cellular level. Every deep inch of her ached for him. She'd never felt anything like it before. She pictured him climbing onto the tour bus, bright with expectation, his mind flickering with all the facts he'd learned about the Inca Trail.

And he was thinking about her too.

Heather felt an urge to throw on her shoes and run to him.

Tell me something about this five-hundred-year-old road, she typed back, willing the conversation to continue. His messages felt like febrile magic.

We'll both be on it at the same time.

Heather felt like she was floating and sinking all at once.

Did you know Ollantaytambo has buildings that have been occupied continuously since the fifteenth century?

Why was he messaging? He'd said his goodbyes until they got back . . . hadn't he?

Heather was going over her memories of their last interaction when she got a shock as another unexpected message appeared on her cell.

Hey darling. It's Dad. Give me a call when you can?

He was the last person she expected to hear from. How had he got her number?

Our bus is heading for your hotel, Owen messaged.

I have news. And I can't reach your mother, Dad wrote.

Hell. She couldn't process both sets of messages at the same time.

Owen: **If you're around, I'll give you a wave.**

What was he asking? Did he want her to come out?

Dad: **I'm worried about your mom. Is she ok?**

And what did *he* want from her?

Heather slid out of bed as quietly as she could. She grabbed her jacket and room card and crept out into the corridor. Shit. She'd forgotten her shoes. But she couldn't go back, or she'd wake Mom up. The tile floor was cold on her bare feet as she scuttled down the corridor and out onto the open balcony, which overlooked the front of the hotel and the quiet early-morning street.

It was icy cold, and she shrugged into her jacket as quick as she could, zipping it up to her chin and pulling the hood over her head. Her breath puffed like a dragon's in the pearly morning.

She messaged her brother. **Did you give Dad my Peruvian**

number? He didn't answer. But of course he had, because Mom sure as hell hadn't.

Why hadn't she grabbed some socks? The cold was killing her toes. Heather dragged a wicker chair up to the wrought iron balcony rail and tucked herself up into a ball, stretching her pajama top down over her frozen toes.

There was a subterranean part of her that was always afraid of rebuffing her father, in case he never returned to her. So, she dialed the number.

"Hello?" The sound of his voice made her heart pinch.

"Hi, Dad, it's me." Heather retreated deeper into her jacket, feeling like a tortoise retreating into its shell. She missed him.

"Chris told me you're in Peru," he said, by way of greeting. He sounded nonplussed.

"I am."

"*Peru?*"

"That's right."

"But . . . why?"

"For a vacation," she sighed, although it was turning out to be a pretty stressful trip. "What else did Chris tell you?" Did he know Mom was along for the ride?

"Not much." Dad cleared his throat. "But he said you found out about the engagement . . ."

"Yeah." Heather closed her eyes, not prepared for this conversation but knowing it had to happen.

"Who told you?" He sounded nervous.

Jesus. She wasn't doing this. She didn't want to get into the whole Mom seeing it on Facebook thing. "Does it matter?" Her first instinct was to do the polite thing and congratulate him on his engagement, but she bit it back, because she didn't want to be polite about it.

Dad made an ambivalent noise. "I suppose your mom knows too?"

Heather saw a bus turn into the street. Owen. Excitement to see him tangled with the unease she felt talking to Dad, making her feel a bit nauseous. It was only as the bus sighed to a stop in front of the casa that Heather remembered Shawn. Oh God, it was at the hotel to pick up Shawn and Kyle.

Her life had become a farce.

"Heaths?" Dad prodded.

"I don't know, Dad. You'll have to talk to Mom." Her head was buzzing. Too much was happening at once.

"She's not answering my calls, that's why I'm calling you. I'm worried about her."

"*That's* why you're calling me?" Heather couldn't keep the edge out of her voice. "You weren't calling to see how *I* was taking the news?"

"Chris said you were a bit upset." Now he sounded guarded.

"Yeah, I guess you could say that." Heather kept her gaze fixed on the bus, drawing comfort from Owen's presence, even if she couldn't see him through the bus's tinted windows. "I don't know why you didn't tell me yourself," she said, terse.

Her father sighed, and it was an exhausted sound. "I guess I thought if I told you, you'd tell your mother."

"You're right, that would have been way worse than her finding out on *Facebook*." So much for not telling him. It popped out of her like a cork from a bottle.

Dad swore. "I guess that explains why she's not taking my calls."

"No, Dad." Heather was proud of how frigid she sounded. "Mom's not taking your calls because she's here with me, in Peru."

"*Peru?*" He said it like they were on Mars. "What the hell is she doing in Peru?"

"At the moment? Sleeping. It's only dawn here."

The door to the bus slid open and Heather heard the muffled sound of voices. She leaned forward to get a better view.

"Can you ask her to call me?" Dad said.

"No," Heather told him, amazed at her firmness. "I don't think so. I don't want to be caught in the middle anymore."

There was a wounded silence. "You're still mad at me, then. About Meg?"

Yes, she was, but that wasn't what was happening here. This was about her and Dad, not about Dad and his marriages. Heather had learned a lot in the last few days, she thought numbly. About how messy life could be, and about how hard relationships were. She thought about Bon and Jimmy Keays, and Grandpa, and Junior, and Mom and Dad. About Shawn. And about Owen. People were complicated, and nothing was ever simple. Happy endings weren't real because endings were never happy. Endings were always about grief and pain.

As though she'd conjured him by wishing, Owen stepped down off the bus, his hands shoved deep in the pockets of his jacket, and a navy-blue beanie pulled down tight over his dark curls. The misty gray of the morning was just light enough to show his face as he took in the hotel, and she saw the moment he spotted her on the balcony. His whole body seemed to exhale, draining of tension, and he smiled.

Heather lifted her hand in a silent wave.

Owen took his own hand out of his pocket and pressed his fingertips to his lips. He blew her a kiss. Then he gave her a salute and mimed shivering.

"Love and sex are two different things, Heaths," Dad was saying defensively in her ear. "Your mother never understood that."

Heather returned to the conversation with a sick thud. "They're two different things to *you*," she told him sharply, "and, trust me, Mom understands. Why else do you think she stayed as long as she did? She was being *understanding*. But the thing is, Dad, love and sex aren't two different things to *her*."

There was silence on the other end of the phone. Heather kept her gaze fixed on Owen, who had cocked his head and was watching her. His expression had turned serious.

"Dad," Heather said abruptly, "have you ever thought about *not* getting married?" She took strength from Owen standing there, looking up at her balcony with nothing but concern.

"Jesus, Heather." Dad sounded wounded.

"Why not try being single? You could fuck who you want, when you want."

"Heather!"

"I'm just saying that you don't have to make Meg the new Mom."

She could feel the tension building on the other end of the line.

"Meg understands me," he told her, striving for patience.

"Mom understood you." Heather felt sadness like a cloud lowering. "It doesn't help anything. They still get hurt."

"You don't know the first thing about my relationship with Meg." He was getting angry now.

"No, I don't. Because you don't talk to me." She felt tears coming on now, as the surge of power at speaking her mind ebbed, revealing the pain underneath. Hell. She was going to cry.

Dad sighed. "I know this is hard for you."

Heather's breath caught as she felt the warmth of him acknowledging her feelings.

"It's just that I'm in Peru," she said, the tears tumbling down now. "And I'm supposed to go trek up Machu Picchu. And . . . there's just a lot, Dad. And I don't know what you want from me right now."

"Want from you . . . ?"

"Well, you didn't call to just say hi, did you?" Oh, it hurt to say. Because it was true. "You never call to just say hi." She scrubbed the tears away. "I wish you would, though. Because I love you." Her voice cracked. Shit, she was going to lose it and she didn't want to ugly cry on the phone. "I love you, Dad. I'll talk to you when I get home."

"Heather—"

"Bye." She hung up, unable to be in the conversation for a minute longer.

Her phone vibrated.

It was Owen. **You ok?** He was busy typing with his thumbs, glancing up at her. **That looked like a hard phone call.** There was a beat. **Not that I was spying on you. I was just worried.** Another beat. **Ok, I was spying a bit.**

Heather took a shuddery breath. **It was my dad.**

Ah.

Yeah.

You want to know something else about Ollantaytambo to take your mind off it?

Heather laughed through her tears. **Yes,** she typed. **Tell me everything.**

There was an eruption of noise in front of the hotel, as Shawn and Kyle and a couple of other people emerged into the bluing morning. Heather pulled back from the edge of the balcony, not wanting to be seen.

Not sure I can fit hundreds of years of history into a text message. Owen backed up until he was standing all the way back by the curb, so he could still catch a glimpse of her.

You underestimate yourself, she texted him.

Shawn and Kyle were loading their packs in the luggage compartment under the bus and chatting to the tour guide. Heather pulled right back, against the wall, out of sight.

Her phone vibrated in her hand, and she looked down to see Owen had sent her a photo of steep terraces cut into a mountain, sunshine cascading over the brilliant green steps.

Where we're running to today, he wrote.

Heather felt her breath loosen in her chest. Yes. That looked like somewhere worth running to.

Juliet?

Yes, Romeo?

I wasn't expecting to miss you as much as I do.

Warmth hit her, right where her heart was. **I miss you too.**

Good.

Good?

I'd rather miss you together than miss you alone.

Heather inched forward as she heard Shawn and Kyle disappear into the bus. Owen was about to get back on too. He gave her a wave.

She touched her lips and blew him a kiss.

He grinned. **Catch you on the flipside, weirdo.**

* * *

"Where have you been?" Bon demanded. She was sitting on Heather's empty bed when she slunk in, trying to be quiet.

There was no point in being quiet, as the overhead lights were on and Mom was sitting up in bed, looking wide awake and annoyed already.

"I couldn't sleep," Heather said defensively. "So I went to get some air." She had no plans to tell either of them about Dad or Owen. "What are you doing here, Bon?"

"Waking us up," Mom said grumpily.

"I wanted to give you something."

Heather noticed Bon had circles under her eyes. She looked drawn. "You couldn't sleep either?" Heather asked.

"I need to talk to you. Come and sit down." Bon pointed to Mom's bed.

Too tired to argue, Heather sat on the edge of Mom's bed. Mom wriggled over and pulled the covers back. "You might as well get in," Mom sighed. "It's cold."

Heather did as she was told.

"I got you a gift at the markets." Bon held out a small paper bag.

"Thanks." Surprised, Heather took the bag.

"Are you okay, Mom? You're being weird." Heather's mother peered around Heather, suspicious of Bon's behavior.

"I'm fine. Just let me do this."

"You bought us bracelets," Heather exclaimed, as she pulled out a pair of black and red beaded bracelets.

"I got one for me too," Bon said, holding her arm up so they could see the slender bracelet knotted at her wrist.

Heather passed one to Mom. "Thanks, Bon." She was puzzled. Couldn't the gifts have waited until breakfast?

Mom was clearly thinking the same thing because she shot Heather a troubled look. "You sure you're okay, Mom? You're not having a blinding headache, or shooting pains down your right arm or something?"

Bon rolled her eyes. "I give you a gift and you think I'm having a heart attack."

"Or possibly a stroke?"

Bon swore at her, but it didn't have any heat to it. "Put the damn thing on, Sandra, and say thank you."

"This is how she gets me talking to her when I'm mad at her," Mom said to Heather. "She acts like she's having a stroke and gives me gifts. Bingo. Argument over." But she held her hand out, so Heather could tie the beads around her wrist. "Happy now?" Mom asked, once they were knotted tight and she was busy tying Heather's on.

"Thanks, Bon," Heather said, wondering if Mom was right, and eyeing Bon for signs of a stroke. But Bon looked fine, just tense.

"It's a huayruro bracelet," Bon told them softly. "They're seeds. It's a protection amulet. I thought it might be a good idea, considering . . ."

"Considering what? That we're about to go hiking up thirteen and a half thousand feet of mountain after some cursory training on a StairMaster?" Mom said dryly.

"The woman at the markets said it will bring you luck."

"You don't believe in luck." Mom was sharp.

"No, but you do."

"It's really thoughtful of you, Bon," Heather said sincerely, elbowing Mom. "We love them, don't we?"

"We do. We also wonder why you felt you had to give them to us *now*."

Bon sighed and rubbed her face. The seeds on her wrist were glossy in the overly bright overhead light. "You both seem pretty set on knowing about Jimmy Keays," she said wanly.

Heather and Mom stiffened and exchanged glances.

"Oh," Mom exhaled. "Well, *yeah*. Given that he's my *father*."

"It's hard to start talking about things you never wanted to talk about." Bon pulled one of Heather's pillows to her chest and wrapped her arms around it. She looked haunted. "But I guess we've been opening a lot of cans of worms on this trip, haven't we?" She met Mom's gaze. "Your dad—I mean, Dale— could never let it go. What happened to Jimmy, where he was, if I saw him. It bugged him. Because I wouldn't talk about it. It didn't matter how many times I told him there was nothing to be jealous about, he stewed on it." Deep lines bracketed Bon's mouth as she spoke. "For the record, I never once cheated on Dale with Jimmy Keays, or with anyone else. But also, for the record, Jimmy *was* the reason Dale cheated on me."

Mom seemed to have stopped breathing. "I *knew* it."

There was a long, charged silence. Then Mom spoke.

"You know where Jimmy is, don't you?" Mom prodded Bon. Her hands were clenched, and she was trembling. Heather thought she looked like all the blood had pooled in two bright spots in her cheeks, leaving the rest of her the thin white of skimmed milk.

Bon nodded, looking defeated. "I couldn't tell Dale, because I couldn't tell you. And I couldn't tell Junior, because I couldn't tell you." Bon met Mom's stare. "It was always for you, honey. I didn't . . ." Bon's eyes were wet, but no tears ran. It was like she was a vessel of tears, with nowhere for them to go.

"You know where Jimmy is," Mom said, sounding like someone had told her she owned the moon, and she had no idea what to do with it. "Where *is* he, Mom?" She stressed the present tense.

"Minnesota," Bon said flatly.

The hair rose on Heather's arms.

"Jimmy's in Minnesota, honey. He's been in Minnesota this whole time." Bon was breathing funny, shallow, like an animal in distress.

"He ran off to Minnesota?" Mom was outraged. "Did he know about me? Did you tell him about me?"

Bon glanced at Heather, spooked, looking like she was on the edge of panic.

"Hey," Heather soothed, leaving Mom's bed and joining Bon. She had some idea of the weight Jimmy Keays carried for her grandmother, after the stories she'd heard this past week. "It's okay. It's in the past. It can't hurt you."

Mom and Bon both gave brittle laughs at that.

"You're young, honey," Bon said sadly. "You don't know how much the past can hurt you."

"Mom," Heather's mother said firmly. "Tell me. I want to know. He knew about me, didn't he? He knew and he still didn't want me." Her blue eyes were stark and clear, with a bleakness Heather had only glimpsed in her before. "I can handle it."

Bon swallowed and gave an odd smile. "You can. But can I?"

Chapter 18
Bonnie

Shitsville, Arizona, 1970

Bonnie didn't know how young and stupid she was until after she got married. It turned out that loving someone and living with them were two very different things. And in 1970, no one knew jackshit about mental illness or how to stop things from going from bad to the very worst.

Jimmy got a job pumping gas, the all-night shift down at the Texaco out on the interstate, and Bonnie had no idea that would be a bad move. She was just glad he got a job. Between his minimum wage and her job at Doc Slaughter's, they had just enough money to move out of Pa's trailer in Shitsville and into another trailer . . . also in Shitsville. But Bonnie didn't mind it so much, since this trailer had Jimmy Keays in it.

The two of them had a ball getting married. They'd bought sparkling wine and pretended it was champagne, and Bonnie had her new ice-blue dress and a bunch of pink roses that she threw in Dee's direction as she and Jimmy were leaving. But Dee, being Dee, had fumbled at the last minute and lost out to eleven-year-old Tina Buck. Bonnie had rolled her eyes and waved goodbye, giggling, and then she and Jimmy had spent the night in an honest-to-goodness motel room, with a radio built into the headboard of the bed and everything.

Jimmy stole the Gideon's Bible for her the next morning and told her to keep it as a souvenir of their wedding night. And Bonnie had thought that was the most romantic thing she'd ever seen.

And they had fun after the wedding too, picking out a trailer and acting the grown-up married couple. Bonnie had scrubbed the shabby old thing and decorated it herself, even sewing curtains for the windows out of fabric she found in a discount bin. They had big purple and white daisies on them, and she'd loved them to bits.

"One day," Bonnie had chirped as she'd walked around twitching the curtains, so they hung *just right*, "we're going to live in a trailer just like your grandparents, with a lounge that looks like something out of *Bewitched*."

"Forget that," Jimmy scoffed dismissively. "We're gonna have a *house*. Out in California where the rock stars live, where it never rains."

"It never rains *here*," Bonnie reminded him with a giggle.

God, she'd loved Jimmy Keays, with his silver eyes and his carefree ways. And she loved the way he loved her. Jimmy would do just about anything to make her happy. Including working at the Texaco.

Bonnie and Jimmy Keays had worked hard. She left in the morning for the dental clinic and got home after he left for his night shifts. And those nights he was gone really started to wear on both of them. But they had Saturday afternoons and Sundays together, and those were the best times of Bonnie's life up to that point, hands down, even though she was living in Shitsville in a trailer that was rusted to its blocks and smelled like chalky dust.

But Bonnie was all of nineteen and being married didn't mean she wasn't still naïve. She'd lived around drinkers and all kinds of messed-up people, but for some reason she never thought of those messes as something that could grow in a person. Only years later would she be watching Oprah when a story came on about a man with a mental illness and she thought, *That's my Jimmy.*

Because Jimmy wasn't well even before the Texaco. It wasn't that he didn't love Bonnie, he did. He loved her more than he'd ever loved anyone, and she knew it in her deepest bones. But love isn't a cure, and Jimmy had a wildness in him, a moodiness that he had no control over, and working nights and not sleeping, and the stress of having to make rent, and keep Bonnie happy, was too much for him.

He got mouthy, with his boss and with the customers. And then with Bonnie too. One minute he'd be his sweet self, and the next he'd be furious about every little thing. He railed at his grandparents when they wouldn't loan him money; he railed at Pa for not letting them borrow the TV; he railed at Bonnie for waking him up by walking too loudly in the kitchen when he was trying to sleep.

"I can't sleep," he'd yell. And he'd punch the wall sometimes, scaring her.

Only years later did she learn about bipolar disorder and the waves that swamped Jimmy Keays, lifting him high, before almost smashing him to pieces. Jimmy's mother told her about the episodes back in Minnesota, the doctors he hated, all the times he'd run away. And Jimmy's mom saw Bonnie as just another symptom of his disease. But Bonnie knew none of that in 1970, when things were tough.

When Jimmy's sleeplessness went on too long, Bonnie got worried. He really wasn't sleeping. He didn't even seem to need it after a while. He talked a mile a minute and was full of plans. They'd get a house, he decided, scouring the listings, even though the two of them could barely afford to live in the worst trailer in Shitsville.

And then one night Jimmy lit out in the middle of a shift, taking fifty dollars from the till of the Texaco and a car from the garage. He drove off in the stolen Ford, leaving the Texaco unattended, and he'd blown the fifty on booze and sat out by the air force base drinking until the sun came up. He'd had an idea about joining the air force and was waiting until the base opened.

Bonnie got the call to come bail him out when she was getting ready for work. She listened, chilled, as the cop told her that her husband had boosted a car and trespassed on air force property. And when she went to pull the bail money from the bundle she kept in the sugar bowl, she found all their cash was gone . . .

Jimmy Keays had spent their monthly rent money, along with all their pathetic savings, on a down payment for a barbecue. To go on the patio of a house they didn't have the money to buy.

"You're mad at me," Jimmy said fretfully when she eventually bailed him out. She'd had to borrow the money from Dee, and Dee hadn't been happy about it.

Jimmy's angry fire had burned itself out and he was limp and tired. His silvery eyes were dull.

"I'm not mad," Bonnie said, and she meant it. They were walking back to Shitsville, and Bonnie had a frightening sense that she was dealing with something far too big for her. Something she didn't understand. "I just don't get it, Jimmy."

Jimmy Keays shuffled along next to her, his hands in the pockets of his Texaco jacket. "I don't get it either, Bon. I don't know what gets into me." He kicked at the dust by the side of the road. "I'm just a fuckup, like my old man says."

"We can't make rent," Bonnie said carefully. "Do you think you can get that down payment back? We don't need a barbecue."

He nodded, looking ashamed. "I'll try."

But he couldn't get the money back. And he'd lost his job at the Texaco. And Bonnie was looking at trying to make rent and also paying Dee back. It was a lot.

Jimmy Keays went into a deep, dark hole over it. All the sleep he'd been denying crashed down on him and he didn't get out of bed for days.

Bonnie had her own hole of a moment too. She felt like Jimmy was on the dark side of the moon, like one of those astronauts, and she couldn't reach him. Sometimes she'd crawl into bed next to him and stroke his face. He'd nuzzle into her like a cat, and she'd hold him tight, feeling like she had to do something, but she didn't know what to do.

And then the storm passed, and Jimmy Keays came back to her. Bonnie felt herself exhale at a cellular level when Jimmy emerged from his black hole, his silver eyes shining, his smile bashful.

"I guess I made a mess," he said, shuffling up behind her as she cooked breakfast. He'd wrapped his arms around her and rested his chin on her shoulder. "I guess you didn't know you married such a loser."

"You're not a loser," Bonnie protested. She leaned back into him, blinking back tears. "Mostly because if you were, then I'd be Mrs. Loser, and I'm no loser."

"I'll fix it, Bon, I promise." He kissed her neck. "Trust me, I'll make it better."

She turned in his arms. "I missed you," she said.

"Hey." He saw she was crying and shifted uncomfortably. "Don't do that. It was only me off on a tear. It's okay." He kissed her. "It's okay, bonny Bonnie. I'm here."

"Don't do that again." She smacked him gently on the chest. "Promise me."

He was rueful. "I can *try* and promise." He kissed her again. "I love you," he said fiercely. "Whatever happens, you've got to know I love you."

Bonnie had never doubted it.

Jimmy hunted for jobs, but it was the era of stagflation, when America's economy was in the toilet. He couldn't find a job to save his life. And he treated it like it was a life-or-death battle. He and Bon couldn't make rent and had to move out of their trailer, and in with Bonnie's pa.

Jimmy grew moody again.

"Don't," Bonnie begged him. "Please, honey. *Try.*"

And he kept himself on a leash, for her, because he'd promised, holding on to her at night like she were a life preserver. It cost him to keep control. It frayed him. Bonnie had no idea at the time that there was no trying your way out of mental illness. She had no way of knowing how to help him, and no money to help him even if she had known how.

"It won't always be like this," she promised him, naïve beyond belief. "This is just a bad patch."

And they made love silently, filling the long, worrisome nights with each other. And as tough as times were, they were also wonderful, because there were never two people more in love than her and Jimmy Keays.

"You deserve more," he whispered to her, as they lay tangled in her old single bed in Pa's trailer.

"I sure do," she laughed. "But so do you." And then she kissed him hard. "But if someone said to me, you have to live in this trailer all your life, but you get to have Jimmy Keays, *or* you can have all the riches in the world, but you can't have him . . . honey, I'd pick this. Every time."

He sighed and held her. "I don't like that choice."

"Luckily I don't have to make it." She patted him. "I'm going to have you *and* all the riches in the world."

"You got me, so at least you're half there."

Yes, she was. And she was happy in those moments. And happiness is a rare jewel, best hoarded when found.

And then early one Sunday morning, Bonnie woke to find Jimmy gone. There wasn't even a note. But there was a knock at the trailer door.

Bonnie opened it.

And standing on the cinderblock step were a pair of cops, their caps in hand.

"Mrs. Keays?" they said. And she knew. It was the somber tones. The inability to look her in the eye. "Mrs. James Keays?"

Bonnie nodded jerkily, her stomach clenching up so small and tight it hurt.

She knew then, before anything was said. Jimmy Keays was gone.

Chapter 19
Heather

Cusco, Peru

"But Jimmy wasn't dead," Bon said, her voice ashy with old pain. "He rammed his grandfather's stolen Caddy into a tree at almost ninety miles an hour, and the damn thing was totaled. But Jimmy didn't die. Not then."

Heather and her mother were spellbound, shocked into utter stillness.

"He'd taken the car and was driving north to Minnesota. He'd left a note for his grandparents, explaining why he'd stolen their Caddy. He was going to his parents, to beg for money. He wanted to get me a place of my own; he wanted to get us out of Pa's trailer, to give us back some dignity. Or so his grandfather told me." Bon cleared her throat. "But who knows. Jimmy wasn't there to tell me if that was true or not. He'd gone and crashed himself into a tree and couldn't tell me anything. He wasn't dead, but he might as well have been."

Heather felt a cold wave. Bon's grief was fresh, as though it had just happened.

"Any trace of the Jimmy Keays I knew," Bon said, clearing her throat painfully, "Jimmy with the silvery quick eyes, the sass, the tenderness . . . any trace of him was gone. In the hospital they kept him stable and waited for his brain swelling to go down, and I prayed like I'd goddamn never prayed before, holding that Gideon's Bible he'd stolen from the motel like it were a life preserver. But God wasn't listening to Bonnie Keays from Shitsville, because when everything settled the doctor told me Jimmy was brain dead. There was nothing to heal, and he was only alive because of the machines.

"His parents came from Minnesota, and they had insurance, while I didn't have jackshit. And his mother was a screaming wreck, refusing any talk about turning off his life support. About three weeks after the accident, Jimmy's parents took him home to Minnesota, and his mother visited every single day and read to him from the Bible—which he would have hated. But Jimmy couldn't hear anything, and Jimmy couldn't hate anything. There was nothing left of Jimmy Keays but his body. No brain activity. Just a machine making him breathe." Bon wasn't crying. She was staring at the ground, seeing things they couldn't. "I was his wife, I could have stopped it. But they had money and lawyers and I . . ."

"Didn't have jackshit," Heather finished softly.

Bon swallowed and looked up at Mom, who seemed frozen.

"He was alive?" Mom managed to say, her voice strangled and strange. "He didn't run off?"

"He wasn't really alive, honey." Bon looked unwell. "It's just that his mother couldn't let go. She believed in miracles."

"How long?" Mom's voice broke. "How long was he like that for?"

"Until 1989," Bon said flatly.

"My senior year . . . when you went back to Minnesota."

Bon nodded.

"But you said it was Granma who died. You said you went back for her funeral."

"It was." The muscles in Bon's throat were clenching. Like she was choking. "Louise died about three years after Jimmy's dad. And left Jimmy to me."

"Oh God," Heather breathed. "That's awful."

Bon nodded. "It was. By then Jimmy was thirty-six or -seven, and he'd been stuck in that bed for almost as long as he'd been alive before the accident. He was doughy and soft, with a baby face. He had all these tubes in him." Her lips shook. "And I sat there for two hours before I could do it."

Heather was breathless with horror.

"But I did it because I loved him. And because he'd been gone all this time, and it wasn't him there in that bed. And he would have *hated it*. According to his death certificate, Jimmy Keays died on the seventh of May 1989, but I knew better. Jimmy Keays died in 1970, on a road somewhere south of Holbrook, Arizona."

Mom was shivering like she was caught in an ice storm. Heather carefully reached out and put a hand on her arm, feeling like her mother might shatter if she pressed too hard.

"Did he know about me?" Mom whispered.

"No, honey," Bon sighed. "Your dad was gone by the time I knew I was pregnant. I mean, I told him—told the person in that bed, with all the tubes—I told *him*. And your Grandma Louise used to tell him all about you. She'd read him your letters and show him pictures of you."

Mom started crying, big, ugly sobs. Heather had seen her mother cry before, but this was different. Heather scrambled closer and wrapped her arms around her, feeling Mom's sorrow in her bones.

"But Jimmy wasn't there to hear her." Bon's eyes were glassy, but she still didn't cry. "I told him I loved him every day that we were together. And I told him I loved him at the end, when they took him off life support. I loved him every second of every day he was on this earth, and I have loved him every second of every day since. And I *know* he knew it. Jimmy died knowing he was loved, and that was what I could do for him," Bon said fiercely. "And *you* were what I could do for him."

"Why didn't you *tell* me?" Mom wailed. She buried her head in Heather's neck and cried like she was quaking off her axis.

"I couldn't," Bon said, and Heather could see the effort it was taking to hold herself together. She looked thin as glass, and just as breakable. "He never would have wanted you to see him like that, to know him like that."

"But to tell me he ran off . . ." Mom made a low, guttural sound.

"It wasn't untrue. He did run off. And maybe he was trying to make things right, by driving to his folks and begging for money, or maybe he fell into a pit of despair and drove himself straight into a tree . . . I won't ever know, because he was gone and couldn't ever tell me." Bon's hands were clenched together, like claws.

"And you never told Grandpa?" Heather asked, as she held tight to her mother. "Dale never knew any of this?"

Bon shook her head. "If Sandra didn't know, no one could know. It wasn't fair."

Heather marveled at how tight Bon had kept the secret.

"Poor Dale," Bon said. "It ate him up. He knew there were secrets, he just didn't know what they were. And he was a straightforward man who went to a straightforward answer."

"That you were having an affair?" Heather stroked her mom's hair.

Bon nodded. "And I was such a mess after Minnesota. It was like something shorted out. I just stopped feeling for a while, because feeling was too much. And Dale took it as rejection . . ."

"And cheated to get back at you." Heather felt a wave of sadness for Grandpa and Bon, so isolated from one another, even in love.

"That's why you forgave him," Mom hiccupped.

"There was nothing to forgive." Bon seemed smaller, deflated. "He was in pain. And I didn't . . . I couldn't . . . I had nothing to give."

"And Junior?" Mom asked, bright jealousy in her voice. "Did *he* know?"

Bon shook her head. "No, honey. If you didn't know, no one could know."

Heather felt like she was looking at a stranger as she stared at her grandmother. Who knew Bon had been hiding so much inside of her? So many stories, so much pain. Perhaps, Heather thought, feeling like a veil was being drawn back, everyone had secret doors they kept closed, no matter how you battered at them. She didn't think she'd ever look at people the same way again, now that she knew the unmapped terrain that lay within her grandmother.

The last thing any of them felt like doing after their emotionally grueling morning was heading off to trek the Andes, but the tour guide turned up to collect them on schedule, nevertheless. Bon and Mom were hidden behind their sunglasses, both drained, their faces swollen from crying.

Their guide, Pidru Humala, was a Quechua man; he wore a red baseball cap low over his eyes and had a gentle smile that never flagged, even in the face of their dull misery; he was accompanied by his niece, Hulya, whom he'd brought along because he was nervous about being on a trek with three women.

"The rest of the team will meet us in Ollantaytambo," Hulya said cheerfully in heavily accented English. She spoke English more fluently than Pidru and chattered away to Heather during the hour and a half drive to Ollantaytambo. Mom and Bon sat silently in the back, pretending to be absorbed by the views flashing by, but actually lost in their own thoughts. Mom had retreated deep into herself, while Bon seemed shattered.

"You will be very spoiled," Hulya told Heather. "Everything will be carried ahead for you on the trail by our porters, you will have a campsite and a dining tent all to yourselves, and we have a very good cook to look after your meals." Hulya was around Heather's age, and she had a ruddy-cheeked oval face and a wide grin. She wore hiking gear with a bright red patterned poncho thrown over one shoulder and a traditional brown bowler hat perched on her head. She told Heather that the porters were mountain farmers who were earning a healthy addition to their yearly income by dragging tourist packs up to Machu Picchu during hiking season; none of them spoke English or Spanish, so Hulya had given Heather a few Quechua phrases she could use, so she could politely say please and thank you, yes and no. Heather was glad of Hulya's distraction because Bon's revelations had thrown her. There had been too much conflict and too many emotional shocks in the past few days. She needed a moment of calm.

When they reached Ollantaytambo, Heather searched for a glimpse of Owen's bus, but she couldn't see it. His tour had a head start and were probably already at the trailhead. She took in the town, remembering Owen's historical facts. She wished he was here to tell her more, because it was like stepping into another world; the steep terraces cut into the mountainside were awe inspiring, and the stone buildings were pitted with the ages of history. Heather would have liked to go for a wander, but they didn't linger long in Ollantaytambo. It was just a pause to get them equipped for the trail. Hulya sprayed them with bug spray and gave them light rucksacks, which held water, super-light rain ponchos, sunscreen, and a candy bar or two in case of low blood sugar. Bon slid Junior into her rucksack with the candy bars.

Pidru also handed out walking poles, giving them quick in-struction for how to use them. "This will take up to a third of your weight. Makes things easier. Especially downhill."

Mom and Bon stood there like zombies throughout his dem-onstration.

"Hey," Heather murmured, turning in her seat to talk to them as Pidru drove them the short distance from Ollantayt-ambo to the trailhead. "Earth to Mom and Bon . . ." She clicked her fingers in front of their faces. "Are you going to be joining me on this trek?"

They both nodded and gave her wan smiles, but neither spoke.

The trailhead where they entered the Inca Trail was at the kilometer 82 checkpoint by the Urubamba River. A line of trek-kers in their bright weatherproof jackets wound through the checkpoint, which was on the other side of the fast-flowing muddy river. Hulya had them pose for a photo under the red sign, which read "Camino Inka-Inka Trail."

"Say cheese," she called.

Mom and Bon barely managed a grimace.

As they stood by the rushing river, waiting to cross, Mom

seemed to finally surface from her state of shock. "How hard is this hike going to be?" she asked nervously, examining the trekkers up ahead.

"Not hard." Pidru sounded sure. "Well, a bit hard today. Tomorrow is easier."

"But what's his definition of hard?" Mom whispered after he'd moved off.

"It's only twenty-four miles," Hulya said, completely undaunted.

"Of *mountain*," Mom whispered to Heather. "Twenty-four miles *up a mountain* isn't the same as twenty-four miles along the street."

"There are old people going through that checkpoint," Heather told her, pointing to the people shuffling through the checkpoint with their passports out. "If they can do it, I'm sure we can do it."

"I really thought we'd be having fun by now," Bon sighed, bringing up the rear. It was disconcerting seeing Bon limp. She was usually a force of nature.

"That's called delusion," Mom said under her breath.

As they hiked, Heather realized how little she knew of the history of this place. The Incan Empire was mind blowing. For some reason, Heather hadn't been expecting an actual road. She'd been imagining hiking tracks, like back in Arizona, but the Incan road was an astonishing feat of engineering; steep cobbled stairs climbed the slopes, each one hundreds of years old. It was like the old Roman roads in Europe, but somehow starker and more impressive, because the Incans had networked the *Andes*. The scale of it all was hard to grasp. Especially when Pidru told them that the Incas had co-opted *existing* roads. Civilization stretched back through the centuries up here.

They trekked along the river, the white-tipped Andes looming over them. The air smelled like sap and flowers and flowing water, and Heather breathed deeply, gradually feeling herself settle into her body, dropping out of her buzzing thoughts about Bon and Jimmy Keays, and landing solidly on the trail. Her boots made a crunching, scraping sound on the cobbled stone path, and the river tumbled and swooshed down the steep bank on her right.

Her quads burned from all the stairs and inclines.

"Llaqtapata," Hulya told them, pausing at the trail side and pointing to a ruin emerging like a dream from the green valley below. "This was an Incan rest stop, or maybe a holy place. Maybe both. Maybe something else as well. It is an important place, so close to Machu Picchu."

At the top of the ruined terraces was a maze of walls, and Heather could clearly see the footprints of the buildings. The thought of people living here, centuries ago, made her feel vertiginous. Like time was sliding away and the past was looming toward her.

"We'll go down and walk around now," Hulya said, inviting them to follow her down to the ancient place in the green valley.

Llaqtapata was huge—not a village so much as a significant outpost. Heather paused at the lip of the top terrace and craned her neck to look up at the steep mountain rising behind the ruins, spiny gray rocks showing through the green. Now that she was standing down in the valley, everything seemed bigger; gargantuan. She felt insignificant as she looked down the steeply raked terraces. From the trail above, the terraces had seemed wide and gracious, but now she was here, she saw they fell away dramatically.

"It makes me feel a bit ill," Mom breathed, joining Heather on the edge of the terrace. She took Heather's arm as her fear of heights kicked in. "But I can't look away."

Along the terrace, Heather saw Bon sit herself down and open her rucksack. She eased Junior's box out. Then she sat the box on her lap so Junior could enjoy the view with her.

"She really misses him," Heather sighed, nudging her mother to get her to look.

"Yeah." Mom's expression clouded. She was still shocked by Bon's confession and not ready to forgive her for the years of secrecy.

"He actually reminded me a bit of Grandpa," Heather confessed, "but cheekier."

They fell into their separate memories.

"Mom?" Heather spoke abruptly, breaking her mother's reverie. "You said you knew Grandpa cheated on Bon? That when you met Dad you weren't talking to Grandpa, I mean Dale, or using his surname?"

That was part of the story that Mom had slid over as she told it, so focused on Dad that she hadn't dwelled on Dale.

Mom blanched.

"How did you find out that he had an affair?"

Mom gave a short bark of a laugh. "He *told* us. Can you believe? It was so Dad. I told you, he was straight down the line. He sat us all down and *confessed*. And I was so *mad* at him." She made a small noise. "Poor Dad. Thinking she was off cheating on him with Jimmy Keays. And I guess," she said in a small voice, "she kind of was."

Heather watched Bon, sitting on the terrace step, with Junior's box in her lap. How lonely she must have felt, all these years, unable to tell the people she loved the truth. Heather could see why Mom was angry, but Heather felt a pang for her grandmother. "I don't think she was cheating, so much as hurting and not able to be comforted."

Heather felt her mom staring at her, not unlike the way she was staring at Bon.

"I mean, can you imagine the grief she must have been feeling all those years? Imagine when you were born . . . doing it all alone, without Jimmy, but with him not *gone*, just . . . gone." Heather felt tears rising for her grandmother, and for her mother. And for Jimmy Keays, who had been hurting in ways even he didn't fully understand. "Imagine how isolated she must have felt from Dale . . . and from you."

Mom made a wordless noise, part rage and part pain, and went back to staring at the crumbled citadel at the foot of the steep terraces. Abruptly, she changed the topic. "I know you don't believe me, but I was trying to help with the whole Shawn thing."

Heather startled. "I know you don't believe me, but I don't need help."

"You'd be the first of us," Mom said ruefully. "The thing is, Heaths, you've got a chance at something there. Something good."

"I know." Heather thought of Owen, who she'd half hoped to see poking around these terraces. But he was already ahead on the trail, adding to his encyclopedia of knowledge as he went.

"Not *him*." Mom gave her the side-eye, following her thoughts without needing to be told. "You've known *him* for all five minutes, and sure, he's good looking and charming and . . ." Mom threw her hands up. "But he's not the kind of man who *stays*. He's the kind who'll leave you, over and over again, off on his adventures, *without you*. Just like your dad."

But Owen wasn't Dad. And Heather wasn't going to spend this precious lifetime atoning for her mother's mistakes.

"You said you didn't regret Dad," she reminded her mother. "That you'd do it all again."

"I feel panic at the thought of doing it again, but *not* doing it over again makes me feel like dying," Mom confessed. "But I *want* to regret it. I just don't. I know how messed up I am, Heather." Mom was flushing pink. "You can stand there, all superior, but you're twenty-hardly-anything years old! It's easy to judge when you haven't made all the mistakes."

"You judged Dale, didn't you? Before you'd made all the mistakes."

"Yeah, I judged Dale. *Dad*. I was a snotty little teen who thought she knew better. And then I acted out all my worst fears, all my life. I know about Freud, and about emotional scripts, and narcissism and abandonment and goddamn sex addiction. I've studied it. I've *lived* it. And now I find out I wasn't even acting out the right scripts . . ." For once Mom wasn't bursting into ugly sobs. She was just staring down at the citadel, her hands shoved deep into the pockets of her down vest. "Because my dad . . . Jimmy . . . never left me."

"Yeah, well," Heather said tightly, "I'm acting out my own stupid scripts, and you don't get to try and rewrite them now.

You wrote them the first time round; this time it's my turn. Shawn is a needy, self-focused, manipulative dude who is using me to fill some hole. And I don't want to be a hole-stopper."

Mom snorted. And then the snort became a giggle. "Hole-stopper would be a good name for a band."

"A Courtney Love/Hole cover act," Heather couldn't resist adding.

Mom laughed.

Heather wasn't quite ready to laugh yet. "I'm sorry Dad was such a dick. *Is* such a dick."

Mom groaned. "Don't be. You're not responsible for him. And I love him. It's insane. But I do. However screwed up it is, it feels real. I love the way he made me feel."

"Not when you were sobbing on the stairs, you didn't."

"No, but when he came back . . ." Mom's voice cracked. "Because he always *came back*. In the end, he always chose *me*."

"Unlike Jimmy Keays," Heather said softly. "Or so you thought."

"I know, I'm such a cliché," Mom sighed.

"I don't think you're a cliché. I just think you're really angry, and you've been really angry for a very long time."

Mom nodded.

"I guess maybe I am too," Heather confessed.

Mom nodded. "You have every right to be," she sighed.

They stared at the ruins of Llaqtapata, where people had once lived and died.

"I just wanted to be important to someone," Mom said. "To be needed, you know? So needed that I wouldn't be forgotten." She pulled a face.

Heather could have pushed her off the mountain. "You *are* needed. By me. And by Chris. *We* need you. You're the only mom we have. You're not just important, you're *essential*."

Mom blinked, shocked. Her eyes grew shiny. She made a small helpless noise.

Heather didn't look away.

Mom roughly rubbed at her tears and nodded, taking the criticism on the chin for once. "Okay," she said softly. "Okay."

"I need you, Mom."

Mom met her gaze, and the naked gratitude in her blue eyes made Heather want to cry.

"I'm sorry," Mom whispered.

"For what?"

"For all of it. For not . . . for always . . ." Mom shrugged. "I love you."

"I know. But you don't know how much it hurts when you *forget* me. It's like Dad is your only source of love. But doesn't the fact I love you matter? Why can't it be enough? Or at least be important enough to . . . I don't know . . ." Heather shrugged, not sure what she was trying to say. "To know how worthy you are. You're not replaceable to me. Even if sometimes I wish you were."

"Funny." Mom gave her a gentle elbow bump, but she was listening.

They stared at each other, and Heather could see her words sinking in.

"I thought we were here to climb a mountain, not to go to psychotherapy," Mom said mildly.

"Yeah, well, that's what comes of traveling with family," Heather sighed, as they turned their backs on the silent ruins and trudged back up the path.

Chapter 20
Heather

The Inca Trail, Peru

"You'd never know you grew up in Shitsville," Heather told Bon, as she took in their camping accommodations for the evening. The porters had erected three yellow and white octagonal tents in a grassy clearing by a cedar grove; the tents were tall enough to stand in, and each had a double bed on a raised platform. "This isn't really camping, is it?"

"It's glamping," Bon amended, heading straight for the middle tent.

Camp chairs had been set out by their tents, with thick blankets neatly folded on their seats. Heather sat herself down and pulled a blanket up over herself.

Mom groaned. "Don't you want to go to bed? Aren't you exhausted?"

"It's only seven thirty!"

"Yeah, but we've got to be up at five thirty." Mom sat in another chair, though, and wrapped herself in a cozy blanket. "And it's been one hell of a day."

"Bon," Heather patted the middle chair. "It's not a party without you." Heather was worried about her grandmother, who had been silent through dinner, and who was holding Junior close, as though for comfort.

"So, we're just going to pretend this morning didn't happen?" Mom said.

"Mom," Heather sighed, "can't we just look at the stars?"

"By all means, let's look at the stars and pretend Mom didn't drop a bombshell on us."

Bon pressed her lips together.

"You are the most infuriating person in the world," Mom said tightly. "Why didn't you *tell* me?"

"I didn't want to hurt you."

"Well, I'm hurt." Mom was clenched. "I've spent my whole life thinking I wasn't good enough, that he didn't want me and I'd been abandoned. And now I find out it's not even true!"

"I did what I thought was best," Bon said stubbornly.

"Why does conversation have to be a contact sport in this family?" Heather sighed. "Why can't you both just admit that you're in pain?"

"Because life is a contact sport," Bon said, her voice sharp.

"As is love," Mom snapped.

And then they both went to bed, leaving Heather sitting alone in the camp chair, staring at stars that she couldn't name.

They'd barely set out after breakfast for the day's hiking, when they ran into a bear on the trail. It was black, with a brown patch across its face, and it was happily sitting in the sun right in the middle of the cobblestones.

"Just stay back," Pidru said calmly. He moved them back and squatted on the ancient road, to wait out the bear. "Glasses bear. It's not a big meat-eater, but you never know."

"Are we far enough back?" Mom asked, fascinated by the bear. She still wasn't talking to Bon, but she was in better spirits.

"The bear is lazy. We'll be fine."

Mom squatted down next to Pidru.

Bon hung back. She was still holding Junior closely, Heather noticed. Yesterday she'd mostly kept him in her backpack, so she could use her poles, but today she kept hold of him in the crook of one arm, holding both poles awkwardly in the other hand.

Eventually the bear made a soft growling noise, like a complaint, and ambled off, disappearing into the forest with a rustling of leaves.

"Well, that was something you don't see every day," Mom said as they set off again. The road unfurled implacably, the cobbles rolling over the mountainsides. Sometimes the ground fell away by their side, suspending them above the river, and sometimes they crossed narrow wooden bridges that were tethered together with agave twine. Heather heard Hulya gently scolding Bon and forcing her to put Junior's box away, so she could use her poles safely. Bon was looking down, her face drawn. She looked her age, Heather thought sadly. Older and sadder.

They walked for an hour or so through the cool forest, pausing to see the tumble of waterfalls and to admire the orchids, but after that first hour, things got hard. The rest of the day was more than four hours of challenging hiking up Warmiwañusca, Dead Woman's Pass.

"I thought you said today would be easier," Mom huffed at Pidru.

"I was being gentle with the facts," he said, easily bringing up the rear. "I didn't want to discourage you."

"Oh my God, kill me now. This is so steep."

"You're doing better than me if you've got breath to complain," Heather managed to gasp out. She had to stop every dozen steps to catch her breath. The altitude was brutal.

Bon was completely silent, head down, slogging up the stairs. Heather kept her gaze fixed on Bon's muscular calves as she climbed. If Bon could do it, she could too. She was a fraction of her age, for heaven's sake.

"Which dead woman is this place named after?" Mom groaned. "And did she die trying to do this hike?"

Hulya laughed—how she had the breath or energy was beyond Heather—and shook her head. "It's called that because the mountain takes the form of a woman."

"A dead one?"

"Lying down."

"Dead." Mom was fixated on that bit. But she sounded in pretty good cheer. She was just enjoying being a pain in the ass.

They'd climbed well beyond the tree line, into the bare cordillera, and the wind was gusting; everything was rocks and dry shale and sheer drops. But the ancient cobblestoned road, worn smooth by centuries of travelers, kept climbing.

"Bon's a mountain goat," Heather groaned, having to take another break.

Hulya kept climbing with Bon, while Pidru stayed back to babysit Heather. He stood politely, looking annoyingly unstressed by the climb.

"If there's one thing your grandmother is good at, it's pain." Mom joined her for an impromptu break.

"You'd never know she was older than us. Look at her go." But while Bon might be ahead of them, she didn't look great.

"She's been in training longer than us, hiking everywhere with your Owen." But Mom's eyes had narrowed. She saw it too. Bon was shaky.

"Ready?" Pidru prodded them, gesturing at the road ahead. "Not much further."

"Are you being gentle with the truth again, Pidru?" Mom asked.

"You don't think she's having a heart attack or something?" Heather felt heavy with dread as she watched her grandmother up ahead. Now and then her pole slipped jerkily against the cobbles.

Mom didn't reply, but she picked up the pace, so she was closer to Bon.

They lapsed into pained silence for the rest of the climb. Heather could hear her breath rasping in her ears. The world narrowed to the uneven cobbles just in front of her feet, and the pain in her legs, and the weight of her body, which seemed to get heavier with every step. As she climbed, her mind grew still. There was nothing to think about, nothing to do, but climb.

Step, breath, step, breath. And nothing but pain.

Then she summited.

Collapsing on the ground, Heather tried to gather her breath, which was labored to the point she started to panic. The wheeze was so loud in her ears, it blocked out all other sound. Mom had rolled onto her back and was doing an impression of a beached fish, while Bon was still standing, but bent double, her hands on her knees and her poles sticking out behind her like the skeletal remains of wings.

"You did it," Pidru said, grinning at them and gesturing at the view. "You climbed nearly fourteen thousand feet!"

"Fourteen thousand!" Mom exhaled like an accordion, squeaking. "That's just sadistic."

"Bon! Mom!" Heather breathed, as she followed Pidru's gaze to the view beyond Dead Woman's Pass. "Look."

Falling away in front of them was a view unlike Heather had ever seen in her life. The summit wasn't a proper summit, as there were still mountainsides rising on either side of the pass, but it made Heather feel like she'd summited Everest. She felt closer to the sky than to the valley below. The centuries-old Incan road rolled through the pass and down, giddily dropping away. Ahead, beyond the dramatic dip of the valley, were ranges like an ocean of waves, their snowy peaks blazing white in the sun.

"Wow." Heather sat on the tussocky grass and stretched her legs out in front of her, feeling them scream in protest, and took in the grandeur. Now that the climb was over, she felt soaring elation, bordering on the transcendental. The meaning of everything was somehow wordlessly tangled up in that view before her.

"Oh." Mom had rolled into a sitting position too and was struck dumb by the view.

Bon straightened, poles still jutting. Her back was to Heather, but something about her rigidity gave Heather a pang.

"Hey, Bon," she called. "Come sit."

But Bon didn't move.

"Bon?" Heather frowned, worried. That was a brutal climb for a twenty-five-year-old. Imagine how it felt when you were seventy. She struggled to her feet to go check on her.

"Bon?" She shuffled over to her grandmother, only to find Bon staring across at the snowy mountains, crying. "Hey," Heather said, worried. Bon's face was like a mask. "Hey, are you okay?" It seemed a woefully insufficient question, because Bon was clearly not alright. "Mom! Come here."

Mom rushed toward them, looking stricken.

Heather put her arm around Bon, and Mom reached for Bon's wrist to take her pulse.

"Is it a heart attack?" Mom had forgotten her anger over Jimmy Keays, totally consumed with fear for Bon.

"Or a stroke?" Heather added.

Bon shook her head, still crying. Her whole face seemed to melt with grief, and she let out a wail that made Heather's blood run cold. She sagged, and Heather and her mom had to hold her up.

"Mom?" Sandy sounded scared.

But Bon wasn't capable of speaking. She closed her eyes and buried her chin in her chest, like an animal in pain. Her whole body shuddered with the force of the tears.

Heather shot Pidru and Hulya an alarmed look.

"We will leave you now," Pidru said tactfully.

"No," Heather protested. Bon was having a heart attack or something, how could they leave!

"It's okay," Hulya said gently, "we'll come back when she's done what she needs to do." She pointed over the crest. "We'll just be sitting over there." Her gaze drifted to Bon. "I'm sorry for your loss, Mrs. Jenkins."

"Mom," Heather's mom said shakily. "Is this about Junior?"

But Bon still wasn't able to speak. They stood there in a huddle while she cried, the sound of her pain small in the vastness of the high cordillera. Heather felt tears welling in sympathy, and she saw Mom had started weeping too. Eventually Bon gave a deep, wracking sigh and looked up. She was shiny and sodden, the whites of her eyes networked with blazing red vessels.

"Mom, are we here to scatter Junior?" Sandy pulled away. "Is that what this whole crazy Peru trip is about? Is that why you're hauling him about with us? To say goodbye?"

Bon nodded jerkily, not quite able to speak yet.

"Honestly, why didn't you *tell* us?"

Bon removed her backpack and fumbled to open it. She was shaking. She pulled out Junior's wooden box and dropped her pack. She made a strangled noise. "I'm not ready yet," she said in a thick, wobbly voice. Then she went and sat down on the poncho Hulya had spread out for them. Pidru had left a thermos of sweet tea and a bag of trail mix for them.

"You told *them*?" Mom complained. "How come you can tell our tour guides, but not us?"

Bon ignored her. She made herself comfortable, with Junior's box cradled in her lap. Heather poured her a tea from the thermos.

"He wanted to be scattered to the winds," Bon said eventually, once she'd had a mugful of tea. Her lips trembled. "But I didn't want to let him go."

Mom sighed and sat down with a thud next to her. "You don't *have* to let go, Mom. You can hold on to him for as long as it takes."

Bon snorted. "I've come all this way, Sandra. I'm not backing out now. Have you got any idea what this trip is costing me?"

Heather felt a wave of relief. There was Bon. Sharp as knives still, despite the pain.

"Well, you could have *told* me. Hell, I might have been nicer to you if I'd known."

Bon snorted again. "You should have been nicer to me anyway. I'm a goddamn widow."

"Yeah, well, I'm a goddamn . . . what's the female version of a cuck?"

"A cuckquean," Heather supplied. She'd looked it up once.

"A cuck *queen*? Seriously?"

"I'm glad you came, Sandra," Bon said thinly. "I've missed you since I moved to Tucson."

Mom blinked, startled.

"Life isn't the same without you in it."

"Um. I missed you too," Mom said. She frowned. "Okay, what's going on? You bringing us all the way to Peru, the spilling of secrets . . . do you have cancer? Are you dying? Is this a situation where you're a widow *and* you're dying?"

Heather felt a stab of fear. "Oh God. *Are* you?"

Bon swore at them good-naturedly. "Is that the only reason you think I'd bring you here?"

"You have to admit, it's a dramatic gesture. Is this some kind of last-wish situation?"

"If I was dying, Sandra, listening to you bitch up and down hills would not be my last wish." Bon gave her a withering look. "If you must know, I didn't know how I was going to let Junior go. Because what's left, then? I'm old and alone and there's nothing to look forward to anymore. I wanted to run to something." She cleared her throat. "And you were part of what I wanted to run to."

Mom looked stunned. "Oh." She took a minute and blinked a lot, her eyes shiny with tears. "Don't tell Jacqui, or she'll pitch a fit. She thinks *she's* your favorite."

"Jacqui knows what I'm doing, I told her when I was in Phoenix."

"Oh. So she *is* your favorite."

"You and I grew up together," Bon said, steadfastly refusing to rise to Mom's bait. "I was just a baby when I had you, and during the worst of times it was the two of us against the world."

They were so similar, Heather thought. Headstrong, feisty, and vulnerable as hell on the inside.

"And you gave me a reason . . ." Bon's voice weakened. "You always gave me a reason. To keep going. To do better. To try harder. To forgive. To say yes, when all I wanted to do was say no. I know I made a mistake not telling you about Jimmy . . . your father . . . but as the years went on, I couldn't see how to un-make the mistake. And you loved Dale so much . . . your father. I didn't want you spending your childhood sitting at Jimmy's bedside, in that living hell of loving someone who was gone but not gone. And then I didn't want to tell you after he was gone, because of the living hell of knowing you never got to meet him and never got to say goodbye. Everything I did made a bad thing worse. I'm sorrier than I can ever tell you. I only ever wanted to keep you safe, and if I had my time over, knowing what I know now, I would tell you. I'm sorry from the bottom of my heart for not telling you. I know we don't do sentiment"— Bon swore softly—"and you better believe I feel like an ass for doing it now . . . but you're the best bit, Sandra. And when I run out of belief, you're the one I need."

Mom was chewing the inside of her cheek and trying not to blubber. Eventually she nodded and swallowed hard. "I don't know how I feel about it all, Mom, but I understand. And thank you, for apologizing." She rubbed at her eyes and tried to make a joke. "If I'm all you need, what's Heather here for, then? Understudy for the role?"

Bon got her sentiment under control. "No. Bait."

"Wait. What?" Heather scowled. "What do you mean, *bait*?"

"I knew you were blanking her, and I knew she would walk over hot coals to get your attention. So, I figured if you came, Sandra would come."

"So, I'm just Mom-bait?" Heather tried to sound disgusted, but she also felt oddly pleased. Because Mom would come all the way to Peru for her. "You disrupted my whole life to use me as bait?"

"It worked." Bon shrugged. "But you've got your charms too. I don't find you a chore."

"A chore!" Heather was insulted.

"I said I *don't* find you a chore. I don't know what you're so offended about. Besides, you bagged Owen, so you did okay out of the deal."

"See what I grew up with?" Mom sighed, but for the first time in a very long time, she sounded happy about it.

"I guess we should do this thing before I lose my nerve," Bon said, after they'd finished crying, and had drunk the tea and eaten the trail mix.

"Why didn't you pack tissues if you knew we were doing this," Mom complained, fishing through her backpack for something to wipe her nose on.

Heather got to her feet and helped Bon up. Her legs were still like jelly after the climb up Dead Woman's Pass. "Where shall we do it?" she asked, glancing around. "Where do you think Junior would like to be scattered?"

Heather didn't think she'd like to be left at the top of a mountain in a foreign country, herself.

"Oh, I'm not scattering *him*," Bon protested. "That wouldn't be fair to his daughter Holly, would it? First, I wouldn't do it without her, and second, I wouldn't leave him somewhere she couldn't visit. Besides, Junior wanted to be scattered with his wife, Sarah." Bon stretched and yawned.

"Are you telling me you've been hauling an empty box around this whole time?" Mom said, exasperated. "I thought we were here to let him go?"

"It's not empty. And we are here to let him go."

"Why do you always talk in riddles?" Mom grunted as she got to her feet. "Are we here to scatter him or not?"

"Not." Bon walked to the edge of the clearing, where the ground fell away into a ravine. "He's already been scattered. Holly and I did it before I left. He and Sarah are at his beloved golf course—we donated a bench, with a plaque to him and Sarah, so Holly and her children can sit and visit with them. They're not far from my back fence."

Mom swore. "So why did we climb almost fourteen thousand feet, then?"

"To say goodbye." Bon opened the box.

Heather inched closer, burning with curiosity to see what was inside.

Bon removed two gold bands.

"You've been carrying your wedding rings around?" Heather said softly.

Bon nodded. She took a breath and stared out at the expanse of the cordillera. "Junior loved traveling. Did you know he'd visited every continent, even Antarctica?" She sighed. "But we never got around to traveling together." She looked down at the rings. "Until now. What did you think of Peru, Junior?" She muttered under her breath. "He never answers anymore."

"I think you'll find that's because he's dead," Mom said dryly.

"No, it's because of the damn golf course. Can you think of anything worse than spending eternity by the seventh hole?"

"Spending eternity alone," Mom said honestly.

Bon nodded. "Yeah."

"You're not alone. I'm here," Heather consoled them.

They both snorted, sounding eerily alike.

"Until Owen turns up." Mom gently elbowed her. "And then you'll be off living your best life. As you should."

"So, find yourself an Owen," Heather suggested. She had a warm, melting feeling as she said his name.

"Sure, so one day I can scatter his ashes on a golf course."

"Mom!"

"What!"

Heather couldn't believe she could be so insensitive to Bon.

"It's true," Bon said philosophically. "They up and die on you."

"Or cheat on you," Mom sighed.

Heather felt a wave of bleakness. What was the point of it all, then?

"But God, it feels good until they do," Bon told Heather wistfully, reading her mind.

"Doesn't it," Mom sighed. "I hope I feel it again before I die."

"Me too." Bon looked down at the rings in her palm. "Don't be jealous, Junior. You're off with Sarah now, so I think you can suck it up if I find a fourth husband."

"And who knows, maybe next time you'll die before he does," Mom said blithely, putting her arm around Bon. "And you'll never be a widow again."

"You two are sick," Heather complained. "It's no wonder I'm in therapy."

"You're ruining my moment," Bon warned. She shook Mom's arm off. "Come on, now, pull yourselves together. This is serious."

"Right."

Mom and Heather stood respectfully by Bon's side. Heather removed her hat and sunglasses and Mom followed suit, wincing at the glare of the sun at altitude.

"Junior," Bon said, holding up the rings, and addressing them as if they were a person. "You were nothing but good to me. No man ever treated me like an equal before I met you."

"What about Dad?" Mom interrupted, offended.

"Which one?"

Mom frowned. "Well, both of them, I guess."

"Jimmy treated me like a goddess to be worshipped, and Dale treated me like a treasure to be hoarded. It was Junior who showed me I could be an equal."

That mollified Mom, although Heather didn't think either goddess or treasure sounded great.

"They were immature loves. Junior was my first mature love."

First, Heather noted. But maybe not the last.

"I miss you, Junior, every single day," Bon said fervently. "And I love you, enough to know that Sarah was the great love of your life. And because I love you, I wish you happiness together in eternity." She turned and whispered an aside to Heather, "And better her than me, spending her afterlife on a golf course."

Bon lifted the rings to her lips and kissed them. "These are the rings we exchanged, and it doesn't seem right to separate them. I don't need to keep part of our marriage, when I carry the whole thing with me, always."

"That's nice, Bon," Heather said, her throat tight with sadness.

"You gave me a new love, Junior, now I'm giving you what we never had: travel. Together." Gently, Bon placed the rings on a rocky outcrop, where they glinted in the sun.

Chapter 21
Heather

The Inca Trail, Peru

"That was some bitch of a climb," Bon told Pidru. "It didn't say anything about that in the brochure."

"The brochure shows the mountains," Pidru disagreed mildly.

They set off down from Dead Woman's pass. The road fell vertiginously in curling loops. Bon gave one last look back at Junior, who wasn't there, and who had never been there. But Heather felt him falling behind, even so. Left in the past, where he belonged now.

"Pidru says that the worst of it is over," Mom said cheekily over her shoulder. "Today was our hardest day."

"And you believe him?" Heather was incredulous.

"I can read between the lines of his gentleness, and I think he's telling the truth."

"Good," Bon said firmly. "Because I can't take many more days like today." She didn't just mean the climb.

The three of them lapsed into a warmer dynamic as they descended from Dead Woman's Pass. They looked around the ruined cities of Intipata, the Sun Place, and Wiñaywayna, Forever Young. And then it was their final night on the trail together. Heather felt a pang as she realized their time together was almost over. Who would have thought she'd miss them? But she was going to. A lot.

"We should do this again," Heather said as they prepared for bed. She didn't remember the last time she'd felt this calm and happy, especially while with her family.

"But next time, no mountains," Bon insisted. "I've done enough climbing."

"And next time no ex-boyfriends," Heather said dryly.

"Or Facebook," Mom added, "I don't want to see Nick getting engaged again."

"Again? How many times do you think he'll be getting engaged?" Bon asked.

"I don't know. How many adult women are there in the world?"

Heather giggled. And then Mom started laughing too.

"You have to rule out the ones he's already been through," Bon said.

And their giggles became guffaws.

"Hot chocolate for bedtime," Wilipi announced, handing out tin mugs of steaming hot chocolate.

"Drink in your tents," Pidru said firmly, "start time is four a.m. tomorrow."

"Four a.m.!" Mom groaned. "What happened to gentling things, Pidru?"

"There's no gentling four a.m."

"You can say that again."

"There's no gentling four a.m."

"Everyone's a comedian." Mom winced in pain as she stood. Taking her hot chocolate, she saluted Pidru. "See you in . . . I mean, *before* . . . the morning."

Heather paused in the rain, listening to them rustle around, readying themselves for bed. The sound of them filled her with love. Tonight, she was grateful for them, in all their messy glory.

Four a.m. was insanely early. The forest was buzzing with night sounds still, and it was misty and cold. Heather trod carefully through the mud, not wanting to step in a puddle on her way to the toilet tent. Her fingertips were frozen; she blew on them, but it didn't really help. Her breath was a white plume in the streak of light from her head torch.

Heather heard muffled voices coming from the staff tents and turned, her head lamp illuminating the row of tents, and she almost lost her footing in the slippery mud in shock.

It was Mom. And *Pidru*.

Mom was emerging from his orange cocoon of a tent, and he was following. They froze in Heather's torchlight.

"Mom?"

Mom swore. She pushed Pidru back in his tent. "Talk later," she apologized, and then jogged over to Heather, mud splattering with every footstep. "Now, Heather . . ."

"Mom!"

"It's not what it looks like . . . well, it is what it looks like . . . but there's no need to be upset about it."

Heather didn't know if she *was* upset. She was shocked beyond speech, but not upset exactly.

Mom grabbed her by the arm and frog-marched her in the direction of the dining tent. "Now, there's no need to tell your grandmother about this," she warned. "Or I'll never hear the end of it . . ."

Mom had slept with someone other than Dad!

It was like the Earth had ceased to orbit the Sun.

But not necessarily in a bad way . . .

"Good for you, Mom," Heather said mildly, and she saw Mom smile.

Heather felt lighter as they prepared for the final day. Maybe Mom would be okay . . .

They reached Intipunku, the sun gate, just as dawn was breaking.

"Be glad you're not here in busy season," Pidru told them as they exclaimed at the crowds. "This is a lighter month." He was in a great mood, Heather noted.

"Thanks for making sure we didn't oversleep," Heather said,

elbowing Mom and trying not to smirk. "Aren't you glad Pidru got you up, Mom?"

Mom scowled at her.

Behind them, Bon was quiet, lost in her own thoughts; she completely missed Heather's insinuation.

Clouds rolled around the sun gate above Machu Picchu, hiding the view of the city beyond. Dawn was sleepy and slow. The first filigree of gold was only just lighting the cloud edges, and it was surreal, standing on this shelf above a sheer drop, looking down on nothing but cloud, surrounded by a flock of strangers in hiking gear and head torches.

"The city was hidden for more than three hundred years."

Heather startled. She knew that voice, even though it was muffled by the cloud.

"It was abandoned around the time the Spanish came."

Owen. She felt a fizz of joy. *Owen.*

"Why did they leave? I doubt the Spanish would have found it, even with the road. I mean, they *didn't* find it, did they?"

Oh God, she knew that voice too. *Shawn.*

Heather craned her neck to see them, but the cottony thickness of the cloud was blurring the world. She thought maybe they were to her left, but they also sounded like they might be behind her.

"No one is sure," Owen's muffled voice said.

"It seems like an odd place to build a city. Like, a total nightmare for the builders."

Were they *getting along*? Heather was shocked as she listened to them converse. It was definitely Owen.

"Is that . . . ?" Bon craned her neck too.

"Owen," Heather supplied. "Yes, I think so." Heather couldn't keep the excitement out of her voice.

Now it was Mom's turn to elbow and smirk.

The darkness was easing, and all around became a lilac-gray shadow world. The clouds were moving swiftly, rolling in fat churns. Long streamers drifted through the maze of hikers. Heather looked down to see the cloud sliding around her feet, so thick that she couldn't see her own boots.

"Sounds like S-H-A-W-N is there too," Bon said.

"Oh, don't mention Shawn," Mom groaned. "I want Heather to keep talking to me."

"I don't mind anymore," Heather said, her desire to see Owen stronger than her need to avoid Shawn.

"You don't?" Bon asked suspiciously. "You're sure?"

"*Now* you don't mind," Mom complained, but she sounded happy enough.

"Well, if you don't mind . . . Owen!" Bon abruptly screeched. "Yoo-hoo! Owen!"

There was a discontented muttering from the crowd around them.

"This is a mystical moment, missus," a young English guy behind them complained.

"Sorry," Heather apologized.

But Bon wasn't sorry. "Not yet, it's not. Right now it's just a bunch of clouds. You would have seen better views from a plane window." She set to screeching again. "Owen!"

"Bonnie?"

Now Owen was at it.

"Where are you?" he called.

"Where do you think she is?" the young guy behind them complained. "Machu bloody Picchu is where she is."

A head torch faintly bobbed in the cloud. And then Owen emerged from the swirls, like an action hero looming into shot.

God, he looked good. The pearly sheen of early dawn made him glow. His head torch had pushed his dark curls back, so they formed a mane, like a moody lion, and his square jaw was stubbled with three days of growth, giving him an added edge.

His gaze went straight to Heather, and she was suddenly aware that she hadn't showered since they left Cusco. He reached up and turned off his head torch so it wouldn't blind them. "Fancy meeting you here," he said, his pointy lips twitching.

He was glad to see her.

"You never told me about Dead Woman's Pass when you

talked me into this," Bon scolded him as she gave him a hello hug. "I could have died on that hill. I'm seventy, you thoughtless oaf."

"I never talked you into anything. You were impossible to shake. Like a tick."

"A tick," Bon scoffed. "What kind of way is that to talk to a lady."

"Hi, Heather." Shawn was directly behind Owen, standing awkwardly in a puddle of cloud, holding the straps of his backpack and staring at her in his usual longing way. She gave him a curt nod but didn't speak.

"Owen said he knew you guys." He shifted on the spot.

Heather wondered how much Owen had told him. She tried to catch Owen's eye, but he was busy with Bon. She felt her mother draw close, for support. Mom stood shoulder to shoulder with Heather and smiled politely at Shawn.

"Have you had a good hike?" she asked him. Like she was asking him how his day at work had been. Heather felt the old irritation with her rise.

"Shawn! Shawney!"

Shawn winced as a high-pitched voice floated through the early morning.

"Oh, Shawwwwwwneeeeeeeey."

Shawney?

Heather watched as Shawn curdled with embarrassment.

"Shawn!" Kyle's voice boomed. "I can't handle all these girls on my own!"

"Ah, excuse me," Shawn stuttered, backing away. "Let me just tell Kyle where I am—I'll come back. . . ."

"Please don't," Heather said firmly. "Stay with Kyle."

Looking wounded, he backed away.

"Who's hollering for him like that?" Bon asked Owen as Shawn slogged off.

"Ah, there's a bunch of University of Texas girls on our tour," he said. "They've been partying together."

"Go Longhorns," Mom drawled.

Heather felt a stab of jealousy. Owen had been on a tour with college girls? "You've had energy to party?" she asked in disbelief, not able to keep the sharpness out of her voice.

"Not me," he said calmly. "I get headaches if I drink at high altitude."

Heather didn't find that reassuring. He could still hang out with girls sober . . .

"Besides, who has the energy after hiking all day." He grinned at her, and she could tell he knew exactly what she was thinking.

"This isn't a bloody disco!" The English guy was now bellowing at Shawney and Kyle and the coeds. "Keep it down."

"Dawn," Pidru told them urgently, pointing to the clouds below.

Mom and Bon took their phones out to take photos, both of them on the lip of the terraced shelf.

"Oh." Heather couldn't help but exclaim as the sun broke the boundary of the horizon and the clouds burst into golden life.

Heather held her breath as the green spears of the mountain eyrie around Machu Picchu became visible. Those spears held a bowl of sliding, tumbling cloud formations, all blazing gold as the day was birthed.

Heather was aware of Owen beside her. She looked up to find him staring at her, not at the view.

"Hi," she said softly.

"Hi." His twitchy mouth was just on the verge of smiling. "Your head torch is right in my eyes."

"Oh!" She reached up to turn it off.

He caught her hand as she lowered it from the head torch and held it, turning back to admire the view, as the clouds swirled into vapor and lifted, revealing the full footprint of the Incan citadel of Machu Picchu below.

"You don't have an encyclopedia entry for me?" Heather whispered.

"Sometimes even I'm speechless." He squeezed her hand. "How's your trek been?"

Heather leaned into him. "Life changing," she admitted.

* * *

It took an hour to descend from the sun gate into the citadel below. Owen regretfully fell back to his own tour group, after Pidru told him he hadn't paid for the private experience.

Heather watched him go.

"You've got it bad," Mom sighed. And she grew serious. "I really am sorry I pulled the Shawn stunt. But how was I to know you'd meet Mr. Perfect in Lima?"

"If you'd talked to me, you might have known," Bon said tartly.

"Or to me," Heather added.

"Point taken." Mom rolled her eyes. "I promise I'll talk to you both next time I ask your exes along for a vacation."

Heather groaned.

"Joking," Mom said defensively. Then she headed into the citadel. "Just think," she told Heather and Bon, "this place was built more than five hundred years before I met Nick Russo and will be here five hundred years after I divorce Nick Russo. It puts things in perspective, don't you think?"

The forest flowed thickly right to the cleared greensward of the citadel, which ran along the spine of the mountains, draped like a saddle across a steep ridge. Heather, Mom and Bon fell silent as they reached it. Machu Picchu was bigger than Heather had expected. The remains of the stone city were substantial enough to hold their own against the mountains. In fact, they dominated the eye.

"The city was only occupied for just over one hundred years," Hulya told them softly, careful not to break their awe. "Archeologists think it was a royal estate, which was abandoned and hidden from the Spanish invaders."

Heather tried to imagine it as it must have been five hundred years ago, but it was a hard task. She felt humbled as she took in the sophistication of the hundreds of reinforced terraces and the clumps of stone buildings.

"What do you think it would be like to be buried up here?" Bon asked, growing quiet when they reached Funerary Rock. "Do you think they get lonely?"

"With all these tourists?" Mom's attempt at a joke was half-hearted.

"The *apus* are with them," Pidru told them. "The *apus* are the mountain spirits. No one is alone in the mountains. The mountains reach from the kingdom of humans to the kingdom of the gods; here, we are close to *Hanan Pacha*, the superior kingdom."

"This would definitely be better than a golf course," Mom whispered to Bon.

They left the hut and wandered the wide terraces, which had once been used for farming. Heather could see Owen standing off by himself on one of the terraces, gazing into the cloudy jungle down the steep drop below. Shreds of cloud were caught in the treetops. She wondered what he was thinking about.

"Ahead, we will see the urban area, where the common people lived."

Bon perked up at that and walked ahead with Pidru and Hulya.

Heather watched her, noting the slight stiffness with which Bon took the stairs down the hill. Bon was the one who might need a massage when they got back to Cusco. She felt sad for her grandmother, going home to her empty house. But then she realized she was going home to an empty house too, and so was Mom.

"Mom?"

"Yeah, honey?" Mom was distracted. She kept trying to spot chinchillas, ever since Hulya said they were living wild in the ruins.

"How are you holding up, living alone?"

Mom seemed pleased to be asked. "I have to say I don't mind it. When I'm not bedridden with depression, that is."

"You don't mind it?" Heather was surprised.

Mom shrugged. "I haven't done it much in my life. It's surprisingly okay. The house stays clean; I don't have to do anyone else's dishes; it's quiet." She glanced at Heather. "What about you?"

"I like it," Heather admitted. "But I think I'm a little house-bound at the moment. I need to get out more."

"This isn't out enough for you?" Mom gestured at the rain-forest.

Heather laughed. "Yeah, well, this is Bon's doing."

Mom smiled. "She was always one for making things happen. She doesn't sit still, my mom." Mom pulled a face. "Not like me. I think I've got a lot to work through. For instance, I might need to do some running away when your dad actually gets married . . . Somewhere even farther away than this . . ."

"You could try running *to* instead of running away," Heather suggested.

"Yeah, I like the sound of that. Come with me?"

"Sure."

Mom blanched and swore. "Oh shit, sorry, honey. I forgot you'll want to go to the wedding."

Heather's stomach curdled, but not as much as it used to at the thought. "If I'm invited . . ."

Mom gave her a one-armed hug. "Well, you can always crash it?"

"Hey," Heather called to Mom and Bon as they reached the end of the tour. "Don't rush. We don't have to go until noon." She stood forlornly on a terrace by the fountains, down near the main gate.

"Yes, sit," Hulya said graciously. "There are snacks left, and tea. Have a picnic for your last hour."

"Well, I can't deny it would be good to sit down," Mom sighed, and they picked their way across to one of the wide agricultural terraces, where it was quieter. In the distance they could see llamas tearing at the grass and chewing ruminatively, looking into the jungle through their curly fringes. Mom was thrilled. "Now, if only we could spot a chinchilla, I'd be perfectly happy," she said as she poured out the tea.

"How are you doing, Bon?" Heather asked.

"I've got sore knees and I smell worse than my pa used to

after a bender." She pulled off her hat and her silver hair stood up in clumps. "Our hotel room better have a bath tonight or there'll be hell to pay."

"Thanks for bringing me here, Bon," Heather said quietly. "And thank you for telling me about Jimmy and Dale and Junior."

"You're welcome, chicken." Bon rubbed her face. "Although it was some hell of a telling, wasn't it? I may need a vacation to recover from this vacation."

"Me too," Mom said dryly.

Bon gave her a thoughtful look. "Huh. You're not even done yet."

"What does that mean?"

"It means we haven't done everything we came here to do."

Mom groaned. "Let me guess, you have another husband to tell us about," she joked.

"Ha. No." Bon brushed the cracker crumbs off herself. "Come on, up you get." She stood and clicked her fingers at them. "I'm not done yet either."

Bon reached down and dug Junior's old box out of the backpack. Then she led them down the terrace to the very precipice.

"You're not throwing that box, I hope?" Mom said dryly. "You'll squash some poor chinchilla flat."

"No." Bon opened the box.

"More rings! How many do you have in there?"

"Just these." Bon held up two more gold rings. "I think it's time to set them free too, don't you?" Bon gave a bittersweet smile. "These ones are mine. Jimmy and Dale were buried wearing theirs."

"Oh, Mom." Mom was clearly hurting at the thought too. Tears had sprung to her eyes.

"You first, Dale." Bon closed her eyes and took a moment of silence. "Dale, you were solid ground when I needed it, and you gave me a kind of certain, regular love that I'd never had before. You treasured me, like no one had treasured me before. You wanted to care for me and give me everything I'd never had. And I loved you for it. But I also loved you for *you*. I didn't convince you of that enough. I should have tried harder. Because you were never second best." Her voice broke.

Heather's heart ached for Grandpa, and for the thought he felt second best to Jimmy Keays. Well, love didn't work like that. That's one thing Heather had learned from Bon's stories. Loving one person didn't mean you loved another person less.

You want to add anything, honey?" Bon asked Mom, turning to her, holding the ring out.

"Yeah." Mom was weeping, her lower lip trembling like a child's. "You were a good dad, Dale. *Dad*. And I loved you. And I'm sorry if I didn't tell you enough too."

"He knew," Bon said, sure.

Mom nodded. "I knew you loved me. And that means the world to me, Dad." She brushed her fingertips over the ring. "Bye, Daddy."

Bon swallowed hard. "Heather?"

Heather startled. She wasn't expecting to be included. "Ah . . ." Heather had cried like a baby at Grandpa's funeral, but she wasn't crying now. Instead, she was filled with an immense feeling of love for him, and of gratitude for the love he'd given her. "I love you, Grandpa."

Bon smiled, and then she gave the ring a gentle kiss. "Goodbye, honey. I love you." She took a deep breath and then placed the ring gently on the stone edge of the terrace, overlooking the cloud forest.

Heather's heart felt like it was falling. She heard Mom sniffle.

"And Jimmy." Bon took the cheap little JCPenney band between her fingers and lifted it up to the sunlight. "I never wanted to let you go. Not ever." Now Bon was the one who looked like a little kid. Her entire face collapsed in on itself as she cried. "I have kept tight hold of you all these years. But you got held up long enough, stuffed full of tubes in that hospital bed. I don't want to hold you up anymore."

Mom was making gulping noises as she tried to draw breath through her tears.

Bon exhaled. "I will never, ever not love you. Or the me I was when you were with me. I loved that you adored that kid from Shitsville. I loved that you set me on fire. I loved that you made me laugh. And I loved that you gave me a future when you gave me Sandra. I wish you could have known her, because she's *everything.*"

"Oh God, Mom, you're killing me." Mom wrapped her arms around Bon from behind, looking like she was just about all that was holding her up.

"I loved getting struck by lightning," Bon wailed. "And I wouldn't give up one second of it, not to save all the pain to come."

One by one they said goodbye to Jimmy Keays, and then the JCPenney ring was lowered, a small hoop of memory on the ancient terrace.

"Alright, Sandra. Now it's your turn." Bon turned to Mom.

Mom frowned, wiping at her swollen eyes. "What do you mean it's my turn? You're not planning on leaving me on this mountain, I hope."

Bon rolled her eyes and took Mom's left hand. She held it up in front of Mom's face. "Your turn."

The rings. Heather saw the moment her mother realized, her eyes flaring wide. Mom made a strangled sound as she stared at her hand.

"Not the diamond, of course," Bon said dryly. "That would be crazy. You can sell the engagement ring and use the money to do something nice for yourself."

Mom's gaze flicked to Heather.

"You don't have to do it," Heather told her hastily.

Mom closed her eyes and tears splashed down. "Damn," she said softly.

There was a long, drawn-out few minutes, where the only sound was Mom's crying and the play of the wind in the trees.

"Nick," Mom managed to say in a strangled voice. "I loved you. I still love you." She drew a long, very shuddery breath. "I wish you could have worked your shit out." She stopped and stared at the rings. Then she pulled them off. She examined the engagement ring and then held it out to Heather. "You have it," she said shakily. "Keep it. It's proof that your parents loved you when they made you, even if they were screwups."

"Everyone's a screwup," Bon said sharply. "You don't have to apologize for it. It's just being human."

Heather stared at the diamond ring. She didn't know if she wanted to take it or not.

"Your father loves you," Mom sniffed. "He will always love you. He's just . . . messier than most."

Heather took the ring. She didn't have to decide right now whether she would keep it or not. And she didn't have to decide right now how she felt about Dad. She closed her hand around the diamond ring, feeling the press of it against her skin.

"I love you, Nick." Mom pressed a kiss to the gold wedding band. "But I'm letting you go." And she put the ring down, choosing a soft pillow of grass, away from the edge, as though protecting it from harm.

I love you too, Dad, Heather thought, and felt a softening behind her rib cage as she stared at the grass, which had swallowed the ring in its pillowy depths. She didn't know if she was letting him go, exactly, so much as letting go of the wish that he would be any different. He was who he was. She couldn't change him. All she could do was draw her boundaries and love him from behind the line.

Heather stepped forward and put her arm around Mom, who was leaning against Bon. "You okay, Bon?" she asked, looking over to see her grandmother staring at the cloudy forest.

"Honey," Bon said, smiling wryly at her, "I'm always okay. It's in my DNA." She sighed, but it wasn't a sad sound. "It's in yours too, you know."

Heather nodded. After this trip, she thought that was true. "Thanks for bringing us here," she said softly. "It's been the most . . ." Heather wasn't sure what the word was.

"It has," Mom agreed. "It has been the *most*."

"You're welcome." Bon considered the path. "You ready to try and get off this mountain now?"

Chapter 22
Heather

Aguas Calientes, Peru

Heather had two things she had to do before the vacation wrapped. The first was unpleasant, the second was nerve-wracking, and they both took some working up to.

"I have these Post-it notes stuck behind my computer at home," she told Mom and Bon, when they met for dinner after they'd cleaned themselves up. "And there's a purple one that says, *Don't look back, you're not going that way.*"

Mom and Bon gave her their undivided attention. It was unsettling. She was used to them talking over her.

"I'm going to take it down when I get back," Heather said. "I think it's wrong."

"Right." Mom pursed her lips. "And . . . ?"

That was more like it. She could feel Mom's attention slipping. "I think you're always going in the direction of your past. Even if you're trying not to."

"God, I hope not." Mom passed her the wine list. "Pick something good. I'll buy this one."

"I mean, I think you *have* to look back," Heather corrected herself. She wasn't expressing this very well. It was a big thought. "I think you can't go forward without looking back."

"You're writing that on a Post-it, are you?" Bon said approvingly.

"I'm trying to say that I've learned a lot these past couple of weeks." Heather felt a spurt of the usual frustration with them. "About both of you, but also about me."

"That's nice." Mom tapped the wine list. "Order something, would you. I'm thirsty."

"May I suggest a Post-it that says, *Bon changed my life*," Bon offered.

"*Mom changed my life more*," Mom said dryly.

"*Thank God, I survived them*," Heather sighed, opening the wine list. She gathered her courage to ask what she wanted to ask. "Do you think I'd be making the right decision, if I . . ." She trailed off, not sure how to say it.

"Is this about Owen?" Bon guessed, shrewd as ever. "Because if it's about Owen, the answer is yes."

"Do you think it's insane to pursue a relationship with someone you've only known for a couple of weeks? Can you love someone when you barely know them?"

"God, yes," Bon exhaled. "To both."

"Agreed," Mom said. "Yes, it's insane. Yes, you can."

"That doesn't help," Heather wailed.

"Heather." Mom leaned forward and put her hand over Heather's. "Look who you're asking. You think either of us are good at relationships?"

Heather blinked. "Yes," she said, stunned. "I do."

Mom seemed shocked. "Have you *listened* to what we've said?"

"Yes."

"Good girl." Bon was approving. "I always knew you were a better listener than your mother."

"I married a man who cheated on me constantly," Mom protested. "I fought to keep him when I should have kicked him to the curb."

"But that's life," Heather said. "That's what I learned. Life is hard and messy and painful, and everything ends. Sure, you should have kicked him to the curb. And you *did*. You *have*."

"Thirty years too late."

"Or right on time. Because I have an orange Post-it too, and it says, *Good things are coming*. Because you ended it, because you loved Dad, because you got hurt and learned, because you valued yourself enough to move on, *good things are coming*."

"Sandra," Bon said patiently, "what the kid is saying, with all her random talk of Post-its, is that your life lessons are *her* life lessons." Bon patted Mom's arm. "She'll make the Owen choice because you taught her how to."

Heather smiled at Bon. Yes. That was what she'd wanted to hear. That *yes* was the answer. Because she didn't think she could have said no to the possibility of Owen, even if she'd tried.

"Has *he* said yes?" Bon asked.

"I haven't asked him yet."

"Well, Heather, let me tell you his theory that he's like a mammoth in a tar pit," Bon said, "that might help you. And order your mother some wine; she looks like she needs it. Then we can explain to her what yes means."

"I know what yes means."

"You do? Good. Then you can start saying it more often. Like when I ask you to come with me to this amazing hotel I found right in the Amazon Rainforest, instead of going home. You'll love it. They have villas right in the canopy, and you'll have all the animals to gawk at while I go to the day spa." Bon fished in her bag and pulled out a brochure, tossing it to Mom. "Go on, open it. Look at all the monkeys: capuchins and tamarins, howler monkeys and squirrel monkeys. You'll be in heaven. Not to mention the macaws. Imagine having a macaw perched next to you at breakfast. You can play David Attenborough to your heart's content while I get a facial and a pedicure."

"What about Heather?"

"Heather's got her own adventures to have."

"Go on, Mom, say yes," Heather ordered.

"Fine. Yes." Mom looked at the brochure. "Oh, there are otters in the river!"

"There you go. It's fate." Bon winked at Heather.

And for the first time she could remember, Heather didn't feel guilty for leaving her mom to live her own life.

"Good luck." Mom kissed Heather on the forehead and gave her a push out the front door of the hotel. She and Bon were going off to the hot springs to soak their sore muscles. "Don't do anything I wouldn't do."

"Or me," Bon added. "And here, tell S-H-A-W-N he can probably use this more than I can." She held out her unread copy of *Eat Pray Love*.

"I'm not giving him that." Heather refused to take it.

"I'll read it." Mom took it. "I saw the movie." She tucked it under her arm. "If it's good enough for Julia Roberts, it's good enough for me."

Heather smiled as she watched them head off up the street, their towels slung over their shoulders. They looked like a couple of schoolgirls skipping school, loose and easy and free.

Heather grabbed a takeaway coffee and sat down on a low stone wall by the rushing river. She inhaled the zesty scent of rainforest and water, enjoying the sight of the mountains cradling the town. She'd never had a better vacation, she decided.

"Hey." Shawn approached, looking sheepish. He stood there, rocking on his heels, his hands shoved deep in his pockets, looking like the hero in a romantic movie. It just wasn't her movie, or her hero.

"I guess this is about me crashing your vacation, isn't it?" he said cautiously.

"Yep." Heather invited him to sit next to her on the wall. "How was your trek?" she asked, striving for distant courtesy.

"Amazing," he admitted. "I mean, I had no idea what I was getting into when I came . . ."

Heather pulled a face and he flushed.

"I'm glad I did, though," he said huskily.

"Shawn," she interrupted, "I know everything was messy before I left. So, I thought I should say things plain and get this sorted once and for all." She cleared her throat. "If there's one thing I've learned on this trip, it's that a little plain speaking can save a lot of pain."

"Okay," Shawn looked apprehensive.

"I don't want to be with you, Shawn. Maybe I confused things and sent you mixed signals, so I just want to be as clear as possible. I don't want to be in a relationship with you." She didn't qualify it. She didn't tell him he was a nice guy or tell him he'd make some woman very lucky. "I don't want to lie to you. Or to me. This isn't ever going to be a thing."

Shawn blinked, and she could see that he was struggling with tears. She felt sorry for him but didn't comfort him. He had the capacity to comfort himself; it wasn't her job.

"You have to stop knocking at my door. And sending me flowers and buying me gifts. And you absolutely have to stop hanging around waiting for me at coffee shops and following me on vacation. It's not okay."

"But—"

"No, no buts. This isn't up for negotiation. You can't convince me. I don't want this."

"Right." Shawn's voice wobbled. "Well, I guess you've made yourself clear."

"Good." She stood up, taking her coffee with her. "All the best, Shawn." And she left, not once turning around to see if he was staring after her with a longing look. It didn't matter. She was moving on.

Owen's hotel was over the river, in the forest. She had to cross a long wooden bridge from the street to reach the complex, which consisted of crushed gravel paths winding through the thickly wooded slopes. She checked his message. He'd said he was in villa 4.

There were signs along the way, and she followed a winding path through the shady green until she reached a quaint Spanish-style villa, with terra-cotta tiles on the roof, and a chimney puffing out woodsmoke. Heart hammering in her ears, Heather knocked on the door.

Her body was going into overload standing on the doorstep

waiting for him. She was hot and cold, frozen and buzzing, all at once.

But then the door opened, and there he was. Everything fell away.

"Hi," he said softly.

It was just Owen, in his soft old blue T-shirt, with his dark curls tumbling, and his lips twitching. Heather felt the *click* of invisible marbles softly colliding.

"Hi," she said, smiling.

He pulled the door wider, to let her in, and she laughed. The room was staged, with lights and a camera set up on a tripod. "You're working!"

"I am."

"I thought it was odd that you were staying at a five-star resort . . ." She walked in, marveling at the beauty of the little villa, with its hardwood floors, sloping ceiling and open fireplace.

"You don't think I'm a five-star guy?" he asked, closing the door.

The room was toasty from the fire. Heather shrugged off her jacket. "I think you're a Casa Suerte kind of guy." She gave him a sideways look. "A farmhouse kind of guy . . ."

"I'm the kind of guy who likes everything," he said huskily. He turned off the bright lights above their silver reflective umbrellas. The villa went from being a spotlit stage to an intimate haven. "But this is courtesy of Condé Nast, who are doing a feature on this place and need some photos."

"I thought you were on vacation."

"I was. Now I'm earning a buck." Owen was staring at her like she was an exotic animal that had wandered in from the cold. He watched as she prowled the room.

Heather bit her lip. She didn't know where to begin. "Did you find Machu Picchu worth running to?"

"Yes." His voice was rough, uneven. His hands were resting on his hips, and his dark eyes were sultry. "How about you?"

Heather swallowed and approached him. "It's not bad, for a wonder of the world."

His lips twitched. "Not bad, huh?"

"Owen?"

"Yeah?"

She put her hands on his chest. She could feel his heart skidding beneath her palm. "*¿Oye hermoso, vienes aqui a menudo?*"

He laughed. "Does that line ever work?"

She stretched up and brushed the lightest of kisses against his twitchy lips. "Every time," she whispered.

"Heather," he sighed, holding her by the arms and pulling her away. "I can't promise anything beyond Peru. If that's what you're hoping for . . ."

She wasn't hoping. She *knew*. She didn't know how she knew, but she did. Lightning didn't happen for no reason.

"Owen? You're not a mammoth and I'm not a tar pit."

"What?" He flinched.

"Bon told me about your mammoth thing."

"I never told her about that." He swore. "I'm going to kill my grandmother the next time I see her."

"I'm not a tar pit. If anything, I'm just another mammoth."

"Heather . . ."

"Look, Owen, life is a total mess. There's no logic to it, but sometimes there are . . . I don't know . . . signs . . ."

"Signs?" He sounded wary.

"Like finding a stranger, who is sharing a bathroom with you, and who knows your grandmother, and who somehow was the reason you came all the way to Machu Picchu, even though you didn't know him . . ."

"I don't believe in fate," he reminded her.

"You don't have to. I do." For the first time she could see the worry in him, the fear. She didn't know anything about his past, or his parents, or his grandparents. She didn't know why he was scared of tar pits, but she *wanted* to know . . . And that's all that mattered for now.

"Owen, I know you travel a lot."

"No." He shook his head. "You don't. Hooking up with someone on vacation is just a form of tourism—living with someone is something else. I love my job. And when I go, you'll be lonely. And you'll hate me for it. You'll look for comfort elsewhere."

"Maybe I won't. Maybe I love my job and my life, and I'll just be fine while you're gone. And maybe you can send me photos and we can message, and we can talk every day. And maybe I love who you are, and don't want you to change."

Owen swallowed hard at the word *love*. "We just met."

Heather nodded.

"Don't you think it's weird? That we feel like this, when we only just met?"

Heather felt weak. He felt it too. She *knew* it.

"Are you calling me weird again?"

"Unusual," he amended.

"Isn't unusual what you're looking for when you go traveling the world with your camera?"

Owen pulled her closer and pressed his forehead to hers. "What if . . ." His voice was low and vulnerable. "What if I end up not wanting to leave you . . . What if I lose my life . . . ?"

"What if you don't? What if it all works out?"

His heart was stumbling and surging under her hand.

"Owen. Maybe we could try being less alone? Together." Heather lifted on tiptoe and kissed him again, so lightly she could feel his breath sighing.

Owen's eyes slid closed, and he kissed her back. "Yes," he sighed against her lips.

"Yes?"

"Yes."

Yes. Because, *Good things were coming.*

Author's Note

Best, First, and Last is inspired by my grandmother, who was once divorced, twice widowed, and who trekked up Machu Picchu in her seventies. She was a force of nature, someone who never lost her lust for life, even after grief and struggle. She flirted, chased fun, and was also tough, troublesome, and irrepressible, right to the end. Bonnie has all her best qualities and her journey is one of embracing life, even when it hurts. Love to you, Grandma, wherever you are now.

Acknowledgments

Firstly, I'd like to acknowledge that this book was written in Tarntanya, on Kaurna Country, and I'd like to pay my respects to elders past and present, and to recognize the long traditions of story and knowledge and connection to Country. This land has never been ceded; it has always been and always will be Kaurna Country. I would also like to pay my respects to the Indigenous people of Peru, especially the Quechua people, and to the ancient traditions of the Incans of the Sacred Valley and to acknowledge the rich and complex cultural heritage of Peru.

This book is dedicated to my mother and her mother, and to my kids. My grandmother actually did trek to Machu Picchu in her seventies, and had three husbands, and was ribald and irrepressible. My mother, however, is nothing like Sandy. And she is still married to my kind prince of a father fifty-three years after the wedding (and counting). I learned a lot about being a kick-ass woman from both my grandmother and my mother, and I learned a lot about love from my parents. I hope I can teach my kids to kick ass and love too. I may even drag them up to Machu Picchu one day . . .

Speaking of those kids: Kirby and Isla, as Bonnie says to Sandra, you are the best bit, and you're the ones I need. Know in your bones that you are loved and treasured, and go forth believing that *good things are coming.*

And Jonathan, you may never get a proper dedication, even though you've been mentioned in many. I do that to you repeatedly and *cheerfully* because I love you. And because you're a smart-ass. Loving you is lightning.

To my family and friends, all the assorted in-laws and drinking buddies and writing buddies: thank you.

Special mentions go to Lynn (always), Tully (for putting the pro in Ass Pro), Sean and Alex VH (for putting the words in Word Docs), Alex C (for the coteaching and coresearching), my postgrads (can't start naming you or I'll leave someone out and get in trouble—but particular love to those of you who know who Hubert and Hugo are), my undergrads (waaaaaaaay too many to name), Kathleen and Georgia (my fellow lovers on Love on Campus), and everyone at Flinders (Creative Arts especially) and Assemblage Centre for Creative Arts.

Now the super important people: thank you to Shannon Plackis for working on this book. This was a hard one, and I appreciated every single note. And thanks to everyone at Kensington for making and selling glorious books! Especial thanks to Lauren and the team for the 'grams and 'toks and all the stuff that helps readers find books.

And thank you, always and ever, to Sarah Younger, my divine agent. I love you and appreciate you and am so glad that I met you in that bar way back when and dragged you out to my hometown that time. It was *fate*.

Finally, thanks to all the readers out there. Don't tell Jonny, but you're the loves of my life.

Discussion Questions

1. *Best, First, and Last* explores the question of regret. What happens when we make choices that lead to heartbreak? Is it possible to celebrate failed relationships without regrets? Or is there value to regret? What do you think?

2. In the novel Owen talks about *running to* something, rather than *running away* from things. What is Bonnie running to? What is Sandra running away from? Have you ever had a moment in your life when you've run away? What would you run towards?

3. Heather struggles to feel compassion for her father. Why do you think that is? What do you think she needs/wants from her father?

4. Bonnie keeps booking fancy hotels that seem divorced from the "real world" of Peru: the luxurious suite in Lima, the casa in the resort at Paracas, the glamping on the trek up to Machu Picchu. Why do you think she does this?

5. Do you think Bonnie was wrong not to tell Sandra about Jimmy? Why/why not?

6. In the end, Heather and Owen say *yes*. What do you think they're saying yes to?

7. Do you have a dream destination you'd like to visit? Where would you go and who would you take with you? And why?

8. Bonnie had three great loves in her life; Sandy is open to a second one; Heather has just discovered her first. Do you believe in the idea of The One? Or, like Bonnie, do you think there's more than one The One for everyone? What do you think makes someone The/A One?

Visit our website at
KensingtonBooks.com
to sign up for our newsletters, read
more from your favorite authors, see
books by series, view reading group
guides, and more!

BOOK **CLUB**
BETWEEN THE CHAPTERS

Become a Part of Our
Between the Chapters Book Club
Community and Join the Conversation

Betweenthechapters.net

Submit your book review for a chance to win exclusive
Between the Chapters swag you can't get anywhere else!
https://www.kensingtonbooks.com/pages/review/